FLIRTING
with the
MOON

ANDY M^cD

Flirting with The Moon
By ANDY McD
www.andymcd.com.au

Published in Australia by McDermott House 2022
P.O. Box 395 Coolangatta
Queensland 4225 Australia
info@andymcd.com.au

Copyright © ANDY MCD 2022
All Rights Reserved

 A catalogue record for this book is available from the National Library of Australia

ISBN: 978-0-6453709-2-8 (pbk)
ISBN: 978-0-6453709-3-5 (ebk)

Cover design by ANDY MCD © 2022
Cover image: © Fotolia_96453311

Typesetting and design by McDermott House © 2022

All characters and events in this publication are fictitious, any resemblance to real persons, living or dead, or any events past or present are purely coincidental.

No part of this book may be reproduced in any form, by photocopying or by any electronic or mechanical means, including information storage or retrieval systems, without permission in writing from both the copyright owner and the publisher of this book.

For Jane . . . my lighthouse in the storm

Other titles by
ANDY McD

X
The Tiger Chase

Quest of the New Templars series:
Book 1 – Resurrection

Children's books:
The Last Tiger

1

Detectives and uniformed police officers filed into the crime incident room and took their seats.

I glanced over my shoulder at the gruesome gallery of victims. Eleven young people each murdered and left in a public place, their bodies mutilated beyond recognition. Beside this, was a projector screen showing a map of LA, and next to that a whiteboard covered in newspaper clippings. A front-page headline of the *LA Times* blared: 'Is Detective Joe Dean Flirting with The Moon?' The press and I shared a mutual loathing. And it was they who had coined the phrase "The Moon" due to the killer's penchant for striking on the first night of the new moon.

My partner, Detective Jacqueline Sanchez, handed out copies of the latest profile report.

Being old-school, I had mixed feelings about the presence of Doctor Charles Dudley, aka 'Chuck,' our in-house FBI profiler. The fact that he looked like a freshman didn't help, but I figured he'd at least be able to field some of the questions.

When everyone was present, I began.

'As we know, tonight is the start of the new moon.' On the overhead projector, I drew a circle on the map, its diameter covering East LA to Santa Monica, North Hollywood to Inglewood. All the killings had occurred within this relatively small area, and all over the last eleven months.

A detective at the back of the room thrust his hand in the air.

'But it's New Year's Eve and we've got just about every cop this side of Texas in town, surely—'

Chuck stepped forward and stood beside me. 'We can't assume that he won't strike. The pattern is unlikely to change. If anything, I believe the added risk will spur the killer on.'

'We have to be extra vigilant,' I interjected. 'Look for anything out of the ordinary.

You all have your assigned areas; it's going to be a wild night.'

I placed a second slide on top of the one already on the projector lens. Sanchez had marked the position of the previous murder scenes. 'According to the profile, it's unlikely that the killer will return to any of these spots, but we also can't rule it out. Going by… shall we say … his past creativity, if a killing does take place tonight, it'll be staged in a way that'll be completely different to the others. Are there any questions?'

'Yes.' A burly, balding detective with the face of a prize-fighter lumbered to his feet. 'Can whoever gets to nail this bastard have some time off?'

I knew where he was coming from. Unshaven, red puffy eyes, shirt hanging out the back of his pants—all signs that he too had been working around the clock. The rest of us didn't look any better.

'How's a week in Vegas sound for the cop who catches The Moon?'

Sanchez raised a questioning eyebrow.

I needed to solve the case and put this psychopath behind bars. I needed to get my life back. At this point I'd promise anything to achieve this.

'Woo hoo!' the detective cried. 'Vegas here I come!'

The room erupted with applause.

After the briefing, Sanchez and I made our way to the communications room.

'I'm sure the LAPD won't be springing for no trips to Vegas, Joe.'

'I know. But I will, and gladly!' I stopped mid-stride as if I'd had a sudden thought. 'I'll catch you up, just got to get something from my office.'

The little crease between Sanchez's eyes, the clamping of her lips and the subtle shake of her head told me she knew exactly where I was going.

'It's okay, I'll just be a minute.'

Grateful that my office had no windows, I closed the door behind me, strode to my desk and pulled out a bottle of Jack Daniels from the bottom drawer. Once you've descended into the gutter of addiction, one of the first things you lose is a need for ceremony. I twisted off the bottle top and gulped down the bourbon like a marathon runner at the last water stop.

There was a knock and before I could answer, Sanchez was poking her head around the door.

I fumbled the bottle back into the drawer. 'What is it?' I snapped.

She gave me her usual knowing look. 'You got visitors.'

'What? Who?' I rustled among the piles of papers on the desk, found what I was looking for and scooped a mint into my mouth.

Sanchez opened the door fully and stepped aside. My wife swept into the room carrying Johnny, our three-year-old son.

'Kathy?'

'Seeing as you haven't been home since God knows when I thought I'd catch you here. I reckoned at least here we'd be able to talk while you were sober. She looked at my mouth working on the mint. 'I see I was wrong.'

Ignoring her, I reached out for my son. 'Hey Sport.'

Johnny frowned and pulled away as if he didn't know me.

'It's okay,' Kathy comforted him. 'Go with Aunty Jacky. I won't be long.'

Sanchez quietly took Johnny from his mother's arms and left the room.

Kathy closed the door behind her.

'What's going on?'

'What's going on?' She threw back her head and laughed. 'You're the big-shot detective, surely *you* can figure it out!'

I offered a searching shrug, but a feeling of dread was cooling the hot liquor in my belly.

'Okay, I'll spell it out for you, and I'll keep it short because I'm sure you're just dying for another drink.'

Part of me already knew what she was going to say but even so, when she said the words, they pierced my guts like a knife.

'It's over, Joe, I'm leaving you.'

The effects of the bourbon were now completely gone, and I began to shake. 'Seriously? You're telling me this here? Now? On tonight of all nights?'

'And there we have it ... Joe Dean the victim. How could *I* possibly do this to *you*? Especially when you've been working *so* hard. What a *heartless* bitch I am!'

'Not now, Kathy, please.' I glanced at the desk drawer longing for the comfort and escape that lay inside. 'You know what's been happening with the case and the pressure I've been under—'

'I don't know anything. You don't talk to me. I only learn what's happening from what I see on the news.'

'That's not true. Let's get tonight over with, then we can talk.'

'When was the last time we had a conversation? When was the last time you spent any time with your son?' Her voice rose with each word until she was screaming.

'Shhh ... keep it down.' I rushed to the door as if doing so would dampen the sound from the rest of the building.

'I just came to tell you it's over. You can pick up your things from the house, but you won't be staying. I've been a single parent for a long time now, may as well make it official. We *don't* need you anymore!'

'You can't just kick me out of my home and stop me from seeing my son.' Now *I* was yelling.

Kathy repeated that humourless laugh. It was as ugly as the

scorn on her face. 'Your home? *This* is your home right here. Always has been. And as for your son, ha! He doesn't even know who you *are!*' She stormed out of the room.

I should've followed her. I should've begged her to reconsider and promised her I would change. I should've fought to save my marriage. But I didn't. Instead, I closed the door behind her, rushed to my desk and dived through the escape hatch.

Sanchez sat at one of the control panels in the communications room wearing headphones and a mic. She didn't look up as I entered.

There were two walls filled with monitors, each showing a close-up view of a specific area in the city. A row of uniformed officers worked in front of consoles, making the room look like NASA mission control.

I took the vacant seat next to Sanchez and put on a matching headset. Static and short radio bursts from the cruisers and mobile units on the streets filled my ears. On one of the monitors there was a view of Hollywood Boulevard. 'Unit Five, do you read me?' I said into the mouthpiece.

'Loud and clear.'

I watched as The Roosevelt Hotel appeared to driver's right, while the ever-present crowd from Grauman's Chinese Theatre spilled onto the road on his left. My God, what an impossible task this was going to be.

On another monitor, Santa Monica Boulevard and the entrance to the pier were also heaving, and it was only eight-thirty. 'Unit Nine, do you read me?'

'Copy that.'

I didn't need to ask them how things were going; the monitors showed me exactly what they were seeing. I felt useless here; I wanted to be out on the streets, I wanted to catch this bastard myself and nail him up on the nearest wall.

By eleven-thirty, the streets of LA were one big open-air party. I tried to remember the last time I had let loose and enjoyed myself. Being drunk and enjoying yourself are two completely different things—on the former I was an expert, the latter a novice.

Basically, all we had done for the last three and a half hours was watch the monitors, listen to radio transmissions and, in our minds, try to piece together the jigsaw that The Moon had created. When the City Hall clock struck midnight, I was damn right miserable.

'Happy New Year!' one of the young female cops cried out, snapping me out of my stupor.

The others rose from their seats and shook hands, slapped each other on the back, and hugged. I stayed put but Sanchez leaned across and wrapped her arms around me. 'Make a resolution, Joe,' she whispered in my ear.

'Already have.'

'I don't mean catching The Moon.'

I knew exactly which way the conversation was heading. I turned back to my console and was about to put on my headset when Sanchez grabbed my arm.

'I'm talking about the drinking.'

'I know you are. I'm okay, it's under control.'

'Is it?' Those arching eyebrows again, speaking a language all of their own. 'So, if you knew of a detective who was drinking while on duty would you say it's okay?'

'I said I'm okay, goddamn it!' I growled at her but instantly regretted it. Sanchez was tough, not the kind of woman who'd back down from a male outburst.

'Stop drinking, sort things out with Kathy, and spend some time with Johnny no matter the outcome of tonight.'

Well, that was easy because in my mind that's exactly what I'd decided to do. 'Okay, I promise!' It might have come out as a mutter, but it was a promise I desperately wanted to keep.

Over the next hour the festivities on the streets continued but were noticeably thinning out.

'Let's pray for a miracle, Joe.' Sanchez's voice was heartfelt. I suspected she still attended Catholic services, but she rarely spoke of her private life.

As we watched the monitors gradually grow quiet, the churning in my stomach was telling me it was *too* quiet.

'You hungry?' Sanchez said.

I realised I was and nodded.

'Mexican?' She was already rising to her feet.

'Speedy's still open?'

'Yep, all night.'

Sanchez didn't need to ask me for my order. We ate takeaway from Speedy's Casa de Mexico a lot. More adventurous than me, my partner liked to try different dishes, but mine was always the same—burritos and chilli. 'Anyone else want Mexican?' she yelled turning to the rest of the crew.

Her question was met by grunts and headshakes.

Most of the monitors were now showing street cleaners going about their work and a handful of drunken revellers here and there reluctant for the party to end. There had been the usual arrests but nothing serious, which was good but still my stomach churned, and the hunger wasn't helping. Sanchez had been gone a while. I checked my watch—3.00 am. I swung around to the room. 'Anyone see Sanchez come back?' I asked loud enough for everyone to hear.

There was a chorus of 'Nopes.'

I tried her cell phone. It rang until her message bank clicked on: 'This is Detective Jacqueline Sanchez of the LAPD. Leave a message. I'll get back to you.'

Speedy's could've been busy, but at three o'clock in the morning? Fresh air seemed like a good idea for me too. I'd sat at that console playing Big Brother all night. 'If anyone needs me, I've got my cell.' I grabbed my jacket, made a detour to my office, and downed a conservative estimate of two doubles—which in reality was probably more like four—then headed out of the building.

Speedy's was only a block away from the Parker Center off East 1st Street. It was the last establishment at the far end of a narrow alley that hosted a few other small businesses: a Chinese restaurant, a tattoo parlour and a gym. The light from Speedy's window barely illuminated the way. It was the only place still open. The rest of the storefronts were quiet and dark. The little, middle-aged hombre with the biggest smile this side of Tijuana was cleaning the counter tops.

'Hey Detective José,' he said with a tired grin when I leaned in through the door. 'You catch el bastardo?'

'No, not yet.'

'So, you steel hungry?'

As soon as he said that, I knew. In fact, if I'm honest, I'd known the last time I'd checked my watch back at headquarters.

I must've suddenly looked ill because Speedy stopped cleaning and rushed to my side. 'What's wrong, Mr Dean?'

'When was Detective Sanchez here?'

'About an hour ago. She buy usual burrito with chilli for you and special New Year rice for her.'

I don't remember leaving Speedy's and heading back to the Parker; I don't know if I ran or walked. When I entered the lobby, the duty officer called me over. 'It just arrived, sir. I was about to call up to you.' He handed me a Speedy's takeaway carton.

Looking down at the unopened box in my hand, I could feel its warmth.

'Everything all right, sir?'

'Who brought this in?'

'A young delivery guy.'

'Speedy doesn't deliver. No sign of Detective Sanchez?'

'Haven't seen her since she left earlier, sir.'

I went straight to my office, closed the door and placed the carton on my desk. 'Sonofabitch.' I paced the room, taking shots of bourbon, stealing glances at the carton, still pacing, pacing. In a matter of minutes, the bottle was empty. I tossed it into the waste paper bin then suddenly felt the need to busy myself. I checked my watch but didn't see the time. I glanced along the files on my shelves but didn't see a single one. I wanted to do anything but look inside that carton. I opened the bottom drawer of my filing cabinet, knelt on the floor, and reached into the back to where my stash was hidden. I was a prepared alcoholic.

When I finally sat at my desk with the now half-empty bottle of Jack Daniels, my life had changed forever. Detective Joseph Dean of the LAPD was no more. Joe Dean, husband and father was no more.

I slammed down the bottle, grabbed the carton, opened it, and looked inside.

2

Twenty-five years later

The air conditioning in Boca Raton Public Library brought a welcome relief from the heat of a typical Florida day. It was 1.15 pm. If the intel was correct, my mark would be here at any moment.

I wandered down the centre of the room, passing aisles of bookshelves on either side then navigated around a circular display of magazines.

At the end of the room, I turned and strolled back along the opposite side. In no time at all, I was back at the checkout counters and the information desk. Not far from the entry doors was a large display of books with a sign announcing: Murder Mystery Month. This seemed like as good a place as any to wait.

On the bottom shelf of the display, a little black book with bright red lettering caught my eye. *Flirting with The Moon.* What the hell? I was about to reach down and pick it up when something breezed past me—a twenty-six-year-old blonde with the air of a pageant queen and the body of a porn star. She hurried down the centre of the hall, glancing from left to right as if searching for a lost child.

My client was Howard B Eastman, aka 'Big Howie.' He owned the Toyota dealership in Boca where I'd recently purchased a second-hand Camry. And that was how he became my client.

'And what kind of business might you be in, Joe?' my new bestest buddy asked as I'd signed my life away.

'A private detective,' I mumbled, wanting to move the process along.

'Really?' His voice lowered but his face retained a carnival grin. 'Happen I might have some work for you, Joe.'

I picked up the nearest book and flicked through its pages while keeping one eye on the blonde. She turned into the non-fiction aisle F – H, pulled a book from one of the shelves and proceeded to do a similar job of pretending to read.

I knew the routine. She'd wait there until he arrived. He was always late, a real bad boy, just how girls like Gabrielle Eastman preferred them.

I figured he'd be a few minutes yet, so I replaced the book I was holding and reached for the little black one on the bottom tier. *Flirting with The Moon*. The author's name, Stephen Powell, I didn't recognise, but the title? A coincidence? Thumbing through the first couple of pages, I came to the dedication:

For my old friend, Joe.

My gut tightened and my head suddenly throbbed as if I'd been hit with a baseball bat.

'When are you coming home, Daddy?' The voice was a faint echo in my mind.

'Stay away from us, Joe Dean,' Kathy screamed. 'We don't need you anymore!'

Then a montage of images from the lost five years of my life flooded my mind: a pathetic bum sifting through garbage to find his next meal, begging for pennies on the street to buy cheap wine, sleeping under a pile of rags in Venice Beach.

I threw the book to the floor like it was a hot coal, steadied myself against the display and took a deep breath. Thirty seconds earlier, I'd been a reasonably content middle-aged man who had fought hard to get his life back in order after a major breakdown. But now, here I was on the verge of panic. I couldn't believe that such a reaction would have been possible from just reading the dedication of a book. But of course, there was much more to it than that. It was like a door in my mind had been opened a tiny bit, just allowing me a glimpse of something inside that I'd locked away all those years ago. My hands were shaking, and I realised that for the first time in twenty years, I needed a drink.

'Shit!' Gabrielle's beau had arrived. I rushed over to the adjacent aisle and, while pretending to browse the shelves, I retrieved my smartphone and activated my new-fangled recording app.

'Oh Jay, you know how much I want to, but I can't.'

'Yes, you can. The old bastard won't miss it!'

'Oh, he'll miss it. Fifty thousand isn't loose change.'

'It's the only way we can be together.'

There was a pause and although I didn't look up, I imagined Gabrielle searching the Wahlberg look-alike's eyes for sincerity.

'With that money, Gabs, we can go west. Get a place of our own. Never have to see or hear Big fucking Howie ever again—'

'I have money of my own. We can use that.'

Wahlberg's leather jacket rustled as they hugged. 'And you'll come away with me? You'll leave him for good?'

Don't just nod, Gabby. Don't just nod. I needed the evidence on tape. I held my breath.

'Anything for you, Jay ... anything!'

Gotcha.

More rustling leather and the wet sound of kissing. I turned off the app and returned the cell phone to my pocket. My work here was done.

I can't say I get a lot of satisfaction from my job; it's certainly not like being on the police force, but it's a living. And it's helped me get my life back together.

I stayed behind the shelf until I heard their goodbyes. 'Wahlberg' seemed to be in a hurry to leave. I gave them a few minutes then emerged from the aisle and made my way back to the display. The little book still lay on the floor where I'd thrown it.

I picked it up gingerly as if it might burn. The cover was bland, designed to look like a black leather diary. The title was in thick red ink in a font that looked like splatters of blood.

I flicked through the pages and, at random, stopped near the end of the book. Although they were part of a sentence, six words in the centre of a page sprung out at me—the heart of the Latino bitch …

Vomiting in a public place was something I'd put behind me long ago, but I had to breathe deep and swallow before I was able to carry the book to the checkout counter. Ten minutes later, I walked from the building with a brand new, still warm, laminated library card in one hand and a copy of *Flirting with The Moon* in the other.

3

As I drove along Spanish River Boulevard, my mind drifted back to a time twenty years earlier following my stint in rehab. Five years after walking away from my family, my career and my sanity, I'd decided it was time to get my life back in order.

It felt strange returning to the LAPD headquarters. Would I still know anybody there? Would they remember me? Would I still be a laughing stock?

The young female officer at the duty desk looked at me with impatient eyes. I was about to speak when someone slapped me on the back.

'You've got to be kidding me … Joseph Dean?'

I'd have known that deep gravelly voice anywhere. I spun around. His face had hardly changed. 'Burt.' I was happy and anxious all at the same time. 'Burt Williams!'

We shook hands and hugged.

'What are you doing here, Joe?'

'I'm looking for Kathy.'

'Oh … I've just finished my shift, how about we get a coffee? We got a lot of catching up to do, friend.'

'That would be great!'

An uneasy silence escorted us the short distance down the street to the nearest coffee shop. There was so much I wanted to ask my old buddy, but I didn't know where to start; the same thoughts were probably running through his mind.

We sat at an outside table. Burt seemed agitated and excited all at the same time. 'So where have you been, Joe?'

'The truth?'

Burt nodded and looked a little embarrassed.

'To hell and back!'

He shook his head and ordered two coffees from a young waitress.

I told him of what little I could remember from the last five years. Of course, he already knew what had actually sent me over the edge. No doubt too there would've been plenty of gossip, but he knew nothing of what had happened to me after I left the police force.

The waitress brought our coffees. I hadn't drank coffee for a while, even in those early days of rehab I'd become more conscious of my health. Tea was my preferred post-drunk beverage and still is.

'So where are you living?'

It was the question I'd been dreading. 'Trips.' Trips was a sleazy hostel for the homeless in downtown LA. Every LAPD cop knew of the place.

Burt spluttered into his cup. 'Trips?'

'I'm fresh out of rehab.' I stirred my coffee. 'Baby steps, you know?'

Burt mopped up the spillage from his coffee then looked at me directly. 'Well, I'm getting you out of that place right away—'

I assured him it was only temporary.

At first I saw disappointment in his expression, but then his features warmed. 'You're back, Joe! That's the main thing, you're back!'

'Yes, Burt, I am.' We gripped each other's hands, old friends reunited.

We sipped our coffees; I guessed he was waiting for the inevitable question. I cleared my throat. 'So, Burt, where's Kathy and Johnny?' The words came out in a murmur.

He stared into his half-empty cup. 'You been to the house?'

I nodded. 'She no longer lives there.'

'That's right. She moved out. Had to.'

The oh-so-familiar guilt welled up again, threatening to swamp me.

'Kathy's ... changed, Joe ...' Burt paused.

I didn't say anything, just waited.

'She found religion.'

'You mean she's gone back to the very thing that she hated her parents for?'

Burt nodded. 'We tried—both Nance and I—but she's made a clean break. She won't have anything to do with anyone, unless—'

'They're a part of her religion. What about Johnny?'

'Well as far as I know, he's okay. He's in the fourth grade at Highland Oaks Elementary.'

'In Arcadia? You know that?'

'Sure. I've been keeping an eye on them for you, old friend. I knew you'd be back some day!'

I saw the moisture in his eyes and loved him for it.

There was another pause while Burt shuffled in his seat. 'There's one thing, Joe, something you need to know.' The lines on his brow deepened like tiny canyons.

I thought I knew what he was going to say. Kathy had found someone else, and my little Johnny had a new father. I braced myself.

'Johnny thinks you're dead!'

The turning afternoon sun had been gradually creeping towards us like a slowly opening door, now it bathed us in skin-scabbing heat, but I hardly felt it. I was cold and numb.

'You okay, Joe?'

I couldn't lie to my best friend. That was what the old Joe would've done. 'No ... I'm not okay.' My hand shook as I placed the coffee cup back on the table. 'He thinks I'm dead?'

'Kathy told him you were shot and killed on duty.'

'Why would she do that?'

'I guess it was her way of handling things. It was a pretty bad time.'

'I need to talk to her.'

Burt shook his head. 'That's probably not a good idea.'

'But Johnny's eight years old now.'

'That's what I mean. You can't just walk back into his life. Remember, he's been brought up thinking you're dead.'

He was right. The one thing that all cops have in common is we're all amateur psychologists. Every day we have to work out what people are thinking or why they are doing what they do. I hated the thought of my son being affected by my actions; I'd caused enough harm.

'It will have to be when he's older, Joe, because Kathy's influence is too strong at the moment. You could risk losing him forever.'

I finished my drink then Burt sealed the case. 'Go get your life back, reclaim your place in this goddamn world, and let time do its work. If anyone can rise to the top again, old pal, it's you.'

I shrugged. 'I'd never get back into the police force.'

'There's more to life than being a cop. You'll work it out.'

That was twenty years ago. Johnny would be twenty eight years old now.

4

I manoeuvred my car into my allotted parking space beneath my apartment and grabbed the book from the passenger seat. Somehow it felt heavy, like it was kryptonite.

I climbed the single flight of steps to my front door. All the apartments at La Casa en la Playa were identical, two-storey hacienda style buildings. The resort-style complex was a haven for elderly retirees.

Once inside, I placed the book on the kitchen counter. If nothing else, my apartment was practical. It came fully furnished, and although the décor had that 1980s 3-star hotel room look—pastel fabrics, dark pink carpets, Wal Mart pictures on the walls, and wicker furniture—it suited me just fine.

I brewed some tea then escaped through the rear sliding door with the little book under my arm, and out to my tiny balcony.

I set my tea down on the small outdoor table and took a seat in the one and only purchase I'd made since moving into the apartment—a single, padded and comfy-as-hell outdoor chair I'd bought at a garage sale for eight bucks. I'd been dreading this moment ever since I'd checked out the book from the library. After a sip of tea, I opened the book to the first chapter. My hands were trembling.

Flirting with The Moon – Chapter 1

As usual, I had picked my star well. Star? Surely you mean victim? I hear you ask. No, no, no, the first lesson of The Moon is this: the star is the one who takes centre stage, holding glory in the spotlight.

It is the star who will be immortal. Without the stars the moon is just a dense rock. This and much more you will come to learn in due time, dear reader.

I first spotted my January Star outside a nightclub in West Hollywood. Not your typical working girl, she was quite beautiful and seemed intelligent too. My arousal heightened at the thought that she might be doing this to get through medical school, or perhaps she was a single parent working the streets to put her kid through college. Oh yes, I liked the idea of that. A true star!

You don't need a chat-up line when your star is a whore. All you need is a supply of greenbacks and a friendly smile. My January Star was no exception.

I didn't take her into a bar, couldn't chance being seen. Remember, dear reader, obscurity is everything. I needed to get her away from the street as quickly as possible. 'I have a place we can go,' I said. She had an annoying little giggle. I was looking forward to fixing that. 'So why are you doing this?' I didn't ask her name. She was January and that was that.

'I'm training to be a nurse.'

Ah-ha, I was right. My arousal continued to rise. I had to get her on to the stage as quickly as possible.

I feel the need for a break in my narration at this point, dear reader, to explain how I operate and what you must do if you are to be successful in your own creative career. Here are my golden rules:

- *Venue – scout for the perfect venue for your production as early as possible. Ensure you are familiar with the layout of the theatre and the comings and goings of the area. Remember you need silence on the set once the performance begins.*

- *Nothing is left to chance. Rehearse the scene you are about to direct and remember your lines. Ad-libbing is discouraged to prevent slip-ups. By opening night, the script has been tried and tested so stick to it. Remember, you are the writer, producer and director of each production.*
- *Choose your stars carefully and find them before opening night. Watch them from a distance, but be careful, this is a vulnerable time. If there is need to come into contact with them, don't let them know anything about you. No one else must see you at any time.*
- *Scenes and props—you might use the same props for each performance—that favourite surgical blade for instance—or you may want to vary them depending on the type of scene you are directing: hammer, hacksaw, butcher's blade, etc. Whichever you choose, you must be able to conceal it on your person at all times without it being noticed, and you must always return it to the props department when finished. Never leave props lying around for anyone to find!*

If you follow these rules to the tee, you too, dear reader, could become a great director like The Moon.

Now, back to January:

When we entered the theatre, the stage was set and ready. I led my star to centre stage and gave her a final hug of encouragement. 'Go break a leg, kiddo!' I'd always found that term amusing, didn't quite understand it, but at my productions at least, it had some meaning.

The venue was West Hollywood Park. It was a typical cool winter's night, but the absence of the moon gave it that touch of ambience that I so enjoyed. Stepping back, I smiled at my star and called, 'Action!'

The twitch of her brow and the hesitant frown told me she was new to the stage. I had chosen my star well, a true starlet in the making. She looked around, then her cheeks reddened slightly as the penny dropped. The grin was totally fake, a mixture of fear and wanting to get this over with as quickly as possible. She peeled off her faux fur jacket and tossed it to the ground. Reaching for me, she stepped forward.

When I raised my hands in protest, she understood right away—or thought she did.

The relief on her face showed with the assumption I was just a voyeur. Easy money. My star lifted the thin shoulder straps, and the cheap cocktail dress slipped down her body revealing a shoelace thong. Of course, her breasts were fake, but we'd see those in more detail shortly. That annoying giggle was exhibited once again, while she lost her balance slipping the thong over her high-heeled shoes. Now she stood before me naked, apart from the shoes. She had a tattoo on the inside of her left thigh. Hate that! She was shaved. Hate that! And she had those fake titties. Fucking hate that! My arousal was turning to anger, the perfect emotional mix for a great performance.

When she started to approach me again, once more, I held up my hands, gesturing with my raised eyes for the performance to continue. She backed off.

I was a little disappointed with her acting ability. It came across as rushed and without feeling, but this was something we could workshop. There would be plenty of emotion soon.

She was on her knees now, rubbing her breasts in a circular motion, the tip of her tongue rotating her lips in the same way. I noticed her bottom lip was beginning to tremble from the cold, but she continued as true stars do. Sinking back on her butt, and opening her long legs, her eyes were fixed on me.

My eyes moved down her body, I had to look just once to make sure the camera angle was right, and it was. 'Turn over,' I said, trying to control the rising rage.

She did as she was told and lifted her butt into the doggie position. I approached her, reached into my pocket and grasped my prop. She giggled and wiggled her bottom as I straddled her.

In one swift and fully rehearsed movement, I grabbed a handful of hair in my left hand, jerked back her head, swished the blade from my pocket like a sword from a scabbard, and slashed it hard and sweeping across her long, taut throat. Deep, hard and wide (very important, the coup de grâce—no screaming, no struggling, do the job once, do the job right). My trusty blade, always sharp, always handy, did its job well, cutting straight through the trachea and the oesophagus, and severing the carotid arteries until scraping bone. Her neck opened like the floodgate to a dam, and blood erupted and sprayed six feet ahead of us. "Careful in the front row, we did say there would be surprises!" Her body jolted and there was an eruption in my crotch. Her legs and arms collapsed, and she fell forward like a splayed deer. As she did, I yanked her head back harder and the two opposing movements caused the blood to squirt even more, like squeezing the last bit of toothpaste from the tube. I slashed again, this time to the back of the neck. The heavy blade slicing through the vertebrae. As the last sinews gave way, I swayed backwards, lifted the severed head and held it before my face by the hair. It rotated slowly until our eyes met. 'And what type of nursing is it you want to specialise in, January?'

Oh she was good. A star as I knew she would be. Placing her head on the ground so it was looking up at me – cute – and flipping her body over, I had to be quick. Remember, timing in the theatre is everything. Inserting the blade down there, I drove it upwards like carving the Thanksgiving turkey. The thin flesh peeling back on either side. Not much blood, most of that had landed on those cheeky kids on the front row. Bet they aren't laughing now.

The blade rose and sank, carving its way towards the soft area of the lower abdomen. Pausing, I stilled the blade for a moment, relishing the thought of what was about to come. Then jabbing deep there was a delightful little pop as the air from her bowel escaped. I continued sawing up through the abdominal muscles and Kapow! Her guts suddenly spilled, making the most wonderful slithery slurp *as they slopped onto the ground. I continued up through the cleavage valley until the blade bit into the hard sternum. Wardrobe were to be congratulated for their choice of prop. Withdrawing the blade slightly I cut through the flesh above the bone until it exited from the diagonal cut at the throat. True art!*

The breasts flopped either side and assisted nicely with the official opening ceremony. The rib cage was now exposed.

After carefully placing the blade on the ground, I reached into my left pocket and retrieved prop #2. The handy-dandy-sized pair of bolt cutters that I loved so much. This made easy work of the sternum and the ribcage parted nicely.

Oh my, I had almost reached the end of the act. I had to smile when I imagined the future eulogy of this pathetic creature: 'She was a lovely girl, always smiling, and she had such a good heart.' How would they know? Had they seen it? Retrieving the blade, I reached into the cavity and sliced through the aorta and the pulmonary artery. The heart was warm and spongy in my hand. It was amazing how similar it was to the pigs' hearts I'd practised on in rehearsals.

There was a need for haste, the curtain would fall soon. After arranging the corpse in a spreadeagled pose, careful not to disturb the natural resting place of the grey bag of guts, I placed the head close to the neck but stood it upright so it was looking down on its body. The heart rested on the pubic bone. 'Oh yes, she had a lovely heart!' And for a bit of a laugh, I scooped out the fake boobies and placed them on either side of her head.

All that was left was the final task—that last, very important moment of the scene and one, my dear reader, which you must always remember to perform. I cleaned the blade and bolt-cutter-junior right there in centre stage using January's coat. 'Sorry about that, dear. Bit of a mess I'm afraid.' Finally, the production was over. Placing my props back in my pocket, I took a last look at my star, blew her a kiss then took a bow.

Leaving the stage behind me, I was looking forward to the morning reviews.

5

I threw the book for the second time in a day, only this time against the wall.

You can get a bottle from Mr Patel's anytime, Joe, remember? My supressed alter ego—Joe the Bum—offered support as always.

I regained my composure, reached over the chair and picked up the book from the concrete. I flicked to the imprint page, looking for the publication date. Strange, it was only published last year. For some reason I'd assumed the book was older. Then a terrible thought struck me. Judging by its worn condition, it had been read by a lot of people. I couldn't comprehend the kind of people who would read this crap. But it wasn't crap, was it? Whatever anyone thought of the book, or whoever was disgusted or horrified by it, the book was actual real-life accounts of cold-blooded murders written by one of the most notorious and successful psychopathic killers of our time.

There was one thing that didn't add up, however. There had been no clues or suggestions of a theatrical element at any of the murder scenes. I wondered what bearing this information might have had on the profile if we'd had it at the time of the killings. Psychopaths have the need to show off, as do thespians and, if The Moon had wanted to be known for the acting/directing angle, why hadn't he exploited this more?

Then *bang!* A Eureka moment hit me. 'You idiot.' My words climbed the wall. 'You stupid cocky sonofabitch! You couldn't let it rest.' I began to laugh and, grasping the book in both hands, I shook it in front of my face like a bully shaking his victim. 'Even though you'd won, you couldn't leave it.' A realisation was fuelling a new excitement that was growing inside me. This could actually be what I'd been waiting for—the opportunity to get my life back, justice for Sanchez and all those victims … getting my son back.

Old instincts flooded back as if finally being released by the slush gates that had restrained them all these years. I suddenly felt like Detective Joseph Dean of the LAPD again. I took a deep breath, trying to calm myself, then reopened the book to the imprint page. My finger twitched as it scrolled down the lines of text and came to the publisher's name—Ruby P Publications. Below this were two words: Sydney, Australia.

6

I fired up my laptop and easily found the Ruby P website. At the top of the page there was a "Contact Us" link. On this page there was an email address and a single phone number. *'Gotchya.'*

The international and local dial codes were also easy to find on Google, so I wrote down the long number in my notebook. After another quick search, the Internet told me that Sydney was fourteen hours ahead of Florida. I checked my watch and did the math. It was 5.30 pm here, which made it 7.30 am in Sydney. I'd need to wait at least another hour before making the call. If I could talk to the publisher, I could learn about the author, possibly even be able to find out where the author lived. Did I really think it would be that easy? Of course not. This was The Moon.

At 6.35 pm, I anxiously dialled the publisher's number in Sydney. It would be 8.35 am in Australia. There were a few clicks followed by a little electronic jingle, then the phone began to ring. It was picked up after about the tenth ring. A grunt echoed down the line.

'Hi, I'm calling from the US, and I'm looking for some information about one of your authors.'

The early morning voice of a young man. 'What's the title?' No 'Hi' or 'Thank you for calling.'

'*Flirting with The Moon* by Stephen Powell.'

There was the sound of fingers tapping rapidly on a keyboard. 'The book is $12.99.'

'Yes, I know, but I already have a copy of the book. I just need to get in touch with the author.'

'We can't give out personal details, only the details that the author provides for the cover and promotional use.'

'And where would I find those?'

'Did you look in the back of the book?' The tone of his answer came through loud and clear. He might as well have come straight out and said it: 'Are you stupid?'

There were no details in the back of the book, and I'd already checked the imprint page. I'd also checked to see if the author had a website and a following on social media, but there was nothing. 'Yes, but there's no—'

'Well, that's it then.'

I was getting pissed at this little shit. 'What's your name, son?'

'Huh?'

'I said, what's your name?'

'Gavin.'

'Okay, Gavin, my name is Detective Joseph Dean of the Los Angeles Police Department.'

Silence.

'I'm going to tell you what's gonna happen—'

'You want me to lift his file?' He sounded less bored now, excited even.

There was a fumbling sound then a woman's voice came on the line. 'Hello, who is this please?'

'Hi, my name is Joseph Dean and I need some information about one of your authors.' I heard the rustle and the scrape of a chair. I pictured her taking a seat in front of the computer.

'Ah, *Flirting with The Moon*. Interesting.'

'Interesting? In what way?'

'There's been a lot of interest in this book.' She was tapping the keyboard now. Not as quickly as Gavin, but adequately.

I lied for the second time that day when I reiterated that I was a detective with the LAPD. 'We need to speak to the author as soon as possible. It's very important.'

'Okaaay!' She sounded impressed. Thankfully she didn't ask any more questions. More tapping. 'It's a strange one this. We've never actually had any contact with the author. The manuscript was posted to us on a disk, already edited and with explicit typed details of the requirements: cover design, layout, and that kind of thing. The envelope also contained instructions for us to send an invoice for the work.'

'So, the author paid for it to be published?'

'Uh huh.'

'Right. So … do you have the contact details?'

'Sure do.'

I had my pen and notepad ready. 'Okay.' I tried to sound casual.

'PO Box 24, Candle Stick Bay, Queensland 4898.'

'That's it?'

'Yep. That's all we've ever received, and it's where all our correspondence goes.'

'Candle Stick Bay.'

'That's right and judging by the postcode, it's quite a way up.'

'I beg your pardon?'

'Close to The Top End. Bunch o' flamin' galahs up there, mate!'

I'd never been called 'mate' by a woman before and found it quite endearing. 'Galahs?'

'Queenslanders. All a snag short of a barby if you know what I mean.'

I had no idea what a snag or a galah was, but I guessed by her tone she was implying that Queenslanders were all a bit slow. 'Right. Well thank you for your time … miss?'

'Ruby.'

After hanging up, I looked down at the address I'd scribbled on my pad. Candle Stick Bay. I went over to my laptop and Googled the place. A list of sites came up, including Wikipedia and the Tourism Tropical North Queensland website. Third on the list was the Candle Stick Bay homepage. I clicked on the link and a picture of a slim, white lighthouse scrolled onto the page. It stood sentinel on the edge of a short peninsula. Behind it was a crescent-shaped bay with a small town clustered around its edge. 'Wow!' I said out loud. I thought the ocean in Florida was beautiful, but this was pure blue heaven. Below the picture was a little about the town's history.

In September 1770, Captain James Cook was the first European to discover the site of what is now known as Candle Stick Bay.

When gold was discovered at the Palmer River, west of Cooktown, in 1872, optimistic miners migrated to the area en masse, beginning a rush that would see Cairns eventually established in 1876. In 1887, the first European settlers arrived at Candle Stick Bay led by Englishman William Holbrook. Originally called Holbrook Bay, the township grew to service the expanding cane and banana plantations that were being planted in the surrounding rich tropical soil. The lighthouse was built in 1899. The structure's unusually narrow girth gave it the appearance of a candle when seen from the sea, hence seafarers and the locals adopting the name of Candle Stick Bay. In 1925, the name was officially changed.

I learned that the town's population was only 600, and that it was extremely hot and humid in the summer with the likelihood of cyclones. Sugar cane and banana plantations were once the main industry of the surrounding area, but the town now relied on tourism for its income.

This had to be a hoax. Candle Stick Bay wasn't the kind of place in which you'd expect an infamous serial killer to reside. From reading that first chapter of the book, the words were definitely those of The Moon. Only the killer or a cop on the case would've known those details. So, had the killer written them? Or someone close to the killer? My hunch was that the killer *had* written the book. The egocentric style matched the profiler's description. And having the story in print for posterity would fuel his or her ego. Candle Stick Bay though? Had to be a red herring to throw anyone off the scent. The Moon was far too clever to reveal details like where he lived. Then something struck me. I rose from my seat in front of the computer and paced the room. In a way, this actually did match the killer's pattern. All the murders had taken place over twelve months, all in LA, and all on the night of the new moon. We knew exactly where and when the murders were going to take place. Is he playing the game of risk again? I imagined The Moon sitting back and enjoying this. But why now? And would he kill again?

I couldn't erase the gruesome images of the first chapter from my mind. The visions were worsened by the fact that I had witnessed the actual scene, and the ones that followed, except that until now it had been like coming into a movie late and missing the start. Now I had the whole story. My next task was to find the killer and find closure. If only it were that easy.

7

My early morning walks were always brisk. I'd walk as far as the Boca Raton Inlet and back to Spanish River Park, breathing in deeply. All the fresh air helped to clear my brain and set me up for the day ahead.

I was mulling over my next move as I strode along the sand. Over the last twenty years, my earnings hadn't been that great, but I'd managed to put a bit by for a rainy day. And thanks to Big Howie's generosity—an extra cash bonus after handing over the audio recording—my funds had received an unexpected boost. A trip to Australia was within my budget.

One part of me was saying: This is it, Joe! This is what you've been waiting for, your chance to nail this bastard once and for all. But the other, more logical me, was saying: What are you thinking, man? Flying to Australia? What will that achieve? Call the police and let them handle it.

Why the hell was I even contemplating this? This time yesterday the farthest thing from my mind was The Moon. And as for Australia, all I knew about that place was kangaroos and …? Off the top of my head, I couldn't think of anything else. I'd made a life of sorts for myself in Florida. I'd beaten the booze and was enjoying each day as it came. Wasn't I?

Some life! Sneaking around following cheating wives. Grassing on guys for fiddling their insurance. Slowly turning into a member of the grey army. Great little life you got here. Joe the Bum seemed to be growing in strength.

I'd known ever since I first stood before my AA group and said, 'I am an alcoholic!' that every baby step, every achievement and every day without a drink had been directed to one thing and one thing only ... a reconciliation with my son. But I'd also known that it wasn't just a matter of showing up on his doorstep announcing: 'Hello son, I'm your long-lost Dad!' I needed to be validated in some way. Might sound cheesy, but that was how I felt.

What better way to validate myself than to bring The Moon to justice? I stopped and stared out to sea. If The Moon was active again, of course the authorities, both here and in Australia, would need to know about it and no doubt reopen the case.

Where will that leave you, Joe? The Moon wouldn't be the only one hunted. The media will come looking for you. They'll tear you to shreds and Johnny will know you're still alive and think you've been hiding for the last twenty years in Florida, which is what you've been doing, isn't it?

If I did the right thing and reported this to the authorities, it would be over for me. I'd have no input and probably end up a laughing stock all over again, but if I didn't report it and The Moon started killing again, it would be old Joe Dean still Flirting with The Moon.

I needed some advice from an old friend.

The new LAPD headquarters, which opened in 2009, was a short stroll from City Hall. It was a far different building from the old Parker Center in Downtown LA. This place was all white concrete and tinted glass, straight lines and sharp angles. My stomach was churning as I neared the front steps. It was early morning on 1st Street but already the place was alive with people: civvies and uniforms, lawyers, office workers, and a few undesirables.

The lobby was huge and very modern. I had no sense of familiarity—of coming home—as I would've had with the old building. This was an alien world to me now.

Before travelling to LA, I'd done my research and discovered that my old pal, Burt Williams, was now Captain Burt Williams. I waited for the elevator that would take me up to the Detective Bureau. The familiar pangs of guilt were tugging at me because I hadn't kept in contact with Burt. In fact, the last time I'd seen him was twenty years ago at our coffee shop meeting when I was fresh out of rehab.

I could've called him at home; I still had the number, and I didn't know why I hadn't but, after a phone call to his secretary, I'd secured a meeting.

I stepped from the elevator and followed the signs along a corridor that led me to the offices of the Special Investigation Section—SIS. There, I was greeted by a young receptionist called Cindy, and was invited to take a seat.

By the time I was finally shown into the captain's office, I was beginning to feel like a kid again going up before the headmaster.

'Joseph Dean!' Burt bounded from his desk to meet me at the door. 'Is it really you?' We bear hugged like old buddies, which I guess we were. 'Look at you. You look ten years younger since the last time I saw you!' He shepherded me into the room.

I wished I could say the same. Burt Williams was a year younger than me, but he didn't look it. His hair was still cropped in the good old buzz style but was now grey and his face was bloated—and blotchy. I wondered if he was drinking. I hoped he wasn't. I could tell he'd lost condition by the paunch that protruded between his open jacket and overhung his belt. No early morning walks on the beach for a captain of the LAPD, I guessed.

Burt poked his head out the door. 'Cindy, this is really important, I have a 9.30 with Detective …'

He lowered his voice so I didn't catch the detective's name. I glanced at my watch. It was 8.30 am.

'Whatever you do, make sure he waits outside the office until I call him in, okay?'

'Yes, sir.'

Burt turned to me. 'Coffee, Joe?'

'Tea would be great if you've got it.'

He relayed my request and ordered a coffee for himself. 'And don't forget the cookies!' he added.

'Wow! Belated congratulations, Burt. Captain Williams, eh? And the SIS too.' I easily read his embarrassment as he took his seat, like he was thinking, *This should have been your job, Joe!*

'So …' he said.

'So …'

'How've you been?'

I told him all about my life in Florida.

'A private dick? 'He interrupted me with a friendly chuckle just as Cindy brought in the drinks and set them down. I noticed she didn't bring cookies and guessed she also took orders from her other boss, Burt's wife.

We thanked the young woman and I continued. I was shocked to realise that everything I'd done in the last twenty years was easily related within a few minutes.

For the next thirty minutes or so I listened while Burt regaled me with his life of recommendations, promotions, overseas vacations, wedding anniversaries, grandchildren, and his plans for an early retirement. I felt no envy, just pride and happiness for my old friend. We chatted about the old days some, but I noticed Burt starting to check his watch. I remembered he had a meeting at 9.30 am. It was 9.10—time for me to get to the point of my visit. I desperately wanted to ask him if he knew anything about Johnny and Kathy, but it would have to wait.

'Burt, the last time we spoke—'

'I know, Joe.' He stood up, thrust his hands deep into his pockets, walked around to the front of his desk, and rested his butt on the edge. 'I've thought about what we talked about a lot over the years, and I've often wondered if I gave you the right advice.'

'Your advice was sound, Burt. There was nothing I could've done at the time.'

Burt nodded. 'As soon as you contacted me, I knew what it was about.'

'You did? How?'

'I've been half expecting it for a long time. I knew the day would come when you'd get your act together and make this decision.'

'But I only came across the book a couple of weeks ago.'

'Book?'

I took a copy of *Flirting with The Moon*—one that I'd purchased from Amazon—from my shoulder bag and handed it to him.

He read the title. His face and neck flushed a deep crimson. 'What's this?'

'The reason I'm here.'

He returned to his seat and slumped down, staring at the book.

'You all right, Burt?'

'*Flirting with The Moon* ... what the hell?' He checked his watch again.

'It's a diary, Burt. Written by The Moon, describing in every single detail how he committed the murders.'

'Has to be a hoax, surely.'

'No, I've read it ... well, some of it. It's him, Burt. This book is filled with stuff that even we didn't know.'

He looked up at me. His expression was wary ... suspicious.

'It means we can get him.'

He checked his watch again and fidgeted in his seat. 'Is this really why you're here, Joe?'

'Absolutely. Don't you see, Burt? This is my chance to make things right. To get my life back.'

'You know the LAPD won't be reopening a case just because of some book.'

'I've got an address.'

A flicker of interest crossed Burt's face.

'A PO Box. The first proper lead that could direct us to The Moon.'

'An address? In LA?'

'No ... that's the thing ... it's in, um ... Queensland ... Australia.'

His shoulders dropped along with the small peak of enthusiasm. 'Australia?'

I nodded, knowing full well what was coming next.

'Do you realise how absurd this is, Joe?' He slapped the book down on his desk and scooted it towards me with the ends of his fingers. 'Like I said, the case is closed.'

It was the response I'd secretly been hoping for. 'I agree that this is probably nothing but I'm going to follow it up all the same. I just wanted to let you know I'm flying to Australia in the morning.'

'What?'

'It's something I have to do, Burt!'

He stared at me for what seemed like forever. A captain's tool for unnerving young detectives that he'd perfected over the years no doubt. Except I was no young detective. I met his stare in silence.

There was a buzz and Cindy's voice came through the intercom. 'Sir, your nine-thirty's here.'

Burt's face grew pale.

'Tell him to take a seat.' He levered himself to his feet and returned to my side of the desk. 'I understand, Joe. Of course I do. Hell, I'd probably do the same if I was in your position.' He leaned his butt against the front of the desk again. I guessed this was the position he used when reassuring young detectives. 'Putting all that aside for a moment ... we have a bit of a problem.'

'A problem?'

'I assumed your reason for coming here today was for an entirely different matter. I never dreamt we'd be sitting here talking about The Moon.' He was sweating and choosing his words carefully. 'I thought you'd made the decision, Joe.'

'What decision?'

He lowered his gaze until our eyes met once more. 'Johnny.'

I was a bit slow on the uptake. Then I realised what he was trying to say. He thought I'd come back to LA to attempt reconciliation with my son. 'No … no, that's not on the cards yet, not until I …' I suddenly realised how foolish it sounded, declaring that I couldn't be reunited with my son until I brought The Moon to justice.

Burt cupped a hand over his chin and lowered his head. 'On the other side of that door, Joe, is my 9.30 appointment. A young detective … a fiery young guy, outspoken and cocky as hell but with a brilliant career ahead of him.' He exhaled loudly as if making room for the words to come. 'His name is Detective John Dean!'

Suddenly our cross-purpose conversation made sense to me. The last time Burt and I had spoken, twenty years ago, I'd said I was going away in order to get my life back, and would only return when I was worthy of my son's forgiveness. And here I was. He thought I'd come back to claim my son.

'Johnny's a cop?'

'John. He hates being called Johnny. He's my best detective.'

'But he's only twenty-eight.'

'Yep, there's only one person in the history of the LAPD who soared through the detective ranks as quickly as this young man.' He raised his eyebrows at me.

After all these years out of the force, I had no idea who he was talking about.

He chuckled. 'You, you idiot!'

I felt the heat rise to my face—a mix of embarrassment on my part plus pride in my son.

'There's something else you should know, Joe.' Burt cleared his throat. 'He married recently.'

It was too much to take in all at once. All I could manage was a choked out, 'Really?'

'Damn right. Nance and I attended his wedding.'

'My son's married?' Staring down at my feet, I wasn't sure whether to be happy or sad.

Burt must've had an inkling regarding what I was feeling and attempted to cheer me up. 'She's a wonderful girl, Joe. Smart and beautiful. Her name's Beth. She's a zoologist, can you believe?'

Burt continued telling me something about how they'd met on a very important case, but I couldn't take it in. All I could think about was my son, the three-year-old, now the man, the detective, the husband. 'And he's sitting outside this office?'

'Yep. He doesn't know why he's been summoned. He's working on an interesting case at the moment. He'll be pissed at me for calling him in when he's busy and will no doubt tell me so.'

I rose from my chair and started pacing. Joe the bum taunted: *Should've had a drink, Joey. Boy you'll need one after this.*

Burt's voice silenced my alter ego. 'What do you want to do, Joe?'

Panic surged into my throat. 'I can't meet him … not yet … it's not the right time.'

Burt twisted and depressed the intercom. 'Cindy, please inform Detective Dean that I'll be a few minutes yet. Ask him to go to the tearoom.'

A deep voice came on the line. 'What the hell's going on, Captain? I haven't got time for this. You know I'm leaving for Pennsylvania this afternoon.'

'I know, I know. Bear with me, John. This won't take long.'

I froze in the middle of the room like a waxwork dummy.

There was a loud *'Hmpfff'* from the intercom, then silence. Despite his added girth, Burt's speed as he strode to the door was impressive. He opened it slightly, enough to peek through the gap. Then he waved me forward. I peered out and my heart just about exploded. A tall, young man with dark-blond hair, wearing a crumpled suit, was marching down the corridor away from us. My son.

8

I've never felt good in confined spaces and I'm a terrible fidget. I need to spread out to be comfortable, and that's an unheard-of luxury when flying economy class. I watched three movies during the fourteen-hour flight, snoozed some between meals, and even managed an hour's solid sleep towards the end. When I woke from my slumber, the little inch-an-hour plane on the screen at the front of the cabin was about an inch away from the east coast of Australia. I lifted the window cover—it was dark outside except for a pink curve on the horizon, like a furnace burner on low. I'd changed my watch to Australian time when we'd left LA. I checked the time—4.55 am.

By the time we were on the descent into Brisbane, the sun was up, and I got a good view of the coastline and a glimpse of the city glistening in the distance. The massive arch of the Gateway Bridge shone like gold.

It took almost an hour to get through customs. My first impression of Australians, whether customs officials, attendants, or even janitors, was that they were friendly, happy, and seemed content with their lot.

I headed for the exit. I'd get some air then find the shuttle bus and head over to the domestic terminal to catch my connecting flight to Cairns.

On the way out I noticed a currency exchange so I changed a wad of greenbacks into multi-coloured Aussie notes.

What I'd expected to be an uneventful two-hour flight, turned out to be anything but. Thank God for window seats. The view as the plane flew north, following the Queensland coast from Brisbane to Cairns, was spectacular. Mile after golden mile of beaches and turquoise bays, sometimes dissected by rivers. The farther north we flew, the tropical rainforests of the hinterland became denser and the mountains more rugged. All the while the ocean glistened and shone to my right, rippling like molten glass.

9

After a night at an airport hotel in Cairns, I arrived at the bus depot bright and early the next morning.

'G'Day, folks. I'm Reg, and I have the pleasure of being your driver today.' Reg was middle aged, wearing khaki shorts and knee-length socks. He was loading our bags into the compartment on the side of the bus. 'If you'd like to take your seats, folks, we'll be away in a jiffy.'

The bus was not much more than a minibus. There were three other passengers: an elderly lady wearing a leather cowboy hat, and a young woman with a baby.

I'd read somewhere that it was important to stay awake during the day after a long overseas flight and to try to sleep only at night if you wanted to restore your normal sleep/wake cycle. Good advice but my body clock was totally out of whack. I'd retired at 10.00 pm the night before but hadn't slept a wink. Now my body was shutting down. I fought to keep my eyes open.

The bus headed out of town and north along a coastal road. The scenery was very tropical: stunning blue ocean and palm trees to my right, forest to the left. A fiercely red early morning sun sat just above the water. The air con hummed along with the music of Michael Bublé. My eyelids were growing heavier until the friendly chatter of Reg dissolved into, 'The Way You Look Tonight.'

When I awoke, the interior of the bus was dark. Peering through the window, I realised we were driving along a narrow dirt track through a dense rainforest.

Reg eyed me through the rear-view mirror. 'Back with us, eh, mate?' He chuckled then informed me that the other passengers had got off at Cooktown over an hour ago.

I was a little pissed at myself. I was hoping to have seen the town.

'Starcke National Park,' Reg addressed my unasked question. 'Bloody thick, eh?'

It was like nothing I'd seen before. Massive *Jurassic Park*-like trees grew amid a profusion of vines and ferns to form a dense canopy over the road. I wondered what would happen if a vehicle approached in the opposite direction. There wouldn't be room to pass or turnaround. Again, Reg seemed to read my thoughts.

'Just got to hope no one's coming the other way. Luckily there's bugger all traffic out this far.'

'Is this the only way into the bay?'

'Yep. Apart from the ocean.'

I hadn't realised Candle Stick Bay was so isolated. I'd expected it to be just a jump up the coast from a town or a major resort.

'Not hard for them to get cut off out here. S'pose they're used to it but,' Reg said.

The scenery was amazing—lush and green—and Reg seemed happy to chat but despite all that, or maybe because of it, I began to grow a little agitated. We still had some way to go, and I was now wide awake. My thoughts returned to The Moon. I had my copy of *Flirting with The Moon*. I'd read up to Chapter Eleven. With each page, the rush of vivid memories, the feeling of being right back there and out of control, was very painful. I knew I'd never be able to read Chapter Twelve. I reached over to the adjacent seat and retrieved the book from my jacket pocket.

Chapter 11 – November Moon

After receiving great reviews for my last production, "October Moon", it was time to hit the boards again. Hey-diddle-dee, an actor's life for me.

My new Star was waiting in the wings. He'd passed his audition with flying colours, although he didn't know yet that he'd landed the part. As with all my Stars, he was an unknown, an ingénu, just waiting for his moment to shine.

The club he frequented was in downtown LA. I won't mention the place's real name, but Sodom and Gomorrah will suffice. He had lots of friends—a very popular boy. His name was Gerald, pronounced Sheraald, but to me he'll always be November. He was a hairdresser. He lived alone in a one-bedroom apartment in Glendale and had frequent visitors. I'd been watching him very closely.

The location was perfect, close to a nightclub that he frequented—our very own little theatre with whitewashed walls, tiled floors, peepholes linking each stall, and the stench of urine. Soon it would be as famous as The Old Vic.

The November new moon was finally here. The police—and old Joe, God love him—had put two and two together after my March presentation. So now, with each performance there was a greater police presence on the streets, which made my task even more exciting.

But I'm jumping ahead. The props were to be the same as always. This is one area where there were similarities in each performance. Perhaps one day I'll donate them to the Hollywood Museum so they can be exhibited alongside Judy Garland's red slippers, Chaplain's cane or Marilyn's white dress. What a touching thought!

I'd introduced myself to Gerald one day while he was out walking his dog in the park. The fact that we shared the same tastes seem to delight him. He liked me. I made sure of that.

On opening night, I knew he'd be on his way to the club around 8.30 pm. When he spotted me standing across the street, his face lit up, and he waved like an excited schoolgirl. I beckoned him across the road.

'Hi, Joe?' he said.

Oops, did I forget to mention, dear reader, that I'd told him my name was Joe? Joe Dean? I used the name as a little joke in deference to my old friend. While you're reading this, Joe, as I know you are, please accept my apologies. My humour was in bad taste and beneath me.

I suggested we go for a walk. He seemed reluctant—had he arranged to meet someone at the club? 'It's early, how about we have a little drink somewhere first then come back to the club later?' My tone was seductive, and he took the bait. We walked through the Arts District and turned dark corners until my little theatre was in view. Thanks to the absence of the moon and the fact that the building was a little way back from the road, the ambient lighting was perfect.

'I really need to go in here first, Sheraald.' Taking his arm, I headed towards the stage door. I'm unsure whether his expression was one of shock or excitement. He halted. Gazing at him, I flashed a seductive grin. It did the trick. He grasped my hand and led the way into the public toilet. His familiarity indicated this wasn't his first time here. Following him past the sinks and the urinals to the stalls, I slipped on my surgical gloves without him noticing. When we reached the cubicle at the far end, he kicked open the door, turned and pushed me inside. With fumbling fingers, he locked the door, then swung

around so we were standing face to face. Leaning forward he tried to kiss me. Placing my left hand on his chest, I smiled and whispered, 'Action!'

For a moment, he looked confused, then he returned my smile and leaned in again, pursing his lips.

'Take off your jeans,' I whispered, pulling away from his lips.

He zipped open his jeans and let them fall around his ankles. I gestured for him to drop his boxers. He obliged.

Once more he tilted forward for a kiss.

Act II

Pushing him backwards and, without breaking eye contact, I retrieved the blade from my pocket and thrust it up into his diaphragm. Warm, minty breath hit my cheek as air burst from his mouth. His eyes opened wide, staring in shock, disbelief. I kept pushing upwards, skewering him, almost lifting him off the ground, angling for his heart. His mouth opened as if he were about to cry out, but his throat had already filled with a foaming upsurge of blood. It poured out the corners of his mouth, making it look like a ghastly downturned smile. Withdrawing the knife—the blade came out with a 'phup'— then I thrust it in again, guiding it at a right angle, carving into his abdomen. He toppled forward. Careful not to get any blood on me, I managed to side-step just in the nick of time like a matador outmanoeuvring a bull. With the dull thud of his forehead hitting the stall door, I let go of the knife and he grabbed the handle with both hands as if he were going to pull it out. But he no longer possessed the strength. I retrieved Baby Bolt from my other pocket and smashed it across the top vertebrae at the back of his neck. There was a loud crack. I hit the same spot again. His legs buckled and he collapsed awkwardly onto the floor. I gave him another whack, this time on the back of the head. There was a satisfying eggshell crunch as Baby Bolt broke through his skull. End of Act II.

I had to be quick or Act III would run into overtime. Grabbing his jacket at the back of the shoulders I manoeuvred his dead weight backwards until I managed to sit him on the can. Shifting my stance, I lifted him higher, plonked him down on the porcelain faucet, withdrew the knife from his stomach with a squishy shlop, *and placed it on the floor. I unzipped his jacket, unbuttoned his shirt then retrieved the knife from the floor and stood watching the blood as it flowed from the two wounds in his gut and into the can. With my left hand, I grabbed his head by the hair. We were almost at eye level again. Then I pressed the point of the blade into his neck just beneath the chin and sliced downward. 'When Daddy carves the turkey,' I hummed in my mind as I laboured. November's torso opened like unzipping a wetsuit. I reached the top of his abdomen. The next scene would be quick—and it was. I pushed the blade deeper then yanked it down towards his groin. Like a calf slipping from the womb, his guts spilled out, landing in the can. The bulging mass of entrails and membrane filled the toilet and overspilled. But there was more to go in yet. Baby Bolt took centre stage once more, this time cutting through the sternum. The ribcage parted and I went to work making the necessary cuts. The kidneys and lungs were now lodged nicely on top of the intestines like petals with his little heart sitting between them—the centrepiece of my design.*

As I sliced off his penis, I couldn't help giggling at the thought of how the profilers would interpret this statement. There wasn't a reason of course, pure poetic licence on my part, but I loved the thought of keeping them guessing. Memorabilia perhaps? No, no, no.

It was a struggle, but I managed to pull up his boxers and his jeans and fasten his fly. I buttoned his shirt and zipped his jacket before lifting him off the faucet and sitting him down gently onto his special throne. Act III was nearly over. I opened his mouth and placed the severed end of his penis between his lips. The phallus hung down like a floppy cigar.

Bravo, Bravo! Absolutely first class. My bow was filled with pride.

There was a sudden shaft of light through the thick trees. Lifting my eyes from the book I stared out the bus window. In my mind's eye I saw the actual crime scene that Sanchez and myself had witnessed when we'd peered into the toilet cubicle. It was exactly as the author had described.

The bus emerged from the rainforest into bright sunshine. The road veered sharply to the right, rising into a pass with steep rock sides.

'Brace yourself for this, mate,' Reg said just before the vehicle traversed through the pass. 'Eyes left.'

I'd assumed that the pictures on the net had either been touched up a little or cleverly filtered. You know, the way they do to make the ocean seem bluer in the holiday brochures? But there had been no exaggeration. In fact, the pictures hadn't done justice to the view.

The bay curved below us in a half moon. The beach was a strip of the whitest sand I'd ever seen, fringed with lush green vegetation, which spread inland as far as the eye could see. But the ocean! Oh my goodness. It wasn't just blue, or turquoise or green. It was all those colours and many more shades in between, glistening and shimmering under an enormous clear sky.

The bus charted the steep decline, coasting from left to right around the bends. The closer we got, the more beautiful was the vista below. The small town was nestled against the sweeping curve of the bay with the lighthouse standing guard on the tip of the peninsula.

'Could you drop me here, Reg?'

'No worries. Bit of a walk in this heat, but.' He pulled over to the side of the road, opened the door, jumped from his seat, and retrieved my bag from the luggage rack.

I followed him off the bus and the heat hit me like I'd stepped into a sauna. 'Is it always this hot?'

'Nah mate, not quite summer yet.' Reg grinned. 'Pretty much unbearable then. There you go, sport.' He placed my bag on the road. 'Good as gold.' Then he reached up into the bus, grabbed a plastic bottle of cold water and a cap with the bus company's logo emblazoned across the front. 'You'll need these.'

'Thank you. How much do I owe you?' I put the cap on my head.

'She'll be right.' That grin again.

We shook hands, then he frowned. Opening his palm he found an orange note.

'I'll be offended if you don't take it,' I said. 'You've earned it.'

'A twenty? Struth! Well … don't mind if I do. Good on ya, mate!'

'No worries,' I said in my first attempt at the Australian lingo.

Reg winked. 'Mate, if you need anything, I'll be filling up at the servo before heading back.'

'Thank you.'

I took a sip of water, watched the bus pull away then headed in the same direction.

10

The omnipresent hum of insects laid down the backing track, the chirping of lorikeets and the warble of a magpie, the melody. Then the chorus broke. I swung around and spotted the star of the performance. Sitting on a power line on the other side of the road was a kookaburra. I'd read about this amazing bird but never expected to see or hear one. A large comical-looking member of the kingfisher family, motley coloured and about the size of an owl but with a squat head and a long sharp beak, the kookaburra is also known as the laughing jackass. I couldn't help but feel as if the little fellow was aiming his laughter directly at me. Of course, I knew he wasn't really laughing, and certainly not at me—the sound was a territorial cry. You see I'd also done some research on Queensland's diverse fauna and flora, that's how I knew the little chirping parrots were rainbow lorikeets. But it was the not-so-nice fauna that had been the reason for my research: snakes, spiders, crocodiles, deadly jellyfish, and sharks etc. I'd heard about them, of course, but until I'd actually started reading the facts, I hadn't anticipated how dangerous Australia was.

Hoping that I wouldn't be meeting a redback spider or a brown snake anytime soon, I continued down the road.

After a little way, a side road veered off to the right, leading upwards. A sign on a steel pole read:

>Private Road.
>No Entry.

Flirting with The Moon

I wondered who might live there. A wealthy landowner perhaps?

Around the next bend, a truck was parked on the right-hand verge with the word "Telstra" emblazoned along its side. In its shade, I noticed two workmen sitting on cooler boxes. One was a large Hawaiian-looking chap. He was hoeing into a huge sandwich. The other guy resembled a very thin Russell Crowe. He was smoking a rolled cigarette and reading a newspaper. They wore shorts, work boots and fluro, high-viz vests.

'How ya goin?' the big guy said with a friendly smile.

'I'm very well, thanks.' A nametag on his vest read, "Tana".

"Russell Crowe" looked up from his newspaper. 'American?' His nametag read, "Kenny".

'Sure am.'

'Sweet!' Tana said.

'Here on holiday, mate?' Kenny said.

'Yes.'

'Top spot, eh?' Tana's wide grin revealed perfect white teeth. Recognising a New Zealand accent, I realised Tana was Maori.

'It sure is.' I glanced over the bay and the town below.

'Bit of unrest down there at the minute though, mate.' Kenny folded his newspaper.

'Yeah?'

'Oh yeah.' He stood, stubbed his cigarette under his boot, opened his cooler box and looked inside. 'Ahh, bloody ell!' He pulled out a can of soft drink. 'Bloody passionfruit again.'

Tana sniggered.

'She knows I hate this shit, s'like cat piss!' He slammed down the cooler lid. 'Do you wan it?' he said, holding out the purple can to his co-worker.

'Sweet, bro.' Tana took the can.

'What kind of unrest?' I asked as Kenny began to roll another cigarette.

'Uhm ... communication problems, I guess you'd say.'

Tana laughed. His voice was high-pitched, and I guessed he had a great singing voice.

'Communication's always been up the shit around here. Lousy reception, ya know?' Kenny continued. 'Poor buggers have been complaining for years.'

'So, you're here to fix it?'

'That's right. We're putting in a 4G mast, which'll bring em into the twenty-first century.'

'So, what's the problem?'

'Well, we've ripped out the old mast, no worries. New mast's here in pieces ready to be assembled.' He pointed back with his thumb towards a cleared track that led up to the top of the ridge. 'Hell of a big job, but.'

Tana nodded. 'Union's just called us out on strike, eh,' Tana said.

'So, they've gone from lousy reception to sod all,' Kenny said and both men grinned. 'And they're not happy.'

'I bet.' I wished them a speedy resolve to their industrial dispute, bid them farewell, and continued on my way. No Internet, no phones and no TV? I wondered how people could survive nowadays without these twenty-first century staples.

After a sweaty but pleasant ten minute or so stroll, I reached the first of the buildings that clung to the ocean side of the hill. It was a simple off-white timber construction, held above the ground by stubby legs with a wraparound verandah and a green corrugated tin roof. I later learned the design was called The Queenslander.

The next property looked ultramodern and stood on steel stilts. It had sharp lines and dark timber cladding. I compared the building to its older neighbour and recognised the similarities. The principle was exactly the same, and one that obviously suited the Queensland environment. Both places had the most amazing views over the bay.

A little farther on and more buildings—mostly of the older design—began to appear on either side of the road. By the time I

Flirting with The Moon

reached the bottom of the hill, the houses were hunkered side by side. From there it was a short stroll into the town.

I stood at the end of the road for a moment, taking in the smaller-than-I-had-expected town before me. Although I couldn't see the beach from here, I could hear the slow lapping of waves and found it easy to imagine how the relaxing sound, coupled with the heat, might dictate the pace of the town like a slow metronome.

The first building on my left was a gas station, the old-fashioned type with two shiny chrome pumps and a store the size of a shipping container. I noticed Reg, the driver, at one of the pumps filling up with gas for his return trip. He waved when he saw me. I waved back.

I strolled down the street. A short laneway at the side of the gas station led to a closed-up mechanic—Davo's Garage. Next to this was a large, two-storey, red-brick building with a tin roof and a wraparound balcony with fancy metal scrollwork encompassing the second floor. On the ground floor there were frosted concertina windows, all closed, and a wide entrance with a brass-framed double doorway. Above this, in large, somewhat flaky writing, were the words, "The Great Northern Hotel". This was the place where I was hoping to get a room.

Approaching the building, I noticed the stench of stale beer. A smell I hated. I'd read on the Candle Stick Bay homepage that the hotel—actually the local bar, or pub—offered bed and breakfast at a reasonable price, with an unbeatable location. They were right about that. It was in the heart of the town and backed onto the beach. I hadn't booked anywhere to stay, as I'd expected there'd be accommodation available. I suddenly realised how dumb this was and began to panic. What if there was nowhere to stay? The pub was a likely choice except now I realised it would be like a diabetic staying at The Cheesecake Shop.

I needed to ask someone for an alternative, but I obviously couldn't go into the pub and ask their opinion. Gazing across the street, I noticed the General Store and headed over.

The building's entrance was between two typical shop windows. The one on the left was dedicated to movie posters and there was a neon sign that read, "DVD Rentals Here". The other side offered only a poster advertising the lottery but gave me a view of the store interior where I could see—past newspapers, magazines and rows of groceries—two women in conversation. It was time to make contact with the natives.

As soon as I entered, the two women at the counter—one in front, the other behind—stopped talking.

I smiled. 'Hi, I'm going to be staying in town for a few days and I wondered if you'd know of a good place to hold up?'

'Oh hello,' the woman behind the counter said. 'The pub across the street.' She pointed through the window. 'That'll be your best bet.'

'An American, eh?' the other woman said, looking me up and down. 'I expect you're here for the wedding?'

'Maudie!' The woman behind the counter was shaking her head at her companion.

'Joe Dean.' I held out my hand.

'I'm Maud, and this ere's Silvia.' Maud shook my hand … tentatively like I might bite her.

Silvia came around the counter and shook my hand. 'Hello Mister Dean, I'm Silvia Stanton.'

'Joe, please, call me Joe—'

'You're a copper!' Maud said.

'A what?'

'A copper … a policeman.'

'What on Earth makes you say that?'

'I can spot a copper a mile off.'

I had to smile at the woman's intuition. 'You can, eh? Well, I hate to disappoint you but I'm not a cop.'

Maud narrowed her eyes at me as if she knew my darkest secrets.

'Maudie!' Silvia had raised her voice. Then she turned back to me. 'Don't tell her anything, Joe. She's a terrible gossip.'

'I've been to LA,' Maud piped up.

'Yeah?'

'Horrible place, full of crooks and undesirables.'

Silvia gave an exasperated sigh and shrugged her shoulders at me.

'Like I said, I just came in to ask if you'd know of a good place to stay.' I directed my gaze at Silvia.

'The pub's the nearest and cheapest. There's lots of holiday lets in town but they're quite expensive. You'll find Pat and Frank at the pub very obliging,' Silvia said.

'Thank you, I'll check it out.' I bid them good day and left the store.

I was lying when I said I hated the smell of stale bear. The smell actually frightened me, taunted me. And Joe the bum didn't help: *You can't fight it, Joe. It's a part of you. Good old Joe could be back with just a single sip.*

The large door was heavy and buffed the carpet as I opened one side, making it feel even heavier. It took a moment to adjust to the dark interior, but I was in the lobby. Before me was a wooden staircase. Once it would've been quite majestic but now, its chips were showing under the dark, waxy varnish. The dull, red-patterned carpet, splattered with years of beer stains, and faded wallpaper made the building appear old and tired. To the right of the staircase was a passageway where a sign, showing male and female figures, led the way to the bathrooms, and to my right there was a glass-panel door with the word "LOUNGE" etched into the opaque glass. This must've once been the more upmarket part of the pub but, going by the flashing lights and the familiar electrical jingles coming from inside, I figured it was now some kind of gaming room.

I stepped tentatively through an open doorway to the left and into the main bar. There was only one patron perched on a barstool nursing a beer—a skinny, middle-aged man with curly red hair and a weathered complexion. He wore a tiny pair of shorts and a loose singlet. He didn't look up from his glass or acknowledge my presence.

The room was surprisingly spacious. The bar stretched three-quarters of the way along the right-hand wall with a row of barstools. The concertina windows I'd noticed from the street made up most of the left wall and below these were a half-dozen-or-so booths with dark-green upholstery. Across the entire back wall was a row of French doors, also closed, leading out to what appeared to be a beer garden, and offering me my first glimpse of the beach close up. Small, circular tables and wooden chairs were placed randomly around the room, and there was a pool table and a dartboard in the far corner past the bar.

A stout man with thin hair and ruddy cheeks appeared behind the bar carrying a wire tray of glasses. 'G'day, can I help ya mate?'

'Good day.'

'Ah, American.' He placed the tray on the bar.

'You can tell that from, "Good day"?'

'My oath.' He grinned. 'If you was an Aussie, you'd have said, "G'day".'

'Ga'day.'

'G'day. Kind of like one word.'

'G'day.'

'There you go. A fair dinkum Aussie already.'

'Fair dinkum.'

The barman leaned over the bar with an outstretched hand. 'Frank Smith, good to meet you.'

I shook his hand. 'Joe Dean.'

'Here for the wedding, then?'

'No, just a short vacation. The lady at the store said I could probably get a room here.'

'Good old Silv.' He began to put away the glasses. 'Hey, Pat,' he shouted over his shoulder. 'Got a minute?'

Pat Smith—a large lady with curly blonde hair, rosy cheeks and a friendly smile—stepped through a side door behind the bar and joined her husband.

'Pat, this is Joe. Joe, this is Pat, my lovely wife.'

'G'day, Joe.'

'Hi.'

'Ah, American. They said you lot'd start arriving soon. A bit early though, aren't you? Or have you got something to do with the building work up there?'

'Joe's on holiday, luv,' Frank said. 'He's looking for a room.'

'Oh, no worries. We're not exactly heaving at the moment—starting to get too hot for the tourists now.' Pat ran her hand through her hair in a fruitless attempt to tame her curls. 'That and the rains should be here anytime,' she added before bustling through a doorway only to return within moments with a booking form. 'If you'd like to fill this in, Joe, I'll sort you out a room.'

I filled out my details. Where the form asked for the number of nights the room would be required, I wrote two weeks.

'Would you like a beer, Joe?' Frank said as I wrote.

'Uhm, no thanks, but I'll have an orange juice.'

'Health kick or on the wagon?' He grabbed a glass and thrust it under a tap.

'The latter I'm afraid. I haven't had a drink now for about twenty years.'

'Well, good for you mate.' He placed the glass on the bar beside me.

I thanked him and finished filling out the form.

'Come on, let's get you up to your room,' Pat said after breezing in from the lobby. She picked up my bag while I finished my drink. In protest, I reached out for the bag.

'Don't worry, Joe, I lift a lot heavier than this around here.'

She wasn't going to take no for an answer, and I could see she could handle the weight quite easily.

I followed Pat up the stairs. The banister felt old and sticky under my hand. My stomach rumbled and I realised I hadn't eaten since breakfast. A corridor at the top of the stairs branched out on either side. We turned right. There were three doors on either side of the narrow passage. I figured one side looked out over the street, while the other overlooked the bay. We continued until we reached the last door on the left—it was open.

The room had a double aspect with French doors on the back and sidewalls leading out to the timber verandah. Pat had already opened the doors. The gentle sound of the ocean and the warm salty breeze filled the room.

11

I was feeling a little tired and hungry, but too excited to relax. All I wanted to do was explore the town, so I had a shower and changed into a fresh pair of shorts and T-shirt, then headed straight out.

As I stepped from the building, the heat and bright sunlight hit me once more—like I was walking into a floodlit sauna.

Next to the pub was an open grassy area that, from where I stood, looked a little like a well-kept vacant lot. Farther along were two or three smaller buildings, not much more than shacks, and a large white building stood at the end of the street.

On the opposite side and to the right of the General Store, was a steep road that headed up behind the town to rows of houses nestled on the hillside. The sign on the corner read, "Eleanor Street". Close to the store there was a parked delivery van with the words "Bluey" painted rather crudely along its side.

I decided to begin my expedition on that side of the street.

To the left of the General Store was a row of six old houses that were set back from the sidewalk by their front yards. They were Queenslanders, but slightly different from each other in style and colour.

Sitting on the verandah of the first one house were two elderly women, obviously sisters if not twins, who smiled at me as I passed. I nodded and smiled back.

The other houses each had a "Holiday House To Let" sign out front.

A row of three stores were next. The first one was empty with a "For Lease" sign outside.

In the window of the second store was a variety of fish lying upon a bed of broken ice. Above them was a crooked neon sign that read, "Fish and Chips".

Next was a second-hand bookstore. It appeared closed but, as I peered in, I thought I saw movement. A handwritten sign on the door announced:

Candle Stick Bay Writers' Group
Meetings, third Monday of every month 7.00 – 9.00 pm
Guests are welcome

Writers. I thought of *Flirting with The Moon*. Could The Moon be a member of the Candle Stick Bay Writers' Group?

There were more houses set back from the road, continuing for about a hundred yards. Once again, they were older-styled homes, all except for the last two. These were identical two-storey contemporary buildings with balconies, built right up to the street. On closer inspection, I realised they were holiday-let apartments over three floors.

I ambled on until I found myself standing outside the police station—a modern, low-set brick-and-tile building about the size of an average family home but with a parking lot out the front. In the planning stage of my trip, I'd decided it would be a good idea to introduce myself to the local police, and try and get them on side. But not yet. I wanted to get a feel of the place first. The police station stood on the corner of another street, which also headed up to the back of the town and was called William Street. On the opposite corner was the post office.

I made my way across the street to the chunky Queenslander building and suddenly realised I was shaking. The importance of my visit had come flooding back and regardless of the heat, I shuddered.

The wooden structure sat on top of a walled foundation about as high as my chest. There was a shallow verandah along the front and right side with wooden steps to the entrance. A ramp clung to the right-hand side and led up to a row of post boxes. I gripped the railing, pulled myself up the ramp and headed for post box number twenty-four. I'm not sure how long I stared at the small cast iron box before I stroked my finger along its façade. Like a psychic trying to pick up vibrations, I circled the key barrel with my fingertip then traced the edge of the little trapdoor. In twenty-five years, this was the closest I'd ever been to The Moon.

I gave myself a shake then walked around the verandah to the front of the building. A small bell jingled as I opened the front door. I stepped through, scanned the room quickly, then pretended to browse the rows of birthday and anniversary cards that were displayed down one wall. The store's air conditioning was a welcome relief, and there were two fans rotating slowly from the high-vaulted ceiling above rows of stationary supplies, books and envelopes. I noticed there were no customers. The relaxing swish of the fans was drowned out temporarily as a young woman began to stamp a pile of envelopes from behind the service counter at the far end of the room. To the right of the counter there was an office with a window into the store. A man with wispy hair was writing at a desk and didn't look up.

The stamping stopped. 'Can I help you?'

I looked up from the cards. The young woman was watching me. 'No, I'm fine thanks, just browsing.'

'No worries, just give us a hoi if you need anything.'

'Thank you, I will.'

I didn't need to purchase anything but didn't want to seem rude by rushing out. What I did need was to find out who rented postal box twenty-four, but all in good time. I perused the stationary goods for a few minutes then thanked the young woman and bade her goodbye. The balding man was no longer in the office.

Past the post office there was a sharp curve to the left and, tucked away in the corner of the bend, was an old building that looked like an English cottage from a Thomas Hardy novel. A sign outside read "Dr Hamish Elliot, Medical Practice".

A narrower road branched from the curve just beyond the cottage, which I guessed led up to the lighthouse.

I didn't fancy trekking up to the lighthouse just yet so I continued along the main curve—the road ended at the jetty of a small marina where I could see a few various sized yachts and boats moored and bobbing gently on the water. To my right and overlooking the marina was the white modern structure I'd spotted from the other end of the street. A large sign across its wall read, "Candle Stick Bay Dive Centre" and, beneath this, smaller signs advertised fishing charters and reef tours. There were two roller doors along the street side of the building. One was open. As I passed, I saw racks holding diving gear and wetsuits. Looking up through the windows of the upper level, all I could see were rows of ceiling fans, but on the outer wall above the windows was another smaller sign that I hadn't noticed before which read "Candle Stick Bay Yacht Club".

A swing gate made from a single copper log blocked the way to the marina for traffic while still allowing pedestrian access.

A man wearing only a pair of red board shorts peered out of the dive centre as I passed. 'G'day.'

'G'day.'

'Up here on holiday?'

'Well, kind of. I—'

'Blimey, an American? Jeez you had me there for a minute.' He strolled over and held out his hand. 'Bruce Stanton.'

We shook hands. 'Joe Dean.'

'Pleased to meet you, Joe. You're looking a bit knackered mate.'

My expression must have conveyed my lack of understanding.

'Tired.'

'Yes, now you come to mention it, I am feeling a little tired.'
'Where you staying?'
'The Great Northern. I should probably head back.'
'Well, if you want to hold on a tick, I've got to see Frank, so I'll come up with you.'
'Ok.'

Bruce returned to the building and closed the roller doors. I gazed out over the marina and noticed it was part of a small man-made harbour.

A couple of minutes later, Bruce appeared from the front of the building wearing a yellow T-shirt.

My stomach rumbled and my legs were starting to feel heavy as we headed in the direction of the pub.

'When did you get in?'
'Yesterday afternoon.'
'Right, still on American time, eh? First big trip?'
I nodded.

On the left of the marina was a small boatyard surrounded by a chain fence with a shack in the middle. In the yard was a small yacht, a speedboat, a couple of aluminium boats, and the paint-stripped hull of an old forty-foot yacht, which looked like somebody's restoration project.

'Pete Bingle's place,' Bruce said as we followed the fence. 'Have you met Pete yet?'
'No.'
'You will.'

Beside the boatyard was a narrow sandy path that led to the beach. From here I could see the bay beyond, but it was the sign at the edge of the path that had caught my attention. There was a picture of a crocodile's head and a jellyfish with long tendrils, and below these were the words "NO SWIMMING!"

Bruce saw me eyeing the sign. 'Yeah, no swimming here, mate. It's not stinger season until next month but the crocs are always there.'

'A stinger's a jelly fish, right?'

'Yep, box jellyfish. Nasty little buggers. Can cause an agonising death within minutes just by touching you.'

'Really.'

'Crocs stay mainly up the creek in the mangroves but do venture closer to town every now and then.'

'Wow!'

I wanted to take a look at the beach but there would be plenty of time for that later.

Next was a bait and tackle shop which was little more than a shack. Out the front was a chest freezer on wheels and a handwritten pricelist of different baits. Through the windows on either side of the door I could see a variety of fishing rods and angling gear for sale and hire.

'Also Pete's place. A proper entrepreneur our Petey boy,' Bruce said with a chuckle.

After a gap of ten yards or so, there was another timber shack, but this one was very old and looked more like an antiquated playhouse for a child. A plaque to the left of its cute little verandah read:

Historical Building
First home of William and Eleanor Holbrook
Built 1879

'The founders of Candle Stick Bay,' Bruce said.

I suddenly noticed a man sitting on the ground with his back up against the side of the building. He was glaring at me.

'Fuck are you looking at?' he spat.

'Shit, pay no attention, Joe,' Bruce said shepherding me past.

The man stood up and swaggered towards us. He wore a dark grey Def Leppard T-shirt, dirty, faded black jeans and odd flip-flops—or "thongs" as the Aussies call them. His arms were covered in tattoos. His unruly hair and unshaven face told me he was sleeping rough. A bum.

'Seen something ya like have ya big fella?' he growled as he reached us. In his eyes was pure anger, fuelled, no doubt, by alcohol and drugs.

'I beg your pardon?'

'Fuck me … a Yank.'

Bruce placed his arm on my shoulder. 'Leave it, Joe. Let's keep moving.'

'Leave it, Joe. Let's keep moving,' the bum mimicked. 'I had you down as a Pom.' He turned his eyes back on me.

'Fair go, Geoff,' Bruce said.

'But a Yank's even lower in my book.' He grinned through yellow-stained teeth as if trying to taunt me.

'Come on, Joe.' Bruce took my arm.

We continued walking in the direction of the pub.

'Why don't you fuck off back to where you came from?' the bum yelled after us.

A little farther on, Bruce said, 'Sorry about that, mate.'

'Don't be, it's not your fault.'

We reached the entrance to the pub. I was glad Bruce opened the heavy door. During the last few minutes, my tiredness had noticeably increased, and strength was draining out of me like water through a sieve.

In the bar, Frank and Pat were busy. They looked up as we entered. Suddenly, my head started swimming. I grabbed one of the barstools and plonked myself down.

'You look buggered, mate,' Frank said.

'If that means tired then yes, I'm buggered.'

'That'll be the jet lag,' Pat said coming around the bar. 'An afternoon nap'll fix you.'

Bruce heaved a sharp intake of breath. 'I wouldn't. You'll be up all night if you do. Stay awake until bedtime, then you'll be right.'

'I've heard that.' It made sense what Bruce was saying, it really did, but my eyes were now as heavy as dumbbells. I doubted I'd last much longer. 'Sorry guys, I just need to go and rest for a while.' I rose from my stool and sauntered towards the door.

Bruce and Frank chimed in unison. 'See ya later, mate,'

'Yes, see you later … mates.'

Their tittering accompanied me as I left the room.

12

When I opened my eyes, I was lying on my stomach on a big comfortable bed. It was dark. I could hear the ocean and crickets resonating on a gentle breeze. The muffled sound of people talking and laughing drifted in. Raising my head, I gazed around the room. Moonlight shone through the open French doors, making long shadows in the dark corners. A bright light suddenly swept across the decor and chased the shadows to the far wall. Then it was gone.

I yawned and stretched like a cat that had slept for a week. My eyes felt puffy and dry. My mouth tasted like garbage.

The beam swept the room again, like a prison searchlight. I clambered slowly off the bed, shuffled over to the French doors, and stepped out onto a timber-decked balcony. Looking to my left, I realised I could freely walk the entire circumference of the building if I chose.

I leaned on the iron railing and surveyed the bay stretching out on either side. The moon was large and fierce, looming very close, or so it seemed, sitting right here on top of the bay like this was its home. The lighthouse beam swept around the bay like the hand of a stopwatch so that for a fraction of a second it threw every inch of the beach into relief under a light as bright as day.

I took a deep breath, filling my lungs with fresh air.

'Oiy ... Yank the Wank!'

The bum from earlier in the day interrupted my appreciation.

'Down here, you dumb cunt.' He stood on the sand below, arms akimbo.

'What's your problem, pal?'

He smirked then took a swig from a bottle held within a brown paper bag. His eyes never left me.

I looked towards the lighthouse. I wasn't going to let this guy wind me up.

'Just watching the *Moon*, eh?' His emphasis on the word 'Moon' seemed deliberate.

He suddenly had my attention.

He must have noticed my reaction because he threw back his head and laughed.

I wanted to go down and confront him but instead, I watched him stagger away across the sand. I'd be seeing him again, I was sure.

I took a shower and put on my shorts and T-shirt, hoping I looked every inch the travelling American.

While heading downstairs towards the sound of the bar, I checked the time. It was 8.00 pm, 6.00 am in Florida, and only 3.00 am in LA. I wandered into the bar expecting it to be full. It wasn't. Only a few people were scattered around the room and there was a middle-aged couple sitting at a table. Through the open concertina doors I could see a man and a woman smoking outside—the allocated smoking area.

A voice boomed out, 'G'day, Joe!' It was Frank the barman.

'Hi,' I said making my way towards him. I recognised Bruce and Silvia Stanton.

'G' day, Joe,' Bruce said. 'You got some kip then?'

'Yes, I did.'

'Hello, Joe,' Silvia chimed in. 'You look nice and refreshed.'

'Thank you. I feel great.'

Frank handed me a glass of orange juice. 'I expect you're hungry, mate?'

'Starving.'
'Pat'll be back in a minute. She'll fix you up.'
'So,' Silvia said, 'how are you enjoying Australia so far, Joe?'
'It's a fantastic place, especially here.'
'Sure is. So, where you headed?'
'Leave it out, Silv …' Bruce said. 'Sound like bloody Maud.'
'I'm just inquiring that's all.'
'That's okay,' I said. 'I'm heading around Australia.'
'All the way around?' Bruce signalled Frank for another beer.

I shouldn't have said that. Travelling around the whole of Australia would be a huge trip. I'm a lousy liar, always have been. 'No, I'm just moving around randomly, you know, wherever takes my fancy.'

'So, what brings you to Candle Stick Bay?' Bruce said.

'Now who's sounding like Maudie?' Silvia slapped her husband playfully on the arm.

'Saw the brochures. Liked what I saw. Thought I'd check it out.'

Silvia narrowed her eyes and grinned. 'Are you sure you're not here for the wedding?'

Pat arrived just in time to save me from any more questioning. 'G'day, Joe. I bet you're starving.'

I chose a fillet of steak from the menu. Pat breezed away on a mission. I wished she'd stayed. The questioning resumed.

'So, you were saying you're here for the wedding, Joe,' Silvia said.

'Silv …! Struth, that's pure bloody Maud if ever there was.'

Silvia ignored her husband, waiting for my reply.

'Look … I have to be honest with you guys. I don't know anything about this wedding.'

'Crikey,' Frank said from behind the bar. 'You're joking, aren't you?'

I shook my head.

'It's William Lambert, Joe,' Silvia said. 'He's getting married in Candle Stick Bay.'

I frowned. William Lambert? Where had I heard that name before?

'You know …' Silvia urged as if trying to jumpstart my memory. '… William Lambert … the writer.'

'Ahh.' William Lambert the bestselling author—and an Aussie. I remembered seeing a news report recently about his up-and-coming wedding to a young English pop singer and, although I wasn't familiar with his work, I was aware of his fame. 'He's getting married here?'

'Yep!' Frank wiped down the bar top. 'He's from around here.'

'Really? I didn't know that.'

'Oh yeah, wrote a book when he was a young bloke, went to America and—'

'Made a fortune making movies,' Bruce said, interrupting Frank.

'Really?'

'And now he's back,' Silvia said. 'You never see him though, just the big cars going in and out of the gates. Maudie reckons he's become a bit of a hermit.'

'What does flamin' Maudie know?' Bruce threw his arms in the air.

'Too bloody much if you ask me,' Frank said.

Pat reappeared carrying a plate piled high with French fries, salad and an enormous steak.

'Wow!' I ate my dinner very informally, sitting at the bar. Best fries and steak I'd ever tasted.

13

The next morning, I awoke very early with just a hint of daylight seeping into my room.

I padded onto the balcony wearing only my boxers. The air was already sticky. A glowing strip of tangerine on the horizon was washing away the last of the night. I couldn't wait to walk around the bay.

I threw on a pair of track bottoms, a gym shirt and my trusty sneakers. Within minutes I was bounding down the backstairs of the balcony. On the beach, another sign warned of the dangers of crocodiles and stingers. The ocean was calm and inviting—hard to believe it could be such a deadly place.

Now the sun had risen above the rim of the horizon and was hanging there like a shimmering ember nestled upon a streak of purple cloud. I realised that Candle Stick Bay and Boca shared something else—amazing sunrises.

I was surprised to find there were already a few walkers and joggers, but not as many as on Boca Beach, thank goodness. I strode along the water's edge swinging my arms in tempo for extra cardio. The breeze had shifted offshore, which accounted for the slight chill in the air.

I'd been walking for about ten minutes. The beach was quite narrow now and I found myself closer to the bush. Tall palm trees seemed to be leaning forward as if reaching for the water, while a spread of thin trees as high as basketball rims filled in the space below them. Cicadas provided an undulating drone. Birds skipped and shrieked in the branches. In the distance, a couple of kookaburras laughed in a rising crescendo.

Something out of place among the trees not far from the edge drew my attention. Something blue. I stopped and squinted, trying to make out what it was. Then it took shape—a tarpaulin, spread out and tied off beneath the tree canopy, kind of like a tent. Empty beer bottles and litter were strewn around. There was movement beneath the tarp. It was the bum from yesterday. He'd rolled over but was still sleeping. I didn't relish another abusive exchange, so I continued on my way.

About thirty minutes later, a creek entrance blocked my way and, although I could see it was quite shallow, another sign showing a crocodile's head stopped me in my tracks. The banks of the creek were thick mangrove swamp, and the air had a pungent aroma. Crocodile heaven!

I had followed the curve of the bay as far as I could go and now had a picture postcard view of the town and the lighthouse at the far tip. The sun had changed from blood red to a pale yellow. The day was heating up.

Heading back, I began to plan my day. I needed to find out who owned post office box twenty-four. Sticking with the naïve, tourist-from-the-states routine seemed to be my best option—it wasn't really a lie. I was looking forward to meeting more locals and discreetly asking a few questions. But if I pissed these people off, they'd clam up—as would close-knit communities anywhere.

Within no time at all, or so it seemed, the blue tarpaulin flapped into view again. Now the bum was flat on his back. Probably sleeping off last night's booze.

A couple of hundred yards from the pub, a man and a young woman jogged towards me. The man was tall and well-built, with short dark hair. I could tell he wasn't a natural runner—his gait was awkward, his breathing heavy and he was covered in sweat.

The girl however was a natural, her stride effortless. 'G'day,' she called as they neared me. She had a pretty face and great skin.

The guy didn't look up. I think he was in pain. 'Good morning!' I said back.

The stroll back to the pub took only a few minutes. I grasped the brass handle and pushed the door. Nothing. It was locked. Damn! I'd left the key in my room. I cupped my hands around my face and peered through the glass. Someone was moving around in the bar. I knocked.

A moment later, the woman I'd met in the store the previous day opened the door.

'Good morning, Mr Dean.' She wore a blue pinafore and pink rubber gloves.

'Good morning, um … Maud?'

'Been out for a walk, have we?' she winked.

'Yes, a morning ritual.' I tried to dodge past her, the stairs in my sights.

She stepped in front of me. 'So, how's it going?' she said in a hushed voice.

'Great. You've got a beautiful little town here.'

'I mean with the investigation?'

'I beg your pardon?'

'You know … the real reason you're here.' She looked around as if to ensure no one was listening.

'I can assure you, Maud, I haven't the slightest idea what you mean.'

'Oh, come on, Mr Dean. I know why you're here.'

'You do?'

'Of course. And I want you to know that I'm here to help in any way I can.'

I nodded and smiled at her, edged past and grabbed the banister. 'I'm here on vacation.'

Maud placed her hand on top of mine. 'I understand. You've got to check out everyone in the town first before you decide who to trust. Well, believe me, I could tell you things about some of the folk in this town that would make your hair curl.'

'I bet you could.'

I was about to head up the staircase when Pat appeared from the bar. She too wore pink rubber gloves. 'Oh, there you are, Maudie. Good morning, Joe.'

'Good morning, Pat.'

She narrowed her eyes at Maud and then at me. 'Is everything all right?'

'Yes, fine,' I said.

'Maudie … what are you up to?'

'Nothing. Mr Dean forgot to take his key, so I let him in.'

There was exasperation in Pat's sigh. She shook her head. 'Whatever she's up to, Joe, take no notice.'

Maud huffed and returned to the bar.

14

After a shower, I was feeling relaxed and refreshed when I entered the bar.

Frank was replacing a bottle on the optics. Maud was on the other side of the room pushing a vacuum cleaner.

Frank looked up. 'G'day, Joe, sleep all right?'

'Not too bad. That's one comfortable bed up there.'

'Bloody oath.'

From the corner of my eye, I noticed Maud moving closer. She'd turned off the vacuum cleaner and was now polishing the bar top.

Pat breezed in behind the bar. She was the kind of woman who rustled when she moved, always in a hurry, cheeks flushed, but in full control. 'Breakfast, Joe?' She handed me the breakfast menu.

I ordered mixed fruit, some toast and a cup of English breakfast tea.

'Want Vegemite on your toast?' Pat grinned.

Frank and Maud stopped what they were doing and stared at me.

'I have no idea what that is.'

'No, then,' Pat said then disappeared into the back.

'Bloody horrible stuff,' Frank grumbled. He lifted the bar phone receiver and punched in a number.

Maud had done a quick polish of the bar, working her way round until she was next to me.

'What have you got planned for today, Mr Dean?'

'Joe ... call me Joe.'

She continued polishing the same spot. 'I expect you'll be looking forward to meeting some of the townsfolk?'

'Yes. So far, people have been very friendly.'

Frank slammed down the phone. 'FLAMIN NORA!'

'Uh-oh.' Maud moved to the tables behind us and began wiping them down.

'Sick of being without a bloody phone. Them lazy bastards up there, I'm not kidding …' Frank continued to rant, grabbing a rack of clean glasses.

I remembered the two Telstra men who were on strike. 'So, your phones are completely down?'

'Yep.'

'What are they striking about?'

'What do they always strike about? Money.'

Pat pushed through the swing doors at the back of the bar, carrying a bowl of sliced fruit and a glass of orange juice. 'Tea and toast'll just be a minute.'

'Give him a bit of Vegemite,' Maud called over from the back of the room.

Pat giggled and disappeared again.

'We're a tiny speck on the map, Joe. Miles from anywhere. Nobody gives a stuff about us.' Frank continued to vent.

My first taste of fresh Australian fruit was memorable—sweet and juicy as nature intended.

Pat returned and placed a mug of tea and a small plate of toast on the bar in front of me. On the side was a separate piece of toast about the size of a playing card. It was spread with a dark brown substance.

I picked it up and scrutinized it.

'Vegemite,' Pat said.

Maud inched next to me while Frank cocked an eyebrow.

'An Australian icon,' Pat added.

It smelled like the outside of the pub—stale and yeasty. 'It's not made from anything gross, is it?'

'Only kangaroos' balls!' Frank chuckled.

Pat elbowed Frank. 'Don't listen to him, Joe. It's made from concentrated yeast.'

That explained the beery smell.

Frank anticipated my next question. 'There's no alcohol in it.'

I took a small bite. The taste was … different. Salty, sharp. I put the toast back on the plate.

Pat grinned. 'It'll grow on you.'

'I doubt it.'

Stepping from the pub, I retrieved my sunglasses from my shorts pocket. The sun was bright, the air warm and pleasant.

Farther down the high street I stopped to look in the window of the fish shop. The display was a work-in-progress—except for the ice and a pile of massive prawns, it was bare. The front door was open, and someone was inside whistling jauntily. I peered in and, at that very moment, a man as short and stout as a barrel emerged from the back of the store, almost dwarfed by a tray of fish.

'Good morning, my friend. I'm afraid we are not open yet.' His accent was European, possibly Greek.

'Oh, that's okay, I was just passing.'

'Ah, the American.'

I chuckled. Small towns.

'Here for the wedding, yes?'

'No, here on vacation.'

'Well how about you come back at lunchtime? I serva you best fish in all of Australia!'

'I will, thank you!'

'Good, good.' He placed the fish on the ice then bustled back into the storeroom.

Inside the bookstore, a teenage girl was stacking books. I entered. She was loudly chewing gum and listening to music through earplugs and paid no attention to me—either she hadn't noticed my entrance, or she didn't care. The store had a homely feel. To the right of the entrance was a counter, and in front of this an open space with a couple of leather couches and a coffee table. Rows of shelves laden with books, mainly paperbacks, led towards the rear.

I began to peruse the shelves when the teenager yelled: 'Aunty Mol. You've got a customer!'

A woman came out from the back of the store. She was attractive in a natural, no-need-for-make-up kind of way. Her hair—shiny with a hint of red—fell just below her ears. A little younger than myself perhaps. Her body was trim, and I guessed she worked out.

I don't know why but for the first time in a long time, I was flustered. 'Hi, I'm on vacation and I, uh … need a good book.'

She smiled warmly. 'Well, you've come to the right place. What do you like to read?'

'Oh, murder-mystery, that kind of thing.'

She led me to one of the aisles at the back of the store. The scents of her morning shower—shampoo, body lotion—followed in her wake, as did I.

'There's quite a selection here. Do you have a favourite author?'

'I just remembered, there is a book that I've been trying to find. It's called *Flirting with The Moon.*'

Was there a change in Molly's expression? Just for an instance, the friendly smile seemed to slip. 'Haven't heard of that one … do you know who the author is?'

'Stephen Powell.'

She shook her head and shrugged. 'I can look it up if you like?'

I nodded and we returned to the front of the shop.

My name's Joe, by the way. Joe Dean.' I extended my hand.

'Molly Quinn.' She placed her hand in mine.

Her skin was warm and soft, her grip firm. I didn't want to let go.

'You're that copper!'

I swung around to see the teenage girl, minus the earplugs, standing behind me.

'Kimmy! Don't be so rude,' Molly said, blushing.

'Maudie reckons he's here looking for someone.'

'Maudie?' Molly threw her arms up in the air in fake surprise. 'Has to be true then. Who're you chasing, Mr Dean?'

'It's Joe, and no, I'm not chasing anyone. Maud seems to have an overactive imagination.'

'You got that right. You'd be here for the wedding?' Molly appeared to forget about doing the book search.

I explained I was just passing through.

'Were you supposed to be doing something, Kimmy?' Molly said.

Kimmy frowned, turned on her heels and marched away.

There was an awkward silence. I looked around the store. 'Nice place you have here.'

'Thank you. Not the best business proposition in the world, but I enjoy it.'

'I notice you have a writers' group. Are there many writers in Candle Stick Bay?'

'Absolutely. Some talented folk around here.'

Kimmy marched back and slammed a mug of very milky tea or coffee on the counter.

'I'm sorry, Joe. Would you like a tea or—'

'Septics drink coffee, everyone knows that.'

Molly came around the counter and wagged her finger. 'Don't think I won't ring your mother, young lady.'

Kimmy huffed and returned to the back of the store.

'I'm so sorry. I don't know what's gotten into her, Joe.' Molly blushed.

'It's okay, really.'

'Teenagers. She's at that awkward age.'

'I know.' Except of course I didn't. I'd missed those years with my son. 'You were telling me about the writers in town.'

'That's right.' She took a sip of her drink, screwed up her nose and shuddered. 'That's disgusting.' Molly excused herself and followed her niece.

I took the opportunity to have a closer look around. On a

shelf below the counter, I noticed a hardback with a picture of the Candle Stick Bay lighthouse on the front cover. I picked it up—*A History of Candle Stick Bay* by Molly Quinn. On the back cover was a blurb and a recent photograph of Molly. I was about to read the short bio next to the picture when Molly returned.

'Ah, you've found my little book.'

'Congratulations!' I opened the book to the first page.

'Yep, that's one of my little efforts. Self-published earlier this year.'

'Cool, can I get a copy?'

'Of course.' Molly smiled. She signed it simply, "For Joe. Best Wishes Molly Quinn", placed it in a bag and rang it up on the till.

'Now you were asking about the writers' group. What would you like to know?'

'I'm a bit of a book nut myself so I'm interested in your writers.' I handed over twenty dollars and took the bag.

'If you're still in town next week, come along to our meeting. We're not just a writers' group, we're a book group too. We read a book each month then critique it.'

'I'd love to come.'

'Writing anything?'

'No, more appreciative of the art.'

'You'll get to meet all the town's writers then. Well not all of them. Lambert doesn't come and Miss Berry doesn't leave her house much nowadays, and—' Molly stopped. 'Sorry, I'm rambling. There'll only be a handful of us, but a good little group.'

'So, you mentioned a Miss ... Berry?'

Molly gave me an are-you-sure-you're-not-a-copper grin.

'Sorry. I've had a long journey, haven't spoken to anyone much.'

'That's okay, I'll be happy to help with your investigation—'

'I'm not a cop.' I laughed. 'I'm just curious.'

'I'm having a lend of you. Miss Berry's the English teacher at the school, getting on a bit now, but she's written over forty romance novels for one of the Mills and Boon type of publishers. Bangs out a couple of books a year.'

Kimmy reappeared carrying a sports bag and marched towards the exit. 'I'm going to work.' The door slammed behind her.

'So sorry about my niece's behaviour—she gets very bored in this little town.' Molly told me why Kimmy was staying with her. Apparently, the girl had been getting into a bit of trouble in Sydney, mixing with the wrong crowd. The final straw was when she was kicked out of school for threatening a teacher. Her mother, a single parent, was having difficulty handling her. That's when Molly stepped in. 'I wonder if I've done the right thing now.'

'I'm sure she's a good kid,' I assured her.

We continued to chat freely as if we'd known each other for a long time. She asked me about my trip and a little about my home and my life back in the States. I was enjoying our talk very much but didn't want to outstay my welcome. 'I think I've taken up enough of your time, Molly.'

Molly smirked. 'As you can see, I'm swept off my feet with customers at the moment.'

I noticed an open laptop on the counter. 'Are you writing anything?'

'Always.'

'Another history book?'

'Are you sure you don't want to take me down to the station, Joe?'

I apologised once more. 'Well, I better keep moving. It's been great meeting you.' I turned to leave.

'See you later, Joe.'

I opened the door, paused, then turned back. 'Can I just ask one more question?'

Molly smiled and folded her arms.

'What's a septic?'

15

"Back in 5 mins" read the sign taped to the door of the police station.

The post office was on the opposite street corner, so I headed that way. The mailboxes mesmerised me, especially number twenty-four. It was as if this little box in the wall was like a portal to another world—a world which The Moon inhabited. Once more, I bent down and rubbed my finger around its edge.

'Can I help you?'

A short, balding man carrying a parcel and a stack of envelopes was looking down at me. He was the man from the office the previous day. I uncurled from my squat. 'Hi, I'm—'

'Ah, the American. May I ask what you're doing around the boxes?'

'Just looking, they're kind of different to the ones we have in the States.'

His piggy eyes narrowed behind small round spectacles. He frowned and I realised how pathetic my excuse sounded.

'Actually, I was wondering if you could help me.'

He cocked his head to one side, his frown deepening.

'Could you tell me who owns number twenty-four?'

'Certainly not, Mister Dean. That's confidential.'

'You know me?'

'Small town, gossip spreads like bushfire.' His expression was a mixture of tetchy and smug.

I took an instant dislike to the guy, and I'd bet he felt the same about me, but I needed to stay on the right side of everyone. 'Good old Maudie, eh?' I held out my hand.

After awkwardly shifting the parcel and envelopes to his other arm, we shook hands.

'Dennis Hodge.'

'Good to meet you, Dennis.'

'Likewise, I'm sure. Here for the wedding then? Bit early.'

'No, just here on vacation.' At this point I wondered about the possibility of getting a T-shirt made so I'd no longer have to answer the inevitable question:

> Septic Tank (Yank)
> Not here for Wedding

'Oh well, got to keep moving.' He turned and shuffled towards the front door, and I noticed he had a severe limp.

Postmaster with access to the mailboxes and confidential information about the people who rented them. If nothing else, Dennis would definitely know who owned number twenty-four. Dennis Hodge. I placed the name in my memory bank, with a red flag beside it.

I returned to the street and headed back towards the police station while reviewing what I'd learned in the last twenty-four hours: William Lambert, famous author, once lived in LA, now resident of Candle Stick Bay; Miss Berry, the English teacher, a published author of around forty books; Molly Quinn, the writer of *A History of Candle Stick Bay*; The Candle Stick Bay Writers,' a group that met once a month, an aggressive town bum who hinted that he knew why I was here, and the postmaster with beady eyes and an abrupt manner. Was The Moon one of these people? I needed to dig deeper but without raising suspicion.

Since deciding to come to Candle Stick Bay, I'd toyed with the idea of bringing the local police into my confidence but instead had decided to introduce myself and play it by ear. The little sign on the door had disappeared so I entered the building. The air conditioning was a welcome relief from the heat outside. The interior was a single open office with windows along both sides. There was a small reception area with a front counter; behind this were four desks, two on either side of the room. I removed my hat and sunglasses.

A police officer sat at one of the desks jabbing at a computer keyboard. The name plaque on his desk read: "Sergeant Robert Radford".

'Won't be a minute, mate,' he said, glancing over the top of the monitor. After a flurry of clicks and a final resounding jab, he jumped to his feet and marched to the counter. 'What can I do for you, mate?' He wore a Florida-style police uniform—dark-blue shorts, a light-blue shirt and badge, and around his waist was a holstered gun. I recognised him from the beach earlier, jogging with the young woman.

'My name's Joe—'

'Ah, the FBI agent!'

'I've been promoted?'

The cop chuckled. 'Probably be CIA by tomorrow. Good old Maudie.'

'Good old Maudie indeed.'

'So, you're looking for someone I hear.'

'No, just on vacation.'

'We're not all country bumpkins.' He grinned. 'How long have you been out of the force?'

My surprise must've shown on my face.

The grin widened. 'Sticks out like dogs' balls, mate!'

'Huh?'

'Means it's obvious.'

'Really?' I'd almost let my ruse slip, but I stopped before confirming his suspicions.

'Nah … Maudie told me.'
I shook my head.
'Didn't believe it, though … but now I do!'
I knew it would be no good trying to lie. 'I'm Joe Dean.'
'Fat Bobby.' His handshake was firm.
I squinted quizzically. 'You're not fat.'
'No, used to be, but.' He patted his stomach with both hands. 'Lost thirty kilos, but the name's stuck. Not very PC these days I guess, but I don't mind. It's Phat Bobby nowadays!' His cheeky grin was contagious.
'Wow! Sixty-six pounds. That's pretty inspiring.'
That explained the early morning run with the fit young woman. His personal trainer perhaps. 'I saw you this morning.'
'Did ya?'
'Yeah, you were running on the beach with a young woman. I said good morning.'
'Did ya? Well bugger me. I can't say I remember. I do struggle a bit with the old running. Anyway, what can I do for you, Joe?'
The decision was an instant one and completely opposite to the one I'd made in the States. I hoped I wouldn't live to regret it.

'Fair dinkum.' Fat Bobby said when he could finally speak.
I remembered the phrase—Bruce Stanton had used it the previous day.
'So, you reckon this … this psycho's here in Candle Stick Bay?'
I nodded. 'A big possibility.'
'Bloody hell!'
'Do you know anyone who might fit the profile?'
Fat Bobby shook his head. 'No, we might get the odd rowdy tourists passing through but the folk who live here, they're all diamonds.'
'Sorry. It was a stupid question. The Moon is far more than just a killer, he's … or *she's* a psychopathic mastermind.'

'Bizarre, Joe, that's what it is. At the moment, my days consist of keeping an eye out for the odd missing cat, chatting with the tourists and checking the weather. Now you're telling me there's a psycho running loose in town.'

I shook my head. 'No, I think The Moon is well and truly retired.'

'But it could be anyone!'

'That's right. Do you know of anybody who might've been in the States twenty-five years ago?'

'Uhm …' He stroked his chin. 'Let me have a think about that … listen, I'm just about to do me morning rounds. Care to join me?'

'That'd be great.'

He went to his desk, retrieved a pair of sunglasses from the top drawer and grabbed his police hat.

I put my own hat and sunglasses back on and followed him out into the sunshine.

16

Fat Bobby scanned the street on either side of the police station like a sheriff of the Old West. 'So, you really think this mongrel could be here, eh?'

I nodded as we started up the street. 'Can you fill me in on some of these people?'

'S'pose so.' Fat Bobby's stride was long but slow and confident. In no time at all we were outside the bookstore.

'Have you met, Moll?'

'Yes, I have. A nice lady.'

'You're not wrong. She's only been in the bay about five years. Almost a local. Fell in love with the place and never left.'

'I can see why.'

'She's having a bit of trouble with a young niece who's staying with her.'

'Yes, I've met Kimmy too.'

'I take me hat off to old Moll, how she brought her up from Sydney. It's hard enough trying to keep the good kids occupied up here, never mind a delinquent.'

'So, what's Molly's background?' I realised as soon as I asked that my question stemmed from more from a personal interest than a professional one.

'Originally from Sydney. I think she worked for one of the big newspapers down there. Hey …' he turned to face me. 'I reckon she worked in LA for a bit too. *The LA Times.*'

'Really?' I was surprised. 'She didn't tell me that.' Molly was sitting in the shop with her back to us, probably writing on her laptop.

Fat Bobby shrugged and was about to continue walking when he suddenly pulled up and froze. He turned towards me again and lowered his voice: 'Bloody hell …I've just thought of something else.'

'What?'

'If the killer's written a book, it means he'd have to be a writer?' Fat Bobby had adopted the use of the masculine noun when referring to The Moon just as I had all these years, even though we both knew the killer could quite easily be a woman. 'Bloody hell,' he said again as more permutations filtered into his mind. 'Do you know how many writers there are in this town?'

I'd already learned there were a few.

'This isn't going to be easy, Joe.'

The man in the fish and chip shop was sweeping the floor of his store.

'Hey Dougie,' Fat Bobby called.

'Dougie leaned the broom against the counter and strode into the doorway. His smile was wide. 'Ahh, so you got a new partner, eh Fatty?' He nodded in my direction and grinned.

'No, this is Joe. He's on holiday. Joe, this is Dougie Costas. He runs the chippy.'

'I've already had the pleasure,' I said, meeting Dougie's smile.

'I nearly go a broke a last year, Joe,' Dougie said with mock sadness.

'Yeah?'

'Yes, it's a very bad, I lose a my best customer.' He placed his hand on Fat Bobby's shoulder. 'Now he eats lettuce and little birdie food.' Dougie's laugh was a churning boom.

'Ah, come on. I still have a bit of fish and a few prawns now and again.'

Dougie's head wobbled in compromised agreement. 'No more of Dougie's famous beer batter, though.'

'Too right, Rox'd bloody kill me. See ya later, mate.'

'See you later.' Dougie returned to the store.

Lovely bloke, Dougie. Greek. Came up to the bay from Melbourne about fifteen years ago after losing his missus. Used to be on the trawlers. Coaches the kids' footy team nowadays and runs the chippy. The tourists love him.'

We passed the empty store and the row of four houses.

'These are all holiday lets apart from the King sisters' house.'

As we came abreast of their home, the sisters, who were in the garden, said in unison, 'Good morning, Sergeant Radford.'

'Good morning, ladies.'

'Good morning, Mr Dean.'

I shouldn't have been shocked that they knew my name. I looked at Fat Bobby. Now it was our turn to speak in unison. 'Maudie!'

We kept moving.

'Some bloody expensive real estate there believe it or not,' Fat Bobby said.

I did believe it. The location would put the land these tiny houses sat on in the millions. I wondered how long it would be before the developers moved in.

'Doc Elliot owns them. Some Brisbane mob's been making him offers for years. Last time he told them to go get fucked!' Fat Bobby chuckled. 'He's a fiery old bugger, is Hamish. Scottish, lived here for years, but I still can barely understand a word he says.'

'And the sisters?'

'Elizabeth and Violet King. Spinsters. Lived in that house all their lives.'

We approached the General Store.

'Ah, Silvia and Bruce,' Fat Bobby said. 'A lovely couple.' He had to duck beneath the doorway as we entered.

'Hello, Bobby, hello again, Joe.' Silvia was placing DVDs back on the shelves.

'How's business?' Fat Bobby said.

'Not too bad, still a few tourists about.'

'How's Bruce?'

'Yeah, he's good. Down at the Yacht Club, probably perving on Roxy's yoga class.'

They giggled.

Non comprende my expression must have said. They looked at me like you would a non-English speaking tourist—a Mexican perhaps.

'Silv means old Bruce is probably having a perv on the sheilas doing yoga.'

From my research I knew "sheilas" meant women. I was slowly getting used to the Australian use—or misuse—of the English language. I figured having a perv meant Bruce was peeking at the women doing yoga. They must have noticed the change in my expression when I realised the meaning.

'Not literally speaking, Joe.' Fat Bobby chuckled. 'Old Bruce ain't a peeping Tom or anything. It's more of a term of endearment we Aussies use when admiring the opposite sex.'

Fat Bobby bid Silvia cheerio. I bowed my head and followed him out of the store.

'Have you met Bruce yet?' Fat Bobby said as we stepped back into the street.

I told him he was one of the first people I'd met in the town.

'A good bloke. Runs the dive centre and volunteers at the Rural Fire Brigade. Great to have around at the barbeque—really knows how to fillet a steak. Used to be a butcher.'

'Really?' My attention was piqued.

As soon as the words left his mouth, he must've realised the implications. 'Nah, not old Bruce.' Then he stopped in his tracks and bit his lip.

'What is it?'

'Nah, it's nothing.'

'What?'

Flirting with The Moon

'Apparently he was a bit wild when he was a young bloke. Got into some trouble but nothing serious. All long before my time.'

'Criminal activity?'

'Just a bit of petty stuff, nothing to write home about.' Fat Bobby stepped to the edge of the sidewalk, turned and stood with his hands on his hips, looking down the length of the street. Wyatt Earp overseeing the O.K. Corral. The heat from the sun was literally bouncing back off the tarmac. A few people seemed to be wandering aimlessly—I guessed they were tourists.

We crossed the road and strolled across the forecourt of the small gas station.

'I'll just pop my head in here. Old Johno's a cranky bugger, not the kind of bloke to stop for a chat. JOHNO, YOU THERE, MATE?'

A thin old man with skin like leather and wearing a coverall grunted as we entered the store. There were shelves of different oils and car accessories around the room, and candy bars that looked as if they'd been there since the fifties.

'Johno, this is Joe!' Fat Bobby yelled.

The wiry old man was obviously a little deaf. He grunted and nodded in my direction.

'Do you need anything, Johno?'

It was as if the grunt, a nod and the shake of his head were Johno's only tools of communication.

'All right then, mate. We'll leave you to it. Just give us a hoi if you need anything, eh? Hooroo.'

Grunt and a nod.

We continued passed The Great Northern Hotel and the park next to it—a small rectangle of mowed grass with a row of palm trees and a children's play area under a shade cloth roof.

'Have you met Pete?' Fat Bobby said as we approached the Tackle and Bait Shop.

I shook my head.

'Old Pete's good value.'

I noticed that Fat Bobby tended to call everybody old—old Molly, old Pete, old mate.

The little wooden store was dark and cool inside and I was forced to duck my head under the array of rods and nets that hung from the ceiling. Rows of shelves were piled high with fishing reels, hooks, lines, and everything you'd need for a day out on the bay. The shop was empty.

'Petey, boy! You there, mate?' Fat Bobby called out.

A bear of a man ambled into the store from behind us. 'Hey, Bob.' His deep voice matched his size.

'Hey, mate. This here's Joe,' Fat Bobby said.

'G'day, Joe. Pete Bingle.' His huge hand enveloped mine as we shook.

'Hi.'

'Ah, the American copper!' he said, bending beneath a net to get behind the counter.

'No, not a cop, just here on vacation.'

'Well, it's good to have you. So how long you here for, Joe?' Pete said.

'A couple of weeks, maybe.'

'Great. Do you fish?'

'Not really.' I'd never fished in my life and wasn't planning on starting now.

17

After leaving the tackle shop and continuing down the high street, we peered across the road towards the post office.

'I expect you'll be wanting to talk to old Dennis?'

'I met Dennis a short while ago. I asked him who owned mailbox twenty-four.'

'You did? What did old Podgy say?' The smirk on the young policeman's face was unmistakable.

'Podgy?'

'Podgy Hodgy.'

'Oh … he said it was confidential information.'

'Yeah, that'd be right. True but.'

'So, what do you know about Mr Hodge?'

'You know what? Since you told me about these murders that happened all them years ago, my detective mind's been kicking in.'

I knew what he meant. Like me, his mind was probably placing together the pieces of the jigsaw puzzle, trying pieces here and there, discarding those that didn't fit, and putting to one side the ones that might slot in later.

'Way before my time, but I reckon old Podge spent some time in LA. Not sure when or why though.'

'He was working over there?'

'Yeah, I think so.'

'What else do you know about him? What's he like?'

'He's a fair dinkum local—not many of them about.' He pointed to one of the houses up on the side of the hill overlooking the town. 'That's his place there, the brick one. Lived with his mum until she passed away a few years ago.'

'Not married?'

'Nah. Lives on his own. Keeps to himself. Bit of a whinger, but he's all right.'

'A whinger?'

'Likes to complain, especially when the town gets a bit rowdy during peak season.'

We continued past the marina and rounded the bend at the Yacht Club. Fat Bobby pointed to the doctor's surgery. 'I already told you about Hamish. Great bloke!'

'A writer?'

'Not that I know of. Very knowledgeable though.' Fat Bobby pointed again, this time to a thin road to the left of the surgery. 'That's the road to the lighthouse. Been up there yet?'

'No but I'm very much looking forward to seeing it.'

'And here we have the Yacht Club.' I followed Fat Bobby to a glass doorway at the street end of the building that I hadn't noticed before.

'More of a social club and a community centre nowadays, not that many yacht owners in the town anymore.' He opened the door, it led to a stairway to take us up to the first floor. Climbing the stairs, I heard faint Indian music.

'Smoko!' Fat Bobby beamed as we entered a small cafeteria.

I realized my puzzled expression was working in my favour.

'Smoko … smoke break.' He placed two fingers in front of his mouth, as if holding an imaginary cigarette.

'Oh right … but I don't smoke.'

'Neither do I.'

I was becoming accustomed to being the Mexican and picking up the lingo as we went. Smoko meant tea break.

We removed our hats and sunglasses at the same time, placed

them on one of the round plastic tables and headed towards the counter. 'What'll it be, Joe? Coffee?'

'Uhm ... tea please.' My attention was elsewhere, taking in the surroundings.

The cafeteria took up only a small area across the back of the building. A glass partition separated it from a large room, which I guessed was used for recreation—a meeting place for the locals, an area that could be hired for functions and conferences. The far side of that room was a wide expanse of glass cantilever doors leading on to a balcony that overlooked the bay. But the view caught no more than a flicker of my attention because, in the middle of the room was a group of women in a circle, lying on the floor. In the centre, seated in the lotus position, was the young woman I'd seen running with Fat Bobby on the beach earlier that morning. Now she was teaching yoga. This explained the slow Indian music drifting through the building.

From behind me, a female voice said, 'I'll bring 'em over to ya,' followed by a familiar huff.

I turned back to the counter where Kimmy was handing change to Fat Bobby.

'Kimmy!' I said as if I'd known her forever. Bad move. A scarlet tide rose up the teenager's neck, flooding into her cheeks. She quickly dropped her head, scowling as she prepared our drinks.

Fat Bobby grinned and headed to the table. 'Lovely girl—' Just as mine had only a moment earlier, his attention was drawn to the scene on the other side of the glass wall. 'And *there* she is!' He gazed in awe at the yoga instructor.

'Your girlfriend?'

'I wish. Working on it but. That's Roxy, she's me personal trainer.'

'And a very beautiful one!'

'You're not wrong. Her old man's one of your lot.'

'An American?'

'Yep, a retired professor. Lost his marbles but.'

Kimmy stalked over and slammed down two cups on our table. The milky tea slopped over the rims.

'Fair go, Kimmy,' Fat Bobby said. 'Take your time love.'

Kimmy gave a who-gives-a-fuck grunt and slouched back to the counter.

'Molly's got her hands full with that one.'

I nodded as I lifted my tea from the puddle, but I wanted to keep on track. 'Roxy's father?'

'Oh yeah, poor old bugger. He's got Alzheimer's.'

'So, Roxy looks after him?'

'Yeah, they live up there on the hill.' He jerked his thumb over his shoulder.

'Do you know whereabouts in the States he's from?'

Fat Bobby was cautiously taking a sip of his tea. He screwed up his face. 'Shit … that's bloody awful.' He looked at his watch. 'Oh bugger!' He pushed himself up from the table.

'What is it?'

'I was supposed to be at the school twenty minutes ago. I've been banging on with you and forgot all about it. Gotta dash.'

I stood and offered my hand. 'Thanks for spending so much time with me. You've been very helpful.'

'No worries.' Fat Bobby's expression hardened as he put on his police cap. He leaned into me and lowered his voice. 'Listen, take it easy with all the questions now, eh? Let's just keep all this between ourselves, yeah?'

'Sure.'

'I just don't want any of these folk getting upset.' The friendly town cop had gone and in his place stood a no-nonsense police sergeant. I knew where he was coming from, and I admired his dedication in protecting the town and its people.

He marched to the counter and, going by his body language, he chastised Kimmy. As he left, Kimmy gave him the finger behind his back.

I couldn't finish my tea—it was dreadful. I stood, about to leave, just as the yoga ladies filed into the cafeteria.

'Hello, Mister Dean.'

I turned. Maud was dressed in black leggings and a purple T-shirt, and tucked under her arm was a rolled-up yoga mat.

'Maud ... were you in the class?'

'Oh yes, three times a week. Yoga's done wonders for my nerves.'

'Good for you.'

'I saw you talking to Fat Bobby. Get plenty of information did ya?'

'No, nothing like that.' I was trying hard to play down Maud's enthusiasm. 'I'm just getting to know the people of the town.'

'Yeah? What'd he say about me?'

'Nothing at all.'

'Tell you about my Shane, did he?' Her back straightened and her chin rose.

'No, I don't know what—'

'He's a good boy deep down. Some folk need to take a look at themselves before they go around talking about others.' She glanced around the room defensively.

'Maud, I can assure you I don't have the slightest idea what you mean.'

'Yeah, right.' She twitched her shoulders like an emu ruffling its feathers. 'Just keep an eye on that Bobby Radford. Not all he cracks himself up to be.'

I was about to ask her what she meant but she turned on her heel and hurried away.

Roxy was the last to leave the room. She too held a mat under her arm and was struggling to replace a CD into its plastic cover.

'Allow me.' I took the CD and its case from her and reunited them.

'Thanks.' She smiled. 'You're the American copper, eh?'

By now I reckon I could recite my denial in my sleep. I introduced myself and shook her small, sweaty hand.

'Roxy Stephens … I'd love to stay and chat, but I've got a private session with William Lambert.'

'William Lambert? He's in town?'

'Strictly between you and me, yes. Been up at the house for a couple of weeks. He's hired me to get him in shape for the wedding.'

'Wow! That's—'

'Sorry, got to go.' She hurried away, leaving the aroma of sandalwood in her wake.

At one of the tables, a couple of the yoga ladies were drinking fruit juice. Kimmy was standing behind the counter, arms crossed with jaw and brow locked into a sulk. She obviously hadn't caught the yoga vibes. Time, I decided, to apologise for embarrassing her earlier. She watched my approach, her face closing like a clam.

'Hey, Kimmy. I'm really sorry about earlier.'

'Don't worry about it.' She looked away.

'So how long you been up here in the Bay?'

She flinched and her eyes met mine for the first time. 'What, so you think I'm the murderer now?'

'What?' I was shocked. The only person I'd taken into my confidence about The Moon was Fat Bobby and that was only around thirty minutes earlier. Maud, her imagination again working overtime, spreading stories around the town. Just what I needed.

'Kimmy, I can guess what Maud's been saying, but I'm going to have to disappoint you. I'm just a tourist.'

She screwed up her face. 'Why the hell would you come here?'

'It's a beautiful place.'

'It's a shithole.'

Under that brash, fuck-you exterior, I suspected there was a scared little girl, sent miles away from home and family to an aunt she didn't know, and to a place where there was nothing to do. It sounded like a Dickens' novel. I took out my wallet and reached into the back compartment where I still had some American dollars. I pulled out a hundred dollar bill and handed it to her.

Her brow lifted and her eyes widened as she took the note. 'What's this for?' For a brief moment, the expression of an inquisitive child replaced that of the misunderstood teenager.

'It's a loan.'

'Huh?' The frown reappeared.

'For when you buy me lunch in Miami.'

'What are you talking about?'

'I predict that one day you're going to visit me in the States. I'll take you to South Beach Miami and you can buy me lunch at the News Café, but you'll need some money. American money.'

'Are you a fucking pervert?' The angry teenager was back.

'No, just a good judge of character. I'll see you around, Kimmy.' I left her standing there holding the bill.

Call it atonement or guilt, but whenever I meet a kid like Kimmy—and let's face it, teenagers aren't an endangered species—I think of Johnny. I hadn't been there for my own son during his teenage years, and I often wondered what it must've been like for him growing up without my influence.

The heat and humidity hit me like a small explosion when I stepped out from the air-conditioned Yacht Club. I put on my hat and sunglasses then checked my watch. It was only 10.30.

To the right of the doctor's surgery and the post office was William Street, a wide road leading up to the houses which overlooked the town. I followed the road up with my eyes. It was tree lined, quite pretty, bordered on either side by timber houses on stumps. I was wondering what the view was like from the top, but wasn't relishing the thought of the climb, especially in this heat. What the hell—the exercise would do me good.

18

The first building to my left was the one Fat Bobby had pointed out as Maud's house—a tired Queenslander with flaky paint and a blue roof. A dog barked from the back of the house. I continued on.

I could feel the heat of the tarmac through the soles of my shoes. But the higher I climbed, the more the sea breeze reached me—a welcome relief on the back of my neck. I couldn't resist stopping every few yards and turning to look at the view.

By halfway up, all the houses were squatting on stumps and had verandahs to take full advantage of the view and the breeze. The gardens were tropical—palm trees, fan-shaped ferns and frangipani trees.

The summit was about fifty yards ahead where a large cylindrical water tank squatted, almost hidden by trees. There were no more houses up there, so I turned into the street that cut across to the right—Bayview Terrace the sign read. On the corner, the leaves of a huge jacaranda tree rustled in the breeze. On the same block, and shaded by the tree, was a small timber church fringed by a graveyard, all enclosed by an off-white picket fence.

Candle Stick Bay State School was the next building—a small, sand-coloured brick structure that looked out of place in its surroundings. I could hear a female teacher speaking above her class as I passed.

I continued along the street while beginning to see a pattern: between every ten houses another road branched upwards into a little cul-de-sac of three houses. It was at the entrance to the third that I was attacked!

He was only a little guy, but I could tell from his body language that he meant business.

He rushed towards me with eyes fixed on mine.

There'd be no talking this guy down. I weighed up my options—stay here and fight or make a dash. Opting for an escape, I turned on my heels and scooted. Of course, he was much fitter than me, so it didn't take long for him to catch up with me.

He latched onto my right ankle.

I yelped, stumbled and fell. I rolled onto my back, lifted my leg in the air then slammed down my foot, But he held on tight.

The little bastard dug his razor-sharp teeth in deeper and shook my flesh.

I tore off my cap and tried to hit him away.

He released my ankle and was about to pounce when a high-pitched whistle pierced the air. The little white dog twitched at the sound and his entire body seemed to deflate.

Two more whistles tore through the morning.

He looked over his shoulder then back at me.

I understood fully. This wasn't over between us.

Another whistle, then a woman's voice: 'Willy Nelson!'

He regarded me balefully, then turned and trotted away with his little tail high in the air like he was the most delightful little doggy you'd ever want to meet.

I examined my ankle—the bite marks were obvious and little rivulets of blood were running down into my sneaker.

The street ended at a T-junction. The road at the end led up steeply to the left and out of site while the right side veered back down to the town. I headed back down with a limp. When I reached the bottom of the hill, I was slap bang next to The General Store. A few steps across the road was the pub.

Pat was coming from the direction of the ladies' toilets when

I entered the foyer. Judging by her widening eyes she noticed the blood on my foot. 'Not Willy Nelson?'

I fidgeted like a schoolboy who'd just had a run-in with a bully.

'That bloody dog. She needs to keep it locked in her yard.'

I assured her I was okay.

A smile twitched across Pat's face. 'He's a nasty little bugger, eh?'

'Who calls a dog Willy Nelson?'

'Babs Bingle.'

The surname rang a bell. 'Pete's wife?'

Pat harrumphed. Clearly, she was not impressed by Babs Bingle. 'Ex. Bit of a fruit loop if you know what I mean.' She didn't expect a reply and with barely a pause for breath said, 'Have you had lunch?'

'No.'

'You go freshen up, love. I'll fix you a sandwich then we'll have a look at that bite.'

I took a quick shower and was trying to clean the wound when there was a knock.

I opened the door to be greeted by Pat carrying a tuna sandwich on a plate in one hand and a first aid kit in the other.

'Let's have a look at that foot, eh?'

I backed up and sat on the bed. Pat handed me the sandwich then knelt down to examine my ankle. She tut-tutted. 'You'll need to see the doctor.'

Despite Pat's ministrations, my foot was throbbing as I came level with the doctor's surgery. The entrance was typically Victorian—a redbrick portico with a midnight blue door and a leadlight glass panel at the top. On entering, I was greeted by a clinical smell of disinfectant so typical of a doctor's surgery.

Except for the reception desk, which was a curved silver monstrosity, the interior of the house matched the exterior: a wooden staircase, forest green carpets, a grandfather clock and maroon-flocked wallpaper. The reception area itself would've once been the lobby but it had been extended into the front parlour and turned into a waiting room.

The young woman behind the desk smiled. The only other patient was an elderly man sitting on one of the wooden chairs with his head deep in a fishing magazine.

'Good afternoon, can I help you?' The receptionist's voice was bright and cheerful. Her nametag read, 'Steph.'

'Hi, I'm Joe. Pat at the pub said I should just show up to see the doc. Is that okay?'

'Ah, the American copper.'

I smiled, although the novelty of the townsfolk's assumption was wearing thin by now. 'I'd like the doctor to check out this dog bite.' I had no idea why I was sharing this with the young woman, and I felt more than a little silly holding up my ankle for her inspection.

'Willy Nelson?'

'Yes.'

Steph exhibited the same knowing smile that had twitched across Pat's face earlier. 'He's a little bugger, ain't he?'

'He sure is.'

She handed me a clipboard and a pen and asked me to fill out my details. I took a seat opposite the other patient. When I'd finished writing, I looked up to find him studying me.

He quickly raised the magazine so that once more his face was hidden, but I'd seen enough to know it was the old guy from the gas station.

'Hi, Johno isn't it?'

He lowered the magazine just enough to reveal his eyes and grunted.

'Didn't get attacked by a crazy little dog, did you?' It was meant as a joke.

Nothing.

I checked the questionnaire to make sure I hadn't missed anything—I hadn't—then signed it.

'My brother lives in LA,' Johno suddenly said.

'Yeah?'

'You might know him.'

'You think? What's his name?'

'Davo.' He was regarding me with anticipation as if expecting me to say. 'Oh that's right, Aussie guy lives on the next ranch to old Abe Lowenstein. Know him well.'

I shook my head and, with a sigh, Johno dived back into his reading.

A door at the side opened and a middle-aged man with wild, grey hair and eyes to match, ushered out an elderly woman.

'Thank you, doctor,' the woman said.

Any doubt about Dr Hamish Elliot being a second-generation Scot were dashed as soon as he spoke. 'Ye're very welcome, Ivy. Just see as ye noo try te dea te much, eh?' He turned to Johno. 'Now then, young Johno. Would ye like te step this way?'

Johno stood, placed the magazine on the side table, then marched into the doctor's surgery without making any further eye contact with me.

Just before the door closed, I heard the doctor rumble. 'Noo, what canna do for ye today, laddie?'

I handed back the clipboard to Steph.

After what seemed like an hour, the door opened and Johno and the doctor emerged. They shook hands.

Johno grunted then headed towards Steph.

The doctor smiled in my direction. 'Looks like ye're next, ma friend.'

When we shook hands, his grip was powerful. In the surgery he asked me to take a seat while he read my newly uploaded details on the computer screen. 'Och, ye're the American chappie then. The policeman.'

'American yes, policeman no.'

'So how a' ye liking our wee town, *Mister Dean?*' He placed a definite emphasis on my name then leaned back in his chair, scrutinising me.

'It sure is a beautiful place.'

'Aye, that it is. And what brings ye all this way from …' he pushed his half-moon glasses up his nose and leaned forward to read the screen. 'Florida?'

'Just a trip. I've always wanted to see Australia.'

'Aye … Aye. So, what canna do for ye today?'

I held up my ankle for his inspection.

'Don't tell me,' he bellowed when he saw my wound. 'That wee bastard, Willy?'

I couldn't help but smile at the notoriety of this little dog.

'He's the devil himself, I'll tell ye. Wreaks bloody havoc up there.'

'I guess I entered his territory.'

'Something needs te be done aboot that dog. Ye're the second victim this week! Take off yer shoe please.' He snapped on a pair of rubber gloves, lifted my foot onto his lap, and studied my wound through a large, illuminated magnifying glass.

'Evil wee fucker,' he mumbled as he gently stroked his thumb across the punctures. 'It's deep but clean, thank goodness.'

'Deep enough for a lawsuit?' I joked.

The doctor didn't seem to hear. He cleaned up the wound and then to my chagrin, gave me a tetanus shot in my thigh. Damn needle hurt more than the bite.

19

By the time I reached my room, exhaustion was creeping up on me. I tossed my cap and sunglasses on the dresser, kicked off my sneakers and flopped onto the bed. But sleep wouldn't come. My eyes followed the tiny trail of cracks in the ceiling. My body felt like jello, but my mind was racing like an Olympic sprinter's.

I had been in town for two days and, to date, there was absolutely no evidence that The Moon was here. But what had I expected to find? Perhaps Burt Williams had been right when he said this trip would be a waste of time. However, if The Moon was here, he or she would know that I was here, that's for sure.

I mentally ticked off the people I'd seen that day and considered those whom I was yet to meet. There was Miss Berry, the English teacher and William Lambert, the writer, of course. Fat Bobby had also mentioned that Roxy's father was an American professor. All three were definitely worth questioning.

After an early night, I awoke the next morning with the first rays of daylight seeping into the room. The ocean gave out a gentle *whish ... whoosh ... whish ... whoosh* and the waking birds chirped and squabbled loudly.

I checked my watch. It was 5.00 am. I understood now about going to bed early and waking at sun-up the next morning. It didn't seem to be an option. The day's heat and sunshine drained you so much that by the time it got to mid-evening, you were totally whacked.

Flirting with The Moon

The pub was eerily still in the morning light. I double checked I had my key then let myself out the front door.

After reaching the harbour, my plan had been to walk in the opposite direction as yesterday. I figured this would lead to the lighthouse.

'Hello, Joe.' I turned to see Molly Quinn approaching the jetty. 'Going my way?' she said, turning on bare feet and heading onto the beach.

'Sure.' My plans of checking out the lighthouse floated away like driftwood on the tide. The thought of spending a little time with Molly Quinn enticed me.

Molly set a steady pace and although I walked every morning, I had to push hard to keep up.

'So, Mr Dean, what's this about my niece visiting you in Florida?' she said, looking straight ahead.

She sounded a little put out. 'Sorry … I just thought she looked really sad at the Yacht Club yesterday so I—'

'Sorry? Why are you sorry? For the first time since she's been here, we actually had a real conversation last night.'

'Really?'

'Yes, really. Kimmy thinks you're the bee's knees.'

'Wow.' A small surge of pleasure rushed into my chest.

'Wow indeed. I'm impressed.'

We were nearing the section of beach where the bum had set up his camp beneath the trees. He was lying under his tarp in almost the same position as the previous morning.

Molly didn't look in his direction as we passed.

'Who's that guy?'

'How would I know?' Molly snapped. Her body stiffened and she marched at a quicker pace.

I almost had to jog to keep up.

We continued on in an awkward silence for a few minutes.

I wasn't sure why such a simple question had caused this reaction, but I felt the need to apologise again. 'Sorry, just inquisitive. Old detective habit I guess.'

'Ah … so Maudie *was* right.' Her shoulders lowered and she seemed to relax. 'You *are* a copper.'

I suddenly remembered I'd only told Fat Bobby about my past. 'No … well …' I'd always been a lousy liar, and by the quirk of Molly's eyebrow, she'd picked up on it.

'Okay … retired LAPD … but I've been a private detective for the last twenty years.'

'And you're here looking for someone?'

'Kind of.'

'Something to do with William Lambert?'

This question came as a surprise. 'Why do you ask that?'

'Who else could it be? I'm sure you're not here because Babs Bingle's trying to squeeze Pete dry.'

'No … I'm not actually sure why I'm here.' By the time we'd reached the mouth of the creek, I'd told her the abridged version of my story, but I was still unable to talk about Jacqueline Sanchez, so I omitted that part.

'You poor thing,' she finally whispered and placed a hand on my shoulder.

Sympathy was not what I was after. 'Oh, I've turned my life around. I'm not quite where I would like to be yet, but I'm well on the way.'

'A reconciliation with your son.'

'That's right.'

She turned and looked me in the eye. 'There's still something you haven't told me though, isn't there?'

Talk about a woman's intuition.

'But that's okay. I'm guessing that when you can finally talk about it it'll be a big part of your recovery too.'

'You'd make a good shrink,' I said, grinning.

We stood side-by-side gazing out over the bay for a while

before she spoke again. This time her tone was serious. 'Do you really think he could be here?'

'He *or* she. Yes, I do.'

'It's crazy, Joe. Things like this happen in crime novels, not in Candle Stick Bay.'

'It may seem that way but think about it. What better bolthole for a killer? A small coastal town miles away from anywhere, and on the other side of the world from where the murders took place.'

We headed back the way we came. The breeze teased Molly's hair and a sudden urge to gently stroke it down made my fingers twitch. We neared the area where the bum had made camp except now, he was on his feet—watching us.

'Well, look who it ain't, the septic and the dyke,' he boomed, staggering towards us.

'Just ignore him, Joe,' Molly said.

'Just ignore him, Joe,' the bum mimicked and began to stalk us like a hyena.

I stopped, turned to face him and, once again, said calmly, 'What's your problem, pal?'

Although I'd come across thousands of his type when I was with the police, that wasn't why I understood him. I knew he was a victim who, instead of taking responsibility for his own actions, found it easier to blame everyone else for what was wrong with his life. I knew because I'd been there myself. I had a fair amount of empathy for this guy cavorting before me like an idiot, but not sympathy.

He lurched forwards, lifted his chin and pushed his face close to mine. 'What the fuck's it to you?' The stink of alcohol and cigarettes did nothing for his maggoty breath.

I could crush you like an insect the old Joe wanted to say.

'Mr Fucking Detective thinks he can flirt with the moon.'

Normally, the glob of putrid phlegm that landed on my lip would have made me vomit. I'm not good with things like that but I hardly noticed it. 'What did you say?'

'Hah, hah!' He jumped back, then proceeded to stagger around us in a circle with his arms stretched wide like a child playing aeroplanes.

'Come on, Joe.' Molly grabbed my arm. 'He's nothing but trouble.'

'Houston this is *The Moon* requesting permission to land.'

Part of me wanted to get as far away from this guy as possible but another part of me wanted to grab him by the neck and squeeze and shake him until he told me what he knew about The Moon.

Molly dragged me away. 'Don't let him wind you up. Let's go.'

Behind us, he burst into a very warped, off-key version of the Creedence Clearwater Revival song, 'Bad Moon Rising.'

The rest of the walk was in silence. The bum had not only mentioned The Moon, but also the title of the book. How the hell had he known about either of them?

We left the beach along the sandy track and continued up the high street, only stopping when we reached the door to Molly's store.

'So, you coming to the writers' meeting on Monday?'

I nodded. 'You bet.'

20

When I returned to The Great Northern, Maud was vacuuming at the bottom of the stairs. When she saw me, she quickly turned off the ancient upright Hoover.

'Mr Dean, I've got some information for you.' She ducked her head and lowered her voice. 'It's about that murderer you're looking for.'

I tried to laugh off her fervour. 'Maud, I'm not here looking for a murderer.'

'Yes, you are. You're looking for The Moon.'

I could feel the smile sliding from my face like butter from a hot knife. 'Who told you that?'

She tapped the side of her nose with her index finger. 'Can't reveal my sources, Mr Dean, you know that.'

'But you don't seem to have a problem telling the whole town about *my* business.'

She reared back a bit. My tone must've startled her. 'It's all over the town, Mr Dean.'

'Yes, because you've been putting it out there.' I dropped the naïve tourist persona, replacing it instead with that of the detective. 'So, who told you about The Moon?'

'Miss Berry.' The words rushed from her mouth.

'The English teacher?'

Maud nodded and glanced from side-to-side like a nervous

snitch. 'She knows all about you, Mr Dean. Them murders all those years ago—everything.'

'How?'

'I don't know, but she was very surprised when I told her you were here.'

I asked Maud to back up a little and she explained that she cleaned at the school three days a week after school hours. When she'd mentioned to the teacher about the American in town who was asking a lot of questions, Miss Berry had asked for my name.

'So, Miss Berry already knew about me?'

'Yes.' She glanced around again to make sure no one was within earshot. 'But that's not the information I've got for you.' She leaned in. 'Have you met Barbara Bingle yet?'

I was about to tell her I'd met her dog, but realised she already knew that.

'A strange lady,' she continued in a whisper. 'Threatened to kill Pete when they split up. Nearly did too, took a knife to him and—'

'Good morning, Joe.' Pat was standing in the bar doorway. 'Maudie … what's going on?'

'Nothing, Pat, just asking Mr Dean about his walk.'

'Good morning, Pat,' I said.

'Is she bothering you, Joe?'

'No, not at all.'

Maud huffed, turned on the vacuum cleaner and resumed her work.

'Give us a shout when you're ready for breakfast,' Pat tossed over the noise.

I gave her the thumbs up, and she returned to the bar. 'So, you were saying, Maud?' I said loud enough for Maud to hear.

She stood upright but left the vacuum running. 'Barbara Bingle—Babs—she's one of them hippy types, you know, crystals and baggy pants and all that.'

'So?'

'She worships The Moon, Mr Dean!'

I pointed to the sky. 'You mean the moon.'

'Yes, but don't you see? It all fits.'

'It does?'

'Crikey, not much of a detective, are you?'

Maud was obviously insinuating that because Barbara Bingle was a hippy who worshipped the moon, that linked her to the killer. But that wasn't what was bothering me. It was the thought of her spreading this information around the town. 'Have you told anyone else about this, Maud?'

'Not a soul.' She had a superior look on her face like she was the guardian of an ancient secret.

I needed a way of curbing Maud's enthusiasm while keeping her onside. An idea came to mind. 'May I ask a favour?'

'Of course, Mr Dean, anything.'

'I need your help.'

Her face lit up as if her Powerball number had dropped.

'I want you to keep what you know about The Moon to yourself.'

Her face collapsed and she regarded me as if I were crazy.

I changed tack. 'Perhaps we could work together on this.'

'You mean I'd be working with you on the case? Like partners?'

I'd given up all pretence as to why I was in Candle Stick Bay. 'Yes. I think with your valuable knowledge of the town and its people, we'd make a great team.'

I could almost see the possibilities shooting through her mind, lighting up like a pinball machine.

'But all information *must* remain confidential, privileged only for you and me.'

The prospect brightened her up. 'You can count on me, Mr Dean. I won't let you down. I'll ask around and get as much info as I can.'

The possible repercussion of this jolted me to my senses. I could be placing this woman in danger. 'No, no, Maud. We have to tread very carefully ... remember, we're talking about a psychopathic killer who has murdered twelve people.'

A veil of worry lowered over her face.

'I don't want to put you in danger.'

She frowned and her bottom lip tensed. 'Danger?'

'Of course. If The Moon hears that you're spreading gossip about him, what's he going to do?'

Her jaw dropped and her face turned white.

There was no need to say more. I'd planted the thought of her becoming victim number thirteen into her mind, and the seed would sprout by itself.

'So, this is really dangerous?' she whispered, furtively glancing over her shoulder.

'Absolutely. This is why I'm trying to be inconspicuous. We'll need to watch each other's backs from now on. Because I'm sure he or she already knows what *we* are up to.'

'We?'

'Yes, we're in this together now, remember?'

'But I ... I haven't—'

'Shhh ... it's okay—'

'But it's not okay,' she wailed. 'He might come after me!'

I was trying to scare her off, but I didn't want to scare her to death. 'Look, I'm assuming you haven't told anyone yet about The Moon being here.'

She shook her head wildly. 'Like I said, I haven't told a soul. Honest to God I haven't.'

'Then it's not too late. How about we make a pact?'

'What kind of pact?'

'How does this sound? You don't speak to anyone about The Moon or why I'm here, and I'll watch your back.'

'You'll protect me from the killer?'

'Yes, but you won't need protection if you keep the information to yourself because the killer won't know *you* know.'

'Yes, yes right, that makes sense.'

'So do we have a deal?' I held out my hand.

We shook. Her hand was trembling like a leaf. 'It's a deal!'

I climbed the stairs. After a few steps, I turned. 'Remember, Maud, if The Moon *is* here, it could be anybody.'

She bolted upright. This was obviously something else she hadn't thought of. 'That's right … anybody!'

I imagined she spoke to just about everyone in town. She might even speak to The Moon on a daily basis. As I continued up the stairs, I could almost hear the *cha-ching-ching-ching* of the pinball machine.

After a long, hot shower and a change of clothes— T-shirt and shorts—I ate another breakfast of fruit out on the balcony of my room while reading the newspaper. But my mind wouldn't focus on the words. I'd learned from Molly during our morning walk that Miss Berry lived two houses down from the school. Being Saturday, it might be a good time to catch her. Babs Bingle was a different matter. She had a bodyguard called Willy Nelson. I doubted I'd even get close to the house. I wasn't game to try. As for William Lambert, I was toying with the idea of simply going up to the house and knocking on his door.

I'd noticed a small yellow shoulder bag hanging in the closet when I'd arrived. I fetched it, picked up my copy of *Flirting with The Moon,* tossed it in the bag, and left my room.

21

The hill was steeper than I remembered. It wasn't long before my legs began to ache and my sore ankle throb.

As ever, the parrots were chirping in the trees bordering either side of the street and the higher I got, the louder the ubiquitous hum of cicadas got too. By the time I reached Bayview Terrace, I was buggered as the Aussies would say. Molly had said that Miss Berry's place was two houses from the school. A waist high chain wire fence surrounded a quaint Queenslander home. I unlatched the gate and slipped inside the front yard.

Three wooden steps led up to the verandah. From the eaves hung baskets with an array of colourful flowers. A wicker outdoor setting hunkered at the far end. Behind the flyscreen the front door was open.

My knock was followed by a wheezy bark and the *clack-clack-clack* of claws on floorboards.

A pug appeared on the other side of the screen door, its bark low and wheezy.

'That'll do, Oscar.'

The voice was female and stern, making me feel like a school kid.

The dog stopped barking, sat down on its fat butt, and regarded me through bulging eyes.

A Katherine Hepburn look-a-like appeared at the door—early to mid-sixties at a guess. She looked me up and down. 'Can I help you?' All business.

'Hi my name's—'

'Ah, Mr Dean. I wondered how long it would be before you'd visit.'
'You did?'
'Of course.' She opened the screen, waving me in.
Without moving, Oscar's breath rattled, and his eyes followed me as I stepped over him.
'I hope I'm not disturbing you.'
'No, I've been writing since five this morning. Time for a break. Would you care for tea?'
'Yes please, that would be nice.'
The house was small. The front door led straight into the living room: light green tongue-and-groove walls, a worn Chesterfield couch, a matching wing-backed chair, a side dresser, and books stuffed into a floor-to-ceiling bookcase at the far end of the room. I followed Miss Berry's well-shod, *clip-clop* heels into the kitchen.
'Earl Grey, Mister Dean?'
I wasn't a huge fan of Earl Grey tea, but I didn't want to appear rude. 'Yes, please.'
Miss Berry lit one of the gas rings then placed a kettle over the flame.
'So how was your trip from LA?' She spoke as if she knew me.
'Pleasant, thank you.'
'That's good. Hell of a flight. Not as bad as flying to England though.'
I followed her out to the front verandah carrying a tray of tea and cookies.
Miss Berry poured the drinks in silence.
I fidgeted and the wicker chair creaked. 'Miss Berry, how do you know me?'
'Partly due to the local newshound. Sugar?'
'No, thank you, just milk.'
'I was amazed to learn from Maud Baker that there was an American detective called Joe Dean in town asking lots of questions.' She handed me my tea and offered a cookie.

'Thank you.'

'Take two, Mr Dean. And you're allowed to dunk.'

It was polite to do as I was told. 'But you seem to *know* me?' I threw the now soggy cookie in my mouth.

Miss Berry took a delicate sip of her tea. 'Mr Dean, I have lost count of how much romantic pulp I've written. I sometimes feel trapped in this shallow genre.' She lowered her voice as if worried that someone would overhear. 'I'm a closet mystery writer.'

My eyebrows inadvertently arched.

'Unfortunately, I don't get much time to work on my passion but, over the years, I've studied some of the most infamous serial killers: Bundy, Nilson, Durst, Christie, and naturally, of course, The Moon.'

The Moon killings were high-profile at the time and, being the detective-in-charge, my name and picture had regularly been splashed across the newspapers. It's possible she could have learned about me during her research.

'I know all about you, Mr Dean.' She looked like a cat who'd licked the cream. 'But what has me absolutely baffled and *immensely* intrigued is what on Earth are you doing in Candle Stick Bay?'

I retrieved *Flirting with The Moon* from my bag and handed it over. 'This.'

While examining the cover, she uttered a soft, 'Oh.' She opened the book to the first page and began to read. 'My God … it's written by him!' Her voice rose at the end of her statement—excitement tinged with horror. She snapped the book shut, and once more studied the cover.

The colour suddenly drained from her cheeks. Was it the author's name that provoked this reaction?

'Miss Berry, are you okay?'

'Uhm … yes … I'm fine. Sorry.' She thrust the book back as if it carried a pox.

'What is it? Something about the book? The author?'

Rising from the table, she shook her head. 'No, of course not.' There was a snap in her tone. 'It's time I returned to my work.'

'Right. Are you sure you've never seen this before?' I jiggled the book in the air as I too rose to my feet.

'Quite sure. It was nice to meet you, Mr Dean.' She proffered a hand and it seemed to flutter in mine like a trapped bird. 'If you could show yourself out.' She hadn't looked me in the face since she'd read the cover, and neither did she now. Instead, she busied herself placing the cups on the tray.

'Thank you for your time, Miss Berry.'

When she'd been glancing through the interior pages, she'd appeared excited, intrigued, but as soon as she'd studied the cover, her excitement had turned to shock, or fear. Whichever it was, she was definitely rattled. The question was, why? Did she recognise the name of the author? If so, it meant Miss Berry possibly knew the identity of The Moon. I'd need to talk to her again but now wasn't the time.

My legs felt light as I plonked down the hill.

With a grating of gears, an orange VW Kombi turned into the street, crawling noisily up towards me. Another loud gearshift and the vehicle swung into a driveway on my right, shuddering to a stop.

Roxy, the personal trainer cum yoga teacher, jumped out. 'You're game, aren't ya?' she called to me.

'Hi.' I had no idea what she was talking about.

She intercepted me at the end of her driveway and gestured towards the hill. 'Bit of a trek in this heat.'

Ah. 'Worth it for the view.'

'Yep, it really is something. So ...' she pushed her hair out of her eyes so she could see me more clearly. 'What brings you up here, Joe? Not looking for round two with Willy, are you?' she grinned.

'No, I've just had tea with Miss Berry.'

'Wow, you're getting around a bit. Maudie tells me you're only here on holiday after all.'

God bless Maudie. 'That's what I've been trying to tell everyone.'

Roxy regarded me with narrowed eyes.

'So how was your session with Mr Lambert?' I changed the subject.

Her shoulders slumped and she shook her head. 'He's a pain in the arse. Reckons he wants to get fit except I rock up there this morning and he's already into the Scotch.'

'An alcoholic?'

She shrugged. 'Dunno. Anyway, I laid down the law. No more drinking or smoking.'

I wanted her to carry on, but she was already edging away.

The curtain in the window at the front of her house twitched. Someone was watching us.

Roxy had noticed it too. 'That'll be my dad. He's not well.'

'Sorry to hear that.'

The front door swung open. 'That you, Jimmy?'

A tall, grey-haired man with a sharp face strode onto the verandah and glared at me. His accent was Midwestern US. His shirt was buttoned up wrong.

'Daddy, go back inside,' Roxy trotted to her father.

'You should've been here an hour ago, man.'

'It's okay, Daddy. Remember? Jimmy's not coming.'

Roxy's father brushed her aside and stepped forward. 'Goddamn it man, don't just stand there. You'll need to drive like the wind to get me there on time.'

I had no idea what I was expected to say so I stood rooted to the spot, staring, just like the idiot he probably took me for.

'Do you hear me?' His voice was sterner now, more authoritarian.

'Daddy, no-one's going anywhere.'

Thank heavens for Roxy.

She rested a hand on her father's shoulder, trying to guide him to the door. 'Let's go inside.'

He waved a dismissive hand in my direction and retreated into the house.

Over her shoulder Roxy shot me an apologetic smile then followed her father inside.

I had the feeling of déjà vu. It wasn't a detective's instincts—it was a feeling of familiarity. I knew the professor from somewhere, but where? The puzzle occupied my mind all the way to Dougie's. I'd met Roxy's father before.

22

Once again, I'd planned on checking out the lighthouse that afternoon but by the time I'd returned to my room, I was as tired as a cat.

I kicked off my sneakers and sat out on the balcony. The morning had been an interesting one. It had provided few answers but thrown up some serious questions. Did Miss Berry recognise the author's name? Who was Roxy's father? And why did I feel as if I knew him? Was he once a well-known actor?' The book was on my lap. I studied the cover for what must have been the hundredth time. The author's name, Steven Powell, was tugging at me. It was obviously a pseudonym, but could there be a hidden clue?

I flicked through the book and inadvertently stopped a few pages from the end. The words **her heart** blazed out at me like a blinding light.

In a fit of rage—the kind I thought I'd had under control for the last twenty years—I lifted the book and flung it from me. The book spun through the air, pages flapping, to land at the far end of the balcony. I was shaking and that old feeling of helplessness had returned. 'You bastard!' I yelled towards the bay.

A group of startled drinkers in the beer garden were staring up at me.

'Sorry!' I mouthed, blushing.

I retrieved the book—thankfully it wasn't damaged—and returned it to the bedside drawer.

My body was still tired, but my brain was whizzing, so I headed back onto the balcony, down the rear stairs, through the beer garden—not making eye contact with the drinkers—and onto the beach. Finding some much-needed shade under a palm tree, I sat down, leaning against the trunk and peering at the bay.

My eyes were heavy, and the gentle lapping of the water was hypnotic.

It was dark when I opened my eyes. The moonless sky was a shroud of chiffon and pearls. There was a bonfire in the middle of the beach, flames crackling and snapping as they spiralled into the air.

I stood and trudged through the sand towards it.

The bum who had confronted me earlier was sitting beside the fire, and next to him with her back to me was a young woman with long dark hair. At my approach, the bum looked up and began to giggle like a nervous child.

The young woman turned and our eyes met.

I froze. It was my ex-partner Jacqueline Sanchez.

'Where were you, Joe?' she said. Blood oozed from the corners of her mouth.

I turned away and realised the townsfolk had gathered around us. Molly and Kimmy, Maud, Pat and Frank, Bruce and Silvia, Fat Bobby, Roxy and the professor, Dennis Hodge the postmaster, Miss Berry, Dougie—the only one smiling—Pete Bingle, Doctor Elliot, and Johno from the gas station.

I turned back to Jacqueline, but she was gone. The fire was now a pile of glowing embers.

The bum was on his feet, laughing uncontrollably, cradling his stomach with one arm and pointing at me with the other. 'You … you did it again … you took your eye off the prize and lost it … just like last time.'

Where Jacqueline had been sitting, the sand was saturated with blood.

The bum laughed so hard he started to cough and splutter. 'That'll be right,' he gasped. 'Have a good look now ... now she's gone.'

There was something lying in the middle of the dark stain. I didn't need to examine it; I already knew what it was.

The bum picked it up and held it in the air.

Jacqueline's heart was still beating.

I woke with a sharp gasp and a yell hovering at the back of my throat.

It was still daylight. I was trembling, but gradually the recollection of my surroundings returned.

Jacqueline was never far from my mind but, when I had the dreams, she was so real I could almost touch her. The urge to wash the memory away with a bottle of Jack Daniels was suddenly very strong.

'Do it, Joe. Do it!' Joe the drunk said.

23

It was late afternoon and *Flirting with The Moon* was the first thing I noticed as I entered my room. It was lying closed on the bed. I didn't remember leaving it there. I was about to put it back in the bedside drawer when it dawned on me that I definitely hadn't left it there.

I lifted the book and opened the drawer then froze with my hand in midair. 'What the hell?'

My copy was still in the drawer!

Instinctively, I opened the book. On the very first page in the space beneath the title and written in blood-red ink was an inscription:

Best wishes, Stephen Powell.

I sat down hard on the bed staring at the page and ran a finger over the inscription. A chill passed through me. The Moon had been right here, in my room!

I rushed down to the bar with the book still in my hand.

Frank was pouring drinks and looked up as I breezed into the room. 'Hey, Joe ... you all right, mate?'

The few other patrons—Bluey on his usual stool, Pete and Bruce at the far end of the bar, a sprinkle of tourists—didn't notice me enter.

'Can I have a word with Pat and yourself?'

'Sure. Just give us a minute,' Frank said. When he'd finished serving the drinks he raised the hatch on the bar, ushered me through and into the open doorway at the right-hand side of the bar.

We were in a small storeroom. Shelves stacked with boxes of chips and glasses adorned the top half of the walls. Along the bottom were glass-fronted fridges containing bottles of wine and beer. Pat was seated on a stool at a stainless steel bench eating a sandwich.

'Hello, Joe,' she said, wiping mayonnaise from the corner of her mouth.

'Hi Pat.'

'Is everything all right?'

'I'll make it quick. I know how busy you guys are.'

'That's all right. I'm just grabbing a quick bite. What's up?'

'Someone's been in my room.'

'What?' they said in unison, bolting to attention.

'I found this on my bed.'

Frank took the book and flicked through it.

'It was on my bed, but it wasn't there when I went out earlier.'

Frank looked at Pat. 'Wasn't Maudie up there cleaning?'

'Yeah. Maybe she left it there for you to read, Joe,' Pat said.

This thought hadn't occurred to me. Perhaps Maud had come across a copy of the book and left it in my room for me to see. My cheeks suddenly felt warm.

Pat laid a work-worn hand on my arm. 'She's still here. I'll ask her.' She shimmied off the stool and crossed to the wall phone at the back of the room.

'I'm pretty sure that's all there is to it, Joe,' Frank nodded as if agreeing with himself. He returned to the bar.

A roar of group laughter shot out from the bar, but Pat retrieved my attention. 'She's on her way down. What book is it, Joe?'

I handed it over. She read aloud from the cover, '*Flirting with The Moon* by Stephen Powell.' She glanced up at me. 'Sounds romantic.' She opened the book, silently read a little of the first chapter then screwed up her face. 'Yuck. Didn't expect that.' She shuddered. 'Oh, this'd be right up Maudie's street—'

'What'd be right up Maudie's street?' Maud said entering from a side door. When she saw me standing next to Pat she flinched, shoulders back, as if about to face a firing squad.

'Maudie, is this yours?' Pat waved the book in the air, level with her face.

Maud squinted as if trying to focus. 'No. What is it?'

'It's a book. *Flirting with The Moon* by Stephen Powell.'

She shook her head. 'Not mine.' Her tone was adamant. 'Why?'

My turn. 'I found it on my bed just now.'

Maud frowned. 'That's odd.' She jerked her chin at the book. 'Wasn't there when I changed the sheets. It was in the bedside drawer.'

Now it was Pat's turn to frown. She turned to me and raised her eyebrows.

'The book in the bedside drawer belongs to me.' I pointed at the book still in Pat's hand. 'That's a different copy.'

Pat's attention returned to Maud. 'Are you sure you didn't put it there, Maudie? If you did, just tell us, you won't be in any trouble.'

'Positive. God's honest truth.'

Her expression was a mixture of bewilderment and panic. I believed her.

'So, it definitely wasn't on the bed when you were in Joe's room?' Pat asked again.

'Definitely not!'

'Can you just take over from Frank in the bar for a minute and send him back in here?'

'What's this all about?' The old Maud had returned. She looked at me with wide eyes and lowered her voice. 'Is it … you know who?'

'Just get Frank for us, eh?' Pat said.

Maud huffed and marched through the storeroom to the bar.

'What did she mean by that, Joe?' Pat said.

'What's that?'

'When she said, "Is it you know who?" What did Maudie mean by that?'

It was bound to come out sooner or later, I'd just hoped it would be later, but it was not to be. 'I need to talk to you and Frank.'

'Sounds ominous!' Frank's deep voice boomed from behind.

We sat at the stainless steel bench and I proceeded to give Pat and Frank the same watered down explanation I'd given Molly.

Their questions were the same too.

I couldn't reveal too much. I explained I was merely looking for the person who wrote the book. It wasn't a lie.

'Bloody hell! I better get Fat Bobby.' Frank pushed himself up from the bench, the stool's legs scraping along the floor.

I winced. 'No, leave it for now, Frank. Truly. It's not that important that we need bother him just now. I'll talk to him in the morning.'

Frank's expression hardened. 'I don't know about that mate. If we've got someone breaking into the rooms, we need to get it sorted.'

I assured them nothing was stolen and there had been no sign of a forced entry.

'So, how'd they get in?' Pat said.

'My guess would be from the balcony. I hadn't locked that door.'

'Anyone could have nicked up the back stairs,' Frank said.

'I don't think it was a burglary. Nothing was taken or disturbed. Maybe someone just wanted to talk to me about the book.'

Frank's cheeks bloomed red. 'Well, they should've bloody asked then, not just barged into a bloke's room!'

'It'll be all right, love.' Pat placed a hand on her husband's shoulder. 'Whoever it was won't be daft enough to come back. They'll know Joe's found the book by now.'

'That's right,' I agreed. 'They won't come near the place.'

Frank calmed down. 'All right, but you go and see Bob first thing in the morning, or I will.'

I promised I would.

When I returned to my room, I realised I was carrying the weight of a familiar uncertainty. It was a sensation I hadn't experienced since the original murders took place.

The Moon was back in control.

24

My ankle was still sore, and as I realised I was probably doing too much walking, I spent the next morning doing very little—reading newspapers, snoozing. Around lunchtime, I was about to head downstairs when the house phone rang.

'Hello, Joe, it's Pat.'

'Hi, Pat. Is everything all right?'

'Yes, all good but I've got a message for you.'

'A message?'

'It's from Molly. She needs to see you. Says it's very important. Can you go to the bookstore right away?'

'Okay, I'll be right there.'

Molly and Kimmy were waiting for me.

'We heard what happened yesterday,' Molly said.

'What happened yesterday?'

'We heard about the break in.' Kimmy was trying to be casual, but I detected genuine concern in her tone. 'And we thought you might need cheering up,' Molly said.

'Not really a break in, nothing was stolen or anything.' I had no idea where this was leading.

'Well, that may be, but Kimmy and I are treating you to lunch.'

This was the last thing I had been expecting and I was taken aback. 'That'll be great!'

'Come. Your carriage awaits.' Molly led the way out the store.

'Aunt Molly, I'm going to stay here.' Kimmy had stopped at the doorway.

Molly blushed and looked a little put out. 'Why?'

'Ah, you know, two's company—'

'No, come on, Kimmy, I want you to come.'

Kimmy shook her head.' You guys go. I'll be right.'

Molly thought for a moment then nodded. 'All right we won't be too long.'

Kimmy didn't wave as we climbed into a midsize Toyota.

'So, where are we going?' I asked as we pulled away from the sidewalk.

'You'll see.'

We headed towards the Yacht Club but veered off at the doctor's surgery and took the road that led to the lighthouse.

Molly drove in silence, focusing on the narrow track.

I was taking in the view of the ocean on my left. The road inclined then curved to the right until the lighthouse came into view. It stood on what looked like a fist of rock.

A stone cottage was set back from the tower, whitewashed in the same manner as the lighthouse. The rest of the headland was grass and rock with the odd picnic table here and there. The road ended at a gravel carpark.

We parked and sat for a moment looking through the windscreen.

'So, this is the Candle Stick Bay lighthouse.' I stated the obvious not knowing what else to say.

'Yep.'

We climbed from the car. Molly opened the trunk and lifted out a picnic basket.

'A picnic?'

She smiled.

We strolled across the grass until we reached a wooden picnic table in the shade of the lighthouse.

Molly placed the basket on the table.

'Wow!' I thought I'd already witnessed the beauty of the bay from all angles—from the top of the hill, the balcony of my room, from around the bay at the creek—but this was something else.

'Come on,' Molly said, leading me to the edge of the cliff.

Unlike the calm of the bay, here the surf pounded the rocks below then hissed and fizzed into swirling foam on each retreat. Behind the infantry of waves, the water was calmer, the colour changing with the varying depths from clear blue to deep aqua.

We returned to the picnic table and sat facing each other. Molly opened the basket, tugged out a folded cloth and spread it over the slats. 'When Kimmy and I heard about the break in, we thought it would be a good idea if we treated you to something different.' She lifted a homemade quiche Lorraine from the basket.

'Perfect!' I meant it.

'And this is Kimmy's contribution.' She produced a see-through container of salad.

I was impressed.

'I don't know what you said to that girl, but crikey you got through to her. More than I've been able to anyway.'

'I didn't really say anything. Just bribed her.'

Molly laughed and there it was again—that tingling sensation that swelled in the back of my neck and shot down to my toes.

'Thank you anyway. She's actually started talking to me.'

We ate our cold food as the sun beat down and I was grateful for the protective shade the old lighthouse gave us.

Molly produced a bottle of Ariel Chardonnay non-alcoholic wine and poured two glasses. 'So, what are your roots, Joe?'

'Both my parents were Irish—'

'Mine too!'

'My dad's family were sheep farmers—'

Molly nearly choked on a mouthful of wine. 'Mine too!'

'Really?'

'Yep, we've still got a station south-west of here on the Queensland border.'

'A station?'

'A ranch. A sheep farm. My brother runs it.'

I was curious as to Molly's past and after a sip of sweet non-alcoholic wine, I plunged in. 'You've never been married?'

'Unfortunately, yes … briefly.' She looked away and it was clear this was all the information she was willing to divulge for now.

A shipping container edging its way across the horizon attracted our attention for a few moments until Molly broke the silence. 'Are you any closer to finding him?'

'No. I'm beginning to realise how foolish it was to come here on a whim.'

'Impulsive maybe, but not foolish,' Molly said.

'So, you don't think The Moon is here, Molly?'

'No, of course not. This is Candle Stick Bay. Everyone knows everyone's business here and, believe me, there isn't much to know!'

'Yeah, I'm beginning to see that now.' It was a lie but not the kind I would regret. Maud's version of why I was there had spread through the town like vodka injected into a melon. Beneath the friendly, happy exterior of the townsfolk, I sensed suspicion. I needed to reverse my steps. 'My old friend in LA, Burt, was right. He said I'd be wasting my time.'

'Joe, are you enjoying being here?'

'Absolutely.'

'Then you're not wasting your time.'

'I guess not.'

Molly's eyes searched mine. 'But there's more … isn't there, Joe?'

I shuffled uncomfortably and took another large sip of Ariel Chardonnay.

Molly starred at me in silence, and I felt my defences beginning to crumble.

'Yes, there's more.' Unbelievably, the steel-lined wall that had been erected on that night twenty-five years earlier, then reinforced with alcohol and shame and rendered with fear and ignorance, collapsed slowly to the ground. I hadn't seen the other side in a long time. I'd known it was there but had stayed well clear of it like a kid avoiding the witch's house at the end of the street. As I began to speak, the scene of the terrible New Year's Eve replayed in my mind like a 35 mm home movie.

25

I don't cry. Never have. Even as a kid. 'My brave little soldier!' my mother used to say whenever I'd hurt myself. This was always a good topic for discussion at the AA meetings. But now, here I was, not only sobbing like a baby in front of someone I hardly knew but opening up like a tortured prisoner of war. I'd never fully spoken to anyone about what had happened to Sanchez on that night, not even at the inquiry. By that time, I'd become the pathetic drunken bum I would be for the following five years.

I'd just relayed the sight of Sanchez's heart resting inside the carton of Mexican rice. Tears were streaming down my cheeks. I was shaking and my sobs were uncontrollable, like hiccups. It had taken all these years to get to this point. This certainly wasn't the Joe Dean everybody knew.

Molly squeezed my hand tightly then handed me a tissue.

I wiped my eyes and blew my nose. Finally, the sobs subsided.

'You okay?' She sounded like a mother, and I wondered why she'd never had children.

I nodded. My head felt light.

'Do you want to continue?'

I wasn't sure if I could.

'You might feel better for it.'

We sat in silence for a moment. Molly was still squeezing my hand as if experiencing the ride with me. The sun was moving overhead—we wouldn't have the shade for much longer.

'What happened then?' Molly finally said.

I took in a deep breath and expelled it slowly. 'Nothing! Apparently, I went to my bank and cleared out all our savings. After that, the next five years were a complete blur.'

'Didn't you say there was an inquiry, though?'

'Yes, there was, and I had to give evidence.'

'So, you went back?'

'No. They found me sleeping under the bleachers at Venice about three weeks later. I was totally oblivious. They threw me in a cell until I sobered up. Then they forced me to give evidence at the inquiry.'

'And did you?'

'Sort of. The problem was I wasn't just a drunken bum. I'd become mentally inoperative.'

'You obviously suffered a breakdown!'

'Yes ... I realise that now, but at the time—'

Molly took a moment before asking gently, 'Did The Moon kill again after that?'

'Nope. Just disappeared.'

'Until now.'

'Until now!'

A thin cover of cloud had snuck in overhead and a cooling bluster brought some welcome relief from the heat.

Molly jumped to her feet. 'Come on. Let's go for a walk.'

We threw the plates and everything else into the picnic basket and I carried it back to the car. Molly placed it in the trunk. Then she took me by the hand.

26

Molly dropped me back at the pub late in the afternoon and had asked if I'd care to join her for an early morning beach walk the next day. Of course, I'd said yes. I couldn't think of anything better. Was I smitten? You betcha! It had been the first time I'd bawled like a baby in front of anyone. I had no idea why, but I wasn't the least embarrassed by it, not with Molly. The sense of relief, of lightness, was almost palpable.

Ignoring the now familiar sound of the patrons in the bar, I wearily climbed the stairs to my room and something occurred to me. Something about Molly Quinn. She knew just about everything about me, yet I knew very little about her or about her ex-husband. Could I expect Molly to open up to me the way I had to her? Did she owe me the return favour? No. But my curiosity was growing.

A soft metallic tapping drifted into my consciousness, waking me. I climbed out of bed and stepped onto the balcony in my boxer shorts. A strip of light was just beginning to break through the clouds and was sitting on the horizon—but it was still dark. A gust of sea breeze hit my face, carrying moisture with it—it was raining. The wind gusted again and the tapping on the tin roof increased and quickened, sounding like a volley of bullets.

For some reason, I thought of Fat Bobby and suddenly remembered that I was supposed to have reported the break in to him. I would have to do it that morning at the first chance I got.

The rain was more of a drizzle than a downpour and though the air was blowy, it wasn't cold. I had my raincoat and decided I'd still go for a walk, hoping Molly would do the same.

We'd arranged to meet outside the bookstore and, as I walked along the shiny, wet sidewalk, I could see a light on in the shop.

'Wasn't sure if you'd come or not,' Molly's voice rang out. She was standing on the doorstep just out of the rain. I wanted to step in and hug her, but I tucked my hands into my raincoat pockets instead.

'Of course, I would. Although I didn't expect this.' I removed one hand and extended it palm up.

'It's very much needed but not enough to declare the rains are finally here,' Molly said. 'Fancy a cuppa instead?'

I was easily swayed.

She led me into the shop. 'We'll have it down here. Kimmy's still asleep upstairs and, believe me, we don't want to wake her.'

'The wrath of the woken teenager.' I took off my jacket, and a fine spattering of drops fell to the floor. I draped it over a freestanding chair close to the doorway.

Molly retreated into the store's backroom.

I sat on one of the sofas.

There was a gush of a tap filling the jug, then Molly returned. 'You coming to our meeting tonight?'

'Yes. I'm looking forward to it.'

'Don't get too excited. Remember, we're a bunch of novices who each think what we're working on is the best thing ever written.' She bit the corner of her mouth then grinned.

I was growing to love that grin. 'Bit harsh?' My frown was exaggerated.

'Maybe. Most of them are okay. We get the usual soapbox speakers, especially when critiquing someone else's work.'

A rumbling and the sound of water boiling, followed by a click, summoned Molly back into the other room. She returned a few moments later with two steaming mugs of tea. 'So how do you feel this morning?' She handed me a mug.

'Amazing actually.'

'Like a great weight's been lifted?'

'Exactly that.'

Molly sat herself down beside me on the sofa. 'That's good. And thank you for sharing it with me. It must've been hard.'

'On the contrary, I was surprised how easy it was.'

For a moment our eyes met. The room was suddenly sparking with tension. We looked away and sipped our drinks in silence. I felt as embarrassed as a schoolboy and I wondered what Molly was thinking.

Before I could say anything, there was a *boom-boom-boom* so loud it reverberated through the shop. Someone was pounding on the shop window.

I jumped up and dashed out the front door. In the darkness, I could just discern a lean figure running in the direction of the pub and heard the receding *slap slap slap* of feet on wet tarmac.

The figure stopped and turned around. 'The Moon'll get ya, mate!'

It was the bum from the beach.

'Careful who you mix with, copper. You're flirting again!'

The words bounced up from the wet pavements and ricocheted off the empty shopfronts. My impulse was to give chase.

As if she knew exactly what I was thinking, Molly grasped my arm. 'Leave it, Joe, it's just Geoff Lambert. He's not worth it.'

'Lambert?'

'Yes.'

'As in William Lambert, the writer?'

'Yes. He's William Lambert's brother. Didn't you know?'

'No.'

The figure had melted into the dark as if he'd never been there.

'Come on, let's go back inside.'

She had no argument from me.

'So, what've you got planned for today?' Molly changed the subject as we returned to the sofas.

I found it odd that what had just happened didn't seem to affect her, almost like she was ignoring it. 'Does that kind of thing happen often?'

'No ... first time.'

'It doesn't bother you?'

'Not really. He's just a loser.'

A tinge of pink appeared in Molly's cheeks. I could tell she was holding something back again. My first port of call later that morning was to see Fat Bobby and to tell him about the break in. I could ask him about Geoff Lambert too, but for now I was more interested in Molly Quinn.

She shuffled uncomfortably in her seat then repeated her question, 'So what are you doing today?'

'Nothing much. Just going to take it easy.'

'That's good.'

'What about you, Molly Quinn?' I purposely left the question open ended to see how she'd respond.

'Normal day in the shop. Quite boring I guess, although I do love it.' She was trying to appear cool, but her chin was too high to be relaxed and her shoulders had tensed.

'I didn't mean your plans for the day.'

The tinge of pink deepened to red. 'Then what *did* you mean, Joe?' There was a huskiness to her voice now.

I decided to pull back. The last thing I wanted was for her to think she was being interrogated. 'Tell me a bit about yourself.' I smiled at her, hoping to put her at ease.

'Well, I've already told you my family history. Queensland sheep shearers—not much more to tell there. I've been in the bay for five years, already told you that. Got a sister in Sydney and a niece sleeping soundly upstairs. There you go. The life of Molly Quinn.'

I needed to play it casual and cool. 'And your husband?'

'Ex-husband!'

'Sorry. *Ex*-husband.' My emphasis on the 'ex' brought a smile to her face.

Molly sipped at her tea then sighed, seeming to relax.

I wondered if she was coming to the okay-I-suppose-you-did-reveal-your-soul-to-me conclusion.

'My marriage ... my marriage was the proverbial cliché—young girl seduced by the charms of her boss, falls in love and ends up marrying way too young.'

'He was your boss?'

'Yes. Jonathon Clark. He was a deputy managing editor at the *LA Times*. I was the new intern. God he was good looking. A young George Clooney, you know?'

'Your husband was American, and you lived in LA?' I pretended I didn't already know this, but I was still curious as to why she hadn't mentioned it before.

'Yes ... it's not a time of my life I like to talk about, or even think about for that matter.' She wrinkled her nose, staring down into her mug.

'I'm sorry, I—'

'It's okay ... the marriage was a mistake. Let's leave it at that, eh?'

'And LA?'

'I enjoyed my job, but after the split I couldn't wait to get out of the place.' She sipped her tea. 'Look ... there are things about my ex that I can't talk about. Not because they're too painful, but because it wouldn't be right to talk about him. Do you know what I mean?'

I admired her principles. 'Of course. Forgive me.'

'There's no need to apologise. I just didn't want you to think there was a suspicious reason I wasn't telling you certain things about my past.'

'I understand.' I tried to mean it, but my curiosity was rumbling and rising like the water in the electric jug. If only there was an Internet connection, I could've checked out Jonathon Clarke, but I decided to respect Molly's wishes. For now, at least.

27

I walked into the bar. Maud was spraying one of the tables with furniture polish in one hand while swiftly polishing with the other. I knew she'd seen me enter but she hadn't looked up.

Pat was washing the back windows. Frank was behind the bar going through the stock list, I guessed.

'Good morning, Joe!' Pat called out.

'Frank looked up. 'G'day, mate.'

I was dreading him asking if I'd reported the break in yesterday, as I'd promised, but to my relief he didn't.

'Good morning,' I said cheerfully.

'Ready for your breaky?' Pat left her post at the windows.

'Yes, but is it okay to have it in my room?'

'Of course. I'll bring it up. What can I get you?'

'Just some fruit and tea please. And no need to bring it up. I'll wait.'

Frank's face suddenly turned scarlet.

Maud flinched and stood upright as if she'd been caught doing something she shouldn't.

Pat's warm smile disappeared, and her brow lowered into a scowl.

I was about to ask what I'd said wrong when I sensed someone behind me. I turned. Geoff Lambert, the bum, was standing just inside the doorway with a cocky grin plastered across his face.

'You know you're not allowed in here, Lambert.' Frank's voice was even and firm.

'Keep your hair on, Frankie,' Lambert taunted. 'Oops, too late. It's already gone.'

'Get the hell out of here. NOW!'

'I want to talk to the Yank.'

'I said OUT!'

'It's okay, Frank, let him talk,' I said.

'Sorry, Joe, but it's not okay. If you want to talk to him, you won't be doing it in here.' Frank barrelled through the opening in the bar, marched up to Lambert and glared down at him.

Lambert wasn't the least bit intimidated. 'The big man, eh?' he said still grinning.

Frank grabbed him by the scruff of the neck and pushed him through the doorway. 'Get the hell out I said.'

I followed them out onto the street.

Frank flung Lambert onto the sidewalk. 'You come anywhere near this place again, mate, and you're gone. Do you hear me? Gone!'

Lambert glared at the publican with his fists clenched tight.

'You might want to reconsider the kind of company you're keeping, Joe. This bloke's nothing but trouble.' Frank returned inside.

It was a side of Frank I'd not witnessed before. What had Lambert done to provoke such a reaction?

'Dis bloke's nuttin' but trouble.' Mimicking seemed to be Lambert's signature comeback.

'What's your problem, pal?' I realised I'd asked him this question each time we'd met.

'This town's my fucking problem and every cunt in it!'

'Plus, the fact that you're William Lambert's brother.'

'What the hell's that got to do with anything?'

'Must make you pretty mad.'

He shrugged dismissively.

'He's up there.' I jerked my chin towards the hill. 'Living a life of luxury in a mansion, rich and famous …' I paused dramatically.

Geoff Lambert's face remained impassive.

Flirting with The Moon

'You on the other hand ... a worthless bum sleeping on the beach.'

Geoff clutched at his stomach and shook, exaggerating a fake laugh. 'Oh, Mr Profiler, that's so good. Especially from an alky who walked out on his wife and kid. What's the kid doing nowadays? Giving blowies in LA?'

Lambert was far superior at this game than me, so I tried a different approach. 'You said you wanted to talk to me?'

'Mr Detective from *Floreeda*, thinks he's found a decent piece of snatch. You gonna fuck the niece too?'

I wanted to punch his head in except I suspected this was leading somewhere. 'What do you want?'

His expression hardened and he stepped in closer. 'You're flirting with The Moon again, aintcha?'

'What's that supposed to mean?'

'You think you're gonna catch The Moon then return to LA the hero.'

'How could you know all this?'

'I know a lot of things Detective Joseph Dean!'

'Yeah? Like what?'

'I know someone left a book in your room.'

I narrowed my eyes. 'Was it you?'

The shrug again. 'Maybe.'

'Look, Geoff, can you stop jerking me around and tell me what you know?'

He straightened, pursed his lips and rubbed together the fingers and thumb of a grubby hand. 'It's gonna cost ya!'

I retrieved my wallet from my back pocket. 'How much?'

'What you got?'

A twenty-dollar bill didn't provoke a reaction. Neither did forty. I peeled off another twenty. 'That's all you're getting, pal.'

He snatched the three notes from my hand and stuffed them in his pocket. 'Tight bastard!'

I scowled at him while he shuffled from foot to foot.

'I put the book there ... got it from my brother's house ... it belongs to him.' The cocky grin had reappeared.

'You broke into your brother's house?'

'Didn't have to break in. The place was wide open. He was in a piss coma as usual.'

'That still doesn't tell me why.'

'Fuck me. Are you *really* this stupid?'

'So, the book belongs to your brother. So what?'

'Jesus Christ ... you really are a dumb cunt. No wonder you fucked up. When I say it's his book, I mean he *wrote the fuckin thing!*'

'You're telling me your brother is Stephen Powell?'

Geoff opened his arms, leaned backwards and threw back his head. 'Halee-fucking-lujah!'

'What else do you know?'

'Tick-tick-tick-tick ... *diiiiiing!* Sorry, sir, your time is up. Please insert another coin.' He held out his hand.

'You won't be getting another dime from me, Geoff. What you will be getting though is a visit from Fat Bobby.'

'And what do you think he's gonna do?'

'Well, you just admitted to breaking into my room, and stealing from your brother's house.'

'Whoopedoo!' He sauntered away. 'Fat boy won't do a thing. Never does!'

'Is your brother The Moon?' I called after him.

'Jeez, how much help do you need? Detective, my arse,' he said over his shoulder.

'I'll be talking to you again, Geoff.'

He stopped and turned back to face me. 'I tell you what, if you don't believe me, talk to the school teacher again.'

'Miss Berry?'

He walked away.

I returned to the bar, deep in thought.

'Everything all right, Joe?' Frank looked up from his paperwork.

'Yes, fine.'

'What did *he* want?' Maud piped up.

'Ah … he was just trying to scrounge money from me.'

'The cheeky bugger!' Pat said.

'You didn't give him anything did you, mate?' Frank said.

'No.' I lied. 'I did tell him I'd be reporting him to Fat Bobby though.'

'Good, it's about time something was done about that flamin' mongrel,' Frank said.

I took my breakfast out to the balcony. The rain had cleared but the air was damp and steamy.

If William Lambert had written the book, it had to mean he was The Moon, I mused chewing on an enormous crunchy grape. But how did Geoff know so much about the case? His motivation was obvious—hitting back at his brother for being everything *he* wasn't. But was there more to it? Was there more to Geoff Lambert? I suspected there was.

I hadn't been in Candle Stick Bay a week yet, but it seemed longer. I'd found the people friendly and genuine. Certainly not a flock of galahs or whatever the term Ruby P had used to describe the people of the north. A galah, I'd discovered from my research of the local fauna, was a pink and grey parrot and considered jokingly as a bit dense. I needed to sit down with Fat Bobby and discuss my findings. I also wanted to meet William Lambert and, if it were possible, get past Willy Nelson's defences and talk to Barbara Bingle.

The first thing I noticed as I stepped onto the street was Maud Baker cleaning the inside of the windows of the General Store. The woman must have had the monopoly on cleaning. Good for her. Of course, she'd spotted me before I'd seen her. Maud Baker missed nothing. She waved when she saw I was looking across.

First stop, the police station to report the break in and Geoff Lambert's confession. I also wanted to discuss with Fat Bobby Geoff's accusations against his brother.

I could tell right away that Police Constable Scott Williams lived for the water—his mop of blond hair and his tanned skin gave him a natural, unkempt, handsome look.

'G'day,' he said. His voice was deep and slow with an almost Californian twang.

'Hi. Would Sergeant Radford be in?'

'No, sorry. Fat Bobby's out for most of the day. Is there something I can help you with?'

Damn. 'No ... that's okay, thanks. I just needed to talk with Bobby. Do you know when he'll be back?'

'Later this afternoon. He's had to go to Cooktown.'

'Okay, I'll come back then.' I turned to leave.

I wasn't sure what to do next. I found myself walking back up the high street.

The bookstore was quiet; Molly was sitting with her back to the window, typing away on her laptop again. I felt the urge to go in but decided against it.

At the top of the street, I turned left at the General Store and, without consciously deciding to, started to climb the hill. This side was steeper than the other and it wasn't until I was halfway up, with my calf muscles screaming, that I mentally kicked myself for what I was doing.

Bayview Terrace was to my left. I glanced down the street and, as if he'd been expecting me, Willy Nelson stood primed for action at the entrance to his cul-de-sac like a sentry on duty.

Although it was hard going, I increased my speed up the hill without looking back. Thank heavens he didn't follow me.

The last section of hill was steeper again. My breathing was heavy, and I was sweating so much the back of my shirt was drenched. I was grateful when the road finally curved to the right and levelled out.

The outlook from here was spectacular—the kind of premium view that a real estate agent would make a year's commission on.

A little farther on, the street ended at a large, wrought iron gate—the entrance to William Lambert's property.

The heavy gate was chained and there was no other way in that I could see. I leaned against the bars, catching my breath, seeing what I could on the other side. The driveway was a little overgrown as if it hadn't been used for some time. I guessed there was another entrance on the opposite side of the building—a way in that would allow Lambert to enter without going through the town. The front of the block ended at a cliff overlooking the bay. The hill continued upwards at the back of the property for about another two hundred yards and was covered in trees. The parcel of land was a large flat terrace and had the appearance of a botanical garden. From my position, I couldn't see the house.

Stepping back from the gate, I considered the six-foot-high walls on either side. They were rendered smooth and would be hard to climb. I needed to turn back right away and not do anything until Fat Bobby returned. And that's exactly what I was thinking as I climbed over the gate.

28

Stealing through the grounds, I made my way along the edge of the trees, remaining out of view. I reached the tennis courts and got my first glimpse of the house close up. With its whitewashed walls, flat roof and curved turret on the seaward side, it wouldn't have been out of place in Miami. Swaying palm trees added to the effect. Between the tennis court and the house there was a modest sized pool. Along the side of the building was a row of glass doors. These were open and through them I could hear heavy metal music.

Checking my surroundings, I sneaked around the tennis court, past the pool and dashed to the edge of the doors. From here I could peek inside the house.

Music from a Wurlitzer jukebox throbbed through the room and the unmistakable aroma of marijuana wafted through the air.

It took a long moment for my eyes to adjust to the dull interior. The white walls were bare except for random pieces of pop art, possibly original Andy Warhols. On the outer wall was an enormous window framing a view of the bay. Beneath this, William Lambert reclined in a leather office chair. He wore a T-shirt and jeans, and his bare feet were propped up on his desk. With his eyes closed, he jabbed his head in time with the music. His not quite shoulder length hair was blond and greasy. It looked like he had two days' worth of stubble. In his right hand he held a glass of Scotch. The computer screen before him was blank.

I knocked on the glass door.

He bolted upright and swung around in his chair. 'How the hell did you get in here?'

'Sorry to startle you, Mr Lambert. My name's John Taylor. I'm here about the security for the wedding.'

He picked up a remote control from the desk, pressed a button and the music died. The sudden silence was a relief. 'You need to leave immediately before I call the police!'

'Forgive the intrusion. Your manager asked me to come and look around the grounds so we can—'

'Save your breath, Mr Dean. I know who you are.' He rose from his desk and knocked back his drink.

'You do?' I was shocked and wondered if Maud cleaned here too.

Lambert poured another drink from a decanter at the side of his desk. 'Of course I do, Joe. I know everything. You're the private dick from Florida. And you're over here looking for … someone.' He began to chuckle.

'Maudie?'

He shook his head and scowled. 'That woman will never step foot in this house.'

'Then how do you know me?'

He ignored my question, swigged a mouthful of Scotch then stepped towards me. 'Why have you trespassed on my property?'

'I wanted to meet you—'

'Don't insult my intelligence, man. Have the decency to tell the truth at least.'

'Okay, I'm sorry … I wondered if you could help me.'

A butler suddenly appeared at the side door. 'Can I help you?' His voice was effeminate but with an air of authority. His expression was an angry glare.

'It's all right, Andrew. Mr Dean is about to leave.'

I stood my ground. 'Have you ever used the pen name Stephen Powell?'

Lambert flinched but quickly regained his composure. 'Andrew, show him out. NOW!'

I withdrew the book from my shoulder bag and waved it in front of his face. 'Is this yours?'

The colour drained from Lambert's face—he turned away.

Andrew grabbed my arm. His grip was surprisingly strong.

I could've pushed him aside like a lace curtain, but I was on private property. If Lambert wanted to press charges, the law would be on his side.

The butler marched me out the way I'd entered and led me around the other side of the house. I didn't struggle. Instead, I tried the friendly approach. 'So, how long have you worked for Lambert?'

Silence.

'Bet you've seen a few comings and goings?'

Still no reaction. We trudged along a pebbled driveway.

'You'd know an awful lot about your boss. Probably travelled with him? Done a few things now and again beyond the job description?'

We reached an ornate gateway.

'What do you know about the book?"

His face only registered distaste—directed at me. He inserted a key at the side of the gates, and they slowly opened. 'There's a track a little farther on that will lead you back to the town. If you return, Mr Dean, make no mistake, we will have you arrested.'

I had no doubt he was serious. I passed through the gates, and they closed between us without a sound.

'Thank you for your time, Andrew. I'm sure we'll be seeing more of each other.' I watched as he marched back to the house with his chin in the air.

There were no houses on this side of the hill, the road was bordered with scrub as it dipped and curved out of sight. About three hundred yards down, a walking track veered to the right.

On impulse, I set off down it. Soon, I came to a clearing smack bang in the middle of which gaped a perfectly round hole about six foot across. The unassembled communications mast lay in pieces close by. I knew where I was. Minutes later I was approaching two men sitting on crates in the shade of a truck.

I recognised them immediately. 'G'day!'

'Struth!' Kenny almost dropped his newspaper. 'Where'd you come from?'

'Sorry, didn't mean to startle you. Just out for a walk.'

'Hey, I remember you,' Tana said. 'The American guy.' He jumped up as if glad of the distraction and I noticed how huge he was.

'That's right.'

'Bloody hell. You still here? Thought you'd be sick of the place by now,' Kenny said.

'Nope. Still here.' I grinned. 'And so are you guys, I see.'

'For all the good it's doing. It's not like it's a national strike or anything. I mean who gives a shit about what's happening all the way up here?'

Tana shook his head. 'It's wrong, eh!'

'I'm not complaining but!' Kenny added with a smirk.

Both men laughed and high-fived.

'Well, better keep moving. Don't you guys work too hard now.'

The comment was met with chortles and, 'No chance of that, mate.'

I headed down the hill towards the town. It didn't seem to take as long as the first day. At the bottom a feeling of homecoming washed over me. Strange, I'd only been here a few days.

It was late morning. Fat Bobby wouldn't be back until the afternoon. But there was someone else I needed to talk to, and to do this I would need to confront my fear. It was time to do battle with my nemesis.

I entered the General Store where Silvia Stanton was as friendly as ever. 'Hello, Joe. How are you today?'

'I'm really well, thanks.' I made a small purchase and was surprised Silvia didn't ask what it was for.

'Anything else?' she asked as she wrapped it in white paper.

'Just a bottle of water, please. I saw Maud cleaning the windows this morning.'

Sylvia opened the glass fridge behind the counter and pulled out a small bottle of water. 'Yeah, she's a busy girl. As well as the pub, she works here two days a week, and cleans the doctor's surgery, the Yacht Club and helps the caretaker up at the school.'

I gave a low whistle. 'Wow, she *is* busy.'

A slow smile crept across Silvia's face. 'That's how she keeps up with everyone's business.'

The prospect of climbing the hill again was a daunting one. A sucker for punishment perhaps but at least I was building some fitness—at least I hoped I was. Trudging towards Bayview Terrace, I was beginning to regret my decision. Only a tourist would attempt this in the overwhelming heat. A little rest would be good. At the verge of the road, under the shade of a small tree, squatted a rock with a flat top. Just the right size. I eased myself down, retrieved the water bottle from my bag, twisted off the cap and slugged the liquid down. I was still gulping when something suddenly stabbed me in the butt. 'Ouch!' I leapt off the rock, spilling water everywhere. A sharp pain, not unlike the tetanus shot I'd had a couple of days earlier, was spreading like fire across my ass. Remembering the book I'd read about Australia's dangerous fauna, I began to panic. Had a deadly snake bitten me? With the pain increasing, I imagined the toxins spreading through my bloodstream. I tried to recall what the book had said. Keep still? Apply a tourniquet? How the hell could I tourniquet my ass? First I'd better identify the snake. I swivelled around gingerly, peered at the rock and spotted the culprit right away. Thankfully, it wasn't a snake. But the biggest black ant I'd ever seen was zig-zagging on patrol as if searching for me. I considered squashing it there and then, but he was only protecting his territory and I had other things on my mind, namely the pain.

'Jeeez-us!' I hissed between clenched teeth as the throbbing spread.

'Keep calm, Joe, keep calm,' I muttered, rubbing my butt in an attempt to alleviate the pain. I considered aborting the mission but, after some deep breathing and stretching, I began to feel a little better, so I limped on.

Around the corner in Bayview Terrace, all was quiet. The only sound was the slow *whoosh* of the sea breeze.

As if expecting me, my adversary was waiting at the end of his street, his eyes locked on mine. The opening bars of *The Good, The Bad and The Ugly* theme whistled through my inner sound system.

Like Clint Eastwood, I coolly strolled forward while trying to quell the fear that was bubbling inside.

I still had some distance to go.

My nemesis stared me down—this was *his* territory.

When I reached the other side of the street, I felt for my weapon.

My opponent flinched, his lips curled and quivered, his eyes narrowed until they were barely slits. A low growl made the hairs on the back of my neck stand up.

The next moment he was charging towards me. I grabbed for the weapon that I'd placed in the waistband of my shorts. 'Shit!' It was still wrapped in paper. Fumbling, I desperately tore away the wrapping and, just as Willy Nelson was about to pounce, I thrust a piece of sirloin steak in the air.

He snatched the meat in his jaws and shook it violently, growling and snarling.

'Willy Nelson, where are you?' A woman's voice called from somewhere close by.

I couldn't see the speaker.

The dog didn't react other than to tear off a piece of steak and gulp it down.

'Willy, boy, come!'

Even his mistress's voice couldn't break the frenzy.

I wasn't sure what to do next. Could I pass without him noticing? I took one step forwards.

He dropped the steak and growled, his black eyes regarding me balefully.

I raised my hands in surrender. It seemed my plan may have merely given me a brief stay of execution. When he finished his meal, I'd be dessert.

'Willy Nelson, get the hell back here.'

He ignored the command.

I'd deliberately purchased the largest, thickest piece of steak Silvia had, knowing the little dog would have trouble ripping it apart.

A tall, dark-haired woman wearing a sarong, large earrings and golden bangles on each arm, came storming out of the cul-de-sac. 'Where are you, dog?' When she saw her pooch chewing on the steak, she stopped in her tracks. 'What is he eating?' Without looking at me, she ran towards the dog.

Willy Nelson took off with the steak in his mouth.

'Come here, ya little bugger!' Her voice was deep and smoky with the hint of an American accent.

The dog scooted behind me.

She turned her anger and her attention to me. 'Did you give him that?'

'Yes ... I ... um ...'

'You gave my dog a piece of a dead animal?'

'Yes.'

Her face scrunched up like a scarlet raisin. 'He's a fucking vegetarian!' she yelled.

From experience, I knew otherwise. Willy Nelson liked to sink his teeth into prime cut American beef, but it wouldn't do to further antagonise her. 'Oh ... I'm sorry, I didn't realise.'

'You're sorry?' Her fists were clenched, and her eyes burned into mine. 'So, you just walk around with pieces of meat in your pocket?' She threw herself towards the dog in an attempt to grab him, but he was way too quick.

'No, look ... your dog actually attacked me the other day.'

She straightened up. Her eyes narrowed. 'Willy Nelson bit you?' Like it was the hardest thing to believe.

'Yes, and I was hoping I could talk to you.' My butt was beginning to ache from the ant bite again, and I realised I'd been inadvertently rubbing it.

Her eyes followed my hand. An eyebrow shot up and there was a hint of a smile. 'He bit you on the arse?'

'No, I just got bitten by an ant.'

'Jeez, you get bitten a lot.' Her face softened. 'Dogs, ants—don't go out in the ocean, eh? What kind of ant was it?'

'A big one.'

'Come on, I'll have a look at it for you.' She turned and headed back towards the cul-de-sac, leaving the dog to enjoy a rare feast.

My leg was beginning to feel a little stiff as I hurried to catch up with her. 'My name's Joe, Joe Dean.'

'Yeah, I know. Reckon the whole town knows who you are.'

'Maudie!'

'No, I don't need the town gossip to tell me what's going on.'

We entered the front yard of a small pink Queenslander. There was no verandah, just a half dozen steps leading to the front door. As she climbed onto the first step, she stopped, turned and held out her hand. 'I'm Barbara Bingle by the way. You can call me Babs.'

We shook hands. I followed her up the steps and through a screen made of hanging seashells that *click clacked* as we passed through. The twin aromas of sandalwood and incense reminded me of the hippy shops in South Florida. The room was dark and cool, the furniture Indonesian teak. A small Buddhist altar had pride of place in the farthest corner of the room. There was a framed hand drawing of John Lennon and Yoko Ono on one wall, and a photograph of Gandhi on another. In another corner stood a massage table. In the middle of the room was a small, square dining table with a floral cloth. Perched in the middle of the cloth was a crystal ball. My inner fruit loop meter began to click like a Geiger counter.

Babs brushed through an open doorway.

Unsure of whether she wanted me to follow her or not, I stood awkwardly in the living room.

'How big was the ant?' She poked her head back into the room.

I gauged the length of the ant between my finger and thumb and held up my hand to show her. 'About half an inch.'

'Ah, just a little bully then.' Babs disappeared again, only to return an instant later bearing a fruit jar containing a yellow liquid.

'A bully?'

'A bull ant. Painful but not lethal.' She pulled out the massage table and gestured for me to climb onto it.

I hesitated.

She chuckled deeply. 'Come on, don't be shy. I won't hurt you.'

I did as I was told and lay with my face through the hole at the top.

'Whereabouts does it hurt?'

Stretching my right hand behind me, I carefully touched the sensitive area.

'Right, I'm gonna have to see your bum, I'm afraid.' She didn't wait for permission; she yanked down my shorts and my underpants.

I was glad she couldn't see my face. From the heat of it, I knew I was blushing.

'Oh yeah, a little bit red.'

With a view only of the polished wooden floorboards beneath me, I heard the top of the jar being unscrewed. When the cold, sticky liquid made contact with my butt, I flinched.

Babs gently massaged the vinegary smelling liquid into my skin.

Being bare assed and vulnerable, I guessed this was as good a time as any to ask a few questions. 'You said you already knew who I was?'

Flirting with The Moon

'You were on the news all the time when I was in LA.'

'You lived in LA?'

'It was going to be the last stop off before coming home. I'd been travelling for three years: Europe, Africa, India, and the States, but I ended up staying in LA for eighteen months. Then, when I came back to Aus, I met a bloke in Brisbane and we shacked up for a while.'

'Pete?'

She let out a long sigh. I didn't know whether it was one of despair, regret or nostalgia. 'You've met my ex then?'

'Yes.' I wanted to say how he seemed like a great guy but instead bit my tongue.

'We came back to Candle Stick Bay. It was his hometown. Eventually we got married.'

'Right, so you're not from around here?' My questioning was the gentle type you'd associate with a barbershop conversation.

'No. But after the split, I stayed. I'd fallen *in* love with the place and *out* of love with Pete.' She dried me off with a towel then pulled up my shorts. 'There ya go, fella.'

I climbed down from the massage table. My butt didn't feel that different.

'That'll be ninety dollars, thanks.' Babs held out her hand, palm upwards.

At first, I thought she was kidding but her fixed stare and steady hand told me she wasn't. I was pissed but I didn't argue. I rolled out a green hundred dollar bill and assured her that it was quite all right when she told me she didn't have any change.

'I'll fix you up next time I see you. Tea? Got no coffee, I'm afraid. There's no drugs of any kind here.'

I decided to stay and get my money's worth. 'Tea will be fine, thanks.'

She disappeared into the back room again and I could hear the clink of her preparations.

'Are you a fortune teller?' I called out and took a seat at the table.

'I'm a *psychic!*' came her reply, like I'd just insulted her.

'Right. Is that how you knew I was here?'

Babs swept through the banners carrying two full cups. 'Are you taking the piss?' She handed me one of the cups.

'No. Not at all. I'm interested, that's all.' I frowned—the liquid in my cup was dark, crimson.

'Just heard you were here from …' She quickly shook her head then changed the subject. 'So, you reckon Willy Nelson attacked you?'

'Yes, he did. He seems to be very territorial.'

'Just protecting me, that's all.'

'Do you need protection?' I was half joking.

She ignored this and joined me at the table where the crystal ball suddenly caught her attention. 'Looks like you're the one that's going to need protection!'

I remained silent.

She placed her hands around the ball, focusing her gaze at its core. 'It's all coming through.' Her voice was low and mysterious.

I was having none of the carnival act. 'Babs, is this going to cost me?'

She threw her head back and laughed. 'You've been fleeced by a gypsy before I see.'

'Uh, yeah. About two minutes ago.'

She slapped the table and sat upright with a cheeky grin. It was good to see she had a sense of humour.

The herbal tea didn't taste too bad—fruity with a bit of spice.

There was a moment's silence as Babs regarded me with dark, toffee-brown eyes, the kind that didn't allow you to see inside. 'It's of no importance to me whether you believe in any of this or not, but I'm sensing an awful lot of pain, Joe.' She was serious again.

Needing to steer the conversation back to planet Earth, I reached down and rubbed my butt. 'Your vinegar potion seems to be working a treat.'

But she wasn't to be distracted. 'You've come here looking for closure.'

'No, I just came to make amends with the dog. If I'd known he was a vegetarian, I'd have brought a lettuce instead.'

'You've already lost everything, so you've everything to gain.'

My jokes were falling on deaf ears. Time to try another tack. Nothing ventured, nothing gained. 'Is The Moon here?'

There was no reaction from Babs—no facial twitch, no change in expression. It was almost as if she really were in a trance. 'Yessss!' A whisper.

She suddenly had my attention. 'Do you know who The Moon is?'

'Yes!'

The *click clack* of seashells startled me.

Willy Nelson padded into the room with his head hung low.

Babs's concentration broke. 'Willy!' she said in a stern voice.

The dog ignored her, climbed into a basket that I hadn't noticed before, lay on his stomach, and whined.

'Of course you've got stomach ache, Mr Nelson. What do you expect eating one of God's creatures?' She spoke to the dog like he was human.

The basket creaked as the dog turned to face the other way.

She returned her attention back to me. 'Well, I hope your little ant bite feels better, Joe. It's been nice to meet you.' She pushed herself out of the chair to a standing position.

'You were telling me about The Moon.' I also rose.

She looked confused. 'Was I?'

'Yes, you said you knew who The Moon was.'

Her brow knotted. 'I did?'

I wasn't quite sure if she was putting on an act, or if she was just plain old batty. All part of the entertainment, I suspected. 'It was great to meet you too, Babs.' I held out my hand. 'And thank you for fixing my … you know what.'

The knot in her brow eased and she smiled. 'You're very welcome.'

Up close I could see how clear her skin was—she wore not a scrap of makeup but there was a soft glow to her face. 'Perhaps we could talk again sometime.'

'Absolutely. Would you like to schedule a reading?'

I said I'd think about it. 'See you, Willy,' I said as I padded towards the front door.

Willy Nelson jumped up in his basket and growled.

'He likes you,' Babs said.

29

It was late afternoon by the time I reached the police station.

Fat Bobby was pulling into the driveway in the town's only cruiser.

He swung open the door and grinned up at me. 'G'day, Joe. How's it going?'

He climbed from the car.

'Very good, thanks. Any chance I could have a word?'

'Sure. Come on in.'

I trailed him towards the station building.

'Where do *you* live, Bobby?' I said as we approached the door.

Fat Bobby leaned back and pointed to an old Queenslander in the back corner of the lot behind the police station. 'Used to be the old station. When they built the new place, they lifted the old girl and restumped her back there.

'That's handy.'

'Yeah. Too bloody handy sometimes.'

He pushed open the door and I followed him in.

The young constable was still on duty behind the reception desk. He looked up.

'Scotty, be a sport and get two coffees, eh?' Fat Bobby said, hanging up his hat.

As if grateful for something to do, Scotty nodded and darted out of the front door like a kid being let out of school.

Fat Bobby seated himself at his desk.

I took the seat opposite.

'So, what's up?' he said.

I withdrew the book from my bag and placed it on his desk.

'Ah … this is the book, eh?' He picked it up and flicked through the pages.

'That's it, yes. But it isn't mine. Someone broke into my room and left it on my bed.'

Fat Bobby looked horrified. 'Someone broke into your room?'

I told him how I'd come back from my walk and found the book.

'But we're heading into the off season. Not that many tourists in town now, mostly only locals.'

'I know who put it there.' It was impossible to play down the drama.

Fat Bobby's eyes widened with anticipation. 'Who?'

'Geoff Lambert.'

'Geoff Lambert? Of course, that makes sense. But how do you know it was him?'

'He told me. He came to the pub this morning.'

'Jeez, that wouldn't have gone down well with Frank.' He rummaged through his desk drawer and retrieved a notepad. 'What exactly did he say?'

'That the book belonged to his brother and that he'd stolen it from his house.'

'Bloody hell.' Fat Bobby grinned. 'Two counts of breaking and entering, and one of theft. I've got you, ya little bastard.'

'What's the story with those two?'

'The Lambert boys grew up in town. Shirley was a single mum. The old man, Des, was a dero—'

'Huh?'

'A dero—derelict … loser … a pisshead.'

'Got it.'

'Anyway, they lived just behind the General Store. Old Dessie was always in trouble with the law. Never worked, just bummed around like Geoff does now. Shirley finally kicked him out.

Apparently, she gave the old bastard some money, enough for him to get out of town. Last I heard he went to Townsville. Don't know what happened to him after that.

'The boys were right little tearaways. This is all before my time of course, but I've heard how they, especially Geoff, near enough terrorised the town. William was the clever one. He was tall, good looking, whereas Geoff was the runt. One night, when they were in their early twenties, they had an almighty blue.'

'A blue?'

'A fight. Geoff put William in hospital. Nearly killed him. He's a wild little bugger that one.'

'What was the fight about?'

'Wouldn't have a clue. As I said, well before my time but everybody knows about it. William Lambert was back from uni. The hero, you might say. Geoff was turning bad even then and was obviously jealous of his brother. Apparently, the fight happened in the beer garden behind the pub. William had brought his mother down for a celebratory drink without inviting Geoff. William was always a cocky sod. Talked down to people like he was better than them. The kind of attitude that'll piss anyone off, ya know? Anyways, Geoff was already in the pub, started to hurl a bit of verbal abuse and the two of them got into a bit of a slanging match.

'Old Bazza, the previous landlord, told them to take it outside, which they did, out in the beer garden. Thankfully Bazza rang Mac, the then police sergeant but, by the time he got there, William was out cold on the ground and Geoff was kicking him in the head. Vicious as. Continually kicking him. Mac dragged him away, but he went wild. "I'll kill the fucking faggot!" he screamed.'

'So, he was arrested?'

'Yeah, thrown in the cell for the night to calm down. But he didn't. Never did in fact. William spent a week in Cairns Hospital. *And* he pressed charges.'

'So, Geoff went to jail?'

'Yep. The first of his many little stays in Boggo Road.'

'Is the mother still alive?'

'No. She died in a bus crash. Ironically, she was on her way to visit Geoff in jail. She travelled down to Brisbane once a month. Too expensive to fly in them days so the twenty-plus-hour bus trip was the only option. Poor woman.

'I think that *her* death was what finally pushed Geoff over the edge.'

Scotty returned carrying two takeaway cups of coffee.

I insisted on paying for the drinks despite Fat Bobby's protest.

'Keep the change,' I handed Scotty a ten dollar bill. The young constable insisted on giving me back a two dollar coin before disappearing into the back room.

'So, Geoff reckons the book belongs to William Lambert?' Fat Bobby tapped his fingers on the cover. 'Is that relevant?'

'It is if it means he wrote the book. What do you know about the William Lambert of today?'

'Bugger all really, apart from what you read in the news. He left the bay right after the attack, went to Sydney. Didn't even come back for his mum's funeral. He had a book published, which was made into a movie. He moved to the States and made a fortune. I went up to the house a couple of weeks ago to see if he needed anything. Shit faced by mid-morning, can you believe?'

We sipped our coffees. I wasn't going to divulge that I'd actually broken into Lambert's place that morning.

'So, we can nick Geoff for burglary and break and enter.' Fat Bobby glanced down at his notebook. 'He's just about due for another stretch in the big house. Be bloody good to get him out of town again, that's for sure.' He looked up at me. 'Is there any way you can prove William Lambert wrote the book?'

'No, but Geoff did say something else.' I didn't purposely pause for effect but I'm sure that's how it must have seemed. 'He told me to ask Miss Berry.'

'Ask Miss Berry what?' Fat Bobby leaned in closer.

'I don't know but it wasn't an off-the-cuff remark. He said it for a reason.'

Fat Bobby sat back in his chair, took a deep breath through his nose, then sipped his coffee some more.

I wondered if the constable had gone to the house out the back of the station. 'Does Scotty live in the house too?'

'Nah, lives with his olds up on Bayview.' Fat Bobby looked over his shoulder to make sure Scotty wasn't there. 'Listen, while he's gone, do you really think this killer could be here in Candle Stick Bay?'

'I do. And I think someone knows his identity.'

Fat Bobby raised the book. 'Stephen Powell. And you think this bloke's the killer?'

'I do, but that's obviously a pseudonym.'

'Right.' Another pause. 'This is bloody serious shit.'

'Absolutely.'

'If someone does know and the killer gets wind of it …' Fat Bobby's voice trailed off into the air.

It was something I'd already considered. Although retired, The Moon was a psychopathic killer. If he felt the need to protect himself—his identity—killing to do so wouldn't be a problem. I doubted The Moon would start killing randomly. Judging by the theatrical nature of the past killings, which I only learned about after reading the book, I suspected that if The Moon were to come out of retirement, it would need to be, in his, or *her*, eyes, a spectacular performance.

'You know what?' Fat Bobby said standing from his desk. 'I think it's time we had a little chat with bloody Geoff. What do you reckon?'

When we reached Geoff Lambert's beach camp, Fat Bobby called out, 'You there, Geoff?'

No reply.

We walked into the shade of the trees bordering the beach and peered beneath the tarpaulin. The area stank of marijuana and urine.

I bent down and picked up one of many empty bottles of Jack Daniels. 'How can he afford expensive liquor like this?' I shook the bottle in the air. The money I'd given him the night before wouldn't have accounted for the man's seemingly endless supply of alcohol.

'Beats me. I don't reckon he'd be on the dole. Nearest Centrelink's in Cooktown.'

'So, where's he getting his money from?'

'Where indeed.'

After a fruitless search, we headed back to town.

'Now might be a good a time as any to talk with Miss Berry,' Fat Bobby said as we stepped onto the high street.

30

All was quiet when we walked through the shaded schoolyard until, somewhere in the distant trees, a family of kookaburras exploded into laughter. The echoing sound followed us into the building.

We stood in a small hallway with fans revolving slowly above us. Over a line of coat pegs, children's colourful paintings adorned the walls. Below these were large pigeonhole shelves for their school bags. At one end of the hall were the boys' and girls' toilets. On the left-hand side was a closed door with a glass panel at the top.

Fat Bobby knocked on the door then entered without waiting for a reply.

I stayed close on his heels.

Miss Berry was seated at her desk at the head of the room. She looked up, pen poised in mid-air.

'Good afternoon, Miss Berry. Do you mind if we have a quick word?' Fat Bobby said politely.

'Why, Sergeant Radford, Mr Dean, please come in.' The imperturbable smile matched the tone of her voice.

With caps in hands, we trudged to the front of the class like schoolboys.

'I'd ask you to take a seat, but I don't think you'll fit on any of our chairs.' Miss Berry indicated with her eyes towards the rows of small desks.

Fat Bobby shifted from foot to foot. 'Miss Berry, sorry for taking up your time … I um … I wondered if we could ask you a few questions.' His voice trailed away as if he was expecting to be chastised.

I reached into my little shoulder bag, withdrew the book and placed it on her desk.

'Ahh … I wondered when you'd be back with that.'

'Miss Berry, is there anything you can tell us about the author?'

She didn't look at me. Instead, she swivelled her head around, birdlike, and regarded Fat Bobby for a moment. 'Is this an official visit, Sergeant?'

'Crikey, no.' Fat Bobby sounded horrified. 'Nothing like that.'

'When I showed you the book last time, you seemed upset when you saw the author's name,' I said.

Miss Berry picked up the book and examined the cover. I wasn't sure if she was trying to remember something or whether she was carefully choosing her next words.

'Do you know who the author is?'

She rose from her desk, looked at Fat Bobby then back to me. 'I won't be a moment.'

There was a door at the side of the blackboard; Miss Berry entered it and turned on a light to reveal a small stockroom.

Fat Bobby and I waited, hearing the rattle of filing cabinet drawers being slid in and out.

After a couple of minutes, she returned carrying a Manila folder. 'I take notes, always have done, if any of my students show any talent in writing. Back there,' she nodded over her shoulder, 'I've a cabinet full of poems and stories. Some of them date back to when I first came here forty years ago. Silly really.' She opened the folder and thumbed through some papers. When she found what she was looking for, she pulled out a sheet and handed it to me.

The title at the top of the page read: "How To Kill Your Brother, by Stephen Powell".

Like the time I first set eyes on the book, I wanted to run my fingers over every word of the page as if there were clues there that only my touch could find. 'Who wrote this?'

'I've got quite a few in here from this student.' She flicked through the wad of papers inside the folder like a deck of cards. 'Showed great promise, even at an early age.' She held up the folder allowing us to see the name on the front.

William Lambert.

Although obviously written by a child, I could understand what Miss Berry had meant after reading only a few lines of the sheet in my hand. The words the young William Lambert had chosen were pretty mature for a ten year old. The work was a lengthy essay, but in one section he'd listed dot points regarding various methods of killing.

Under the subtitle "Asphyxiation", I read:

If asphyxiation is your choice of revenge, you need to take into consideration the following points:

- *Decide on your method of asphyxiation*
    1. *Strangulation*
    2. *Suffocation*

Choose the instrument of application carefully
- *Strangulation*
    1. *Rope*
    2. *A belt*
    3. *Mother's tights*
    4. *15 lb fishing line*
- *Suffocation*
    1. *Pillow*
    2. *Plastic bag*

Important: Make sure you strike at a time when your brother is unaware. If suffocation is your choice, wait until he is asleep. When choosing strangulation, the best method is to approach him from behind.

'This is pretty gruesome stuff.' I passed the sheet to Fat Bobby.

'Yes, the boy was severely reprimanded,' Miss Berry said defensively.

'But you kept it just the same.'

'I didn't keep that particular piece due to its merit. I kept all of his work once I'd recognised the talent.'

'So, William Lambert *is* Stephen Powell?' Fat Bobby was still staring at the sheet.

'Do you think Lambert wrote this?' I held up the book.

'Oh yes, absolutely. That's his style. Even at ten years old, you can see it.'

I had to agree. The essay, even though written many years ago and a lot less explicate, still bore an uncanny resemblance to the prose in the book.

'May we keep this, Miss Berry?' I took the sheet from Fat Bobby.

'Certainly not!' Her eyes pierced my big boy armour. 'But you may make a copy. Now if you don't mind, I have a lot of marking to do.'

'Yeah right, no worries. Thank you for your time.' Fat Bobby turned and headed to the door before I could ask where the photocopier was.

I bowed my head and followed.

'Bloody Lambert,' Fat Bobby said as we stepped out of the schoolhouse and back into the heat.

'So, what do we do now?'

'We?'

'About Lambert?'

'Oh right. Well, I better take his book back and see if he wants to press charges against Geoff. He probably will.'

'No, I mean this.' I held up the essay.

Fat Bobby sighed. 'I know I might come across as Deputy Dawg, Joe, but I'm actually not that stupid. I know exactly what you're saying. This isn't an investigation. I can't go around accusing William Lambert of being a murderer just because he wrote a book and a story when he was a kid. Do you know how powerful that bloke is?'

I understood, and I'd also worked out when we first met that there was far more to Fat Bobby than the slow, far North Queensland mannerisms he'd chosen to adopt.

We climbed into the cruiser.

'So, you're not going to bring him in?' I said pulling on my seatbelt.

'Bring him in where?'

'To the station for questioning.'

'Don't be daft. Just let it go, eh?'

I decided not to push my luck. I needed Fat Bobby on side. My own investigation would have to suffice for now. I changed the subject. 'Are you going to the writers' meeting tonight?'

'Yeah. You?'

'Yes. Molly invited me.'

'Cool. Listen, let's not say anything about this to anyone, eh?'

'No worries!' I was relieved to see my attempted Aussie response elicit a grin.

31

I'd planned to arrive early at the writers' meeting. An unscheduled nap put paid to that. When I arrived, everyone was present and the meeting was about to start.

I bungled through the door. 'Sorry I'm late.'

A circle of chairs, including the two sofas, had been arranged at the front of the store. In the middle was a coffee table holding wine, nuts and potato chips.

'G'day, Joe,' almost everybody present said in unison.

Molly was standing in front of the shop counter. 'Joe, do you know everyone here?'

A quick scan of the circle told me I did. Fat Bobby and Roxy sat together on one of the sofas, Maud and Silvia Stanton sat side-by-side on chairs, next was Dennis Hodge, the postmaster—the only person who hadn't said g'day—and I was surprised to see Frank, the publican, in the group.

'Yes. Hi everybody.' I greeted each of them with a nod.

'Didn't know you were a writer, Joe,' Silvia Stanton said.

'I'm planning to write a memoir one day.'

'Okay, everyone who is coming is here so let's make a start,' Molly said, silencing the chatter. 'I've got an apology from Babs Bingle, she can't be here tonight. Apparently, Willy Nelson's sick.'

Uh-oh. A thought dawned on me. Perhaps Willy Nelson was vegetarian for medical reasons. Yikes.

'Have we got any achievements this month?' Molly continued.

Dennis Hodge lumbered to his feet.

Fat Bobby rolled his eyes.

Roxy chastised him with an elbow to his ribs.

'I achieved third place in the Eisteddfod open category for my poem *Under the Tree*,' Dennis announced proudly.

There was an underlying weariness in the applause that followed.

He opened a folder and began to read his poem. After five minutes, I understood the apathy. I like poetry but I like it short and sweet. My appreciation won't stretch further than a couple of stanzas.

Dennis was a passionate poet. He delivered the words in undulating tones and with dramatic body language, which was great if you liked that sort of thing—too melodramatic for my tastes and the piece was far too long.

'Thank you, Dennis,' Molly said after a more enthusiastic applause, which I'm sure was due to the poem ending.

'Anyone else?'

Silvia Stanton smoothed her dress and rose from her chair. 'I've had an article accepted by *Cairns Life Magazine*. It's five hundred words on life in the north. It's going to appear in their summer edition.'

'Well done, Silv!' Frank said above genuine applause.

'Anymore?' Molly said scanning the room. 'No? Okay, who would like to start then?'

Dennis Hodge's hand shot up. The silence was as loud as a collective groan.

'*I've* written a short detective story,' Maud said.

'Great. Would you like to read it for us?' Molly ignored Dennis. The relief in the group was almost palpable.

'It's not finished yet—it's more of a prologue and only a rough draft.' She handed each of us a copy then flicked her head back to read through glasses perched on the end of her nose:

'It was a dark, dark, quiet, quiet night, no moon, no stars, even the usual sounds of the city—traffic, sirens, people—all seemed unusually quiet. Detective John Dent stood at the entrance to the alley, staring into the darkness, afraid of what might be there.

'Is anyone there?' he called.

There was the sound of movement, like he'd disturbed somebody or something.

Could this be it? John thought. *After all this time searching to no avail, could I have inadvertently stumbled on the serial killer?*

He moved slowly into the alley and, as his eyes adjusted to the dark, he narrowed them scanning from left to right.

Suddenly, the silence was shattered by an explosion of sound. A dustbin lid came crashing down on his head. He fell to his knees, hot blood trickling down the side of his face. He felt a gush of wind fly past him as the assailant took off. But he was powerless to give chase.

Detective John Dent sobbed as he peered at the body of the young woman lying at the end of the alley.'

The applause that followed was supportive but a little forced. I noticed Dennis didn't join in and that he'd been taking notes as Maud had read.

'That's very good, Maudie,' Molly said sounding a little patronising, which I'm sure she didn't mean.

'You don't like it?' Maud responded with an I-don't-believe-you-don't-like-it tone.

'Yes, I like it but as you said it's a rough draft.' Molly's eyes searched the others for support.

'Well, that *is* what I said!'

"I know. I'm agreeing with you, Maudie.' Molly turned to me. 'Joe, let me just explain to you how the group works.'

Maud dropped down into her seat and crossed her arms.

'The idea is that we each bring in a sample of the writing we are working on at the moment and the group critiques it.'

'But it has to be an honest critique,' Dennis Hodge piped up. 'We're here to help each other to grow as writers, not to pat one another on the back.'

'Perhaps you'd like to start then, Dennis,' Molly said.

Maud bit her lip and shuffled in her seat.

Dennis spoke *at* Molly instead *of* Maud. 'Well, I'm just not feeling it.' He paused for a moment as if searching for the right words. 'I want to feel the fear, I want to visualize the surroundings, the sights, the smells, the sounds—'

'There weren't any sounds,' Maud snapped. 'I said that!'

'Yes, it was dark, dark and quiet, quiet.' A smirk flickered across Dennis' face. 'Here's another example: "Suddenly, the silence was shattered by an explosion of sound". What does that mean?'

'Well, it's obvious. It means exactly what it says.' By the end of the sentence her voice had risen in pitch.

'But what kind of sound? The lack of adjectives shows the author to have a very poor understanding of prose.' Dennis was still addressing Molly as if Maud weren't there. 'The piece is littered with poor punctuation, grammatical errors—*their* instead of *there*. And "He felt a gust of wind flu past him" and "… the young woman was laying at—'

'Fair go, Dennis, 'Fat Bobby said. 'Maudie said it was a rough draft.'

'Yeah,' Silvia and Roxy said in unison.

'I understand, but in the interest of constructive criticism, I would be doing the author a disservice if I weren't to point out the problems I see with the text. I'm sure if Miss Berry were here, she'd agree that the piece wouldn't amount to much more than a lower school standard.'

'Whoa, good on ya, Podgy,' Frank said sarcastically. 'Don't hold back, mate.'

'Well, why don't you tell us what you think then?' Dennis shot back.

I'd sensed a flash of anger when Frank addressed him as Podgy.

Frank shuffled uncomfortably as if he'd just been asked to address the local AA on the benefits of drinking beer. 'Well, I think as a rough draft it's not bad … shows potential. Not sure about the dustbin lid though. It's all wheelie bins nowadays.'

'That's a very good point,' Molly said.

Everyone nodded and agreed enthusiastically.

'Might want to change that bit, Maudie,' Silvia said.

Maud was nodding as she scribbled on the manuscript.

None of the comments that followed were as scathing as Dennis,' but I realised that Dennis was the only member of the group who wasn't afraid to tell the truth. I actually agreed with everything he'd said but I doubted I'd have had the guts to speak out the way he had.

Discussions ensued on the projects each member was working on. Fat Bobby had been writing a novel for three years about a young detective on the Gold Coast. His energy and passion were surprising.

Roxy sent him admiring glances as she listened. The sample he'd chosen to share was well written. Dennis however, had different views.

Frank was compiling a family history. Silvia was writing a biography about her husband's family. Dennis was writing poetry, which he insisted on reading to more unspoken disdain from the group.

Molly had told me previously that towards the end of each meeting the group would discuss which book they'd choose to read then critique the following month.

'Right, we need suggestions for this month's book,' Molly said when the reviews of the previous month's book were all done.

'I have a suggestion.' I reached into my trusty little bag and pulled out my copy of *Flirting with The Moon*. 'This might be a good one.' I placed it on the table and looked around the group, trying to gauge their responses.

Fat Bobby looked back at me warily.

'Let's have a look,' Silvia picked it up. 'Oh, it's about that serial killer,' she added, thumbing through the pages.

'Hardly appropriate,' Dennis said.

Flirting with The Moon

'If we're taking a vote, I'll vote no.' Fat Bobby handed the book to Frank, bypassing Roxy.

'Hey, let me see it,' Roxy protested.

Frank passed it back.

Fat Bobby shot me a what-the-hell-ya-doin' frown. 'It's not the kind of thing I think you should be looking at Rox.'

'I think I'm big enough to decide that for my—' She read a passage. 'Oh … I see what you mean.' She quickly handed it back to Frank.

'Well, I think it's a great idea,' Maud said.

'I'll give it a miss,' Silvia said. 'Not really my cup of tea.'

'I'm not interested in it either,' Dennis said. 'I understand that poetry is too difficult for this group to review, but I don't think it would hurt to try.'

'Roxy? Frank?' Molly said once more, ignoring Dennis.

Roxy shook her head.

'I'm easy,' Frank said handing the book to Molly.

'What about you, Moll?' Fat Bobby said.

'I'm with Frank, whatever the group decides.'

'That's a no then,' Fat Bobby said firmly.

The group decided on another book, one suggested by Silvia.

After everyone had left, I stayed behind to help Molly with the cleaning up.

'What do you think of our little group?' Molly said as she cleared the table.

'Great, they certainly enjoy their writing. I felt a little sorry for Maud, though.'

'Don't be. She can be just as hard when it's someone else's work.'

'Dennis is pretty intense.'

'He's a poet and blinkered about it. He's not interested in any other kind of writing.'

'You don't think then that he'd write anything like this?' I held up *Flirting with The Moon*.

'No. Apart from it not being poetry, he writes about the landscape, the fauna. Not the kind of nasty stuff you have there. In fact, I've never read a single expletive in his work.'

'Interesting.'

'Why so?'

'Well out of everyone I've met so far, Dennis Hodge is the one who *most* matches the profile of a serial killer.'

Molly giggled. 'Dennis? He can be a nasty little bugger, but he wouldn't hurt a fly. He used to be the scoutmaster when the town had a troop. He helps out at the church. Looked after his mother until she died. He's a nice man when you get to know him.'

As we cleared away the cups and plates and rearranged the chairs, I asked half-jokingly, 'So if you had to pick a serial killer from someone in the town, who would it be?'

'Are you kidding?'

'Yes but indulge me.'

'I can't go talking about people like that. It's not in my nature. Except ...' Her voice dwindled away and she frowned, her hands stilled over the plates.

'Except?'

'Geoff Lambert, He'd be capable of killing someone. He's a vicious man!'

The dishwasher was in a small kitchen behind the store. When we'd finished loading it Molly said, 'Fancy a nightcap?'

'Sure.'

I followed her up a flight of stairs to a neat little flat.

Kimmy was sprawled across the couch watching TV. 'Hey, Joe,' she said groggily, turning off the remote, sitting up and stretching.

'Hi Kimmy. Anything good on?'

'No reception, remember? Just the same DVDs over and over. What's that you got there?' She pointed at my copy of *Flirting with The Moon*.

'Just a book. Not a very good one.'

Her face dropped. 'Nothing's very good in this town.'

Molly sat on the sofa next to Kimmy. 'Why don't you go to bed, love?'

'Yeah. Just need to check my Facebook first … oh that's right, there is no Facebook on this fucking planet!' She pushed herself up, flung down the remote and stomped off.

'Kimmy!' Molly shouted after her.

I was a little shocked by the outburst. Molly seemed to read my expression.

'Teenagers, Joe, it can be hard going.'

'How are things going with you two?'

'She's a great kid, but there's a problem on the horizon.'

'What kind of problem?'

'Schooling. She's still supposed to be in school, even though she was expelled from her last one.'

The only school I'd seen in Candle Stick Bay was the junior school.

'The nearest high school is two hours away in Cooktown.'

'Oh … what do the other kids in town do?'

'A couple travel every day, but most board.'

'Four hours commute just to get to school and back would be a nightmare.'

'Yep, and now's not the time to be sending her away, not after her mother packing her off up here.'

'Right. So, what are you going to do?'

'I've applied for home schooling permission, and Miss Berry's offered to do some private tutoring.'

'Great!'

'Great for us, yes. Convenient. But think back to what you were doing in your high school days.'

'Of course … but like you say, she's a good kid.'

'She is, but I've got to work out how to keep her stimulated.'

32

The next morning as I ate breakfast on the balcony, there was a knock on my door.

'Cooeee.'

Before I could reach it, the door opened and Maud popped her head in.

'Maid service.'

'Hi Maud, come on in.'

Straight to business, she breezed in and started to strip the bed. At first, I thought she was ignoring me, so I went to return to the balcony.

'There's a bit of gossip in the town.' She threw the sheets in a pile on the floor.

'Yeah?'

'About William Lambert.' She lowered her voice. 'This is unofficial of course but word is …' She paused for effect. 'Word is the wedding's off!'

'Really?'

'Yep!' Maud picked up the pile of sheets. 'I've scored a bit of cleaning work at the house. That Andrew fella hired me. There's something about him I don't like, Mr Dean. Something not right. You know what I mean?' She carried the sheets out to the hall only to return almost instantly with a fresh set. 'Anyway, I just happened to be there yesterday morning when there was this almighty row going on in the next room. Shouting and screaming they was. I looked out the window and I saw her marching out of the house. She got straight in the back of one of them Range Rovers, then it drove off. Next, Lambert comes running out cursing at the top of his voice like you'd never heard in your life. Calling her a whore and a ... I'm afraid I can't repeat the things he was saying.' She went about making the bed.

'So, she was here?'

'Been and gone, all in one morning apparently.

When Maud had finished tidying the room, I returned to the balcony. I'd inadvertently formed a mental image of the old whiteboard from the Parker Centre but the pictures hanging on it weren't of the victims. These were of smiling, ordinary people. The images had been arranged in the order in which I had met the folk of Candle Stick Bay—starting with the two Telstra workers and ending with Babs Bingle.

'The players!' A compassionate whisper in that delightful Latino accent I remembered well. It was the voice of Sanchez in my head.

Studying each of the photographs on the whiteboard, I made a shortlist. First, I set aside those who'd been in the States at the time of the murders. Of course, none of this was substantial, all I had to go on what I was told. If Bruce Stanton, for instance, told me he'd never been to the US, I had no way of verifying it. My list looked something like this:

William Lambert
Babs Bingle
The Professor
Molly Quinn

The next list contained suspects who may have had the necessary skills to commit the murders:

Geoff Lambert
Doctor Elliot
Dougie Costa – he filleted a mean fish
Pete Bingle – Ditto
Bruce Stanton – Ditto

Looking at the two lists, I realised how pathetic they were. But at least I had the incident room set up in my head. Now I needed to move the investigation up another gear.

The next morning I met Molly on the beach and we managed halfway around the bay. We walked closer to the water edge where the sand was firmer underfoot, and she placed her arm in mine. It felt good.

Something in the water caught my eye.

'What is it, Joe?' Molly followed my gaze.

To my trained eye, there was no mistaking the object rolling in the gentle waves of Candle Stick Bay that morning.

Forgetting the threat of crocodiles and stingers, I waded into the water. Luckily, the incoming tide sent the body rolling towards me. I grabbed a cold, heavy arm and had to pull against the outgoing surge that was sucking it back. I dragged the corpse up onto the sand.

Molly gasped and lifted her hands to her mouth. 'Oh my God!'

From the moment I'd touched the cold, stiff hand, I knew the person was long gone and beyond help. This was confirmed when I rolled the body onto its back.

Molly's gasp turned into an anguished cry.

Although the corpse was bloated and grey, it was obvious from the Deff Leppard T-shirt that it was Geoff Lambert. His lifeless eyes remained fixed and opaque. His lips were swollen, and his enlarged tongue bulged from his mouth. The stench of death was overwhelming.

'Get Fat Bobby, Molly. I'll stay here.'

There were no arguments from Molly. She sprinted across the soft sand.

33

I was amazed at how unequipped the town was for a situation like this. It was twenty-first century Australia, not Gambia or Ethiopia, I thought to myself as PC Scotty Williams and Fat Bobby lifted Geoff Lambert's corpse into the back of Pete Bingle's ute.

Doctor Elliot had been and gone, issuing brief instructions for Fat Bobby to deliver the body to the rear of the surgery as soon as possible.

'I'll need full statements from you two,' Fat Bobby said.

Molly nodded slowly. 'Do you mind if I go home now?'

'That's fine,' Fat Bobby said. 'I'll come around a little later.'

I went to escort Molly home, but she stopped me. Her hand on my arm was shaking and her face was pale. 'It's okay. I'd rather be alone.'

'Are you sure?' She was rightfully upset but I was a little confused by her reaction to me.

'Yes,' she said and walked away.

'She'll be right,' Fat Bobby said. 'I'll get round to her place as soon as I can.' He climbed into the ute.

'Mind if I tag along with you guys?' I said.

I expected Fat Bobby to say something like: This is police business now. Leave it to us. But instead, and after pausing for a moment as if contemplating an idea, he said, 'Yeah, no worries, jump in.'

With Fat Bobby driving, Scotty Williams as passenger and myself in the back seat, we drove slowly across the sand. I looked over my shoulder and out the rear window. Unsecured and wrapped in a grey blanket, the corpse bounced around as the vehicle negotiated the uneven ground.

We drove down the side alley of the surgery to find Doctor Elliot waiting for us at the back door of the building.

'Bring him this way,' the doctor instructed once Fat Bobby and Scotty had unloaded the body. Carrying an end of the blanket each they followed the doctor with me bringing up the rear.

The doctor pointed to a narrow bed in a small surgery room. 'Place him here.'

The two cops did as they were told and stepped back to give the doctor room.

'There isnae much we can do here,' Doctor Elliot said after unwrapping the blanket. He moved Geoff's grey and bloated head to one side. There was a deep purple welt encircling his neck. The mark had the texture of rope. 'Asphyxiation!'

'Strangled?' Fat Bobby said.

The doctor shook his head. 'Naw. Hanged. His neck is broken.'

'Hung himself?'

'Perhaps.' The doctor looked closely at the mark.

Fat Bobby's eyes flicked from the corpse to the doctor then back. 'How come he was in the water?'

'Well, that's where you come in isn't it, Bobby lad?'

'Can you tell how long he's been dead?'

'It's very difficult. We'll need tae arrange a post-mortem as soon as possible, but I'd say a day or two.'

'But the crocs would have had him surely?'

'Aye, that they would, but I'd say he's been in the water no more than a few hours.'

Fat Bobby and I walked back to the station while Scotty returned Pete's ute. 'What do you make of it, Joe?'

'He definitely died by hanging—doesn't make sense how he could be in the water, though.'

'That's right. If he'd hung himself, he'd still be swinging.'

'Perhaps someone found him.'

'And dumped him in the water?'

'Hmm ... if anybody had found him, they would either have reported it or not wanted to get involved and left him hanging. Why would anyone go to the trouble of cutting him down and throwing him in the ocean?'

'Trying to dispose of the body?' Bobby said.

'It's the only conclusion I've come to, but that begs the question as to whether he was murdered or not.'

'It makes it bloody awkward that's what it does. If we found him hanging, we could've recorded a verdict of suicide. If somebody had killed him, they could've gotten away with it ... unless ...' His voice trailed off and his lips puckered as he mulled over a new scenario.

'Unless what?'

'The killer didn't want us to believe it was suicide!'

Fat Bobby got me to write down my details on the top of a statement form while he reported the incident to the Cairns CIB over the airwaves. When I'd finished, he motioned for me to pass him the sheet of paper.

'Okay. I'll get you to check this bloke out.' He read out my details over the two-way.

'Am I a suspect?' I asked when he'd finished making his report.

'Of course you bloody are!' He took the seat opposite me. 'I'm going to need to ask you a few questions.'

Fat Bobby's questions were sharp and direct, but my answers were pretty straightforward and nothing he probably didn't already know. Then I remembered the incident with Geoff when he banged on Molly's window.

'What and he just ran off?'

Scotty Williams returned after dropping off Pete Bingle's ute. He didn't say a word, but his eyes searched the room as if he were looking for something else to do.

'Make some coffee, eh Scotty,' Fat Bobby said without looking up. He continued with his questions: 'Can you tell me why you're here in Candle Stick Bay?'

The question was simple, but it was the one I'd been dreading. I'd have to answer truthfully. And Fat Bobby knew why I was here. 'I'm in Candle Stick Bay to search for a serial killer.'

'In an official capacity?'

'No.'

'You've listed your employment as a private detective. Is this part of a case you're working on?'

'No.' I figured the best way to proceed was to go with the caprice of an old detective looking to solve the one case that had beaten him. And that's exactly what I did for the next hour as I answered questions about my past, from the time of joining the LAPD, to my time as the leading investigator on The Moon case, life as a bum, to my life in Boca.

'Well, that just about covers everything for now.' He slid the papers across the desk to me, and jabbed his pen at the bottom of the last page. 'I'll get you to sign and date this here once you've read it.'

I settled back into the chair to read my statement.

Fat Bobby stood up and reached for his cap. 'I'm going to have a chat with Molly. PC Williams will keep you company while I'm gone.'

'You're detaining me?'

'No, but the CIB are on their way. They'll want to talk to you as well.'

'Sure.'

When Fat Bobby returned two hours later his mood seemed somewhat lighter. 'Sorry about that, mate. I made it as quick as possible for Moll. She's understandably upset.' He quickly bundled something into his top drawer, then turned to his junior. 'Scotty, can you do the beat this morning?'

'No worries.' The young PC jumped to his feet and grabbed his hat. The two-way radio crackled into life just as the station door swung closed after him.

In one large stride Fat Bobby was at the console. He placed the headphones on, flicked a switch and the transmission fell silent.

'You've got to be flamin' joking!' he yelled into the handset. 'So, what the hell are we supposed to do?'

Over the next few minutes, a heated discussion ensued of which I only heard one side.

'Yeah, well thanks for nothing, eh. Over and bloody well out!' He yanked off the headphones and slammed them onto the console. 'Bloody typical!'

'What's wrong?'

He threw his hands in the air, his face red and flustered. 'Bloody mongrels aren't coming. There's some kind of bikie war thing going on in Palm Cove. Can't spare anyone to come all this way just for a suspected suicide.'

'What about the body?'

'A coroner's van is on the way.' Fat Bobby checked his watch. 'Should be here this arvo. They'll take it back to Cairns for an autopsy.'

'At least that's something.'

'Yeah ... bloody bikies.' He returned to his desk and dropped into his chair.

After a minute or so of silence, I cleared my throat. 'What happens now?'

'Hmm, indeed ...' He pursed his lips and regarded me closely. 'Thing is mate ... although you're a suspect, I don't think you killed Lambert, but I think you've stirred up a bloody hornets' nest with all them flamin' questions.'

I couldn't argue.

'Now that there's been a death, I'm going to have to make a

few enquiries of my own. And seeing as you're a suspect whom I can't risk disappearing on me but also can't legally throw in jail, I'm going to have to keep you close.' He grinned and tapped the side of his nose.

'To assist you with your enquiries.'

The grin spread wider. 'I'm happy to let you into my confidence but I'll need you to swear that you won't breathe a word of anything you hear or come across to anyone else.'

I placed my left hand over my heart and raised my right. 'I swear!'

'I think it's about time we got this investigation started, don't you?' He reached into his top drawer, pulled out a wad of cash and tossed it onto his desk. 'After I'd taken Molly's statement, I went out to Geoff's camp site and found this.' He pointed to the money. 'Two grand! Just lying under his blanket.'

I picked up the bundle. 'Where would Lambert get this kind of money?'

'Exactly … I think it's time we paid Sir William Lambert a visit.'

34

When we passed the bookstore in the police cruiser, I craned my neck, but the brightness of the day made the interior too dim to see inside. 'How was Molly?'

Fat Bobby changed up a gear before answering. 'Ah, she's all right. Upset. But she's tough, you know? Kimmy's staying at home with her.'

'That's good.'

'Apparently Lambert had been giving her a bit of a hard time. Hanging around her place, harassing her.'

I remembered how he'd hammered on the storefront that morning, but I'd assumed that had been directed at me. 'Did she report him?'

'Nope. The first I heard of it was this morning.'

We drove out of town and up the hill. Kenny and Tana were still sitting on their crates reading their newspapers. They waved as we drove past.

'Lazy buggers,' Fat Bobby said. 'Now if either of them two were murdered I'd quite understand. Be bloody hard to find the killer, but. Everyone in the town'd have a motive.'

'It's not their fault they're on strike though.'

'No, s'pose not. It's just frustrating. The answer to our communication problem is lying up on that hill in pieces, and them two's sitting on their arses doing nothing.' A few minutes of thoughtful silence followed until Fat Bobby spoke again. 'Listen, if there's anything you know that I need to know, I expect you to tell me.'

'Absolutely.' I checked the whiteboard in my head for any new intel. The only change was a close-up photograph of Geoff Lambert's bloated face. 'To be honest with you, Bobby, I have nothing.'

Fat Bobby swung the cruiser left into the narrow lane with the "No Entry" sign I'd passed on my first day. The vehicle handled the steep incline well. After half a mile or so we were pulling up to the palatial gates of William Lambert's estate.

I hadn't really taken much notice of this side of the property when Andrew, the butler, had ejected me. This entrance was far grander than the one I'd climbed over on the other side of the hill. There was an intercom on a post; it reminded me of a drive-through burger joint.

Fat Bobby lowered his window and pressed a button marked with the sign of a bell.

A crackly voice filtered through a small speaker. 'Yes?'

'It's Police Sergeant Radford, here to speak with William Lambert.'

'Do you have an appointment?'

'Don't need one. Just open the gate, will ya sport?'

There was a long pause and for a moment I thought the request was being ignored.

Fat Bobby was just about to jab the button again when there was an electrical buzz followed by a clunk.

The gates slowly and silently opened.

The entrance to the house was a beautiful, art-deco style, wooden-and-glass doorway that reminded me of the entrance to Macy's department store in New York.

'Worth a bob or two, this bloke.' Fat Bobby guided the cruiser to a stop on the gravel driveway.

Andrew, the butler, met us at the door. His disdainful expression conveyed that communication between us was beneath him.

'Face like a smacked arse!' Fat Bobby muttered as we were ushered into the hallway.

The butler sniffed then intoned, 'Wait here please.' He glided through a double doorway at the far end of the entrance hall.

The interior was cool and light, smelling of beeswax. The 1920s style had ended at the entrance. Inside was all white walls, high ceilings, terracotta-tiled floors, and dark wood doors. Mediterranean.

Suddenly, a door to our left opened.

We both jumped.

Andrew, the butler, reappeared. 'Mr Lambert will see you now.'

We were shown into the room at the back of the house that I recognised from my previous visit.

Lambert sat at his desk, typing on his computer. He didn't get up or acknowledge us.

'Sergeant Radford to see you,' the butler said.

He neither announced me nor met my eye. He hadn't addressed Lambert as 'sir' and he didn't leave the room.

Lambert tapped his keyboard hard and fast in an exaggerated flurry of typing then swivelled around in his chair, jumped up and greeted Fat Bobby with a handshake and a warm smile. 'Sergeant Radford, it's good to see you again.'

'Likewise.' Fat Bobby extended his arm towards me. 'This here's Joe.'

Lambert's chin rose and he regarded me down his nose. 'Yes, I know who Mr Dean is.' He frowned then pointedly turned back to Fat Bobby.

'Mr Lambert, I'm afraid I've got some bad news for you. Would you like to take a seat?'

Lambert's eyebrows shot up. 'Bad news?'

'When was the last time you saw your brother, sir?'

'I don't have a brother!' he replied without a flicker of emotion.

'We both know you do.'

'If you mean that worthless piece of shit that shares my surname,

I haven't seen him for years. Why? What's he done now? Burglary? Rape? I wouldn't put anything past him.'

'He's dead!' Fat Bobby said.

Part of being a good detective is to be able to read expressions. Years of interviewing suspects has taught me to look closely for any signs or changes in a face when a person is given bad news or is accused of something. In less than a second, Lambert's face passed through three definite stages that only a trained eye would've picked. A twitch of a smirk, a stab of recognition, then a back-pedalling frown of fake remorse.

'Geoff's dead?'

'Yes, we found his body washed up on the beach this morning.'

Lambert lifted a hand to his forehead—his face had definitely paled. 'Drowned?'

'Strangled. Probably hanged.'

Lambert tottered back and steadied himself against his desk. He raised his left hand and cupped his mouth, then he began to shake. Pure Hollywood. 'Suicide?'

'We're not sure yet.'

'You're not sure?' He staggered to the table on the other side of the room. A large crystal decanter held pride of place like a showcase artefact. Lambert poured himself a large Scotch.

As well as paying attention to Lambert, I was also watching the butler from the corner of my eye. Two things interested me: one, he'd shown no reaction on hearing the news of the death of Lambert's brother; two, he was offering no assistance to his apparently grief-stricken employer. He just stood there, listening. I'd had enough of this guy's attitude. I strolled over to him. 'And what about you? When was the last time you saw Geoff?'

He stared into my eyes. What I saw in his made me uneasy. They were cold, black, almost reptilian. He remained silent.

'Answer the question, please,' Fat Bobby said.

'If you wish me to answer questions in an official capacity,

Sergeant, I'll be happy to comply. But as the American has no official status, I feel it is well within my rights to ignore his harassment.'

'Harassment?' I allowed myself a short bark of laughter. Then I shook my head but stepped back because, of course, he was absolutely right. Once again, I had no authority here and he didn't have to tell me a thing.

'Fair enough Mr …?' Fat Bobby said taking over.

'Winstanley, Andrew Winstanley.'

'Right, Mr Winstanley… when was the last time you saw Geoff Lambert?'

'I've never met the gentleman, sir.'

William Lambert poured another large drink. 'Sergeant, what's this all about?'

'We won't have the results of a post-mortem for a few days yet, but it looks like your brother may have been murdered.'

Lambert stumbled backwards into the table, almost knocking over the decanter of Scotch. When he caught it without spilling a drop, his shocked expression turned to one of relief. He must've quickly realised that we were watching him, and the bereft brother returned.

'Can you think of anyone who would want to harm your brother, sir?' Fat Bobby said.

Lambert nearly choked on a mouthful of Scotch. He coughed and spluttered into his sleeve. When he raised his face, his eyes were streaming. 'Uhmm …' He frantically wiped at the spill on the front of his shirt with his free hand. 'How about … everyone?'

'Including you?'

'Look, I'm going to be honest with you, Sergeant. My brother and I weren't what you'd call close.'

'Yeah, I heard about the night he bashed you out the back of the pub,' Fat Bobby said.

As if offended, Lambert rose to his full height. 'We haven't spoken since that … night. I've had no contact with my brother in over thirty years.' He finished off his drink. 'I thank you for bringing this sad news to my attention, Sergeant. I'll take care of the funeral arrangements. Now if we're finished here?'

'No, we're not finished. I'll need you to come down to the station and make a statement.'

'Good heavens! What on Earth for?'

'I'll also need you to officially identify the body.'

'You've got to be kidding.' All signs of remorse had dispersed into the ether.

'No, I'm not kidding, and we need to do it now.' Fat Bobby checked his watch. 'I'll expect you at the doctor's surgery in say … fifteen minutes?'

'This is outrageous!' Lambert's voice had risen to a shrill.

'Hoo-roo!' Fat Bobby padded from the room with me following in his wake.

'Does he really need to identify the body?' I asked as we drove back towards the town.

'Nah, I just want to make sure he remembers who's in charge around here. What did you make of the pommy butler?'

The car rounded back onto the main road, narrowly missing a bush turkey as it scurried across our path.

'I found it odd that he stuck around when we were talking to Lambert.'

'Yeah. Shifty little bugger, I reckon.'

We pulled up outside the doctor's surgery beside a white unmarked van.

Fat Bobby turned off the ignition. 'Coroners are already here, or at least the couriers.'

The waiting room was empty except for Steph, the receptionist, and Maud Baker. I was surprised to see Maud straightening magazines and wafting around the chairs with a duster then I remembered she worked there too.

'The doctor's in the back,' Steph said.

I followed Fat Bobby through the waiting room and into the doctor's office. The doctor was talking to a young man in blue coveralls while a woman, identically dressed, was zipping up the body bag containing Lambert's body.

'Doc, we've got William Lambert coming down to identify the body.' Fat Bobby cupped his hand to his nose at the pungent odour still present. 'It won't take long. He should be here any minute.'

We stepped out into the hot but fresh air at the front of the building.

A few minutes later, a black Mercedes CLS with tinted windows swung into the small parking area.

William Lambert, eyes shielded by sunglasses, let himself out of the back of the car like a vampire stepping precariously into sunshine.

The butler climbed out of the driver's side but didn't offer assistance to his employer.

'This way, sir,' Fat Bobby said politely, taking charge. 'You stay by the car,' he said not-so-politely to the butler.

William Lambert seemed taken aback by this and looked at the butler as if seeking permission.

The butler nodded.

'Prepare yourself, mate, because this ain't pretty.' Fat Bobby grasped the body bag's zipper.

William, still wearing his sunglasses, said nothing.

The zip parted with a ripping sound, opening just enough to reveal the corpse's face. 'Is this your brother?' Fat Bobby said.

'You know damn well it is!' Lambert spun on his heels and stormed out of the room.

35

With Fat Bobby's permission, I returned to my room at The Great Northern, picked up something I needed, and was back at the police station just as William Lambert's black Mercedes pulled into the driveway.

Fat Bobby was waiting at the entrance.

Once again, the butler climbed from the car.

I got the feeling he fully expected to be present when William Lambert gave his statement. His face fell into a sulk when Fat Bobby once again ordered him to stay in the car.

Fat Bobby showed Lambert into the station and led him to his desk. 'Take a seat please, sir.' Then, with a flick of his head, he gestured to Scotty Williams to take a walk.

The young PC nodded, grabbed his hat, and headed out the front door.

'Can I get you a tea or a coffee?' Fat Bobby said.

'I suppose you wouldn't have a stash of Scotch?' Lambert said, gingerly lowering himself into the chair.

'I'm afraid that's not on offer, sir.' Fat Bobby sat down at his desk across from Lambert, reached into one of his drawers and pulled out a statement form. 'If you'd like to fill in your personal details at the top there, please.' He rotated the form, pushed it to Lambert and proffered his pen.

Lambert reached into the inside pocket of his sports jacket and produced his own pen.

'Help yourself if you want a coffee, Joe,' Fat Bobby said, hitching his thumb towards the back room.

'Does he have to be present?' Lambert growled.

'Who?'

Lambert glared at Fat Bobby. 'Who else is in the fucking room?'

'Whoa … that's not very nice. I'll put the aggressive behaviour down to a by-product of grief.' He swivelled his chair round and winked at me. 'Would that be a fair assumption, Joe?'

I arranged my face into a suitably grave expression. 'Yes, quite understandable.'

'Why don't you fuck off back to Florida?' Lambert spat in my direction.

'Well, well, well …' Fat Bobby shook his head theatrically from side to side. 'I see you're not so different from your brother after all.'

Lambert pressed his lips together as if clamping down on the words that wanted to flood out. He scribbled down his details then turned the sheet and skittered it back across the desk. 'Let's just get this over with.'

His hands were beginning to shake, an obvious sign to a reformed alcoholic like me. Lambert was an addict, and he needed his fix.

Something he'd said was bothering me. 'How did you know I was from Florida?'

Lambert ignored me, staring down at his lap. His legs were beginning to twitch.

'I understand my police career in LA was high profile, but I doubt there'd be any record of me living in Boca.'

Lambert glared at Fat Bobby while scratching his shoulder nervously. 'Is this an interrogation now, Sergeant?'

Fat Bobby heaved himself up from his desk, poured a cup of water from the cooler, returned and handed it to Lambert. 'Take it easy, eh. We just need a statement.'

'But he's not a cop!' Lambert barked taking the cup. He took a mouthful of water, closed his eyes, and threw back his head.

'Actually, you're right,' Fat Bobby said with another wink in my direction. 'Joe, could I ask you to take yourself off to the waiting room please?' The waiting room was at the front of the building where the only partition was the chest-high reception desk.

I seated myself on one of the waiting room chairs and, although I was out of sight, every word was clearly audible.

'First of all, Mr Lambert, I really am sorry for your loss.' Fat Bobby's tone was warm and friendly.

There was no response.

'I'll make this as quick and as easy as possible, sir.'

The questions Fat Bobby asked over the next few minutes were procedural ones, the kind wherein a lawyer wouldn't need to be present. 'When did you last see your brother?' and 'Was there any bad feeling between you both?' etc. I guessed he was leading up to something though and, when I heard Lambert scrawl his signature on the bottom of the sheet, I waited.

'Well, that's all we need for now. I'd just like to say I really appreciate your assistance with this matter at your time of loss.'

I heard a grunt, followed by a chair scraping across the tiles.

'There's just one other thing, sir. Off the record, so to speak.'

'What?' Lambert snapped.

'Did you know that your brother broke into your house last week and stole something?'

Slowly and quietly, I stood and peered over the reception desk.

'What are you talking about?' Lambert was swaying like a palm tree in a breeze.

'He broke into your house and stole a book.'

'Rubbish.'

'You got that book, Joe?' Fat Bobby called.

'Sure have.' I pulled my little bag from my shoulder, retrieved the copy of *Flirting with The Moon* and marched towards Lambert. 'There you go.' I placed it into his trembling hand.

'What's this?' He turned it over, looked at the back, then flipped it over to the front cover again.

'Your book,' I said.

'It's not *my* fucking book!' Disgust was heavy in his voice.

As if we'd been a double act for years, Fat Bobby and I laughed, then we launched into a routine:

'Did you hear that, Sergeant? He said this isn't his book.'

'That's what I thought he said, Mr Dean.'

'Oh, he definitely did say that. I'm sure of it.'

'What the fuck's going on?' Lambert's tone was a mixture of anger and panic.

'Have a closer look at the book, Mr Lambert, or is that Mr Powell?' I said.

'Fuck you!' He hurled the book on the floor and was about to storm out when Fat Bobby grabbed him by the arm.

'You're not going anywhere, Lambert.' He slammed him back down into his seat. 'Time to start answering a few real questions.'

Lambert looked as if he'd been caught with his pants down. His eyes flicked from Fat Bobby to me and back. His lower lip trembled as if he were about to sob. But instead, he burst out laughing.

Fat Bobby stepped back and directed a puzzled frown towards me.

'He's been acting. Putting on a show,' I said.

'Having a lend of us?'

Lambert's laughter launched into a high-pitched hooting. Tears flowed down his cheeks. Then suddenly, he stopped.

And something hit me bang between the eyes. 'Are you a fan of the theatre, Mr Lambert?'

He was taller than me, an advantage he used to its full benefit as he rose to his feet and fixed me with a cold stare. 'If we've finished here, Sergeant?' he said without breaking eye contact with me.

'Well as a matter of fact, we haven't finished—'

'Then you'll need to speak to my solicitor.' He reached into his inside pocket and produced a white business card. There was no sign of a tremble in his hand now.

'A bit of a thespian, eh?' I said. 'A wannabe actor, is that right?'

'I'll also be pressing charges,' Lambert said, pushing the card into Fat Bobby's hand.

Fat Bobby's eyebrows rose. 'Charges? Against whom?'

'Against Fuckface here. Breaking and entering. That should get him deported.'

The smirk was more than smug. It made me want to put my fist through his face. And he knew it.

'Add a charge of GBH and he'll be back in the gutter in no time. But then again, that's inevitable, isn't it?' He breezed out of the station leaving Fat Bobby and myself speechless.

'Struth, what was all that about?' Fat Bobby scratched his head.

'An act.'

We returned to Fat Bobby's desk, and I shared my new theory. '*Flirting with The Moon* has a thespian theme. The writer refers to the victims as stars, the crime scenes as theatre venues, and the murder weapons as props.'

'Is that right?' He cocked his head on one side as he processed this information. 'So … that means William Lambert's your killer?'

I sucked in air through my clenched teeth. 'Not necessarily.'

'Bloody hell, Joe. How much more evidence do you need? He's a writer, he wrote the book using a pseudonym, he's an actor *and* he was in LA when the murders took place.'

The evidence did seem overwhelming, but we couldn't arrest Lambert. Even if a cold case were opened in LA, there'd been no evidence left at any of the crime scenes—nothing biological, no hair, no semen, nothing that could be tested for DNA. All we had were our suspicions. 'It's not that easy though is it, Bobby?'

I guessed Fat Bobby's wheels of reason had been turning at the same pace as mine and he'd just come to the same conclusion. 'No evidence. Shit, how are we going to handle this?'

'Perhaps we need to keep digging.' I sat down at the desk. Fat Bobby took the seat facing. 'There is something else that's beginning to gnaw at my brain.'

'What's that, mate?'

'That this could be a part of The Moon's game.'

'Stitching up Lambert you mean?'

'Doesn't it all seem a bit too obvious? Lambert's not stupid. If he is indeed The Moon, then this would be the first time he's ever slipped up. I just can't see it.'

'Everybody stuffs up some time or another.'

'True.' I had an idea, and I couldn't believe we hadn't pursued it yet. 'There is one piece of evidence that will tell us who the writer of the book is for sure …'

Fat Bobby nodded, beckoning me to continue.

'Post box number twenty-four.'

'Good call! Let's go.' He jumped up from his desk and grabbed his police cap and sunglasses.

36

Monday was obviously a slow day in the postal business because Dennis Hodge was working the post office alone. 'Bobby, Mr Dean,' he said as we approached the counter.

'Dennis.' Fat Bobby removed his sunglasses.

'What can I do for you?' His tone was rushed as if he suddenly had something important to attend to.

'I need to know who owns post box number twenty-four?'

'That's strictly confidential, Bobby, you know I can't tell you that.'

'This *is* official Dennis. It's not a request.'

'Has this got anything to do with the death of Geoff Lambert?' Dennis' beady eyes blinked rapidly behind his glasses.

'Maybe. Look up the name for me please, mate.'

'I don't need to look it up. I know who all the boxes belong to.'

Fat Bobby took a deep breath, containing his impatience.

'It's Roxy's,' Dennis said. 'Roxy Stephens rents twenty-four!'

I noticed a fleeting smugness as he reached under the counter and lifted up a leather-bound clip folder. He flicked through the alphabetical pages, turned the book around so Fat Bobby could read it, then jabbed a finger halfway down the page. 'There you go.'

We read the details in silence. The insert was a twelve-month renewable contract in the name of Roxanne Emily Stephens of Number 9 William Street, Candle Stick Bay. Roxy had rented the box for the last three years.

'There's no mistake?' Fat Bobby sounded like he didn't want to believe it.

'Positive.'
'And she's had it for three years?'
'Uhm … kind of.'
'What do you mean kind of?' Fat Bobby said.
'For the five years before that it belonged to her father.'

'There's got to be some kind of explanation,' Fat Bobby said as we trudged up William Street.

'What do you know about her father?'

Fat Bobby didn't look up. He was staring morosely at his feet as they moved him up the hill. 'Not a lot. Before he got sick, he used to travel a fair bit. A university lecturer. Seemed like a nice bloke.'

'What did he lecture in?'

'Not sure. I think it was something to do with drama.'

'Acting?' A flutter of excitement stirred in my chest.

We reached the short driveway of number nine. A frangipani tree with huge leaves and two-tone orange flowers stood at one side. The driveway was empty. No Kombi. No Roxy.

Fat Bobby continued towards the house.

As we were about to climb the steps, the front door flew open.

'Thank God you're here!' The professor's distinguished voice presented a tone of authority, but his attire told a different story. He wore a two-piece suit without a shirt, and slippers with no socks. His hair was unruly as if he'd just jumped out of bed. 'Do you have any idea what it's like being stuck out here on one's own?'

'Professor Stephens, I'm here to talk to Roxy,' Fat Bobby said.

'Good god man, are you insane? There's no time for that. Get the bags, get the bags.'

'Are you going somewhere, Professor?'

'The professor pointed to me.' You, you … what's your name?'

'Joe.'

'Joe, yes of course, Joe Dean. Well, come along, you're not paid to stand there gaping. Get the bags.'

My eyes met Fat Bobby's. The question didn't have to be asked. How did he know my last name?

'Professor, do you know where your daughter is?' Fat Bobby said.

The professor breathed deeply then expelled an impatient sigh. 'She's waiting for us.' He spoke slowly as if he were addressing children. 'This is what I've been trying to tell you. She's waiting at the stage door and now because of you I'm going to be late. Late for my own first night. Have you any idea how unacceptable that is? Now move it!'

Roxy's Kombi pulled into the driveway. She rushed from the van. 'Daddy, what are you doing?'

The professor frowned at his daughter then, looking confused, he glanced around as if not knowing where he was.

'Come on, let's get you back inside.' Roxy ignored Fat Bobby and me as she brushed past us.

'Did you get the reviews?' the professor murmured as his daughter led him into the house.

'The reviews were great, Daddy. They loved your performance!'

We stood outside in the shade of the house and waited, not quite sure if Roxy was coming back or not.

Minutes later she appeared at the front door. 'What's going on?' She glared down at us.

'Nothing,' Fat Bobby shrugged. 'We just came to see you and your dad came out.'

Her expression turned from anger to concern. 'He was already out here, or he came out when you arrived?'

'Uhm … he came out when we arrived.'

Her shoulders relaxed and the tension in her body seemed to subside. 'So, he wasn't wandering around?'

'No.'

She covered her face with the palms of her hands then raked them slowly over her head as if she'd just emerged from the shower. 'What did you need to see me about?'

Fat Bobby shuffled from one foot to the other. He was in an

awkward position. He was smitten with Roxy, but I couldn't be sure if his feelings were reciprocated, and I don't think he knew either. 'I just need to talk to you about your post box.'

The tension returned in her tone. 'My post box?'

Fat Bobby's sideways glance at me was a cry for help.

'We just need you to confirm that number twenty-four belongs to you, Roxy,' I said.

'Yes, it does, well … it's Daddy's, but it's in my name.'

'Right, and does your father get much mail?'

'Some. He gets theatrical magazines, bank statements, insurance, that kind of stuff.'

'So, you check all his mail?'

'Yes.' She was tapping her foot on the step—not a good sign. 'Does somebody mind telling me what this is about?'

'Do you recall seeing anything from a company called Ruby P Publications?'

A definite change came over Roxy's face when she heard the words *Ruby P*. Her brow lowered into a searching frown. She was wary of me now. 'Maybe,' she said slowly. 'I mean it rings a bell.'

'Do you read your father's mail?'

'Some of it. The stuff from Centrelink. He's on a disability pension. But most of it I leave for him to read.'

Our silence prompted her to continue.

'He still has good days; they're getting fewer, but they're still there. So, I save up all his mail and give it to him when he's lucid.'

'And he reads it?'

'Yes, even manages to answer a few.'

'Do you know if he's received any cheques in the mail?' I wasn't expecting her to continue answering my questions. I was sure she was about to complain to Fat Bobby at any moment.

Fat Bobby stood silently, poking the toe of his shoe in the dirt.

'Not that I know of. I certainly haven't banked anything for him in a while,' Roxy said.

I could tell by Fat Bobby's fidgeting that he was uncomfortable and wanted me to end the questioning. 'Well thank you for your time, Roxy, you've been very helpful.'

'Yeah thanks, Rox, that's great. Listen, sorry about all this. See you in the morning, first thing?' Fat Bobby said.

Roxy nodded but she was obviously not happy. She went back into the house without saying a word.

'Bloody fucking hell, Joe!' Fat Bobby said as we headed back towards the town. 'I thought William Lambert was the prime suspect. That's all gone to buggery now!'

I nodded, knowing exactly what he meant. Professor Stephens was a writer, an actor, and he was also in LA at the time of the murders. And post box number twenty-four belonged to him. A sense of disappointment overwhelmed me when I realised that The Moon might now be an old man with dementia.

Could he have been capable of killing Geoff Lambert?

37

By the time Fat Bobby and I arrived back at the station, my legs were aching, and I was as hungry as hell. 'I need to go and rest up.'

'Yeah, no worries, Joe.'

I also wanted to check on Molly to make sure she was all right, but I decided to keep that to myself. I was making my way towards the door when it flew open, and Roxy burst in. Her face was flushed, and she was waving a letter in one hand.

'Hey, Rox. You all right, love?' Fat Bobby hurried towards her.

'After you left, I couldn't get the name of that publisher out of my mind.' She was out of breath, and I figured she'd run from her place.

Fat Bobby gently guided her to the seat opposite his desk then fetched her some water. 'There you go.' He handed her the cup.

Roxy gulped down half the drink then continued. 'I'd heard the name before. After you two left, Daddy slipped into what I call one of his comatose periods where he just sits in his chair staring at nothing. He can be like that for hours.'

'Is he going to be okay?' I said, standing behind Fat Bobby.

'Yes. It's a bit of a relief when he's like that actually. At least I know he's not wandering off.'

'He's started taking off?' Fat Bobby said.

'No, but I'm worried he will. He gets so confused. Some days he thinks Mum is still alive or he's still living in the States. I can't lock him up while I'm not there.' The anguish was moving her to tears.

Fat Bobby reached across the desk and patted her hand. 'Hey, it's gonna be okay.'

'But I don't know how much longer I can look after him. If he disappears when I'm not there.' A tear rolled down her cheek.

I was finding it hard to take my eyes off the letter in Roxy's hand. Curiosity had deadened the ache in my legs like morphine.

She sipped on the water then gazed out of the window. 'On his good days it's easy to forget that he's ill. He'll wake up as if nothing is out of place. We'll talk like we used to do. Back to his old charming self, you know?' A little smile tugged at the corners of her mouth. 'Anyway, whenever I collect his mail, I place it on his desk, knowing that when he does have a good day, he'll read it.'

'How often does he have a good day?' Fat Bobby asked.

'Not very often these days. They're getting fewer.'

'So, his mail's mounting up?' I said.

'He still gets an awful lot, but nowadays most of it's junk. I check the important stuff and file it away.'

I couldn't help myself. 'What's the letter you've got there?'

Roxy turned to Fat Bobby. 'That's what I wanted to speak to you about. When Joe mentioned the name of that publisher, it rang a bell so I decided to check through the pile of mail on Daddy's desk.' She handed the letter to Fat Bobby.

I was easily able to read the envelope over his shoulder.
Mr Stephen Powell
PO Box 24
Candle Stick Bay
Qld 4900

Fat Bobby turned the envelope in his hand to read the back.
From: Ruby P Publications
Paddington
NSW 2021
The postmark was dated two weeks ago.

Flirting with The Moon

'Do you mind if I open it, Rox?' Fat Bobby said.

'No, go ahead.'

He reached down, picked up a paper knife from the desk, and slipped the blade under one corner.

The knife sliced through the paper with a *shwip*.

Fat Bobby pulled out a letter, a handwritten receipt, and what appeared to be a bank statement.

Dear Mr Powell,

Please find enclosed quarterly royalty statement #0202 for the period of July 1st to September 30th and attached receipt for proof of donation to the Sydney Theatre Company.

I wasn't sure whose face turned the whiter, Fat Bobby's or Roxy's.

Speechless, Fat Bobby handed the papers to me.

I grabbed a chair and seated myself at the end of the desk.

The receipt was for the sum of four thousand dollars. Scanning the list of transactions on the statement, I noticed that each payment total was decreasing. Over the year to date, the author had earned twelve thousand dollars in royalties, all of which had been donated to the Sydney Theatre Company. At the top of the page, it showed the title of the book, *Flirting with The Moon*.

I looked up at Roxy. 'Does your father receive these each quarter?'

'I'm not sure. It's only because this one is recent it was fresh in my mind.'

'Do you understand what this means?'

Fat Bobby shot me a warning glance.

I chose to ignore it.

'That my father wrote that awful book you brought to the meeting last week.'

'That's right ... do you think that's possible?'

'Possible yes ... probable? I don't know.' She looked wrung out, exhausted.

'Has he written anything as dark as this before?'

'Oh yes. Apart from being a professor of drama, first and foremost

Daddy was an actor, but he …' She was searching for the right words. 'My mother told me that he lost his nerve. He was playing Antonio in *The Merchant of Venice* in London, a role he'd played hundreds of times. In the middle of the performance, he forgot his lines and froze.'

'Dementia?'

'Could've been an early sign, but because he was only in his forties—'

I finished the sentence for her. 'People thought he'd lost his nerve.'

'That's right. But worse, he was slammed by the critics for ruining the performance.'

'So he never acted again?'

'Not in front of an audience—he taught instead.'

'And the writing?'

Fat Bobby was quiet. I guessed he was happy to let me continue.

'That's what makes me unsure. You'd be amazed at how many stage plays he's written—screenplays, books.'

'Published?'

'A novella, which he hated after it had been edited. He accused the publisher of watering down his art. His dream though was to write a successful play.'

'Did he ever stage anything?'

'No … apparently the stuff he was writing was too dark—too violent for those days.'

Fat Bobby's eyes met mine and his expression said, *fuck me, here we go again.*

'Has he ever used the name Stephen Powell?'

'No, not that I know of, although he used to joke that to get published, he'd have to use a pseudonym.'

'Thank you for sharing this with us, Roxy. It's most interesting.' I handed her back the papers.

'Yeah, thanks for your time, Rox. I know how busy you are.' Fat Bobby rose from his desk.

I was glad that Roxy knew little about the book and so hadn't made the link between it and the possibility of her father being a vicious killer.

As I strolled up the high street towards the bookstore, I couldn't help but feel disappointment. I wanted to catch The Moon and bring him to justice but if my nemesis was now nothing more than an old man suffering from dementia, would the feeling of closure be the same?

The bookstore was closed and, when I knocked on the door, there was no answer. Where were Molly and Kimmy? Was Molly upstairs ignoring my knock? Perhaps the shock of finding Geoff Lambert's body had upset her more than I'd thought. I suddenly felt bad for spending the whole morning with Fat Bobby without checking on her. I made a note to call back soon.

I purchased a cheese and salad roll from the bar and ate it out on the balcony. I wasn't sure if it was the hot breeze or just the feeling of a full belly, but I'd dozed off to be woken sometime later by a gentle shaking.

'Joe, wake up.'

I opened my eyes to find Fat Bobby standing over me. 'Hi, Bobby.' It came out as a croak. I was still half asleep.

He drew the other balcony chair closer and flopped into it. 'Good news, mate.' He fanned himself with his cap. 'Now that the bigwigs down south realise that Geoff was William Lambert's brother, they're sending up a detective from Cairns.'

'Excellent.'

He dropped his cap on the floor, retrieved his notebook, and flipped through the pages. 'Detective Inspector Rodney Cooper. He's on his way so should be here sometime tonight.'

'Are you going to tell him everything?'

'Have to. He'll probably want to talk to you too.'

I'd arranged to meet Fat Bobby back at the station in an hour. After a long, hot shower I strolled down the high street in the fading light.

The bookstore was closed, which wasn't unusual as it was after five, but I suspected it hadn't opened all day. I knocked.

Nothing.

I knocked again, a little louder.

Kimmy appeared from the back of the store then opened the door.

'How is she?' I asked.

Kimmy shrugged. 'I don't know, haven't seen her all day.' Her nonchalant attitude took me by surprise.

'What? She's been missing all day?' I snapped.

'Not missing. She went for a walk just before lunch, said she needed to think. She was pretty upset.' Her tone was now defensive.

'Well, do you know where she went?' I didn't want to alarm her, but I couldn't hide my concern.

'No, but she'll be all right. She does this sometimes when she's worried about something. She'll just walk.'

I checked my watch. 'She's been gone a long time.'

'She'll be back soon. I'm sure of it.' Only now Kimmy was sounding less sure.

'Do you know which way she went?'

'No, but she likes walking the bush tracks.'

I didn't like it. She'd been gone over five hours and it was getting dark. 'Will you tell her to come to the police station as soon as she gets back?'

She shrugged again but with a slight nod.

I told Kimmy to stay inside and not to open the door to anyone. A flinch and a frown told me I'd raised her concern. 'It's okay, I'd just rather know that you're here when Molly gets back.' I reassured her then waited as she locked the door and returned to the back of the store.

Back at the station, the dark circles under Fat Bobby's eyes were noticeable. His large frame filled the office chair, and his hair was a little ruffled as he scribbled notes in his pad.

'How are you holding up, Bobby?'

'I'm knackered to tell you the truth, Joe.'

'A long day, huh?' I sat at Scotty Williams' desk; he must've finished his shift. 'Bobby, there's something I need to tell you, something I just realised this afternoon.'

Fat Bobby's slight nod prompted me to continue.

'Today is the first cycle of the new moon.'

For a second or so it didn't register, then his heavy eyelids sprung open. 'Shit ... you don't think ...?'

'Hope not.'

'But Geoff was killed two days ago, so that'd be out of character for your serial killer.'

'That's right.'

'Maybe the business with Geoff is coincidental?' Fat Bobby said. 'What if Geoff Lambert just killed himself?'

My pondering nod invited him to continue.

'What if he hung himself but the rope snapped.'

'And he fell into the water?'

'Yeah.'

'But the tide doesn't come up as far as the trees, surely?'

'That's right. We cleaned up the old camp site this afternoon, but we didn't find any rope or signs on the trees, so what if he'd done it farther up the beach—you know, where it slopes?'

It made sense. There was an area farther along from Geoff's camp where the trees sat above a slope. If he'd hung himself there and the rope had snapped, his body could've rolled down the bank and on to the sand below. The tide could have then carried his body away.

'Best check it out in the morning, eh?' Fat Bobby leaned back in his chair and yawned.

38

For the first thirty minutes Fat Bobby fought to stay awake but it was a losing battle. He drifted off right there, sitting at his desk. The rest would do him good. I glanced up at the clock on the wall and thought of two things. The first was what kind of reaction I could expect from the detective travelling up from Cairns—would he dismiss my theories about The Moon being in Candle Stick Bay as ridiculous? Or even treat me with disregard? Trying to put myself in his place, I guessed it could be a mixture of both.

My second thought was worry—worry about Molly. She'd been out a long time and it was now dark. It's not like there was somewhere in town where she could hang out other than the pub. If she were walking in the bush and with the absence of the moon, it would be pitch black. Even the beam from the lighthouse only penetrated so far into the dense foliage.

A wave of panic suddenly overcame me, and I jumped to my feet. What the hell was I doing? I should've been out looking for her. I was heading towards the exit when my fears disappeared in a gush of relief. Molly and Kimmy stepped through the door.

'Molly, thank God!' I wanted to hug her but as I drew closer, I realised she wasn't feeling the same way.

Her expression was sharp, a mixture of bewilderment and anger. 'What on Earth's wrong?' she snapped.

'I was worried about you.'

'Why?' Her eyes stabbed at me like daggers.

'Well ... after what you witnessed this morning then taking off on your own—'

'Taking off on my own? I don't need anyone's permission if I want to go for a walk. I'm not a child, Joe!'

'I know that ... I just ... sorry I ...'

Kimmy shot me an apologetic glance. 'Joe was just worried about you, Aunty Moll.'

'Well, there was no need.' Her tone was marginally softer, but she was still taking no prisoners.

I was getting myself into trouble with Molly simply by opening my mouth. I stepped back and an awkward silence fell around us like a shroud. Thankfully, Fat Bobby stood up, stretched, and through a stifled yawn, said: 'G'day Moll. How are you?'

The smile I was growing to love returned. I only wished it had been directed at me.

'I'm good thanks, Bobby. Been out walking up to Stanton's Lookout. Clears my head, you know?'

'Yeah. Good to walk it off. Can I get you a coffee or anything?'

'No, thank you, I'm fine.' She turned and put her arm around her niece. 'We need to get home.' She was speaking to Fat Bobby and Kimmy as if I weren't in the room. Obviously, I was the only one in her bad books.

'Before you go, can I just ask you something?' Fat Bobby said.

'Sure.' Her reply was void of enthusiasm.

Fat Bobby leaned down, opened his desk and withdrew the wad of money he'd shown me earlier. 'When we searched Geoff Lambert's camp, we found this.' He placed the money on the desk. 'You wouldn't have any idea where he got it from, would you?'

Being a silent observer worked in my favour at that moment. From where I stood, I was able to analyse Molly's reaction to the question.

'How would I know?' The slight crease across her brow told me the question irked her.

Kimmy's face however, told a completely different story. When she saw the wad of notes, her open-mouthed gaze shifted from the money to her aunty.

'I remember you saying that Geoff had been giving you some strife.' Fat Bobby wasn't sounding quite so friendly now.

'No more than anyone else in town.'

'You wouldn't have given him any money to get rid of him then?'

'Certainly not. Where's this leading, Sergeant?' As had Fat Bobby's tone changed, so too had Molly's.

But I wasn't interested in their interchange—I was more interested in Kimmy.

She knew something. The expression she wore now was easy to read: *but-Aunty-Molly-what-about-that-time-when ...?* I fought against the urge to intervene. Fat Bobby was handling the situation well and besides, I didn't want to piss Molly off any more than I already had.

'So, you've never given him any money?'

Molly's face was flushed with outrage. 'Positive,' she growled. 'Can I go now?'

'Yeah, of course you can.'

She was heading towards the door when Fat Bobby called after her. 'Moll ...' he left the rest unsaid, until she turned back to face him. 'I'm just trying to find out what happened to Geoff.'

Molly shrugged as if she couldn't care less. 'Come on Kimmy.' She pushed past her niece and left the building.

Kimmy followed.

'What do you make of that?' I asked as we resumed our seats.

'She's upset. Understandable. Bit of a nasty shock finding Geoff like that.'

'Did you see Kimmy's reaction when you asked about the money?'

'I did, mate. There's something Molly's not telling us, that's for sure.' He looked at the time. 'Where's this bloody bloke from Cairns? He should've been here by now.'

'Will he stay at the pub?'

'Nah, there's a spare room at my place.'

We sat for another two hours. I drank a terrible cup of coffee after Fat Bobby had assured me that his was better than Scotty's. It wasn't. I told him more about The Moon case. Then for the second time that week, I spoke about my murdered ex-partner.

'Bloody hell, Joe. I didn't know.'

At this point I realised Fat Bobby hadn't shown any interest in reading the book.

The conversation turned to his life. He told me about his upbringing on the Gold Coast and about his parents. 'Old Stell and Clivey, God bless 'em. Dad's gone now. Mum's still on the Goldy. I try to get down to see her as often as I can,' he said fondly. He briefly mentioned a younger sister called Jenny then looked at his watch for the umpteenth time. 'Joe, I'd better check that this bloke is definitely coming.' He pushed himself to his feet. 'Be just like them galahs to change their minds and not tell me.'

He radioed through to Cairns and, after being kept waiting for five minutes, received confirmation that Detective Inspector Cooper had indeed left Cairns at lunchtime to travel to Candle Stick Bay.

'It's 9.30! You blokes might need to see if you can get hold of him because he should've been here ages ago! Over.' Fat Bobby said into the handset.

'Perhaps he thought he was staying at the pub,' I said after Fat Bobby had finished the call. 'Might've checked in there for the night.'

'Yeah, it's possible. Communication isn't our strong point around here. How about we go and have a look, eh?'

Part of me wanted to go to the pub with Fat Bobby to see if DI Cooper had arrived, but the biggest part wanted to check on Molly. Something other than the fact that she saw Geoff Lambert's body that morning had upset her. She was angry with me and, yes, I had to admit that the detective inside me was curious. But it was more that I was really beginning to care for her.

'I'm going to check on Molly,' I said to Fat Bobby as we walked side-by-side along the dark high street.

'Yeah, good idea, mate. She seemed to have warmed to you until now.'

Apart from the three seconds of light that swept across the town every minute, the street sat silent on the moonless evening. The glow from Dougie's fish shop spilled onto the sidewalk. The bookstore next door was in total darkness. Had Molly and Kimmy already turned in for the night? I knocked anyway.

First, a strip of light appeared across the floor at the back of the room, then the door opened, sending shadows fleeing across the bookshelves.

The figure walking towards me was Molly. She hit a switch and the store interior flickered into light. Her puffy eyes and red nose told me right away that she'd been crying. She looked at me for a moment through the glass as if contemplating whether to open the door or not. When she finally did, she stepped back without saying a word, allowing me to enter.

'How are you feeling?' It was all I could think of to ask.

Molly closed the door behind me and turned off the store light. 'Come through,' she said, leading the way.

We climbed the stairs and stepped into the small flat above the store in silence. I noticed Kimmy's absence.

'Kimmy's in her room listening to music,' Molly said. 'Drink?'

'No, I'm fine thanks.'

'Take a seat.' She sounded curt.

I sat on the small couch. Molly sat in the armchair opposite.

'Have I done something to offend you, Molly?'

I saw a mixture of emotions wash across her face. I guessed she wanted to cry, she wanted to be strong, she wanted to tell me something, and she didn't want to tell me anything. 'I'm not angry with you, Joe …' Her bottom lip trembled. 'I'm angry and ashamed of myself.'

The space between the couch and the armchair seemed as vast as the Australian outback. I wanted to throw my arms around her and tell her everything would be all right, but I sensed she needed to get something off her chest.

She was tightly twisting and screwing up a handkerchief in her hands. 'I haven't been entirely honest with you, Joe.' She lowered her head. 'Even after you confided in me, told me about your past, your nightmares.'

'What's happened, Molly?'

She took a deep breath and peered up at the ceiling, as if searching there for her next words. 'Where to begin ... my ex-husband, I guess. Everything I told you *was* true, but ...' Her voice trembled as she spoke. 'My ex killed someone. We were still married. She was a young prostitute in Hollywood. I didn't know, of course. He didn't get caught, not then anyway. He got away with it and carried on as normal. When our marriage collapsed, he kind of lost the plot.'

I was shocked at what I was hearing, but I remained quiet.

'To cut a long story short, he killed again—another prostitute—only this time he was caught. He was drunk and out of control, didn't cover his tracks like he had the first time. When he was charged with murder he broke down and confessed to two other killings. The man I'd once adored had killed three people, one when we'd only been married for three months, when we were still happy.'

The tears were flowing down her cheeks now.

'Molly, don't feel bad for not telling me any of this. It's not like you know me that well. This is deeply private. And what your ex-husband did had nothing to do with you.'

'But everything you told me was also very private. I could've told you when I had the chance.'

'No. The time wasn't right. The fact that I burdened you with all my problems was totally unfair of me.'

She wiped her eyes and blew her nose. 'But I felt honoured that you wanted to share your past with me. I'm angry because I should have reciprocated.'

Whether I liked it or not, mine was the mind of a detective. The next question came straight from my subconscious and even took *me* by surprise. 'So how did Geoff Lambert find out about your ex-husband?'

Molly's face froze. 'Wow!'

'Was he blackmailing you?'

'I can see why you're such a good detective.'

I rose to my feet, walked over to the kitchen counter and from memory of my last visit, I grabbed a glass from an overhead cabinet and filled it with tap water. 'Take your time,' I whispered, handing her the glass.

'I don't know how he knew but he did. He was a nasty, vile creature. He enjoyed conveying every single disgusting detail. One thing I'm ashamed of, Joe, and I can't believe I'm telling you this, is that I'm glad he's dead. This town will be so much better without him.' She took a large gulp of water and trembled.

'So, you gave him money?'

'Yes.'

'And Kimmy saw you?'

Molly looked at me as if I'd just performed the most amazing magic trick ever. 'How could you know that?'

'I saw Kimmy's expression tonight when Fat Bobby asked you about the money.

'Wow again …! I was out the back of the shop flattening a few empty boxes when he appeared at the fence. He had this knack of just showing up, you know? Anyway, that was when I paid him two hundred dollars. What I didn't know was that Kimmy was watching from the upstairs window.'

'You only gave him two hundred dollars?'

'Yes, told him that's all I had ... he said he'd be back for more. And he grinned that sick, smug grin of his.'

'And did he come back?'

'No.'

'When was this?'

'About a week ago.'

'And now he's dead.'

'Yes. And good riddance.' Molly stood up and shivered. 'I'm going to make a coffee; do you want one?'

'Tea would be good.'

While Molly busied herself in the kitchen, I sat back down on the sofa and sifted through this latest information, compiling new questions.

Molly returned, handing me a steaming mug with Candle Stick Bay and a picture of the lighthouse emblazoned on one side. She remained standing.

'When did Lambert first approach you?'

'The evening after we'd had that wonderful picnic at the lighthouse. Not long after you'd left there was a banging on the front door of the shop. I thought you'd forgotten something. When I walked through the shop, I couldn't see anyone through the glass but when I opened the door, he pushed past me and got inside. I was scared, Joe, I didn't know what to expect. Then he blurted it all out, everything he knew about my ex. Said I was a filthy whore and a ...' She lifted the handkerchief to her mouth.

I went to hug her, but she pulled away and sat back facing me.

'It was then that he demanded money. When I said I didn't have any, he started throwing books around, said how he would hurt Kimmy if I didn't come up with some cash. I told him I had money in the post office.'

I sank back into the sofa. 'When did you give him the money?'

'The next day. The Monday afternoon.'

'The same day as the writers' meeting? Why didn't you report any of this to Fat Bobby?'

'Looking back now I realise it was foolish not to have said anything, but I was worried about the adoption case. If the board find out I've been lying about my past, they might take Kimmy away.'

I understood. 'But Molly, you have no reason to be ashamed of your past. You've done nothing wrong.'

'I know. Sir Walter Scott was right: Oh what a tangled web we weave, when first we practise to deceive!' She began to cry.

I couldn't take it any longer. Two steps were all it took to span the wilderness. I knelt in front of the armchair and pulled Molly to my chest.

'It's okay.' I squatted there, stroking her hair until eventually her sobs subsided.

39

Instead of waking early for my morning walk as planned, I'd slept an extra hour the next day. I vaguely remember waking and contemplating getting up but must've drifted back to sleep. I wasn't complaining. I felt quite refreshed when I finally climbed out of bed. After a shower and a shave, I felt like a new man.

Breakfast was orange juice and croissants out on the balcony. The day was another bright and sunny one. I momentarily wondered if Fat Bobby had caught up with DI Cooper, but I swung back to thinking about Molly. She was really beginning to dominate my thoughts. Did I have a crush on her? Of course, I did. The first time I'd met her, I'd witnessed one of those little schoolboy twinges—the kind that makes you want to show off.

But the notion of Molly Quinn and I becoming an item, no matter how appealing, wasn't what I was focussing on. I hadn't ruled out the possibility that The Moon could be a woman. How could I rule out Molly Quinn as a prime suspect? She fitted right in there with the other suspects—William Lambert and Professor Stephens. She was in LA at the time, she's a writer, and she had a good reason to want Geoff Lambert dead. What if he actually knew more about her than she had let on to me? I remembered what he'd said to me the night he'd asked to speak to me outside the pub. 'Beware the company you keep.' Then there was her husband—did he have any relevance to the case?

When I arrived at the police station, PC Scotty Williams was manning the place alone.

'You've just missed him. He's out on his rounds.'

'No worries. I'll see if I can find him en route.'

I knew it wouldn't be hard to find Fat Bobby. I'd walked his beat with him on a couple of occasions by now. It was 9.00 am. My guess was he would be in the Yacht Club having a smoko. I was right.

'G'day,' he said. He was seated at one of the tables, wiping his mouth with a napkin.

I raised my eyes at the plate of crumbs before him.

'Just a little bit of healthy carrot cake, Joe. Nothing Roxy needs to know about.'

I had to smile. 'So did the DI show up?'

'Nope. He definitely left Cairns yesterday though.'

'So, he should be here.'

'Yep … but I reckon he probably stayed the night in Cooktown. They hate coming all the way up here. He probably drew the short straw.'

'Then we should see him this morning.'

'Yeah, he'll show up eventually.' He dropped the napkin onto his plate and burped.

There was a clatter from the stairs and Scotty Williams came running into the canteen, his face nearly as white as the lighthouse.

'What's up, mate?' Fat Bobby was already pushing back his chair and heaving to his feet.

'You better come back to the station, Bob.'

The face of the young man who met us at the police station was familiar, only different. Gone were the mischievous dimples and the carefree smile to be replaced by a strong-set chin and fear-ridden eyes. His posture was that of a young warrior being sent to battle for the first time.

'Tana, isn't it?' Fat Bobby said.

Tana nodded, trembling.

'What's up, mate?' Fat Bobby continued.

'There's a ... at the ... in the ... the mast ... you better ...' He tried to spit out the words, shaking his head in irritation with each attempt.

'Just take it easy ... what's happened?'

'You better come and look, eh.'

Fat Bobby and I followed in the police cruiser as the Telstra van headed out of town. When we reached the site where the van was usually parked, Kenny was standing there ashen faced.

From the moment Scotty Williams had rushed into the Yacht Club, I'd been expecting the worse. It had been twenty-five years since I'd had this feeling, but it was as familiar to me as my own two feet.

We followed the two Telstra workers up the track towards the site of the unassembled communications mast. And there it was. Kenny and Tana looked away as they pointed to the hole they had bored into the ground six weeks earlier.

'Holy shit, you've got to be kidding me!' Fat Bobby said under his breath.

The cleared ground was a sandy red. The circular hole was about as deep as a tall man. As we approached, the first thing I saw were the soles of a pair of shoes just below the rim. There was someone upside down in the hole.

Fat Bobby lifted his leg over the tape barrier, which was the only thing stopping people from falling into the hole, and he knelt by the edge.

Kenny spoke. 'He's long gone, mate. We already checked. Must've fallen down there sometime last night.'

Fat Bobby reached down and grasped the victim's leg. 'Damn, cold and hard. Give us a hand here to pull him out, eh?'

'Shouldn't this be treated as a suspected crime scene, Bobby?' I said.

'Turn it up, Joe. This isn't LA. Someone's fell down a bloody hole for God's sake.'

'So, you think this guy was just walking out here and—'

'Exactly. Now we need to find out who this poor bugger is. Come on, grab his legs.

Tana's face exploded with fear. 'Not me bro, I'll puke, eh!'

'I'll do it,' Kenny said. 'Although we'll be breaching the terms of our industrial action.'

The body they dragged from the hole was male, white, about forty years old, slim build with thinning brown hair. He wore a cheap brown suit and an open-necked shirt.

My mind automatically placed his image on the whiteboard next to Geoff Lambert's.

Fat Bobby reached into the man's inside jacket pocket, pulled out a wallet and flipped it open. 'Fuck me dead ... it's DI Cooper.'

I'd already suspected as much so the news was no surprise. What was a surprise though was the large gash on the back of the victim's head. It was barely visible with the corpse lying face up but I'd noticed it when Fat Bobby and Kenny had first pulled him out of the hole. I knelt next to Fat Bobby and pointed to the wound. 'That's one hell of a nasty cut.'

'Yeah, must've hit his head as he fell.'

I looked down into the hole. Although the dirt was hard and compact, there were no rocks or jagged edges. 'This guy's been whacked from behind, Bobby!'

'Nah, looks to me like he's fallen backwards, cracked his head on the way down.' He turned to the Telstra workers. 'Can one of you blokes go get Scotty for me?'

The two men looked at each other puzzled.

'The young bloke at the station, PC Williams,' Fat Bobby added.

'I'll go,' Tana said, already heading off.

'Tell him to bring Pete's ute,' Fat Bobby shouted after him.

'I really think this is a crime scene, Bobby. We could be destroying vital evidence.'

'I doubt that very much, but I hear you. You just have to

realise, mate, that things are a little different around here. We're still in the bloody dark ages remember.'

I didn't agree with what he was saying but I knew what he meant about things being different. The town was remote and currently cut off from the rest of the world. Only a couple of weeks ago, I couldn't have dreamed of what it would be like not having a cell phone, or an Internet connection, or even a home phone. 'What would he have been doing up here?'

'That's the bit I don't get.'

'And where's his car?'

'Good point.' Fat Bobby rose to his feet and peered down the hill. 'I didn't see it when we drove up, did you?'

'No, it wasn't down there. How about I take a look up top?' I gazed towards the steep track ahead of me and immediately regretted the suggestion.

'Mate, that'd be great. I'll stay here and wait for Scotty.'

I was puffing and panting like a steam train by the time I reached the top of the track.

The narrow bitumen road was clear. No car. Remembering that William Lambert's place was only a couple of hundred yards around the next bend, I decided to take a look.

I wasn't surprised to see a dark-blue sedan parked in front of the large gates. It had almost indistinguishable red and blue lights in the front grille. An unmarked police car. I thought about pressing the intercom at the side of the gate but decided against it. I needed to get back.

A few minutes later, I was bounding back down the slope.

Kenny was sitting cross-legged on the ground, rolling a cigarette.

I told Fat Bobby where I'd found the car.

'So, he went to Lambert's first. Still doesn't explain how he got down here though.'

'Something's amiss, Bobby. Would a city guy really be wandering around here in the dark? And how come he went to Lambert's?'

The rumble of a diesel engine broke through chattering birdcalls when the Telstra truck pulled up below us, then a squeal of brakes as a second vehicle arrived.

A couple of minutes later, Scotty Williams and Pete Bingle appeared.

Pete was gasping and blowing like a fish out of water.

Scotty seemed totally unfazed by the exertion.

Tana had evidently decided to stay at the bottom of the hill.

'Struth … what the hell's going on here, Bob?' Pete said, bending at the waist to catch his breath.

'Old mate here's had a nasty fall,' Fat Bobby said.

'Fuck me dead!' Pete said.

It was only the second time I'd heard that phrase but both times were within the last thirty minutes.

'How about you take a bit of a look before we move him, Joe,' Fat Bobby said.

Kenny lit his cigarette. 'Like that CI … CS … ICS. You know that shit on the telly?'

'CSI,' Scotty said.

Pete Bingle shot Kenny a contemptuous glare. 'Wouldn't know, mate, we don't have the luxury of a telly cos of you bastards.'

'Oi, that's enough fellas,' Fat Bobby said. 'Show some respect for the dead.' He nodded at me. 'When you're ready, Joe.'

The conditions weren't ideal. Although the ground around the scene was cleared only a few weeks earlier, the red sand had baked hard under the hot sun. What footprints were visible were difficult to distinguish. One section of the hole's wall had given way and collapsed inwards, but all the same the blood at the bottom was easy to spot.

I carefully stepped back to the body, squatted and checked the front of it for any signs of trauma. Apart from a few abrasions—possibly caused by the fall—there was little to report. Wishing I had a pair of rubber gloves, I rolled the corpse over.

There was a collective gasp when the wound on the back of the head came into view.

'Jeez, he's been clobbered!' Pete Bingle said.

He was right. I'd bet that forensic analysis would show the angle and depth of the wound to be incompatible with a fall. Whether it was from a blunt or sharp weapon, I had no idea, but to the naked eye, the gash was a sticky, bloody mess. I decided to keep my conclusions to myself, at least until I could talk to Fat Bobby in private.

As if reading my thoughts, Fat Bobby shuffled impatiently. 'Right to go now, Joe?'

'Almost. Pete, would you have a towel and a blanket, or a tarp or something in your ute?' I stood and brushed down my shorts.

'I'll have a look.' He loped down the track with long strides to return a few minutes later, wheezing and coughing once more. 'Struth I'm too bloody old for this caper.' He handed me a dirty towel that stunk of fish. 'All I've got mate, sorry.'

I wrapped the towel around the head of the corpse in an effort to avoid more contamination or loss of evidence such as fibres and possible DNA.

Then the two policemen heaved up the body—Scotty on the legs, Fat Bobby at the shoulders. They slowly carried it down the hill and gently placed in the back of the ute.

'I might have to start charging you for this, Bob,' Pete Bingle said. 'Two stiffs in two days.'

Scotty Williams and Pete Bingle took off slowly in the ute.

Fat Bobby and I followed behind in the cruiser.

'So whatdya reckon, Joe?' Fat Bobby said as we descended into the town.

'He was definitely hit from behind. The fall could've broken his neck and therefore killed him, but there was nothing in the hole that could cause that sort of trauma to his head.'

40

Detective Inspector Cooper's body lay on the same narrow bed that Geoff Lambert's had only twenty-four hours earlier.

'I cannae believe it,' Dr Elliot said, examining the body. 'Two in two days. It must be a Candle Stick Bay record.'

'Is there a chance that the fall could've killed him?' Fat Bobby said.

'Aye, if he fell doon a ruddy great cliff, but then there'd be trauma to the body too.'

'So?'

'So, I think he's hit his head on something.'

'Or something has hit his head,' I said.

'Aye, that'd be my guess.'

'Then Pete was right—he's been clobbered,' Fat Bobby said. 'I better go and call this in.'

The thirty-second drive from the doctor's surgery to the police station was a quiet one.

As we swung into the driveway, Scotty Williams appeared at the doorway. He had that same look on his face that I'd seen when he rushed into the Yacht Club earlier.

Fat Bobby noticed it too. He climbed from the cruiser. 'What's up now, mate?' His tone was cautious like he was bracing himself for more bad news.

'It's bad, Bob.'

We followed the young constable into the cool shade of the station.

Flirting with The Moon

The airwaves on the two-way radio were crackling and humming with broadcasts.

'There's been an accident out on Mt Webb Road,' Scotty said. 'A fuel tanker's overturned, burst into flames. Started a major bushfire.'

'You've got to be kidding.'

'Nope. Driver's dead. Road's blocked.'

'Shit!' Fat Bobby bounded over to the two-way and placed the headset on. The station was thrown into momentary silence. 'Delta Tango 1 over …'

I noted a very slight tremble in his voice. 'When did this happen?' I asked Scotty.

'Not long ago. Bruce and Pete are already on their way out there.'

I remembered Bruce telling me in our first meeting that he was a volunteer rural firefighter with the SES—the State Emergency Services. I hadn't known Pete Bingle was too; he must've been called out just after he'd dropped off the body at the doctor's surgery.

'Apparently none of the services are there yet,' Scotty continued. 'It's lucky that old Bluey was on the way back from his Cooktown run. The truck was behind him heading for Johno's garage.'

'Where's Bluey?'

'In the pub, probably shaking like a leaf.'

'Right, so he couldn't even report it, he had to get back here and tell someone.'

'He went straight to Bruce at the General Store. Bruce called it in from his two-way then came down here, but we must've all been at the doctor's surgery. Luckily Pete was back.'

'Okay, we're on our way, over and out,' Fat Bobby yelled. He twiddled a dial on the consul. 'Tango Delta 3, this is Tango Delta 1, do you read me, over … Pete, it's Bobby, where are you? Over.' He turned to look at us while listening. 'How's it looking …? My God … okay, I'll be there shortly, over and out.' He tore off the headset and threw it onto the console. 'Lock up, Scotty, we're heading out.'

'How bad is it?' I thought of the wildfires in California and wondered if they were the same here.

'Bad. Real bad. It's the road that leads into town.'

'Isn't it the *only* road into town?'

'Yep, and it's impassable. Fire's spread into the bush either side. It's so dry out there at the moment. The whole bloody bush could go up!'

'Anything I can do?'

'No.' He was rushing around grabbing things as he spoke. 'Best just stay here.'

It wasn't until I watched the cruiser drive away that I realised Fat Bobby had forgotten to call in DI Cooper's death. It was understandable under the circumstances, but still, it should've been done.

'Hey, Joe.' Dougie was standing on the step of his store. 'Lionel Messi, Cristiano Ronaldo and a donkey are in a bar—'

'Maybe later, Dougie,' I said.

Molly Quinn had snatched my attention. Stepping out of the bookstore, she wore a casual but pretty floral dress, tasteful make-up and a wonderful perfume that somehow made me think of Paris.

Kimmy appeared somewhat awkwardly behind her, also dressed smartly, but completely out of character in a skirt and blouse.

'Hi, Joe. Well ... wish us luck,' Molly said, smiling anxiously.

At first, I was confused, then I remembered. Today was the adoption hearing. 'Oh Molly.' Either my woeful expression or my tone of voice chased the smile from her face, and I hated myself for it.

'What's wrong?'

I told her about the tanker overturning, the death of the driver and the bushfire.

'You mean we can't get out?'

'No. The road's blocked both ways.'

'But ...' She looked from me to Kimmy then back again. '... But if we can't get down to Cooktown, we'll miss our appointment.'

'It'll be okay. I'm sure they'll understand,' I reassured.

'But we can't even call them. Bugger, this stupid town.'

'It'll probably be on the news, Aunty Moll,' Kimmy said.

'That's right,' I agreed. 'So, they'll know why you couldn't make your appointment.'

'Right ...' She began to calm down. 'That's right. They already know we can't reach them by phone. I've explained that to them.'

'So, there you go. It's all good,' Kimmy said. 'That means I can get out of this old-woman gear.' She disappeared into the store.

The corners of Molly's mouth curled upwards, and a cute blush crept across her cheeks. 'Wow! I spat the dummy there a bit, didn't I?'

'Yes, you did.'

'It's just been a bit of a stressful time lately, what with Kimmy and all—'

'You don't have to explain to me.'

'I feel a bit of a goose now. And look at me all dressed up with nowhere to go.' She curtsied, holding out the bottom of her dress.

'Seeing as you are looking so beautiful, how about I take you for lunch?'

'Oh, I'd have to check my diary. Clear a few appointments perhaps.'

'Fine, let me know when you're available.' I began to walk away.

'Okay, all done.' She skipped up and placed her arm in mine. 'So where are we going?'

'The pub of course!'

We strolled towards The Great Northern Hotel. Molly's smile disappeared after only a few yards.

'Is everything okay?'

'A pang of guilt.'

'About what?'

'There's been a terrible accident, and all I can think about are my own silly problems.'

I decided not to mention DI Cooper's death. 'Your problems, as you call them, are important. Kimmy's important, isn't she?'

'Yes.'

It took a few moments for my eyes to adjust to the dimness of the pub interior after the bright glare outside. News of the accident had spread like the fire itself. Thankfully, nobody had heard about the body we'd found on the hill that morning; it had even slipped by Maud.

She was serving at the beer taps. 'Have you heard about the fire, Joe?' she said as Molly and I passed.

'Yes, terrible, isn't it?'

Maud looked disappointed that I already knew.

Molly and I seated ourselves at a dining table near the open French doors.

I returned to the bar where Bluey was perched on his stool and ordered two orange juices. 'How's it going, Bluey?'

'Not so good, mate.' His hand shook violently as he lifted his glass of beer to his lips.

'You might want to go and see the doctor?'

'I am.'

'Good, he might be able to give you something to relax.'

'No ... I *am*!'

I was puzzled.

He held up his half-empty glass and jiggled it. 'This is the only doctor I need, mate!'

I paid for my drinks and another beer for Bluey.

Maud was twitching with adrenalin-fuelled energy as she handed me my change. 'You going to give them a hand, Mr Dean? Frank's gone, that's why I'm helping out here.'

'Maybe. I'm not sure yet.'

'I saw the poor bastard and I heard him screaming!' Bluey said, staring down at his drink.

Maud's eyes met mine.

'I couldn't get to him. He was trapped in the cab ... but he saw me ... and I saw him ... and I'll never forget the look on his face.' Bluey gulped down a mouthful of beer. 'Then there was an explosion, and he was engulfed in flames but ...' He wiped a dirty hand frantically across his face.

'It's all right Bluey, mate.' Maud reached over the bar and squeezed his arm.

Bluey ignored her and carried on as if he were witnessing it again. 'But I could see his eyes. And they were looking straight at me, begging me to help him ... his screams!'

I also touched his arm. 'I definitely think you should see the doctor.'

'Fuck off, you cunt,' he suddenly snarled, snatching his arm away from me.

I backed off.

'He's right, Bluey,' Maud said gently.

'Oh yeah, and what does he know? Walking around here like he owns the fucking place.'

Maud looked at me with an apologetic expression that said now-you-know-why-they-call-him-Bluey.

I nodded and carried the drinks back to the table.

'I see you've pissed off Bluey,' Molly said as I resumed my seat.

'He's in shock and he needs to see the doctor.'

'He'll be right. Tough as old boots.'

'Yeah, but what he witnessed this morning, it's not the kind of thing you can wash away with alcohol. Trust me, I know.'

'You really do care about people, don't you?' Molly said looking into my eyes.

'I guess.'

'Even an old pub brawler like Bluey.'

'Believe it or not, Bluey and I have a hell of a lot in common!'

41

After lunch, Molly changed into casual clothes, and we walked to the lighthouse. Like a smitten teenager, I wanted to hold her hand, but I guess the fear of rejection is the same no matter what age you are.

'How much longer are you here for, Joe?' Molly asked as we trudged the gentle incline.

'My ticket is for six weeks.'

'Then you've still got plenty of time.'

'I hope so.'

'Are you going to catch him?'

I wished I could have said yes with confidence, but I'd known right from the beginning that this would never be easy. I wanted to confide in Molly Quinn but decided the least she knew the better. 'I'm starting to doubt he's even here or was ever here.'

'Really?'

'When you're dealing with a personality like The Moon, a psychopath, everything is planned right down to the finest detail. They don't leave tracks. It's hard to believe he would've written a book knowing that it could lead me here.'

'Unless he led you here for a purpose.' Molly's face was now awash with concern.

I tried to play the situation down. 'To make me look a fool!'

She stopped walking and turned toward me. 'Or to kill you!'

I couldn't help but blush. I didn't believe either scenario and that was what made this case so baffling—there was no logic, nothing made sense. Suppose The Moon did write the book, did this mean he also killed Geoff Lambert and DI Cooper? Sure, there may have been plenty of folk in this town who had motives to get rid of Lambert, but these were good people. As for DI Cooper, nobody even knew he was here.

Something I hadn't thought of before suddenly came to mind. Fat Bobby, Scotty Williams and I were the only people who knew DI Cooper was travelling out from Cairns. Had Doctor Elliot known? I couldn't be sure. So, apart from myself, there were only two or possibly three other people who knew he was coming. Interesting.

We walked around the headland. Our hands brushed a couple of times but neither of us took advantage of or the responsibility to take hold. I certainly didn't want to look like a goose, as Pete Bingle would say.

It was late afternoon when we got back to town. When we strolled past the police station, I was surprised to see Fat Bobby's cruiser in the driveway.

'I better go see what's happening,' I said.

'I'll come too.'

Fat Bobby was sitting at his desk with his head in his hands. He looked up sharply when we entered. 'Hey, Joe, Moll.' His face sagged with exhaustion, his skin was dirty and sweaty.

'How is it out there?' I said.

'Bloody bad, mate.' He rose from his desk and padded towards the front counter. 'I've never seen anything like it. It's so dry, the fire's raging both sides of the road, and it's spreading fast.'

'Are the firies out there?' Molly asked.

'Yeah, we've got crews from Cooktown and Cairns. The big rigs from Cairns only just arrived. Trouble is they're all on the other side. There's only Bruce, Pete and Scotty on this side.'

'Didn't Frank go out there?' I said.

'Yeah, I sent him back though. Too dangerous. Even Bruce and Pete can't do much. It's that vast. The stretch of road where the tanker flipped is really narrow, trees overhanging either side. Even without a fire, the bush either side is so dense it's inaccessible.' He gently massaged his forehead with the fingers of one hand.

'What will they do?'

'The Cooktown mob tried to cut a track parallel with the fire so they could get around to this side. They went out about three kilometres, can you believe? Then they hit Bunga Ridge and couldn't go any farther. So, they had to retrace their tracks and had just started cutting on the opposite side of the road when I left. But the wind's picking up and driving the flames forward.'

'It's heading this way?' It was hard to tell whether this was a question from Molly or a statement.

Fat Bobby returned to his desk. 'I've come back to round up the town folk for a meeting.'

'Great idea,' I said.

'This bloody communication situation's a joke, but. I haven't got a clue how I'm going to get everyone together.'

'I do,' Molly said with a slight mischievous grin.

We exchanged glances then said in unison, 'Maudie!'

'She'll be round this town quicker than the lighthouse beam,' Molly said. 'Leave it with me. I'll go and see her, and we'll do half the town each. Where and when do you want the meeting?'

Fat Bobby checked his watch. 'Yacht Club in an hour? Tell everyone it's an emergency meeting ... oh and that attendance is compulsory!'

'Right!' Molly dashed out in a flurry of well-shaped calves, her dress belling out behind her. I sighed. What an idiot—a whole afternoon and I hadn't so much as held her hand.

'She's a bloody diamond that woman!'

'Bobby, I hate to bring this up, what with everything else but ... did you report DI Cooper's death?'

'OH, BLOODY FUCKING HELL!' He threw his hands up to his face. 'Shit, shit, shit! I forgot all about that!'

Flirting with The Moon

While Fat Bobby reported DI Cooper's death over the two-way, I made two strong coffees.

We walked silently to the Yacht Club. There was obviously a lot going through Fat Bobby's mind. Life in this little hamlet really had been turned upside down. I'd learned earlier that the last death in the town was an old spinster called Miss Burtles who had lived on her own on Bayview Terrace. She'd been ninety-three years old and died of natural causes. There'd been no murders in recorded history. The only crimes reported were those during the tourist season and usually concerned drunken tourists. The townsfolk seemed an honest and happy lot. Flamin' galahs? I think not.

When we entered the club and climbed the stairs, some people had already arrived. A sudden jolt of recognition brought a sharp pain to my ankle.

Willy Nelson stood facing me like Lee Van Cleef returned from the dead. Thankfully, he was tethered to his owner by a rope.

Babs Bingle winked at me and grinned.

Behind sliding doors along one side of the room was a small storeroom. Inside were stacks of white plastic chairs. Within minutes, Fat Bobby and I had them set out in rows with an aisle down the centre.

The townspeople took their seats without being told.

Red-faced and out of breath, Maud Baker bustled into the room and marched up to us. 'All done, Bobby!' For a moment I thought she would salute.

'Thanks Maudie, you're a legend.' Fat Bobby gently squeezed her shoulder.

The room began to fill. Many faces I didn't recognise, which wasn't surprising because after all, I'd only met a handful of the residents and a lot of the people present were tourists.

Roxy and Miss Berry sat in the front row on either side of the professor.

I was surprised to see Tana and Kenny sitting in the back row until I realised that they were just as trapped here as the rest of us. My guess was Molly would've have driven up the hill to tell them about the meeting.

Maud Baker stood at the front of the room with Fat Bobby and me. There was no sign of William Lambert or his butler.

Molly and Kimmy entered. Molly smiled and gave a slight wave when she saw me, making me feel important and bashful at the same time.

'Okay, if I can just get everyone's attention, please!' Fat Bobby yelled above the din of chatter.

The room grew silent. All eyes—except for two little black ones—were on Fat Bobby.

'First of all, I'd like to thank you all for attending at such short notice. I guess most of you already know why I've called this meeting.' He scanned a sea of nodding heads. 'Good!' He winked at Maud. 'Okay, for those who don't know, a fuel tanker has overturned about twenty kilometres out of town, triggering an enormous bushfire.'

There was a collective gasp. 'There's been a fatality and the fire from the crash is spreading.'

An elderly gentleman sitting next to Dougie rose to his feet. 'Is it heading towards the town, Sergeant?'

'It is but it's still a fair way off, George. But that's not my immediate concern. I wanted to bring you together to keep you informed of what's happening—'

'But are we trapped?' George's voice quivered with anxiety.

A murmur rose from the crowd.

'Trapped with no means of communication,' Dennis Hodge piped up.

The murmuring grew and a few scornful glares were directed towards the Telstra workers.

'Technically yes, but this is another reason I wanted to get us all together.'

The room fell silent again.

'To give you the facts, to reassure you all that everything is under control and that there's no need for panic.' He went on to tell them how the crews from Cooktown and Cairns were at the scene.

'What about supplies?' George shouted. 'If Bluey can't get his truck through.'

There was a surge of manic debate.

Silvia Stanton raised her hand.

Fat Bobby lifted his arms, trying to bring the crowd to order. 'Shhhh ... everybody ... yes Silve.'

Silvia stood. 'Fortunately, Bluey made a delivery to the store this morning so there's plenty of stock.'

Bluey sat nodding.

'Thanks Silve, that's good to know.'

'There's bugger all fuel though,' Johno said.

'Like I said, folks, it's under control. I'll keep you posted as best as I can. Now I really need to get back out there. Are there any questions?'

The folk were talking among themselves again.

Kenny, the Telstra technician, stuck his hand up.

'Yes?' Fat Bobby said.

Kenny stood but the crowd paid little attention to him until, that is, he said: 'What about the dead bloke we found this morning?'

Another collective gasp, this time louder, dissolving swiftly into expectant silence.

All eyes bored into Fat Bobby, and I guessed my expression must've mirrored his which, if could've been translated into words, would have said, 'Fuck!'

42

'What's he talking about, Bobby?' Dennis Hodge demanded.

Panic swept through the crowd.

Fat Bobby's eyes searched mine for guidance.

I had none to give. In all the chaos of the day we'd forgotten to debrief Kenny and Tana. In fact, we hadn't even spoken to each other about a plan of action.

As if deciding her acquaintance with Fat Bobby and myself might suddenly be detrimental, Maud slunk into one of the empty chairs in the front row.

'Has somebody else been killed?' George, the man beside Dougie, asked.

'Let's just calm down folks, eh?' Fat Bobby said. 'There's been an accident, a fall.'

'Who?' Roxy said. Her father sat next to her with his eyes closed, smiling and nodding as if he were listening to a piano recital.

'Someone from out of town,' Fat Bobby said.

There was a surge of chatter.

'Bobby, for goodness sake!' Dennis Hodge's voice drowned out everyone else's. 'Stop beating around the bush and tell us what's happened.'

Fat Bobby took a deep breath, the strain hard on his face. 'A man must've been walking near the site of the communications mast last night when he fell down the hole.'

'Is it another murder?' Maud couldn't help herself, her eyes as wide as saucers.

This ignited a fierce response among the audience, everyone wanting to speak at once.

Willy Nelson started barking.

Fat Bobby had to shout to be heard. 'Quiet please … can we just bring it down? Thank you. Maudie, there have been no murders. This was just an accident.'

'What like Geoff Lambert's?' She looked away sharply as if it wasn't her who had asked the question.

'No … that was a suicide.'

'That's two deaths in two days, isn't it Bobby?' Dennis Hodge looked around the crowd as if rallying support.

Bluey jumped to his feet. 'Nothing ever happened like this before he arrived!' He pointed at me, looking nearly as ferocious as Willy Nelson. Nods and words of agreement from the audience spurred him on. 'He's either brought bad luck with him or he's the cause of it all!'

'Fair go, Bluey. That's not right!' Frank said, turning in his seat.

Maud swung around in her chair. 'I'm with you, Bluey!'

I looked along the rows. It was then that I caught Miss Berry's eyes—she was watching my every move.

The man I only knew as George stood up again and the noise dropped down to a murmur. 'I think it's about time someone told us what's really happening.'

'There's nothing more to tell about the deaths, George. One was a suicide, the other an unfortunate accident,' Fat Bobby said. 'The object of this meeting is to discuss the situation outside of town.'

'But what about this serial killer we've all been hearing about?'

Maud's head seemed to sink into her shoulders.

Fat Bobby raked his hand through his hair. 'Just silly gossip, mate.'

'What if it isn't gossip though? What if there *is* a killer here?'

'I can assure you it *is* gossip. It's just—'

Cutting Fat Bobby off in mid-sentence, Dennis Hodge yelled, 'My God!' He had to grasp the back of the chair in front of him to help him rise to his feet. With wide eyes he perused the audience as if trying to make eye contact with each and every person in the room. 'Don't you all see? We're trapped here. We're completely cut off from the outside world and … and there's a killer among us!'

It took quite some time for Fat Bobby to bring the room back to order. 'There is *no* killer in Candle Stick Bay.' He emphasised each word slowly and clearly. 'Let's keep it real, eh?'

'So why is the American copper here then?' Bluey said.

I held my arms out in surrender. 'I'm just here on vacation!'

Now it was Maud Baker who jumped to her feet. 'He's a liar! He threatened me! He told me that a serial killer from America lives here. Said that if I keep spreading rumours the killer would probably get me!'

The hubbub grew once more.

'Come on, Maudie,' Fat Bobby said, raising his voice again. 'Why would you say such a thing?'

'If you don't believe me, ask him.' She jabbed a finger in my direction then sat down.

No longer was it only Miss Berry's and Willy Nelson's eyes that were fixed on me, but every single person's in the room. 'I'm here on vacation,' I said. Even to my ears it sounded lame.

'Tell them what you told me about the killer and the book,' Maud called out.

During my time as a police officer and later as a detective with the LAPD in charge of a number of high-profile cases, I'd been in some awkward even nasty situations, all of which paled in comparison to how I felt standing in front of a mob of Far North Queensland townsfolk. Should I have lied and lost all credibility?

Or should I have told the truth and possibly caused panic among them? I decided to mix a little of both.

'Let me start at the beginning,' I said.

Fat Bobby shot me an anxious glance.

I returned his serve with an *it's-okay-I-know-what-I'm-doing* nod. 'I'm a retired police officer from LA. I'm a writer, some might say not a very good one, but I enjoy it all the same. I write crime fiction, murder mysteries that kind of thing. Like most writers, I have a vivid imagination. Unfortunately, sometimes I tend to let mine run away with me.

'There is no serial killer living in Candle Stick Bay! You all know that because you all know each other. Am I right?'

Slow at first but the nods of agreement had swung to my side.

'I'm on vacation but that's only a part of the reason for me being here. I'm also doing research for my latest book.'

The nods were replaced with narrowed eyes.

'It's about an American detective who tracks down a retired serial killer to a small town in Australia.'

'Do you expect us to believe that?' Maud said folding her arms and repeating the look-away-sharply routine.

'Firstly, I'd like to apologise to you, Maud. I should've been honest with you right from the beginning. I was, how do you say …? Having a lend of you.'

A hum of laughter quelled my nerves a little.

'You'll make a great character in the book by the way.' A direct hit from my flattery battalion caused a reddening of her cheeks and a slight smile.

'And I'd also like to apologise to everyone in the town. The way I've conducted myself, asking questions, raising concerns. I really didn't mean for any of this to happen.'

'But what about Lambert and this other bloke who's dead?' George said.

'Just unfortunate coincidences.' Fat Bobby's tone was direct and final. 'Now, if we can get back to the reason for this meeting. The fire. I want to ensure that every precaution is being taken to stop it spreading farther but I don't want anybody going out there please. It's way too dangerous.'

I noticed that Doc Elliot remained in his seat as the audience filed out.

Fat Bobby had been busy answering questions from individuals who'd approached him after the meeting. He sighed heavily when it was finally over.

'Bobby, lad, we have a wee problem,' the doctor said rising from his seat.

'What's that, Doc?'

'We have a corpse lying in the surgery.'

'Struth, that's right.'

'The thing is, Bobby, we dinna have nae storage facilities.'

'Bloody hell. It's gonna stink!' Fat Bobby screwed up his nose at the awful prospect.

The doctor's smile was more grave than humorous. 'That's right. We need tae get the poor soul on ice as soon as possible.'

After a brief brainstorming session that included suggestions of ice in a bathtub, and storage in Pete Bingle's bait freezer, we came up with the idea of Bluey's refrigerated truck.

'He's not gonna like it,' Fat Bobby said.

'Understandable,' Doctor Elliot said. 'We're talking about probably violating every health and safety code in the book.'

I doubted Bluey was the type of guy to be fluent in health and safety regulations.

'Desperate times call for desperate measures,' Fat Bobby said and checked his watch. 'I'll sort it out, then I'd better get back to the fire. How about you go to the surgery, Doc, and wait for me there?'

'Aye, I'll see ye there.' He bowed his head and left.

After a heated exchange, it had taken the threat of a permit review by Fat Bobby for Bluey to finally agree to his truck being taken.

The drive down to the surgery was more of a coast with only one gear change required.

Doc Elliot was waiting for us at the back entrance.

Apart from the odd cabbage leaf, shrivelled carrot and a few empty produce boxes strewn around the floor, the back of the truck was empty and relatively clean. During the trip down, Fat Bobby had turned on the refrigeration unit and the air was already beginning to cool.

'I've nae body bag I'm afraid,' the doctor said as we followed him into the surgery.

The corpse of DI Cooper was wrapped in a grey blanket on the narrow bed.

'No worries. Let's just get him in as quick as we can,' Fat Bobby said.

I lifted the feet and swung the body around and off the bed slightly so Fat Bobby could grab it under the shoulders, a manoeuvre he was probably growing accustomed too.

'Can you do me a favour, Joe?' Fat Bobby asked when the task was complete and the back doors of the truck were closed.

'Sure.'

'First thing in the morning go and see Johno, tell him I need first dibs on all the diesel.'

'First dibs?'

'Tell him I'm acquisitioning all the fuel he has. He's not to sell any.'

'Right.' It was a good move. It would ensure that any gas would be set aside for the police, the fire fighters and of course the new mobile morgue, but it would also keep people in the town. No fuel, no travel.

43

As I watched the tail-lights of the police cruiser disappear at the top of the high street, a car pulled into the sidewalk beside me. I bent to see Frank the publican sitting in a small Hyundai hatch. He climbed somewhat awkwardly from the car.

'Hey, Joe. Bob around?'

'No, you've just missed him.'

'Bugger, I was just coming down to see if there was anything I could do—' His eyes suddenly opened wide and his mouth dropped open.

I turned to follow his gaze, and probably adopted the same expression.

Ambling down the sidewalk towards us, wearing nothing but a pair of yellowed Y-fronts, a string vest, black socks, and shoes was Professor Stephens. Trotting beside him, at the end of a piece of rope, was Willy Nelson.

'You've got to be kidding me,' Frank mumbled.

'Good evening,' the professor said politely.

Seeing me, Willy Nelson stopped in his tracks and immediately began to snarl.

The professor also stopped. 'Now then, Hergé, it's only Joe and his brother Dickie.'

'Out for a walk, Professor?' I said.

'Well of course. There's only three weeks left you know.'

'Three weeks?'

'Got to be in shape for the opening night.'

My next question didn't even make it to my lips. If I'd had the time to think I probably would've thrown myself between them. Frank knelt down and reached out to the dog. He'd be mauled for sure. But my rising howl of 'Nooooooooooo!' never made it into the night air.

Willy Nelson's stubby white tail wagged like crazy. He licked Frank's hand then jumped up him.

Frank held the dog's head between his hands and massaged his ears with his thumbs, 'G'day maaaate.'

The dog groaned and whined.

I was stupefied. 'How'd you do that?'

'Always been good with animals,' Frank said, wrestling playfully with the dog.

'Well, must keep moving,' the professor said. 'Cheerio!' He lightly yanked on the rope.

'Mind if we join you, sir?' I said.

'Okay, but I'm almost there.'

'And where's that?'

'Why, the theatre of course.' He stopped again and cupped a hand to his mouth. 'Meeting a gal.'

'Really?'

'Yes. Jennifer La Roche, but you're not to say anything. Her father's the dean. He'll have me thrown out of college if he finds out.'

'How about we give you a lift?' Frank said.

'Seeing as you've already made me late, that would be only proper.'

'The thing is your daughter sent us to get you,' I said.

'Roxanne? She's back all ready?' His mind was obviously all over the place.

'Uh ... yes.' I led him gently by the arm towards Frank's car.

'But wasn't I supposed to pick her up?'
'She got back early. Got a cab.'
'Oh, that's wonderful. Jennifer will be thrilled.'
'The dean's daughter?'
'Her mother!'
'Right.'
We manoeuvred him into the back seat.

Completely ignoring me, Willy Nelson jumped in the car and sat on the professor's lap.

Frank executed a three-point turn then we headed back down the high street and turned into William Street. The small car, carrying three adult men, struggled on the hill.

'So have you found the heathen yet, Joe?'

The question took me by surprise. 'Who might that be, sir?'

'Why The Moon of course!'

'The Moon?'

'He was an artist. And a great actor.'

I turned in my seat. The professor was staring out the window. His skinny arms and shoulders were white, his skin goose pimpled.

Willy Nelson gave a low growl.

'Do you know who The Moon is, sir?'

'Of course. But I could never tell.'

'Why?'

'Because!'

To the relief of the Korean engine, we swung into the professor's driveway.

Frank cut the motor but left the headlights on.

The professor leaned forward between the two front seats. 'Promise you won't tell Jennifer?' he said urgently.

'Tell Jennifer about what, sir?'

'Oh, come on man!' He raised his voice. 'You know very well what I'm talking about!'

'Remind me so I don't put my foot in it.'

He flung himself back in his seat. The air escaped in a little *pffff*. 'Is it any wonder you lost everything?'

'Are we talking about something you did, sir?'

The front door opened, and Roxy appeared. Squinting through the headlights' glare she stared at the vehicle in her driveway.

We only had a few seconds before she would realise her father was in the back of the car. I grabbed the professor's wrist.

In turn Willy Nelson launched himself and fastened his razor-sharp teeth onto my forearm.

I didn't care. 'Are you The Moon?' It came out in a low hiss. Even to my ears it sounded dangerous.

The professor looked me in the eye and began to laugh. Soft and low at first, then building in volume and strength until tears glistened and trembled on his lashes.

'Are you?' I yelled, shaking his arm.

Roxy appeared at the car window. 'What's going on here?' Then, she realised who was in the back seat. 'Daddy?'

Frank climbed quickly out of the car. 'We found him roaming the streets, Rox.'

I released the professor's arm and was relieved when Willy Nelson did likewise with mine. Then I too got out of the car.

'Is he okay?' Roxy's voice was rough with concern.

'Yeah, he's fine, just a bit worked up.' Frank said.

She opened the back door. 'Daddy, where were you? I thought you were in bed.' She helped her father out of the car.

'Oh, I do wish you could have been there, Jennifer,' the professor said. 'Impromptu can be so damn good for the soul.'

'Let's get you back in the house.' She reached for Willy Nelson's rope and handed it to Frank.

'I wouldn't say it was my best performance, not like the old days of course, but I still received a standing ovation.' The professor looked at Frank. 'I want the reviews first thing in the morning, Dickie!'

'Come on, Daddy.' Roxy tenderly led her father towards the house.

'Don't forget to pay Joe and his little brother, they've been most helpful.'

'I will.'

'Book them again for next week.'

'Okay, Daddy.'

Frank put Willy Nelson back in the car then we followed Roxy and the professor into the house.

I checked my arm and was grateful that Willy's fangs hadn't pierced the skin.

'Where was he?' Roxy asked us after putting her father to bed. She wore an oversized T-shirt and track pants.

'Walking down the high street,' Frank said.

'He was in bed. Must've slipped out the back.' Roxy closed her eyes and a collage of sadness, concern and defeat washed over her face.

'Hey.' Frank placed his arm around her.

'I don't know what else I can do.' She stifled a sob. 'I can't lock him up.'

'Can't you get some assistance?' I said.

'This is Candle Stick Bay we're talking about.'

'Has he taken off before?'

Roxy nodded and sighed 'Yes, but it's happening more often. I know exactly what I've got to do … I've just been prolonging the inevitable.'

'A nursing home?' Frank said.

Roxy grabbed a tissue from a box on the coffee table and blew her nose. 'It's the last thing I want to do, but he can't be left on his own any longer.'

'I think you're right, luv,' Frank said softly. 'There's no knowing what could happen to him out there.'

'Do you know when he last took off?' I asked, and immediately regretted it. The sudden crease between Roxy's eyes condemned my lack of tact.

'What … you don't think?' The crease deepened to an angry

scowl. 'Surely you're not suggesting my father had anything to do with the deaths?'

'No. I didn't mean that. I was just—'

'Thank you for bringing Daddy home, I appreciate it.' Her tone indicated we were dismissed. 'I've got an early start in the morning, so if you don't mind.'

Frank shot me a warning glance. 'Sure thing, Rox. You take it easy, eh? And if there's anything me and Pat can do, just holler.'

'Thanks Frank.' She avoided eye contact with me.

We climbed back into the car.

'You don't seriously think the old Prof could be the serial killer you're looking for, do you, Joe?' Frank said.

Willy Nelson jumped onto Frank's lap and smothered the publican in doggie kisses.

'Let's just say out of everyone in the town, at the moment Professor Stephens is at the top of my list.'

'Crikey! But now he's senile so you'll never know.'

The words were like the D minus you got on your school report when you were expecting a B. Disappointment, shock, reality. Could it really end like this?

We drove up to Babs Bingle's house but there was nobody there.

'Looks like we've got another guest at The Great Northern tonight,' Frank said as we headed back to the town.

To my utter shock, Willy Nelson suddenly jumped from the back seat and landed on my lap. My whole body tensed but the little white fox terrier sat upright and looked through the windshield.

'Ha ha! He likes you, look!' Frank said.

I didn't dare move.

Frank chuckled. 'Stroke him, Joe.'

'No, I can't.'

'Go on. He likes it when you rub his ears.'

I cautiously lifted my right hand. With my fingertips, I touched the back of the dog's head.

He responded by twisting his neck slowly from side to side.

'See?'

Digging my fingers into his short fur, he pushed backwards and I could feel the strength in his neck.

'Now tickle his ears and he'll love you forever!'

With both hands I began to massage behind his ears the way Frank had earlier.

There was a groan followed by a little whimper.

I rubbed harder and Willy Nelson began to shuffle on his backside.

'You're the master now, Joe,' Frank said parking the car in a small carport beside the pub.

I was feeling kind of good. Like I'd overcome an adversary. I was in control and Frank was right, I was the master.

When the engine died, Willy Nelson stood up, raised his tail in the air and farted in my face.

44

I'd hardly slept that night—the wheels of my mind weren't just turning, they were spinning out of control. But for some reason, I'd woken with the image of a car in my mind—a dark blue sedan with partially hidden lights in the front grille. DI Cooper's car. I'd forgotten all about it.

At first light, I headed up the hill to where the Telstra truck was usually parked. Behind me, a burning red orb shimmered just above the horizon, its heat yet to reach the land. Small, scattered clouds were streaked with tones of purple, scarlet and orange.

By the time I'd left the road, climbed the track and stepped onto the bitumen at the top, I was what the Aussies would describe as buggered! My legs were crying out for a rest, but curiosity drove me on. When I turned the bend at the summit, I wasn't surprised that DI Cooper's car was still blocking the gate. But on closer inspection, the doors were unlocked and the keys were still in the ignition. Was it strange that Lambert hadn't reported this? Wouldn't the butler at least have moved the car?

I was debating whether to buzz the intercom when I heard a familiar splutter coming up the hill. It was Roxy's Kombi.

She pulled up behind the sedan and stepped onto the road. 'Whose is that?' Her lack of greeting told me she was still angry with me.

'Um … not sure.' I didn't like lying to her, but it was easier to play dumb.

She flung herself back into the driver's seat, slammed the door, reversed, and parked to one side of the gate. Turning off the engine she grabbed a bag from the passenger seat then climbed from the van again. 'Bloody inconsiderate whoever it is.' She typed in a four-digit code on the intercom keypad.

The gates clunked and began to open slowly.

'Do you mind if I come along?'

Roxy frowned.

'I need to talk to Mr Lambert.'

'Still snooping around then?' She spoke as if she were addressing a naughty child.

I tried to play the situation down with a mischievous smile. 'Always.'

The house was quiet, playing host to the early morning shadows.

The sun's heat was beginning to chase away the pockets of cool air and the sky was a pearly grey.

A magpie warbled from the trees somewhere at the back of the property.

Roxy fumbled with a bunch of keys, found the one she was looking for and placed it in the keyhole of the front door. She tried to turn the key, but it wouldn't move. Frowning, she turned the key in the opposite direction and it clicked over. 'Strange,' she said. 'It wasn't locked. Andrew would never leave the front door unlocked.'

I stepped up beside her. 'Maybe he's already awake.'

'You obviously don't know Andrew.'

My concept of an English butler's duties—early to rise, baking bread, polishing shoes, preparing breakfast for the master—was probably romantic, old-fashioned and very American. The tone of Roxy's reply told me there was something about the butler I'd either missed or didn't know. 'What do you mean?'

She shook her head and pursed her lips. 'Nothing.' She pulled down the handle and opened the door. 'Just don't wake him!'

I followed her through the lobby and toward the room I remembered as William Lambert's study.

'Mr Lambert sleeps in here most nights,' Roxy whispered. She opened the door slowly.

The room was a mess. Papers were strewn about the floor. A half-empty glass of Scotch sat on the desk. No Lambert.

'Must've crawled off to bed last night,' Roxy said. 'Wait here. I'll go and wake him.'

Being alone in William Lambert's office was an opportunity I wasn't going to pass up. As soon as Roxy was out the room, I set to work. There were papers on the floor that looked like they'd fallen there from the printer. On close inspection they were letters from the States. I read through a few of the sheets. Some were from Random House Publishing, New York. Others were from an attorney acting on behalf of the publisher. Not only was Random House cancelling Lambert's contract, but they were also suing him for breach of contract. If Lambert lost the suit, he'd be responsible for paying back millions in advances.

No wonder he was drinking. I nudged the computer mouse on the desk and the large Mac came to life. Images of men in bondage being whipped and tortured by leather-clad women filled the screen.

Suddenly there was a scream from above.

I rushed from the office and into the foyer.

Roxy was bolting down the stairs, sobbing hysterically.

'What is it?' I stepped in front of her and grabbed her shoulders.

Unable to speak, she was a gibbering mess, trembling violently.

I pushed her into the nearest chair then took the stairs two at a time.

On the landing, eight doors faced me. The only one open was farthest from the stairs. I raced towards it—my instincts preparing me for what I was about to find. I stepped into the room and almost instantly, the weight of twenty-five years crashed down on me. I was in the alley again staring down on the body of Jacqueline Sanchez, next on Venice Beach, then in the grounds of the Beverley Hills Hotel, then in a public toilet in Downtown LA. Each murder scene flicked before my eyes like a gruesome slideshow.

Returning to the present, I was standing in the doorway of a palatial bedroom. Taking centre stage was a massive four-poster bed. Any doubts I might've had about The Moon being in Candle Stick Bay were washed away into the plush carpet along with the blood that dripped from the walls. The bed linen, soaked crimson, was drawn over someone.

Treading carefully, I approached the bed, leaned over and carefully drew back the sheet.

The stench of fresh blood is one you never forget and never get used to. Even with all my experience, my stomach jolted and I had to clamp my mouth shut to not vomit. Although I could only see part of the torso, it seemed that the body was naked. And headless. As much as I wanted to look for clues, I couldn't. I was standing in a crime scene, and I no longer had any official capacity. I needed to get back to the police station and call Fat Bobby on the two-way.

I replaced the sheet, retraced my steps and left the door open so everything would remain as I'd seen it.

I found Roxy outside, slumped on a wooden bench, still sobbing. I sat down, gathered her in and awkwardly patted her back.

'What is it, what's happened?' The voice was shrill.

I looked up to see Maud trotting towards us.

'Maud, what are you doing here?'

'I work here now.'

Damn. The last thing I needed was the town gossip poking her nose around a crime scene. But she was here so I decided to use her. Taking her by the arm, I led her over to the garden beds and out of Roxy's earshot. 'Maud, something terrible has happened.'

Her eyes looked as if they were going to pop from their sockets.

'There's been a killing.'
She gasped and threw her hands to her mouth. 'A murder?'
'Yes. William Lambert.'
'Oh my God.' Her eyes searched the house. 'Here? Where?'
'You can't go into the house, it's a crime scene.'
'Oh.'
I waited for Maud to say something else, but she simply stared at me as if lost for words. 'Did you bring your car?'
'Yes, couldn't drive in though, there's a car in the way.'
I glanced over at Roxy. 'Can you take Roxy down to the doctor's please? Explain what's happened?'
Maud nodded vigorously. 'Okay.' That industrious, helpful demeanour was back.
'And Maud ... this is really important ... *please* don't say a word to anyone!'
After they'd left, I should've locked the front door, returned to town, and called Fat Bobby right away on the two-way as I'd originally planned to do. But I didn't. Unless a chopper was sent, it would be hours before a forensic investigation team could reach the scene, possibly even days because of the fire. I know it was wrong, but I decided to do a little investigating on my own first.
I headed back into the house.
Scanning each tread above me, I ascended the stairs on tiptoes. I made my way across the landing. No signs of a struggle anywhere. No knocked over furniture, no blood splashes. I quickly checked the other rooms to make sure there was nobody there. The whereabouts of the butler was foremost on my mind. Had he also been killed? Or was he the killer? Then the pieces began to slot into place. Andrew had been in Lambert's employment for a long time. Had they been together in LA twenty-five years ago? As to whether he was a writer, that remained to be checked. He would've known about Lambert's pseudonym, Stephen Powell. Perhaps he'd borrowed his employer's pen name for his own book?

The murder and decapitation had occurred in the one room—the master suite. The carotid artery had been severed, which was why there was as much blood on the walls and carpets. This would suggest that the head had been removed post-mortem.

It was a familiar scene—one I'd hoped never to witness again. As I locked the front door using Roxy's keys, one fact stood out above all—The Moon was definitely in Candle Stick Bay … and was killing again!

45

Using the call code Fat Bobby had written down and left for me, I managed to get him on the two-way. The LAPD code for a homicide was 187—I had no idea what the equivalent was in Queensland.

'We have a 187 situation. Over …'

There was a pause on the other end then Fat Bobby's voice echoed tinnily down the line. 'Do you mean a 204?'

For obvious reasons, I couldn't mention the word 'homicide' and I had no idea what code 204 meant.

'The Moon is rising. Over' were the only words I could think of.

There was heavy silence.

'Would suggest a return to base immediately. Over.'

'Copy that. On my way.'

Twenty minutes later, the town's only police car swung into the driveway of the station.

Fat Bobby jumped out. His face and clothes were filthy, his eyes bloodshot and tired. I met him at the door.

'Tell me you didn't mean what I think you meant, Joe?'

'I'm afraid I did. There's been a homicide.'

He stopped dead in his tracks and paled. 'Who?'

'Lambert!'

'What? William Lambert? He's dead?'

'Decapitated in his bed.'

He staggered backwards and had to steady himself. 'Shit we need to get out there right away.'

I placed a hand on his shoulder. 'Can I make a suggestion?'

He seemed to be lost for words.

'Have a hot shower and get changed into a clean uniform. While you do that, I'll make coffee and something to eat.'

'We haven't got time for that, we—'

'There's time.' On his face I saw a raging battle between desperation and exhaustion. 'Just take a few minutes. Recharge your batteries.'

He reluctantly agreed and left by the rear entrance.

When Fat Bobby returned, he was clean, fresh and raring to go.

I handed him a mug of coffee and a plate of vegemite on toast that I'd rustled up in the station's kitchenette.

'You bloody ripper!' He bit into the toast.

I started to tell him how Roxy had found the body.

'Where is she?' The concern was obvious in his tone.

'Probably at home now. A little shaken but okay—'

'I need to see her right away.' He searched for his police cap.

'I wouldn't recommend it at the moment. Maud's with her. The doctor's probably given her something to help her relax.'

'Maudie?'

'Yes, she was at the house too. So was I by the way.'

'You were there?' He narrowed his eyes as if struggling to read small print. 'What on Earth would you, Roxy, and Maudie be doing at Lambert's at the same time?'

I explained how I'd gone up to check if DI Cooper's car was still there, that Maud was scheduled to do some cleaning, and how Roxy had arrived for an early training session with Lambert. And he listened quietly as I told him about the murder scene.

'What about this butler bloke? Where's he?'

'Good question. He seems to have disappeared.'

Fat Bobby pressed his face into his hands and kneaded his forehead. When he looked at me again there was desperation in his eyes. 'I'm not equipped for this, Joe. I'm just a country copper looking after a little town.'

'Would they fly someone in from Cairns, or send a boat maybe?'

'I would bloody well hope so.' In two large strides he was at the two-way consul. 'Is there anything else you haven't told me before I call it in?'

I shook my head then waited as Fat Bobby requested urgent assistance for a 204.

The reply wasn't very encouraging. He was told that assistance would be forthcoming at the first opportunity. I would've expected assistance as a priority.

Fat Bobby removed the headset. 'That's all I can do.' He took a deep breath, grabbed his cap and headed for the door. 'C'mon, let's get up to Lambert's.'

I wasn't sure if it was the tiredness clouding his thoughts or that he had never been in this situation before but there were procedures we'd need to abide by. I didn't want to appear as if I were taking charge, so I simply asked, 'Do you have all the equipment we'll need in the car?'

Fat Bobby stopped and turned to face me. 'There should be some rubber gloves and a roll of crime scene tape in the boot.'

'We'll need more than that. Booties? Evidence bags? Markers? A camera?'

'Fuck, I'm glad you're here, Joe!' He rushed to the back room.

I followed him through the door, into the corridor and into the interview slash storeroom.

'There's a camera in the bottom drawer of my desk. The rest of the stuff should be in here somewhere.'

46

'Never thought I'd be doing anything like this,' Fat Bobby said as we covered our shoes with plastic disposable booties and pulled on surgical rubber gloves. Ideally, we should have had paper coveralls on too, but there'd been none in the storeroom.

The key Maud had given me for the front door was shiny and new. I pushed it into the lock.

Armed with a roll of crime scene tape, evidence bags, numbered marker cards, and a camera, we decided to stick together, starting in William Lambert's office. I'd already told Fat Bobby what I'd found earlier, including the letters from the publisher.

'So, it looks like he was about to lose his livelihood,' Fat Bobby said, thumbing through the papers.

'Sure looks that way.' He placed them in one of the evidence bags.

The only other thing of note was that the decanter of Scotch was empty. The cabinet that it sat on, which also housed the refill bottles, was also empty. I recalled seeing about half a dozen bottles the last time I'd spoken with Lambert in this very room just over a week ago.

We searched the rest of the downstairs and found nothing out of the ordinary. If one of the knives on the chopping block were the murder weapon, it had been washed and replaced.

'It might be a good idea to check the rest of the rooms first before going into the master suite,' I suggested as we climbed the stairs.

'Yeah, right.' Fat Bobby stopped on the stairs and turned to face me. 'Listen, Joe, you've obviously had a lot more experience with this kind of thing than me.'

It had been a while, but he was right. Even before The Moon killings, I had attended countless homicides and knew the dos and don'ts.

'So ... you're in charge. Just tell me what I should and shouldn't be doing. I don't want to go touching anything I shouldn't. Is that okay?'

'Of course.'

We checked all of the other rooms first. After an inspection of the closets and ensuite bathrooms, it was apparent that the farthest room on the left was the only other bedroom in use and so must have belonged to the butler.

I noted the Armani and Hugo Boss suits hanging in the closet. 'Seems our butler has expensive tastes.'

'You're not wrong.' Fat Bobby lifted a neatly folded Paul Smith shirt from one of the drawers. He sifted through the drawer with his other hand. 'Ralph Lauren, Lacôste.'

He replaced the shirt, straightened to his full height and placed his hands on his hips. 'Joe, is it just me or is it too obvious?'

I knew what he was going to say but I let him continue. 'What's that, mate?' The little noun slotted itself on the end of my sentence without me realising.

'It's a classic case, isn't it? The bloody butler did it!'

I couldn't argue with him. 'It's beginning to look that way.'

We continued searching the room then went into the ensuite. Nothing out of the ordinary there. I bagged a hairbrush, a toothbrush and a bar of used soap.

The rest of the rooms were like hotel rooms ready and waiting for guests. The bed linen was fresh and crisp. The closets were empty except for the hangers, and there was an identical arrangement of soaps and three sizes of towel in each of the ensuites. The main bathroom was also spotless and exhibited the same toiletries and towel arrangement common to high-end hospitality.

'Okay, when we enter, we need to tread very carefully,' I said as we approached the master bedroom. 'I want to take photographs first before we touch or move anything.'

'Sure,' Fat Bobby took the camera from around his neck and handed it to me.

'I'll go in first and take the pictures, then I'll call you in.' I wondered how many fatalities Fat Bobby would've witnessed during his career. Apart from deaths by natural causes, there would had to have been the odd road accident—probably not as bad as the tanker but still a few nasty sights.

First, I took a series of shots from the doorway of the bedroom—the bloodstained carpet and furniture, the walls that looked in places like they were dressed with a contemporary red-and-white wallpaper design. Then I crept into the room on tiptoes, retracing my earlier steps.

'Holy Jesus Christ!' Fat Bobby said, peering through the doorway.

I entered the ensuite first and while snapping away with the camera I noted that nothing was out of place. An open toothpaste tube lay on the granite vanity top, a single toothbrush stood in a glass, and there was a bottle of antiseptic handwash next to the faucet. Opening the vanity doors, I found the kind of items you would expect to find in a man's bathroom: a selection of deodorants, an electric shaver, toenail clippers, etc. The camera's flash bounced back at me off the white ceramic tiles as I continued taking photographs.

Heading back into the bedroom I snapped close-ups of the walls, the carpet and the furniture then started on the bed. The once-white bed linen was soaked burgundy and pink and reminded me of the pad in the bottom of a meat tray. After a series of shots from varying angles and positions, I carefully peeled back the sheet with one hand while using the camera with the other.

Although of a religious nature, I was sure the affirmations Fat Bobby recited, while he watched me go about my work, were of the semi-atheist kind.

Flirting with The Moon

'Can you help me here, please, Sergeant?' I said, turning to face Fat Bobby.

Like a shy schoolkid suddenly being called out in front of the whole school, Fat Bobby stepped forward, his eyes locked firmly on mine. 'What do you want me to do?'

'Just pull back the sheet carefully as I take pictures.'

He tiptoed into the room, careful to tread in my steps, and followed my signal to take up position on the opposite side of the bed. His wide-eyed gaze lowered slowly, and with trembling hands he grasped the top edge of the sheet and peeled it back.

Click, click, click, click. 'Slowly!' *Click, click … click … click.*

'I think I'm gonna throw up, Joe,' Fat Bobby said when the decapitated corpse was revealed.

'That's okay. Go outside and get some fresh air. I'll finish up here.'

'Cheers.' He rushed from the room.

I carried on taking photographs from all angles, close-ups mainly. When I was satisfied I'd taken enough, I exited the room and placed the camera on the floor just outside the bedroom door.

Normally a coroner would be the first to examine the body and would be able to determine a pretty accurate time of death but, as the closest one was five hundred kilometres away, I was it. I'd thought about bringing the doctor in but decided against it. The crime scene had to remain intact. The fewer people trudging through the house, the better.

I returned to the room. Bending to examine the body more closely, I realised I'd seen this before. The clean surgical cut, almost like the head had been removed with a single action, severing the vertebrae with no evidence of sawing. Definitely the work of The Moon.

Going by the amount of blood splattered on the walls and around the room, I concluded that the victim's carotid artery had been severed while he was still alive. When the body had just about bled out then decapitation had taken place.

I turned my attention to the closet and drawers. The contents were pretty much the same as those in the butler's room, except there were more designer labelled clothing and suits. Returning to the ensuite, I bagged the entire contents of the bathroom vanity. I decided against placing markers because there were no signs of a struggle, no weapon, and no damage to any part of the room except for the bloodstained walls.

Fat Bobby was crouching in the shade with his head low.

'You okay, Bobby?'

He glanced up. His face was sickly white. 'Just about puked me ring up, but she'll be right.'

I carried the evidence bags back to the car.

Fat Bobby followed, gulping air. 'Find anything?'

'Not really. Do you know where the garage is?' In our search of the ground floor, we hadn't come across a door that led to the garage.

'Over there,' Fat Bobby pointed behind me.

To the far right of the building in the shade of some trees and separate from the house was a triple garage.

We found an entrance at one side.

Still wearing rubber gloves and booties and with the camera around my neck, I turned the handle—the door was unlocked. I opened it and leaned in. In the darkness, I rubbed my hand along the inside wall until I found the light switch. The strip lights across the ceiling flickered and beneath them classic chrome glistened like gems in a jewellery store. The nearest car was a silver 1964 Aston Martin DB5. 'Wow!' The single breathy word echoed inside the space.

Although three cars were parked inside the garage, there was plenty of room to walk around them. There was a black Range Rover Sport and the Mercedes that Lambert had used when he'd come down to the town.

I stepped into the garage with Fat Bobby on my heels. My attention fell on something along the back wall. A large chest freezer.

Fat Bobby must've followed my gaze. 'You thinking what I'm thinking?'

We walked slowly towards the white chest, a gentle hum breaking the silence. Reaching for the handle, I paused and glanced at Fat Bobby.

With a grim but determined expression, he nodded. 'Do it!'

I lifted the lid, and our fears were confirmed. Inside, placed among boxes and bags of frozen goods, was a severed head.

Apart from the obvious shock, there was another problem however. It wasn't William Lambert's.

47

Fat Bobby stumbled backwards and steadied himself against the Range Rover. 'Is that—'

'Yes, it is!' I bent over the freezer to get a better look. The eyes were lowered under their lids as if in prayer. The hair was curly, black and thick, and two large dangly silver rings adorned each ear. It was Babs Bingle—or at least her head.

'This can't be happening, Joe.' Fat Bobby's voice was strangled.

There was nothing to say. At this stage it was pointless moving the head so, leaving it perched on top of the French fries and frozen burgers, I took some pictures.

We checked the cars—none were locked. The interiors were spotless, the trunks empty, and although it seemed as if nothing was out of place, I continued taking pictures.

Fat Bobby was still shocked. 'Babs. I can't believe she's dead!' He kept shaking his head in disbelief. 'Why would anyone want to kill her?'

I guessed his question was rhetorical, so I said nothing.

Leaving the garage, we split up to conduct a thorough search of the grounds but found nothing, so we returned to the cruiser, removed our gloves and booties, and tossed them into the trunk.

I was pretty sure the killings were the work of The Moon and because of that I feared where Lambert's head and Babs Bingle's body would turn up. A macabre image of the two combined flashed across my mind. Although it was now clear that The Moon was responsible for the killings, there were still obvious differences that couldn't be overlooked. Twenty-five years ago, The Moon killed once a month and always on the night of the new moon, and each time the body was displayed to fulfil the killer's sick idea of a production. Here we'd had four deaths in less than one week: Geoff Lambert, DI Cooper, William Lambert, and Babs Bingle. The Moon had changed his MO. Perhaps these killings were self-preservation? I was beginning to suspect so.

We locked up the property and climbed into the cruiser.

'Okay, we need to get back, write up a report and call it in,' Fat Bobby said as we passed the sensor that opened the front gates. 'And we need to get the coroner and a team out here right away.'

I was glad to see he had regained his composure and was taking charge once more. 'What about the body?'

'Hmmm ... we can't leave him there.'

This was tropical Queensland. It would only be a matter of hours before the flies and heat began reclaiming the flesh. We decided to return with Bluey's truck and place Lambert's body and Babs's head in the back along with DI Cooper's corpse.

Back at the station, while I carefully removed the evidence bags and equipment from the cruiser, Fat Bobby contacted Cairns and requested immediate back-up.

'Affirmative ... assistance on the way,' came the reply.

After returning to Lambert's with the truck, we stood at the front door wearing fresh rubber gloves and booties.

'Are you going to be okay?' I asked Fat Bobby.

'Yeah, should be right. I'll let you know if I'm gonna puke.'

We decided to wrap the headless body in the sheet that covered it. Flies were already present and there was a persistent drone as they buzzed around the gaping wound. The corpse was beginning to smell. The air was thick and cloying.

I glanced at Fat Bobby. Although pale, he looked determined. 'Breathe through your mouth,' I told him. 'It makes it easier.'

This time I grabbed the shoulders while Fat Bobby held the feet.

Like furniture removal men moving a rolled-up carpet, we carried the corpse downstairs and out through the front door to the truck. Damn! We'd forgotten to open the back, so we had to place the body on the gravel driveway. When Fat Bobby opened the doors, cool, butchers-shop-air wafted over us.

'HOLY BLOODY SHIT!' He jumped backwards, almost knocking me over, like he'd been stung by a swarm of bees.

'What is it?' The doors swung open fully.

A head stared back at me. This one was looking upwards, its facial expression frozen in the grasp of fear. And once again, it wasn't William Lambert's. It belonged to Andrew the butler!

'What the hell's going on, Joe?' Fat Bobby said for what must have been the tenth time that day. He began to pace like a fighter minutes before a bout. 'This is out of control.' His voice and body trembled in unison.

There was something else in the truck. I climbed into the back. Beside the shrouded corpse of DI Cooper was another body, except this one wasn't wrapped in anything. It lay on the cold metal floor and, although headless, from the soft shape, the purple sarong and the silver bangles and rings I knew who it was. 'Bobby, you better come here,' I called over my shoulder.

'Babs?' Fat Bobby said from the doorway.

'Yes, afraid so. Let's do what we have to do then get back to town.'

I peeled the butler's head from the floor of the truck. It came away with a sickening *sschlup*.

'So, now there's another body *and* another head floating around somewhere,' Fat Bobby said as we laid Lambert's corpse next to Babs's body.

'That's right. Lambert's head and the butler's body.'

'Bloody fuck!'

I left him there while I returned to the garage. I opened the freezer lid and lifted out Babs's head—a bag of frozen French fries came away with it.

It somehow seemed right to place the head of Babs Bingle not on but close to her torso, but it would've been wrong to do likewise with the butler's head near Lambert's body. Instead, I placed it in an empty Golden Mangoes box then we closed the doors on the gruesome scene.

Doctor Elliot's face was grave as he looked at the row of corpses in the back of the truck. 'So, we do have a serial killer in the town.' He unwrapped the sheet from Lambert's body and began his examination.

'Thing is, Doc ...,' Fat Bobby said. '... we haven't found Lambert's head yet, or the butler's body.'

The doctor jerked his head up, visibly startled. 'Eh? Lambert's dead too?'

'Well, yeah.' Fat Bobby nodded towards the third corpse.

The doctor stood up, reached into the mango box, lifted out the butler's severed head, and placed it unceremoniously on the shoulders of the corpse. 'That's no Lambert!'

The body and head belonged to Andrew the butler.

'Fuck a duck! How'd we miss that, Joe?' Fat Bobby scratched his head.

I couldn't believe it either. In all the surreal pandemonium, we'd assumed that because we'd found the headless body in William Lambert's bed, that it must've been him. I could feel the heat in my cheeks rising under the doctor's probing gaze.

'So Lambert's the killer!' Fat Bobby said.

'And if he is ... he's still in town ... somewhere!' I added.

We locked up the truck and reminded the doctor to run the engine for thirty minutes every couple of hours to keep the batteries topped up.

In silence, we headed back to the police station.

'We need to handle this with the assumption that the coroner and the homicide team won't be here for a while yet.' Fat Bobby handed me a cup of coffee.

'Right. What are you thinking?'

'We must contain the situation. The last thing we need is panic in the town.'

My thoughts exactly. And I was relieved to know we were both on the same page. 'What about Lambert? Can you think where he might go?'

Fat Bobby narrowed his eyes in concentration. 'Nowhere comes to mind.'

'Was he close to anyone in town?'

'Nah, too up himself.'

I wasn't about to take it for granted that William Lambert was The Moon but the evidence sure was beginning to mount up: bodies found on his property; DI Cooper's car abandoned at his gates; Stephen Powell, a pseudonym he used for a school essay. The two opposing halves of my detective's mind were churning away independently of each other, separating the fors and againsts, the positives and negatives, like a postal sorting machine.

48

We decided to call another town meeting. Although it may have seemed strange to want to share the news of the incidents, we also had to take into account the welfare and safety of the townsfolk. We needed to bring the town together in the hope that honest communication might suppress panic. We decided not to use Maud and Molly to get the word out this time. After all, there was a serial killer on the loose. 'Do you have a tannoy on the cruiser?'

'Bloody good idea, Joe!'

With me sitting in the passenger seat feeling kind of redundant, we cruised the entire town in the space of fifteen minutes. Fat Bobby's voice echoed through the streets as he spoke into the two-way handset that he'd switched to external. 'Please be advised, there will be a town meeting at four pm at the Yacht Club!'

It was late afternoon. Fat Bobby still needed to take a statement from Roxy, so we headed out to her place. I leaned forward in the passenger seat of the cruiser and looked up at the sky. Thick cloud was rolling in from the ocean and the wind was blowing noticeably stronger. 'Looks like it might rain.'

'Let's hope so. Firies need all the help they can get. This wind won't help, but.'

We pulled into Roxy's driveway and parked behind a white station wagon.

Silvia Stanton answered our knocking.

'How is she, Silv?' Fat Bobby asked.

'She's as well as can be expected. Just had a bite to eat.'

'That's something I s'pose. Can we come in?'

Silvia ushered us in. Roxy was sitting in her father's winged chair.

Fat Bobby was across the room in three strides. He knelt beside her. 'Hey, Rox. How you feeling, love?'

'I'm okay.' She spoke in a whisper. Her blue eyes were puffy, and her hair was scraped back into a ponytail.

'That's good. Listen I need to ask you a few questions about what happened this morning. Think you're up to it?'

Roxy nodded.

Fat Bobby stood up, reached into the breast pocket of his shirt, and withdrew a notepad and pen.

I already had mine in hand, so I sat down on the couch.

'So how come you were at Lambert's this morning, Rox? Had he booked a session?'

'Mr Lambert hired me to train him three mornings a week. He'd paid a month in advance.'

'When was the last time you saw him?'

'Over a week ago. We've only had three sessions in as many weeks.'

'Why's that?'

'Because he was either too hungover, or just wasn't there.'

'Wasn't there? What ... gone away on business?'

'No, he goes for walks out in the bush. Or he'd likely be at—' Roxy cut herself short and looked away.

'Be at where? Go on, it's okay.'

'I shouldn't say. It's pure gossip.'

'It's not gossip if it's relevant to the case.'

Roxy sighed then said: 'He was likely to have been at Babs Bingle's place.'

'Babs's house. Why?'

Roxy raised her eyebrows and looked directly at Fat Bobby. Her expression said, *think about it Bobby*.

'You don't mean?' Fat Bobby glanced my way.

'Yep!' Roxy said. 'Even Maudie didn't know about that one. That's why Mr Lambert didn't want her anywhere near the house. It would only be a matter of time before she found out. Then of course everyone in the town would know.'

'But he hired her to clean for him,' Fat Bobby said.

Roxy shook her head adamantly. 'No, Andrew did.'

'Right.' While he scribbled in his notepad, under his breath he said, 'Old Lambert and Babs, eh? Bugger me.' He finished writing, then continued. 'What do you know about the butler, Rox?'

'Butler?'

'Andrew the butler.'

Roxy frowned. 'Bobby, Andrew wasn't a butler.'

'What?'

'Andrew was Mr Lambert's manager.'

'You're kidding. But he acted just like a butler.'

'He was a strange man. It's almost like he enjoyed giving that impression.'

All this time I had been quietly transcribing in my own notepad. There was a pattern beginning to form. 'Was he gay?' I intervened.

'Most definitely!' Roxy said.

'What about Lambert?'

'I'm pretty sure he swung both ways.'

'That might explain what Andrew was doing in Lambert's bed,' Fat Bobby said, shooting me a sideways glance.

'That wasn't Mr Lambert's bedroom. It was Andrew's,' Roxy said.

'Oh really?' Another glance in my direction. 'Do you reckon they might have been … you know … in a relationship?'

'I wouldn't know about that.'

'Roxy, can I just ask you about your father?' I said.

The defence shutters slammed down and her whole body tensed. 'He's in bed. Hasn't been out since …' She must have suddenly realised that her father had been out the previous evening. 'Surely you're not suggesting …?'

'Not at all. We just have to explore all avenues.'

Fat Bobby almost appeared to shrink—the baton seemed to have been passed to me again.

'That's ridiculous. My father is ill. He wouldn't hurt a soul.'

I looked at Fat Bobby for support.

'I think all Joe's saying is that he might have seen something while he was out.'

'Bobby, he doesn't remember to put his trousers on.'

'Right, yeah. Sorry, Rox.'

I wasn't about to give in so easily. 'But you said he has his good days.'

'Not so often now.' Her brow lowered and her mouth tightened to a pout.

I hated to see such a beautiful face harbouring contempt towards me. 'Is it possible he could have gone up to Lambert's place last night?'

'No, it is *not*!'

'What makes you so sure?' I said calmly.

'Are you not listening to me?' Roxy jumped to her feet. 'My father is ill. He's fragile.'

Fat Bobby placed a reassuring hand on her shoulder. 'It's okay, nobody's suggesting anything.'

Roxy stood, glaring at me.

'We better head off, Joe.' Fat Bobby made his way to the door. 'You girls know about the meeting, eh?'

'Yes, we'll be there, Bob,' Silvia said.

'If you remember anything else, contact us immediately, please,' I said meeting Roxy's stare.

'Bloody hell, Joe, you was a bit hard on Rox,' Fat Bobby said as we backed out of the driveway.

'You think?'

'Shit, I don't know. Maybe it's me that's too soft.'

49

It was almost an exact replay of the scenario two nights earlier when the townspeople filed into the Yacht Club. They even almost took the same seats. But this time there was no Babs Bingle and no Willy Nelson staring me down.

To my relief, Molly and Kimmy entered the room.

Roxy avoided eye contact as she and Miss Berry helped the professor to his seat.

When everyone was present, Fat Bobby raised his voice to ask for hush. 'What I'm about to tell you isn't easy … I'm not going to beat about the bush but before I start, I need reassurance from every single person in this room.'

'What kind of reassurance?' Dennis Hodge said loud enough for everyone to hear.

'That you all remain calm, keep an open mind, and above all, do not panic.'

'What's happened, Fatty?' Dougie said, his eyes wide with concern.

All I could offer in answer to Fat Bobby's searching glance was a slight nod of support.

As if about to dive off the high board, he took a deep breath. 'There have been two more deaths.'

The room erupted with a collective, 'WHAT?' Questions and cries of disbelief echoed from the walls and ceiling and ricocheted off Fat Bobby as he silently stood his ground.

When the cries died down to a murmur, the man I only knew as George stood up.

Everyone fell silent.

'More accidents?'

'No! Not accidents this time.'

Fat Bobby made no attempt at trying to calm his audience as they erupted once more. Instead, he waited patiently.

George, seemingly the unofficial spokesperson, remained standing and yelled above the crowd, 'QUIET … let the sergeant speak.'

'Thank you, George,' Fat Bobby said. 'There have been two murders in the town …'

If it weren't for George bringing the audience back to order, the meeting would've gone on all night.

'Who, Bobby?' George said.

'William Lambert's butler … um associate … and … Babs Bingle!'

Even George couldn't quell the burst of outrage and fear that followed. I could tell Fat Bobby was exhausted and afraid, and really didn't want to be there, but he needed to take charge. The town needed a leader.

'So I was right, there is a murderer running around the town?' Dennis Hodge said shuffling to his feet.

Bluey, who had been quiet all this time, stood and pointed his finger at me. 'It's him! Can't anybody else see it?' He looked around the room and his bulging eyes triggered a chain reaction of nods. 'Like I keep tellin ya's all. None of this happened until he come!'

'That's right!' Dennis Hodge called out.

Even George joined in. 'There's your murderer, Bobby!'

'Come on folks, that's ridiculous!' Frank the publican said also standing. 'Joe's not a killer. He's a copper!'

'Not anymore he's not,' Dennis Hodge said.

'I reckon it's about time this Yank told us why he's *really* here,' Bluey growled.

I leaned into Fat Bobby's side and whispered in his ear, 'I'm going to have to tell them.'

'Tell them what?'

'About The Moon. About my past. Why I'm here.'

Fat Bobby nodded warily.

For the next hour, I relayed the whole story from start to finish. I didn't leave a thing out, not even the details of the murders twenty-five years ago in LA.

'So now you know everything,' I said, grateful that the audience had remained quiet and allowed me to finish.

'And do you know who the killer is?' George said.

Suddenly Professor Stephens jumped to his feet. 'This is preposterous!'

'Daddy, it's okay,' Roxy said trying to guide her father back into his seat.

'You've stolen my story. You low-life, thieving scum!'

'Sit down, Daddy.'

Miss Berry tried to help by pulling gently on the professor's other arm.

'For over twenty years I have been writing this play. And you think you can just walk in here and steal it?'

'Shhh, Daddy.' Roxy and Miss Berry managed to push him back into his seat.

'I'll sue. He'll never work in this town again,' the professor mumbled to nobody in particular.

'What's being done, Bobby?' Dennis Hodge demanded.

'We've opened an investigation—'

'But how are you going to catch the killer, man?' George said.

'We could be killed in our own beds!' Bluey yelled, rising from his chair again as if preparing to dash from the room.

'The CIB will be arriving shortly from Cairns. There'll be plenty of police officers here to protect us.'

'But how are they going to get in? Roads are all blocked,' Dennis Hodge said.

'By boat. Should be here anytime now.' I looked at my watch as if their arrival was imminent.

Dennis eyed me suspiciously as if he knew I were lying.

The wind had lifted quite noticeably over the last hour. Intermittent gusts, each seemingly stronger than the last, rattled the Yacht Club windows, plastering them with a sheet of transparent beads. As if on cue, the biggest gust yet hit the side windows and shook them like sails.

'Bit rough out there for a boat, Mr Dean,' Dennis said.

Frank the publican stood. 'Listen folks, we've got quite a few empty rooms at the pub. Pat and I will be happy to open them up free of charge to anyone who wants to stay overnight.'

I noticed the loving smile on Pat's face as she looked up at her husband.

'That's a great idea. Safety in numbers, people!' Fat Bobby said. 'In fact, if you don't mind, Frank and Pat, I'm going to insist that everyone return to the pub.' He scanned the room as if trying to make eye contact with everyone present.

Pat rose and stood beside her husband. 'If you can bring some sheets and blankets, that will help. We won't have enough beds or rooms, but we can make do.'

Another gust of wind hit the windows, this time so hard it startled everyone in the room.

After the meeting, Fat Bobby and I returned to the police station so he could check in with Bruce and Pete as to the situation with the fire. As we drove from the Yacht Club, the wind and rain were lashing down across the bay and an uncharacteristic swell was causing the boats in the harbour to bob and groan.

Back at the station, after a lengthy discussion over the two-way with both Bruce and Pete, Fat Bobby learned that the fire was still out of control and although the rain was welcome, the wind that it rode upon wasn't.

'What a bloody mess,' Fat Bobby said, replacing the two-way handset.

'Just suppose you were out in the woods walking.' I raised my hands and emphasized the word walking with inverted commas. 'Would you stay out in the rain or head home?'

'Lambert you mean? Might be worth taking a look.'

I agreed but Bobby suggested we make sure everyone was safely in the pub first. Then our investigation could begin proper.

50

By the time we entered The Great Northern Hotel, people were arriving carrying bedding and supplies. In the true spirit of Australian mateship, Pat and Frank had the situation well and truly under control. There were even plates of sandwiches on the bar. Frank was serving drinks while Pat, Silvia and Maud were bustling around helping folks find a space to bed down. Rather than a first come first serve basis, Pat had allocated the rooms upstairs to the elderly. I'd happily given up mine as had the few tourists that were still present.

Frank was cleaning some glasses behind the bar.

I sauntered across. 'Is Molly here yet?' I tried to keep my tone casual, but even I heard the anxiety in my voice.

'Haven't seen her, mate.'

Concern welled within me like a boiling pot but then the thermostat kicked in as Molly and Kimmy entered the room, arms piled high with sleeping bags, pillows and blankets.

'Okay everybody, if I could just have your attention for a moment,' Pat called out above the din. She stood on a chair so everyone present could see her. 'Obviously there aren't enough rooms, so we'll all have to camp down here. Is everyone okay with that?'

'No worries,' Bluey slurred from his stool, obviously relishing the thought of a night in his favourite place.

Scanning the room, I made a mental note of who was present. Miss Berry sat chatting with a young woman and her two small children. Dennis Hodge sat with Dougie, Johno and the man I only knew as George on stools at the far end of the bar. Most of the other faces were familiar by now. I couldn't see Roxy and her father. Maybe they had a room.

'Perhaps we need to do a head count,' I whispered to Fat Bobby.
'Good idea. Hey Pat, can we get everyone down from upstairs?'
'No worries,' Pat said but Maud was already on her way.

I was relieved when Roxy entered on her father's arm. The professor held his chin high. 'Good evening. Thank you for coming. Oh, you are too kind!' Striding through the crowd, he nodded to his imaginary fans.

There was a sudden boom of laughter from the far end of the bar. I craned my neck—Dougie was acting out the punch line to one of his jokes. He was also the only one laughing.

Dennis Hodge, sitting on one of the bar stools, met my gaze then quickly looked away. Over the next couple of minutes, every time I glanced his way, I caught him watching me, only to look away each time. Something was on his mind. When I approached him, his face turned red, and his body seemed to shrink as if he were trying to hide.

'You all right, Dennis?'
'I'm fine, Mr Dean, thank you for your concern. Well, apart from the fact that I'm probably in the same room as a killer.'
'Is there something else on your mind?'
The pause and the squint told me there was.
'Something you need to talk about?'
He lowered his head and his voice. 'Yes, there is. Something very important.'
'Do you want to go somewhere we can talk?'
He shuffled on his backside then climbed awkwardly down from his stool. 'There's something you need to see.'
Glancing around I saw Fat Bobby talking with Roxy.
Dennis grabbed my arm. 'Might be best you don't tell him.'
'Why's that?'
'You'll see.'

Something was telling me I should've told Fat Bobby where I was going as I followed Dennis out of the hotel, but it was too late. We made our way through the driving rain, his limp making the short distance to the postal van a little way down the street, a wet, uncomfortable journey.

I needed to be on my guard. For all I knew, this guy, however unlikely it seemed, could've been The Moon, and for the first time since leaving the police force, I wished I'd had a firearm with me. 'So, what is it you need to tell me, Dennis?' I asked as we climbed into the van.

'For a detective, you seem to be very trusting, and if you don't mind me saying, a little naïve.'

My silence was an invitation for him to continue.

'You've got to know the townsfolk since you've been here. A friendly lot, aren't they?' He narrowed his eyes. 'Until you scratch below the surface that is. Then they start to pull together, protect their own. Think about this, Mr Dean, would you protect your loved ones no matter what?'

My frown prompted him to get to the point.

'Things are different here in this cursed little town, more primitive than you'd ever guess. Until now, there's been no crime in Candle Stick Bay. Don't you find that odd?'

'There's crime everywhere.'

'That's right, but what happens when a crime is committed?'

'We punish the offender.' I think I knew where Dennis was going with this.

'Exactly. Just as Geoff Lambert was punished!'

'What are you trying to tell me, Dennis?'

'You've spent some time with Fat Bobby. How do you find him?'

'What do you mean?'

'Have you noticed anything out of the ordinary—mood swings, secretive?'

'No.'

'That's odd because he's well known for his bad temper.'

I certainly hadn't witnessed as such. 'Dennis, I'm not sure what this is about but—'

'Remember when you both came enquiring about the owner of the post box?'

'Number twenty-four? Yes.'

'Well Fat Bobby already knew who it belonged to. Sometimes he collected the mail.'

'Are you saying Fat Bobby is protecting the professor?' It was hard to believe.

Dennis shook his head. 'Oh, not just Fat Bobby. Fat Bobby and friends, you could say.' He reached over his seat, produced a newspaper from the back of the van, and handed it to me.

The front-page headline read: "Police no nearer to finding missing backpacker in Far North Queensland!"

I read some of the article about an English backpacker who went missing close to Candle Stick Bay. 'Surely you're not saying Fat Bobby knew anything about this?'

'That's just one of the missing person cases.' He was suddenly the major shareholder in my attention stock. 'Do you know how many backpackers have gone missing in this area over the last twenty odd years?'

'Are you saying there's been more killings?'

'Here's a question for you—apart from yourself, who knew about the detective coming up from Cairns?'

Bang! Bang! Bang! We both jumped at the sudden loud knocking on the side of the van.

Fat Bobby appeared at the passenger window.

I was about to open the door when Dennis grabbed me by the arm once more. 'If you don't believe me, see for yourself.'

Bang! Bang! Bang!

'Don't say anything about what I've said. Just keep a close eye out. Now that you know, you'll start to see things clearer.'

I shook my arm free and climbed from the van.

'There you are. Bloody hell, Joe, you had me worried,' Fat Bobby said.

The three of us headed back to the pub, heads down through the rain.

'Sorry,' I said as we entered the foyer. 'Dennis needed to talk to someone.'

Fat Bobby brushed his shoulders, sending a flurry of raindrops over the floor. 'Oh, he *did*, did he? And you thought you'd oblige.'

'I should've told you where I was going. Sorry again.'

'If you've got anything you need to say, Dennis …' The policeman tapped his chest with his index finger. '… you come and see me. I'm the authority around here. Do you understand?'

'Yes, Bobby. We were just having a chat, that's all.'

'I bet you *were*. Meanwhile, Joe we've got a situation.'

51

'It's the professor, he's gone walkabout again,' Fat Bobby said.
'How did he get away?'
'He went for a leak. Slipped out the back.'
'Wasn't anybody watching him?'
'Roxy was waiting for him in the foyer. Must have nicked out the beer garden door.'
There was a fire door in the toilets leading out to the beer garden. The professor could easily have let himself out.
'Trouble is, Roxy's gone out looking for him.'
'Damn!' The possibility of Roxy being taken by the Moon and the effect it would have on the townsfolk, especially Fat Bobby, was unthinkable. But if the professor was the killer, would he harm his own daughter?
'We'll need to split up. You go one way, I'll go the other. Frank can't get away, but he said we can use his car,' Fat Bobby said.
Frank's little Hyundai was automatic transmission, thank God! The steering wheel was on the wrong side of course, but I wasn't too concerned about that.
Fat Bobby would check Roxy's house and if there was no sign of them there, he'd head up the hill and loop the upper town slowly with his searchlight on.
I'd work my way around the lower streets, stopping off at the Yacht Club and the beach and anywhere else I thought the professor might've gone.

The wind had dropped, but the rain was now pouring straight down, looking like rods of steel. I'd never seen rain like it. In one way, the weather would hinder our search, but in another it could be a blessing. I doubted even a man with Alzheimer's would venture out in it for long.

My search proved fruitless, so I went up to Roxy's house in the hope that Fat Bobby had found them there. The driveway was empty, but I was relieved to find the front door to the house unlocked. 'Hello,' I called out as I entered the building. 'Anybody home?' The living room light had been left on, but there was no one there. I decided to take a quick look around.

From the living room, a small corridor led to two bedrooms and a single bathroom. Peering around the door of the first bedroom, I realised it belonged to Roxy—the fresh smell of perfume, a menagerie of stuffed toys on the bed and a poster of *Kinky Boots,* the stage show, on the wall. I didn't need to look in there. Walking past the open bathroom door, I continued to the final door.

The professor's bedroom was fusty, cluttered. There was a desk and chair, and a single, small bookshelf. Knee-high columns of books, magazines and papers stood randomly around the floor like paper stalactites, and through an open closet I could make out the shadows of hung clothing.

The dark mahogany desk with a leather insert was old and chipped. On it there was a brass writing lamp with a green glass shade, and more stacks of papers. On close inspection, I realised the papers were plays written by the professor. Some were dated as far back as the 1970s.

Many of the books were old clothbound drama teaching manuals. There were also novels by Faulkner and Hemingway.

I opened the top drawer of the desk and gasped. Lying on a criss-cross layer of pens, pencils, erasers, and paper clips was a copy

Flirting with The Moon

of *Flirting with The Moon*. I lifted it out and opened it to the title page where a simple handwritten inscription read: "Thank you!"

A theory was beginning to form in my head. What if The Moon hadn't written *Flirting with The Moon* at all? What if there was a collaboration with a writer? A ghost writer?

Ideas and scenarios were swirling around my head like flashing billboards as I dashed back through the rain and into the car. We needed to find the professor, and there was still the matter of Lambert's whereabouts. Could they be in this together? It made a sick sort of sense.

I pulled into the lane at the side of the doctor's surgery and drove to the back of the building. Our mobile morgue—poor Bluey's truck—was still there. As much as I didn't want to, I decided to check and make sure everything was okay. Thankfully, the rain had slowed quite substantially as I climbed from the car and approached the back of the truck. I was about to open the back door when I heard a voice behind me.

'I suppose you think you're clever.' The familiar voice was encumbered with distain. 'Did you really think I'd stand around while you ruined everything?'

I turned.

The professor was standing right behind me. He was drenched and shivering but his eyes glowed with anger.

'Professor, I've been looking for you.'

He laughed. 'You've been looking for me? And you came all this way to find me, eh?'

'That's right.'

'Well now you've found me. Or should I say *I* found *you*?'

'Perhaps we found each other?'

The professor's laugh turned to a sickly chuckle. 'After all these years you must have known this moment would come?'

'Dreamt about it … planned it—'

'LIAR!' He lurched forward, raising a clenched fist.

I held my ground, didn't flinch.

'You take away the one thing that is dearest to me and you stand there like you own it.'

'You lost nothing. I lost everything!'

'And …' he growled through clenched teeth. '… it serves you right!'

'Why'd you stop?'

This question seemed to alter his focus. He blinked and stepped back, but quickly resumed his upright stance. 'I never stopped!'

'There's been more killings?'

He glared at me as if I were scum. 'How dare you? How dare you dismiss my work in such a journalistic way?'

'How many more?'

'You'd really like to know that, wouldn't you? How about I tell you where they're hidden too, eh? Wouldn't that boost your career?'

We stood for a moment staring into one another's eyes as if searching each other's souls. And it was in his vacant stare that I saw the answer. My heart sunk.

A bright beam suddenly illuminated the lane at the side of the surgery chasing away the shadows.

I was forced to shield my eyes. When the light went out, I was relieved to see it was the police cruiser. My sense of relief doubled when I realised Roxy was in the passenger seat.

She rushed from the car. 'Daddy, where have you been?'

'You all right, Joe?' Fat Bobby asked, joining us.

'Officer, arrest this man at once,' the professor said.

'It's okay, Daddy, let's get you out of the rain.' Roxy tried to coax her father towards the cruiser.

'This is the man we've been looking for.' The professor brushed aside his daughter's hand. 'I just caught him trying to tamper with the evidence.'

'And what evidence might that be, sir?' Fat Bobby said.

'Set a trap for him, didn't I! And he stepped right into it. I knew he would.'

'Come on, Daddy, please, you'll catch a cold—'

'He's right!' I held up my hands in surrender. 'I can't lie anymore. Can you ever forgive me, Professor?'

'Never!'

'Then all I can do is apologise. Officer, I'll come quietly.' I held out my wrists to Fat Bobby, gesturing for them to be cuffed.

'At last. The truth will be told!' the professor hailed triumphantly.

'What's going on, Joe?' Fat Bobby whispered to me.

'Please, Daddy, let's go.'

I handed Roxy the keys to Frank's car. 'Take this. Get him back to the hotel.'

With Roxy on his arm, the professor strutted towards the car with his chin held high.

'What the bloody hell?' Fat Bobby wiped the rain, which had turned to more of a drizzle, from his eyes.

'Nothing, just a harmless old man.'

'You don't think he's the killer anymore?'

I detected doubt in Fat Bobby's frown, which was strange, especially as the professor was the father of the girl he loved. I would've expected relief.

We watched as Roxy helped her father into the back seat of Frank's car.

'He's not The Moon!'

'So, what was he banging on about?'

'He's suffering from dementia. He thinks I stole one of his plays.'

'Are you sure he's not the killer?'

'Yes. I saw it in his eyes.'

'You saw it in his eyes? What's that supposed to mean?'

'You may have to trust me on this.'

Fat Bobby shook his head and eyed me cautiously. 'Is that right?'

52

Ironically, there was a jovial atmosphere as we walked into the pub—not quite a party but a friendly gathering.

'Pat, I've got some people I need to talk to,' Fat Bobby said as we approached the bar. 'Do you mind if I use the back room?'

'No, I don't mind. As long as *you* don't mind me and Frank swanning in and out.'

We entered the small room and could hear the loud chatter coming from the bar. But suddenly, as if someone had flicked an *off* switch, all sound stopped.

The abrupt change startled Fat Bobby and I, and we rushed back into the bar.

Everyone was standing in silence, staring at the entrance.

My eyes followed the collective gaze to see William Lambert standing in the doorway.

'What the fuck's everybody looking at?' He stumbled into the room.

Like a mother hen, Pat breezed past us and took him by the arm.

Although he wore a leather jacket, he was soaking wet from the rain. His blond hair was plastered to his head. His cheekbones appeared more prominent than usual as if he hadn't eaten for some time.

'Here love, sit down.' Pat guided him to a stool. 'Can I get you anything?'

'Scotch. A large one.' There was no thank you or acknowledgement of Pat's kindness.

'We've been looking for you, Mr Lambert,' Fat Bobby said.

'Have you? That's nice! Guess you found me, then.'

'There you go.' Pat slid a drink towards him.

Lambert threw a hundred-dollar bill on the bar. 'Keep them coming.'

The din of chatter gradually returned.

Pat poured another double.

'Mr Lambert, have you been home tonight?' Fat Bobby said.

'Might have. Why?' This time he sipped his drink, savouring the taste.

'Finish your drink and follow me please.' Fat Bobby gestured with his arm to the door behind the bar.

'What's this about?'

'We just need to have a little chat.'

Lambert was about to protest when Fat Bobby grabbed his arm and guided him towards the storeroom.

I followed and closed the door behind us.

'Right, this is just between us now.' Fat Bobby pushed Lambert down onto one of the stools. 'Where have you been for the last couple of days?'

'I'm not saying a word without my lawyer present!'

With the speed and dexterity of a prize-fighter, Fat Bobby drew back his right fist and punched Lambert in the mouth.

A mixture of surprise and shock sparked a debate in my mind. *Should I intervene before Fat Bobby goes too far?* Then I remembered Dennis Hodge's words: 'He's got a nasty temper, that Bobby!'

Lambert gasped and tried to pull away, but Fat Bobby held him firm.

I intervened. 'Mr Lambert, you've got nothing to lose by answering a few simple questions.'

My good cop tactic paid off. Lambert's voice quavered with anxiety as he answered each of Fat Bobby's questions.

'So, you reckon you were just walking out in the forest?'

'Yes, I do it a lot. Helps clear my mind.'

'And you've been out walking for two days?'

'Can I … get a drink?'

'No!'

Lambert's hand trembled as he ran it through his hair. 'There's a place where I go. It's an old logger's cabin. It's quite deep in the forest.'

'You go there with Babs Bingle?' I said.

The sudden jolt of Lambert's head betrayed his surprise. 'How did you know that?'

'We'll get to that in a minute,' Fat Bobby said. 'Did anybody else see you at the cabin?'

'No, I doubt anybody else even knows of its existence.' Lambert went on to tell us how he had first stumbled on the shack around six months earlier. And how he had unwittingly witnessed one of Babs Bingle's secret rituals.

'Secret rituals?'

'The cabin belongs to Babs, or so she told me. Doesn't of course, but she claimed it as hers. She's got it all decked out with her crystals and stuff.'

I noted his use of present tense and wondered if this was a clever ploy.

'She's a pagan, worships nature. Oh, and she's a gypsy. A great shag but a massive fruit loop.' As addicts do, he was beginning to twitch and fidget.

'You were having an affair?'

'If you could call it that.'

'So, why'd you kill her?'

'What?' The fidgeting and twitching came to an abrupt halt. 'Babs is dead?'

Flirting with The Moon

Fat Bobby shot me a glance, but I couldn't tell what was on his mind. 'We found her decapitated head in your freezer.'

'No!' He withdrew.

'Did you kill her?'

'No!' As if I really were the good cop, he looked across at me for support.

'Have you been home tonight?'

'Yes, but there was a padlock on the front gate for some reason. I couldn't get in.'

'So, you came down here?' Fat Bobby continued, his iron stare fixed on Lambert.

'Yes, there was no sign of Andrew. I was hungry and I was out of booze, so—'

'When was the last time you saw Andrew?'

Lambert gazed into the air as if he were checking back through a mental diary. 'The day I left for the cabin.'

'Did you have an argument?'

'No.'

'Bet he didn't like you messing around with Babs.'

'He didn't know … had nothing to do with him anyway.' Now his eyes searched the room as if he were looking for an escape exit.

'But you and he were …?' Fat Bobby twitched his eyebrows.

'Don't be preposterous! Me and Andrew?'

Fat Bobby walked around the workspace. 'William Lambert, I am arresting you for the murders of Geoff Lambert, DI Cooper, Andrew … the butler, and Babs Bingle.'

Lambert tottered to his feet. His face had turned an ashen white and his whole body began to twitch. 'What? Andrew's dead too?'

Fat Bobby read him his rights and cuffed him.

'Sergeant, you have to believe me. I know nothing about any of this!'

For the first time, I spotted something real in William Lambert's eyes—fear.

'I won't say another word until I see my solicitor,' he spat.

My heart thumped and my throat had suddenly turned dry. For the last twenty years, I had thought of very little else other than bringing The Moon to justice. I felt like I'd finally made it to the front of a very long line, holding up a coupon. But it somehow didn't feel right. There was none of the adulation I'd imagined, none of the self-satisfaction. It was as if my coupon had expired.

'Are you The Moon?' I blurted out.

He looked down at the floor and remained silent.

All the facts pointed directly to William Lambert being The Moon. He was living in LA at the time of the original murders, he was a writer, his complicated sexuality and personality was like a textbook extract from the profiler's core curriculum.

Now here he was, the prime suspect, in the thick of four new murders, without an alibi. And it was *that* that worried me.

No serial killer in the history of … ever had covered his tracks the way The Moon had. Why would now be any different?

53

I knew I wouldn't be able to convince Fat Bobby of my doubts. Thankfully, my pleading bought me some time to prove a theory that was forming in my head. I'd need to tread very carefully.

'But what if you're wrong, Joe? I can't release him back in there with all them innocent people.'

'But if I'm right … we've got the whole town in one place. There's no one we haven't accounted for. Am I right?'

Fat Bobby nodded peevishly.

'That means … if Lambert is innocent, The Moon is in that room regardless!' I pointed to the entrance of the bar, waiting patiently while the information filtered through Fat Bobby's mind.

'There's no way I'm letting him out of my sight. He's still under arrest.' Fat Bobby unlocked the cuffs, placed one bracelet on his wrist and one on Lambert's.

I headed for the door, but Fat Bobby placed his arm on mine. 'Have you got any more suspects?'

'Not really.' It wasn't a lie, but I'd had an idea that I couldn't share with him.

'You wouldn't be holding back on me would you, mate?'

'No, what about you? Can you think of anyone that fits the profile?'

'Mate … I'm going to come straight out and say it. If we eliminate the professor and Lambert, there's only one other person it could be.'

'And who's that?'

'You!'

Ditto, I wanted to say, but I needed to keep him on side for now. 'I can assure you I'm not The Moon!'

'Got to admit it though, none of this happened until you came to town.'

'So, nothing strange happened before? No unexplained deaths? No missing persons?'

Fat Bobby narrowed his eyes. 'What are you getting at?'

'Nothing. Just trying to put the pieces together.'

'Has somebody been saying something?'

I shook my head dismissively.

'Cos I already told you all that, remember?'

'You did?'

We walked through the bar and I made straight for Dennis Hodge. Like before, he immediately looked away when our eyes met.

'How's it going Dennis?'

'I'm good. Did you say anything to Fat Bobby?' He spoke as if he were addressing the floor.

'No, I didn't.'

Relief seemed to wash over him like a warm shower. His shoulders dropped and his body relaxed. 'Thank God for that. Listen, just disregard everything I said.' He held my stare. 'About Fat Bobby I mean. He's …' He suddenly froze.

'You blokes all right?'

I turned to see Fat Bobby standing behind me.

Inconspicuously cuffed, William Lambert stood beside him looking sheepish.

What happened next, I can only describe as pure subconscious impromptu.

'Dennis was just telling me about all the backpackers that have gone missing over the years.'

There was an audible gasp from Dennis Hodge, but I hardly heard it. I was busy trying to analyse all three faces at the same

Flirting with The Moon

time. In Dennis' I saw pure fear. In William Lambert's I saw shock. In Fat Bobby's I saw anger.

'Oh, he *was*, was he?'

'Yeah … says they were all murdered.'

'No, I never—'

'What?' Fat Bobby seemed to swell in height and girth as his indignation grew.

'That's not true, Bobby. He's lying.'

'And that you covered up their deaths.'

'BULL … shit!' Fat Bobby yelled but then lowered his voice, realising he was drawing attention. 'That's ridiculous, Dennis. Why would you say such a thing?'

'I didn't. He's lying.' His demeanour had changed from the scared little podgy kid to a cornered, angry rat.

'Well how about we talk about this elsewhere, eh?' Fat Bobby said.

'That's probably what you said to Babs Bingle and Geoff Lambert!' Dennis snapped loud enough for those around us to hear. People began to turn around and stare—in seconds the whole room was quiet.

'Let's go into the backroom, eh?' Fat Bobby gestured calmly with one arm.

While still analysing, my brain suddenly slowed down like a newspaper printing press after rolling out the final page. I couldn't believe it. After all these years, the final piece was hovering before my eyes like a Tetris block, turning slightly and carefully gauging its descent before slotting into place. I looked into William Lambert's eyes and I could tell he knew that I knew. Fat Bobby was glaring at Dennis Hodge. And Dennis? I couldn't read him.

Fat Bobby drew his gun.

There was a scream from the crowd and people scurried to the edges of the room.

'Nobody leaves!' Fat Bobby yelled, the veins in his neck seething like scarlet snakes.

'What's happening, Bobby?' I played dumb.

'Nothing to be alarmed about, folks. Dennis and I are just going to have a cosy little chat.' Fat Bobby reached over to grab Dennis by the shoulder, but Dennis swept away his arm, knocking the policeman off balance.

For an alcoholic, William Lambert moved remarkably quickly. In the split second that Fat Bobby lost his balance, he grabbed the gun with his free hand.

There was another scream from the crowd.

'What the hell are you doing, Lambert?' Fat Bobby yelled righting himself.

'Something I should have done a long time ago.' He raised the gun.

I didn't have time to think. I sprung forward and, with the heel of my right hand, hammered Lambert's forearm across and down.

He immediately dropped the gun.

Still in motion, I swung my left arm around the front of his neck and, like a rugby player executing a high tackle, I slammed him to the ground. Then the air was forced from my lungs as Fat Bobby came crashing down involuntarily on my back.

It all happened in a matter of seconds. Lambert wasn't going anywhere, and neither was I until Fat Bobby decided to move.

By the time Fat Bobby climbed off, I'd already pictured the scene that was about to unfold.

'Give it here,' I heard Fat Bobby say. Then, 'What the hell?'

Lambert flinched as his cuffed hand dragged him from under me. As I stood, I was looking straight at him, and I noticed the blood draining from his face. I didn't need to look to know exactly what he was seeing.

Turning slowly, I was greeted by a face I hadn't seen before. A brand new character. With gun in hand, the eyes danced with an electric energy and a nervous giggle leaked through a self-satisfying smirk.

It was The Moon!

54

Frightened and confused, the townsfolk stared at the person holding the gun.

Although the comb-over and the horn-rimmed glasses were still present, Podgy Hodgy had disappeared to be replaced by his alter ego ... The Moon!

Frank shielded his wife behind the bar.

Dougie, whose face looked completely different without the usual smile—longer, older—stood in silence with Johno and the man I only knew as George.

The King sisters huddled together like mice.

Roxy and her father were seated at one of the tables with Miss Berry, the professor the only person present not looking at Dennis, choosing instead to gaze out the window into darkness. Even Kimmy's attention had been wrenched away from her video game.

Molly's eyes were begging me to be careful as they caught my glance.

Maud Baker stood white and perfectly still as if she'd been turned to salt.

Silvia Stanton froze, holding a plate of fresh sandwiches as if the movie had been paused in mid-action.

The rest of the faces, most familiar, some not, were like those of sheep being herded into a slaughterhouse.

'Are you angry with yourself?' I said, locking eyes with The Moon.

Although there was no sign of damage to his façade, I knew this scored a direct hit.

'You know I am.'

'What a shame, it was a stupid mistake.' I chuckled. A little render crumbled. It was between him and me now. 'Why don't you let everyone go?'

'It's not that easy, is it?'

'Dennis?' Fat Bobby said.

'It hasn't gone to plan has it, Dennis?' I kept my voice at a calm and slightly patronising tone.

'NONE OF THIS WAS PLANNED!' His neck and head seemed to swell and throb.

The theory that had presented itself to me during the interview in the back room with William Lambert had proved correct. But I needed to remain calm, I couldn't risk provoking him too much, not in front of all these innocent people. 'This is between you and me now.'

'I'm so sorry, darling!' He lifted the gun and pulled the trigger.

William Lambert's head jolted backwards. A sickening spray of blood, bone and grey matter exploded from the back of his skull, splattering across the bar like a Jackson Pollock painting. His lifeless body slumped to the ground with an ethereal thud.

Hysterical screams tore through the air and the crowd drew back, huddling against the walls.

Fat Bobby had been pulled down with Lambert's body, he released the cuffs and rushed towards Dennis.

Dennis shuffled backwards and aimed the gun at the cop.

Like a referee, I stepped between them and shot Fat Bobby a let-me-handle-this glance.

Fat Bobby nodded reluctantly and stepped back.

I resumed eye contact with Dennis. 'It was all Lambert's fault, wasn't it?'

'Of course it was! IDIOT!' he growled at Lambert's body.

Flirting with The Moon

A cloud of mental dust rose before my eyes as the final Tetris block dropped into place. 'If he hadn't written the book, nobody would've known you were here.'

Dennis lurched forward and placed the barrel of the gun under my chin.

The women screamed again.

'You think you know it all. YOU KNOW NOTHING!' His eyes bulged beneath his glasses.

'I'm disappointed, Dennis!'

'You're thinking I panicked? Slipped up?' His voice became instantly calm.

'Yes, it's not like you.'

'I can play this game, Joe. If that's what you want.'

Something in the way his expression changed once more, but this time to a nonchalant grin, worried me.

He stepped back and scanned the faces around the room. Then he looked back at me and smiled. 'You never got over your little Latino, did you?'

I didn't answer but I knew exactly where this was going.

'I mean it *was* your fault. You were the one that sent her out, knowing there was a ... what was it you called me ... a maniac on the loose? Not very nice.'

'Let everyone go, Dennis.'

'All in good time. I'm just reliving a fond memory. Humour me, will you?' With the gun still trained on me, he shuffled sideways then walked backwards. His limp was very prominent.

'Don't you do it, Dennis!' I yelled.

'That's the spirit. Gosh it's just like old times. Do you remember how you felt that night, Joe?'

All the emotions—failure, anger, self-blame, and lack of control—came flooding back. I couldn't let this happen again. 'Don't you *dare!*' I snarled.

'See what I mean? It's uncanny. It's just a shame you can't refine it. If only you could have known that a little bit earlier.' He had made his way towards the sidewall where most of the townsfolk were huddled together. Reaching out, he grabbed Molly by the arm and pulled her to him. 'You see you can't really blame anyone but yourself, Joe.' He stood behind her and wrapped his arm tightly around her neck.

Molly whimpered, her terrified eyes searching mine for help.

'You're right. It *is* my fault. I'm the stupid one.' I was struggling to find the right words. 'Let her go, please!'

'Why don't you have a drink, Joe? Then this will all go away again like it did last time.'

'Put down the gun, Dennis!' Fat Bobby said, stepping forward.

'Whoa, careful there, Sheriff. This is between your deputy and me.'

'Then let Molly go!' I said.

'Okaaaay.' Dennis released his arm from Molly's neck and pushed her to one side. He lifted the gun, aimed it at Fat Bobby and casually pulled the trigger.

BANG!

The big man stumbled backwards, clutched his shoulder, and roared like a bear.

The women screamed again and everyone in the room cowered.

Once again, I stepped between Dennis and Fat Bobby so that the gun was trained back on me. 'You alright, Bobby?' I said over my shoulder while trying to remain nonchalant.

Bobby nodded and glared at Dennis.

Dennis threw back his head and laughed. 'See Joe, I'm not such a bad guy after all. I could've splattered his big fat head across the bar with Lambert's.'

'What, so you're showing off now? Just like those bullies you despised so much?' This scored a direct hit. I noted the brief crease in his forehead.

He swung around, pointing the gun at different individuals as if choosing a victim, causing each of them to gasp and tremble.

Flirting with The Moon

As if making his choice, he looked at me from the corner of his eye and grinned. 'Of course. Perfect!'

'No, you don't, you bastard!' Molly snarled, moving in front of Kimmy.

'Oh, I don't mind killing you both. In fact, that would be even better, wouldn't it, Joe?' He lifted the gun to Molly's head.

I suddenly realised that, apart from my son, at that moment Molly Quinn and her niece were the two people I cared about most. 'Leave them be, Dennis. Just take me, do whatever you have to do.'

'But I'm going to do that anyway, Joe. May as well have some fun first. After all, I've gotten the taste for it again.'

'You're better than this Dennis, you're The Moon!'

'DON'T CALL ME THAT!' The angry psychopath was back, but I'd managed to draw his attention away from Molly and Kimmy and back to me.

'Okay. How about Podgy Hodgy then?'

As quickly as his limp would allow, he rushed towards me again and jammed the barrel of the gun between my eyes.

'Or … little man?'

'Don't you try me, Dean!'

'See, I've been thinking about all the killings back in LA—prostitutes, gays. The only one not matching the MO was Sanchez, but then she was a very strong woman, perhaps a bit like your mother?'

'SHUT UP!

He thrust the gun back into my throat, forcing my head up.

'I can imagine how hard it would be for a little guy like yourself.' I didn't know where I was going with it, but my fear was that if I stopped, his attention would return to Molly and Kimmy. Unbelievably, not knowing whether I was about to die or not, I began to sing: 'Podgy, Hodgy, pudding and pie, kissed the girls and made them cry …'

The veins in Dennis' neck bulged once more, and his body trembled and rocked like a volcano about to erupt.

'When the boys came out to play ... Podgy Hodgy ran away!'

I often wonder if there is a moment when a prisoner on death row finally comes to accept his fate. Whether during the long walk from his cell to the place of execution, or the very last moment when the syringe is placed in his vein. I guessed that moment must exist—all fear and anger gone to be replaced by an acceptance of the inevitable outcome. Excuse the cliché but, staring in the eyes of death, I guess you would've expected me to be experiencing that moment. But I wasn't. Even with a loaded gun held at my neck by a psychopathic killer, I somehow still felt in control.

'Everybody's laughing at you, Dennis!'

'SHUT UP!' His trembling voice relayed symptoms of a bullied schoolboy. My hunch was right.

'But you should be used to it by now, surely?'

'You never get used to it.'

I detected a sob. 'So, you made them pay?'

'I showed them ... had too.'

'You did. You were in control.'

He blinked and the corners of his mouth turned slightly upwards. 'Still am in control. You know that?'

'Of course. You're far too clever for my goading. Why don't you let everyone else go?'

Dennis stepped back and lowered the gun slightly 'Okay, everybody out!'

The crowd didn't need telling twice. They raced towards the doorway en masse.

'But Joe, I can't leave you,' Fat Bobby said.

'Go now or die!' Dennis said, aiming the gun at him.

'It's okay, Bobby.'

'It's not okay!' Molly cried out, still shielding Kimmy behind her.

Flirting with The Moon

BANG! Dennis fired the gun into the ceiling. The escaping townsfolk ducked and yelled out in fear as the deafening crack ripped through the air in a cloud of acrid smoke.

I tried to reassure Molly the best I could with an it-will-be-okay look. To my relief, she reluctantly filed out of the room with the rest of the people.

When everybody had gone, apart from the intermittent jingles thrown out from the poker machines across the foyer, the eerie silence that stood between Dennis Hodge and me, was as strong as any wall. We didn't break eye contact. We just stood there scrutinising each other like gunslingers.

'What are you going to do now, Dennis?' I said, finally breaking the silence.

'All in good time, Joe. All in good time.'

'Oh, that's right, I forgot about the need for gratification.'

'Yes. That's what makes us so similar, isn't it?'

I ignored his jibe. 'Why did you stop?'

'Why don't *you* tell me? You seem to know it all.' He chuckled. 'Shame it's taken you so long to figure it out.'

We were in the middle of the room, I with my back to the entrance and the bar to my right.

'Okay, let's see how close I am. Twenty-five years ago you worked in LA as the assistant to an exciting new writer called William Lambert. Soon the relationship, in your mind at least, changed direction when your love for him that you'd harboured since your school days, manifested. But the feelings weren't mutual, were they? William Lambert was a playboy who was enjoying the spoils of his new fame and wealth.'

'He was a slut!' Dennis said affectionately.

'You did have a relationship, but to him it meant nothing, just another casual affair. And you didn't like that because you loved him! How am I doing so far?'

'Don't get smug.'

'It wasn't a good time for you, was it Dennis? All those emotions swirling around in your little head.'

'Be careful, Joe.'

'The bullying from school left such deep scars, didn't it, Podgy?'

'I'm warning you!' The hand that held the gun was shaking.

'And that's where it all started. You first met William Lambert at school, and he was the only one who stuck up for you.' I was delving into the realm of educated guesswork now, but Dennis' reactions told me I was pretty close. 'How old were you when you first fell in love with him?'

'How about we get to the bit where I sliced out the heart of your partner then destroyed your life?'

'I'm coming to that.' I could see that my composure was annoying him. 'At a guess, I would say he was your first and only love. Lambert gave you a purpose. Perhaps you were more than just a pathetic little fat kid who preferred boys instead of girls, after all.' I was very slowly edging my way backwards towards the door as I spoke. I couldn't be sure if he realised it or not, but he was following. 'Lambert didn't give a shit about you. Never did.'

'Just like your wife never loved you, eh? Spooky, isn't it? The similarities?'

'But I never killed anyone!'

'Oh, but you did, Joe. Don't you see? You were responsible for what happened. It was your inadequacy that allowed me to carry out twelve wonderfully planned and executed presentations right under your nose. You were the facilitator; I merely took advantage of the situation. A derisory detective way out of his league. The only thing on your mind was where the next shot of Jack Daniels was coming from. Poor little Johnny grew up without a father. Perhaps it was for the best.'

Ignoring his attempt at turning the tables, I continued relaying my theory. Was I showing off? 'So, unbeknown to Lambert, you followed him to LA, even got a job with the LA postal service for a short time.

Then, after a cleverly staged meeting set up by you to look like a coincidence, you hooked up once more with the love of your life.

'Lambert was pleased to see you. After a year in the eye of the Hollywood machine he was beginning to lose control—too much money, drugs, women, boys, you name it. When a person has everything they could ever desire, they begin to crave the simple things in life. Couldn't get any simpler than Podgy Hodgy—his little bit of ass from Candle Stick Bay.'

He was absorbing hit after hit. I could only wonder what was going through his mind. Until the recent killings, everything in Dennis Hodge's life had been planned with immaculate efficiency.

'But your happiness didn't last. Couldn't. How did it make you feel to have no choice but to sit around while William entertained hookers and rent boys right in front of you?'

'It made me angry.'

'More than angry, I think. You were filled with a bottled-up rage so great, one that had been gradually jackpotting since your schooldays. Something had to give. The little voice you had so far managed to control suddenly became more than just a voice. An alter ego was developing during those teenage bashings, one that evolved and matured over time until it was strong enough to stage a coup!'

'You're a very clever man, Joe. Not clever enough to realise that every little jibe you make will mean more pain later. But clever all the same.' He reached into the waistband of his trousers and extracted a long butcher's knife. Standing with a gun in one hand and a knife in the other, he smiled at me like we were best buddies. He asked me to continue.

'There's just one thing I've never understood.'

'And what's that?'

'Why'd you stop? Was it because William Lambert found out?'

That annoying giggle again. 'Our little story is full of ironies, Joe. Some are so far out there you just couldn't write about them.'

He had obviously realised that we were gradually moving

towards the exit and had counter-moved by slowly shuffling around me until he was between me and the entrance.

'So, what happened?'

'I'm sure you'll agree that the last one—the Latino bitch—was my most daring. I was so proud of myself for that one.' His eyes became distant and glazed as if he were reliving the experience. 'What you don't realise is that it was the one that almost caused my downfall. It was New Year's Eve … well … New Year's Day … morning, still dark of course. The streets were still busy.

'It was shoddy, but I knew it would only be a matter of time before you sent her out for takeaway. Yes, I'd been watching you. There was a pattern. You treated her like a fetch-me-carry-me slave. After … I'd paid a street kid to make the delivery for Detective Joseph Dean. Meanwhile I was making my escape on foot, but I crossed Main Street a little hastily and a drunk driver hit me. Shattered my pelvis and right hip. Hit my head hard. Woke up two days later in hospital.'

'So that's why you stopped, because of your injuries?' I said, still trying to appear calm.

'Ironically, I think your little partner would've been the last one. I'd achieved everything I'd set out to do. And here's something you didn't know …' He paused for effect. '… the last one was actually a toss-up between the Latino and your wife!'

'You bastard!'

'I made the right choice, of course.'

His giggle was really getting to me now, but I wouldn't let him know it.

'I'd have probably done you a favour if I'd taken the old lady, huh?' He suddenly became serious. 'But this way you lost both of them. I did actually toy with the idea of taking the kid.' His eyes were searching mine, now looking for cracks in my render as I had his earlier. 'Not taking him as in taking his life. I considered keeping him as a pet. A toy if you like—'

'But instead, no longer were you just a pathetic twisted little faggot, but now you were also a worthless cripple. It was *your* life that was over!'

There was no sign of a reaction from my pot-shot. 'Aren't we just like two peas in a pod, Joe!'

'So how did Lambert find out?'

'When I was released from hospital six weeks later, William arranged to have me picked up. He even met me at the apartment and stayed with me for a while. It was kind of like old times, that is until he found the knife concealed in my coat.'

'They didn't find it at the hospital?'

'No, it was hidden in the lining. If they'd looked hard enough, they would've found it, but obviously they didn't. We were in the apartment together—William and I. It was my first evening at home. I wasn't much company, kept dozing off. Anyway, William was growing bored. He needed a hit but didn't have any cash, so he went through my coat while I was asleep and found the knife.'

'Did he confront you?'

'No, never said a word. But what I didn't realise until quite recently was that while I was sleeping, he must've gone through my things and found my diary.'

'So, he knew everything!'

'That's right.'

'But surely he didn't get to keep the diary?' As surreal and as unbelievable as it seemed, we were chatting casually.

'The book you've so enjoyed flaunting around town isn't my diary. That's fiction based around facts. The theatrical theme was obviously a creation of William's to spice up the prose. You see, my diary was made up of twelve sonnets.'

'Poetry?'

'That's right—each holding the vital elements that William built his book on.'

'*Flirting with The Moon.*'

'For that alone, I could've killed him.'

'Except you still loved him!'

Dennis sighed. Just like after a good session of therapy he now seemed relaxed and less inhibited. 'I did. Foolish I know.' He glanced lovingly across at Lambert's corpse.

'As soon as you saw the book written by Stephen Powell, you knew it was Lambert's work. With that realisation came the old mixture of feelings: anger, insecurity, fear, but there also came a new realisation, one that I think hit you pretty hard. Over the last twenty-five years, you had inadvertently reverted to the old Dennis. Podgy Hodgy had reclaimed his pathetic life.'

'Gosh, Joe, you really are outdoing yourself. Shame you're going to be dead in a matter of minutes!'

55

The muffled jingles of the poker machines were more muted now that we'd slowly moved back towards the farthest end of the bar. The sweep of the lighthouse fell across the windows of the room on each pass. I'd lost all concept of time, but sensed Dennis and I had been alone for a while.

'Answer me this.' I needed to keep the dialogue going. 'The only people who knew about DI Cooper's arrival were Fat Bobby and me—'

'Lots of people have two-way radios in rural areas.' He cut me off as if his answer was obvious.

'Right. So, you knew the detective was on his way and you met him just before he came into town. Probably told him there was a disturbance of some kind at the Lambert place. Directed him to the property and followed him. When he got out of his car at Lambert's gate, you clobbered him on the back of the head, threw him in the back of your van and drove him as close as you could get to the mast. Not your best presentation, but an effective one, nonetheless.'

'Thank you!' Dennis bowed his head in acknowledgement.

'But of course, this was after you'd killed Geoff Lambert. That was what really gave you the taste for it again. And the revenge for all the school bullying was just a nice added bonus. Were you disappointed when you heard his body had fallen into the water?'

'A little, at first, but then it just turned out to be another of those wonderful ironies.'

'Or the work of a has-been. I guess it would be pretty hard for a cripple to drag a dead body and hang it in a tree. You're certainly not the man you used to be, are you, Dennis? Then again, you were never much of a man!'

I was standing only a few feet away from a psychopathic killer. In one hand he held a loaded gun, in the other a butcher's knife. Why on Earth was I taunting him? Knowing that my life was about to end at any moment, I should've been afraid, pleading perhaps.

I detected movement from the corner of my eye and was momentarily distracted.

The doorway behind the bar leading to the back room had opened very slightly.

My heart sank. Was Frank planning to intervene? I didn't want anyone else involved because Dennis Hodge—The Moon—wouldn't hesitate to kill them.

From where Dennis stood, he didn't have the same view as me, and because the door had opened silently, he hadn't heard it.

Please, Frank, stay in the back room, I prayed. Leave it to me. I was on my own and yes, back-up would've been appreciated but I needed help, not a hero. How wrong could I have been? Because that's exactly what I got. A hero!

Like a Chinese firecracker, a white flash exploded from the opening in the bar. Dennis and I saw it at exactly the same time, but it was already too late. From my point of view, what happened next was in pure slow motion.

Dennis didn't have time to pull the trigger or lift the knife in self-defence. His smug expression morphed into wide-eyed shock. He squealed like a little girl, stumbled backwards, and doubled up in agony ... with Willy Nelson attached firmly to his balls.

Fat Bobby leapt from his hiding place in the foyer and, although his shoulder was covered in blood and the pain showed on his face, he scooped his arms beneath Dennis' armpits from behind.

I lurched forward, grabbed Dennis's wrists, and assisted with

Flirting with The Moon

their upward motion. With the assailant and I both wide open, my natural impulse would've been to knee him hard in his groin, but Willy Nelson had that area under control. Instead, I drew back my head, catapulted it forward and 'kissed' The Moon.

I'd like to say it was a good kiss—the way his nose crunched and popped under the force of my forehead, the high-pitched moan and his spectacles snapping at the bridge. It should have left me satisfied, but one kiss wasn't enough. I let fly with another and felt his arms go limp.

I twisted his wrists and forced him to drop the knife and the gun.

Fat Bobby wrenched Dennis' arms down, skilfully retrieved the handcuffs from his belt with one hand and cuffed the prisoner's hands behind his back.

Willy Nelson held firm, growling and shaking his head with his teeth deeply embedded and his back legs swinging with the momentum.

'Get it off me, please.' Tears, mixed with oozing blood from his broken nose, covered Dennis' cheeks. He had an enormous red mark across his forehead and a cut where his glasses had broken.

I guess the humanitarian thing to do would've been to remove the dog, but neither Fat Bobby nor myself offered to assist. Instead, we watched as the cruel little man with his hands cuffed behind his back swung himself from side-to-side, trying to get some relief from the dog's grip. But this only made it worse.

As barbaric as it may seem, I found myself having to suppress a smirk. Looking back, I can only put it down as an irrational thing to do at an irrational moment in time.

Fat Bobby, however, showed no such restraint. 'Go on, Willy. Rip the little fuckers off.'

56

The sun glistened on the surface of the water like scattered diamonds. The ocean was calm once again, as was the town. I was a little late for my walk with Molly that morning, which was understandable. After all, I hadn't slept—hadn't even been to bed. Instead, I'd spent the night seated in a mobile police unit, drinking coffee, answering questions, and reliving the events of the last few days in the form of a police statement.

In the hours that followed Dennis Hodge's arrest, the bush fire had been brought under control, and a horde of police reinforcement had swarmed on Candle Stick Bay. And the media also came to town. The high street was crammed with cruisers, trailers, trucks, and news vehicles. It resembled a movie set.

I wondered how long it would be before the news hit LA—if it hadn't already. There was a bitter-sweet side to all of this, and one that I have to admit I hadn't given much thought to. 'Would my son hear about me from the news?'

'A penny for them?' Molly said.

Jolted back from my thoughts, I pulled up in the sand and turned to face her. 'Just thinking of LA and Johnny.'

We were heading back to town. I was glad of Molly's company. The fact that we held hands seemed completely natural now.

'When do you go back?'

We stepped off the sand and onto the street.

Flirting with The Moon

'As soon as I can arrange a flight.'

'Then what?'

A simple enough question, but one that churned up the stagnant bottom of my subconscious like a stick in a pond. I literally had no idea what I would do next. In fact, for the first time in years, the future frightened me. I was too old to rejoin the police force and the thought of going back to Boca and resuming life as a private detective in Florida, appalled me. And what kind of reception would I receive in LA? I'd already dodged the Channel 10 news crew from Cairns earlier that day, but Fat Bobby had told me that they were just the beginning. Channel 7, Channel 9 as well as Sky News and CNN were on their way.

'They'll want to talk to you, mate,' Fat Bobby said. 'You're a real-life hero!'

'Perhaps they should speak to Willy Nelson,' I joked.

I wished I'd had an answer for Molly. After trying to account for every possible scenario of how my confrontation with The Moon would turn out, I hadn't given a single thought to the aftermath. All I could muster in response was: 'I haven't got a clue.'

For three days, the little coastal town in Far North Queensland became the focus of the world. The major news crews had indeed arrived, their vehicles outnumbering those of the police by at least two to one. The story, along with my interviews, would've been aired in the States. Most people now would know everything about the case. *Sixty Minutes* had offered me a six-figure sum for my story. I wanted to turn them down cold but instead told them I'd consider it.

The police presence gradually thinned until only the detectives working on the case were left but now, even they were preparing to leave.

Dennis Hodge was in a high security prison in Townsville, and his victims' bodies had been taken to Cairns for autopsies.

It was my last evening in Candle Stick Bay. Pat and Frank had organised a *bon voyage* party to be held in the hotel. All of the townsfolk were invited.

Sadness enveloped me as I packed my belongings into my suitcase. The sun was low and filled the room with a red dimming light. The warm breeze carried the gentle lapping of the ocean in through the windows, crickets chirped, and a far-off kookaburra reminded me of Dougie as it gave its final laugh of the day.

I wandered onto the balcony and, as I gazed out over the spectacular bay, I realised I didn't want to leave this place.

Bluey was seated on his usual stool, nursing a beer. He acknowledged me with a sideways glance and a grunt as I strolled into the bar.

Bruce and Silvia Stanton were chatting with Maud Baker and Molly Quinn, and Kimmy stood close by drinking an orange juice. Pat and Frank were also a part of the conversation but from behind the bar.

'Here's the man of the moment!' Frank cried as I approached the group.

'G'day Joe,' Bruce called out.

I kissed each of the women on the cheek, except for Pat, and I shook Bruce's hand.

'So, you're back off to La La land tomorrow, mate?' Bruce said.

'That's right.'

'You're a celebrity now,' Maud said.

I winced and blushed. 'Not if I can help it.'

'I've just had a thought,' Maud said, bolting upright. 'They might make a movie.'

'Yeah right. *Murder in Candle Stick Bay*—great title,' Silvia joked.

'Seeing as I was your partner, Mr Dean, and helped you solve the case …' Maud lifted her chin. '… who'd you think they'd get to play me? Cate Blanchett? Nicole Kidman?'

'Dame Edna?' Bruce said.

Flirting with The Moon

'I might even get an Oscar.' Maud, ignoring the laughter, stared into Hollywood space.

'Why would you get an Oscar, Maudie? You wouldn't be in it,' Silvia said.

'Could happen, they might insist on the real thing.' She sipped her drink then grinned.

'Hey! And here's the other hero,' Frank cried out, pointing to the door.

We all turned to see Fat Bobby enter with Roxy. With one arm in a sling, he held Roxy's hand with the other.

Like the parting of The Red Sea, a gap suddenly appeared between the patrons. A white streak rushed into the room, and in one fluid movement, sprung up onto a stool and onto the top of the bar. Willy Nelson stood proudly with his chin and tail in the air as if waiting for a fanfare.

'Here's our little bloke,' Pat said, stroking his ears. 'He's the real hero, aincha!'

'I'll drink to that!' I lifted my glass of juice.

Willy Nelson eyed me warily while enjoying the touch of Pat's gentle fingers.

Pete Bingle came bounding into the room. 'Drinks are on me, Frankie Boy!' he yelled, grinning.

I wasn't surprised at Pete's joviality in the wake of his ex-wife's death. Silvia Stanton had told me earlier that this was his way of handling bad situations. I realised having his beloved dog back would go a long way in helping him through this difficult time.

The room was filling up. Even Dougie had closed the fish and chip shop early to wish me farewell, which I found to be a real honour.

About halfway through the evening, Frank raised his authoritarian voice. 'Could I have everybody's attention please?'

The chatter quickly died down.

'Now, we all know why we're here tonight. We're here to say farewell to a new mate of ours, Joe.'

There was a splatter of applause and all heads turned to face me. Molly jabbed me playfully in the ribs.

'Firstly though, I'd just like us all to spare a thought for our fellow townsfolk who are no longer with us and ask for a minute's silence in respect.'

During that long minute, the jingles of the poker machines reminded me of the night when I stood in this room facing death at the hands of Dennis Hodge. I looked over at Willy Nelson. He was still watching me. I actually wanted to go over and give him a big hug, but I wasn't that brave.

'Good on ya, Frank!' Pete Bingle called out after the minute was over.

Frank continued with his speech. 'As you all know, Joe came here from LA and caused quite a stir.'

Murmurs of light-hearted agreement washed through the crowd.

'But we've all come to enjoy having him around. And I'd just like to say, Joe, on behalf of everybody here in Candle Stick Bay, we hope you have a good trip back. But more importantly, we really hope you'll come and see us again. Could I get you all to raise your glasses please and join me in a toast? To Joe!'

'To Joe!'

From behind the bar, Pat passed a wrapped parcel to Bruce Stanton then said loud enough for everyone to hear: 'Joe, we'd like you to accept this little gift as a token of our friendship and as something for you to remember us by.'

'We've had a whip round,' Maud said in my ear.

Bruce shook my hand and handed me the parcel.

Searching for words, I looked around hopelessly at the wonderful people around me.

'Open it then, mate,' Pete Bingle said.

I tore off the wrapping paper to find a plain cardboard box. Inside the box there was an assortment of items: a jar of Vegemite and a packet of Tim Tams—chocolate cookies—a tube of sunscreen, a pair of thongs—flip-flops—and some postcards featuring different views of the bay. There was a bar towel with a woven picture of The Great Northern Hotel, a schooner glass and some XXX beer mats. There was a folded polo shirt with the Candle Stick Bay Yacht Club logo on the left breast, and I was surprised to find a signed romance book written by a Miss Charlotte Berry.

On a small greeting card, written in scrawled handwriting, it said:

> To my friend, Joseph.
> Fish and chip dinner free
> of charge anytime.
> From your goodest mate, Dougie.

There were two photographs: the first was of Fat Bobby, Pete Bingle and Bruce Stanton, all wearing only shorts and standing on a boat in the bay. Three cheeky larrikins grinning back, each holding a fish. The other photograph made me laugh out loud and I guessed it would do so every day for the rest of my life. It was a picture of Willy Nelson standing regally atop the bait freezer outside the Bait and Tackle Shop. As if knowing the picture was being taken for me, his eyes would be watching me always.

In the bottom of the box was something about a foot long, wrapped in pink tissue paper. I placed the box on the bar and carefully lifted out the light, fragile item with both hands. I unravelled the wrapping to find a beautifully crafted ceramic reproduction of the lighthouse. The Vegemite and the Tim Tams had brought a lump to my throat, but now my eyes glistened with warm tears.

'Good on ya, Joe,' Pete Bingle said, lifting his glass.

Molly stroked my arm.

'I don't know what to say,' I blurted, wiping my eyes with the heel of my hand.

Molly placed her arm around my shoulder and drew me to her. 'You big softy!' she whispered in my ear through barely veiled emotion.

Fat Bobby elevated himself above the heads of the crowd by standing on the footrest of one of the stools. 'Can I also have your attention please?'

The patrons fell silent again.

'While we're all here, I thought it would be a good time to share something else with you all.' He looked down at Roxy.

Roxy blushed and looked timidly away.

'Thing is, I've asked Roxy to be my wife.'

A joy-filled gasp ran around the room.

'And she said yes!'

'YOU BEAUTY!' Pete Bingle cried above the cheers.

Everyone, including me, rushed to congratulate the couple. After shaking every man by the hand, left-handed, and kissing all the women present, Fat Bobby returned to his perch. 'And there's just one more thing.'

I followed his gaze until I realised it had come to rest on me.

'Joe, I would like to ask if you would give me the honour of being my best man?'

It took a moment for his request to sink in.

Everybody in the room was staring at me once more, waiting for my response.

'It would be an absolute honour, Bobby!'

Roxy threw her arms around my neck. 'Thank you so much, Joe.'

The handshakes and kisses continued.

'When's the wedding, Roxy?' Pat asked as Roxy paraded her ring.

'Sometime soon, hopefully.'

'So, you'll be coming back!' Molly whispered to me, smiling.

'Wow!'

'Wow good or wow bad?'

I looked deeply into her eyes. 'Wow amazingly good!'

She stood on her tiptoes and kissed me on the lips.

There was one more announcement towards the end of the evening, one that made the townsfolk of Candle Stick Bay extremely happy. Kenny the Telstra worker announced with a grin, almost as wide as Tana's who stood next to him, that the strike was over, and work would resume on the erection of the communications mast the very next day.

'Hip hip!' Pete Bingle cried.

'Hooray!' yelled everyone present.

'You bloody ripper!'

57

The lighthouse swept the town with its protective beam, and a hazy hush hung over the streets like a cleaning agent readying the land for the coming dawn. Standing at the top of the high street in Candle Stick Bay at three-thirty the next morning, the last thing I wanted to do was leave. In the short time I'd been there, I had literally fallen in love with the place, not only for its natural beauty but for its friendly, genuine, she'll-be-right-mate people. A bunch of flamin' galahs they certainly were not. And I will defend that stance to my dying days.

Molly had kindly offered to drive me to Cairns. Kimmy slept in the back seat for most of the seven-hour journey. Their trip wasn't entirely for my sole benefit; Molly had organised a meeting with her family lawyer for the next day, in preparation for the pending adoption hearing.

Our parting at Cairns Airport was a very emotional affair. Molly cried. Kimmy cried. I cried. 'I'll be back in a few weeks,' I assured them. And I meant it even though I didn't have a clue how I would afford another return ticket.

'We'll be *waiting* for you, Joe Dean,' Molly said and the emphasis on the word "waiting" made me feel homesick for Candle Stick Bay already. I felt like Gene Kelly leaving Brigadoon and his love behind, conscious that he could never go back, but in his heart knowing he must.

Flirting with The Moon

It was late evening by the time I checked in at Brisbane International Airport. Relieved of my baggage, I decided to have a look around before passing through customs.

The smell of coffee from the café bar was drawing me towards it like the sirens of Capri. I ordered a latté and a blueberry muffin then searched for a seat among the crowded tables.

I was beginning to worry that I'd be forced to remain standing when I noticed a young woman sitting at a table alone, tapping away on a laptop. There was a vacant seat at her table.

'Hi, is this seat taken?'

She looked up, shook her head, and smiled. 'No, please, be my guest.' Her accent was Southern Californian.

'Thanks.' As I placed my tray on the table and took my seat, the young woman closed the laptop and sipped her coffee.

'Heading home?' she asked.

'Yes, you?'

'No, I'm working over here. My husband's flying in but his flight's delayed.' She looked at her watch.

'Right. What do you do?'

'I'm a zoologist.'

'Cool. From LA?'

'Yes, you?'

I nodded while I unwrapped the largest muffin I'd ever seen in my life. 'Boy, size really does seem to matter over here.'

'It's a great place. I'm Beth by the way.'

'Hi, I'm Joe.'

We shook hands.

'So, are you at the end of a vacation, Joe?'

'Kind of. Australia's a great place to find yourself.'

'Or lose yourself.'

'That's right. Listen, there's no way I can eat all of this. Can you help me out?' I surveyed the monolith on my plate.

'Sure.' There was no, 'Oh I couldn't' or 'Are you sure?,' just a cheeky grin that scrunched up the line of tiny freckles across her nose.

I took an instant liking to Beth. She reminded me of a young Molly Quinn. I cut the muffin in two with a plastic fork and handed over one half.

'Thank you,' she said, taking a bite.

'Are you working here at one of the zoos?'

'Not exactly. I'm over here setting up a tiger reserve.'

'A tiger reserve? Like a safari park you mean?'

'No, it's a bit hush-hush. I'm not really supposed to be talking about it yet.' She lowered her voice. 'It's in far North Queensland.'

'Really? Wow!' I took a bite of my half-muffin. 'I just got in from there. Amazing place.'

A barely audible voice somewhere overhead announced that boarding of my flight would commence in five minutes.

'That's my flight,' I said rather reluctantly.

'Yes, I better head down to Arrivals.' Beth crammed the last piece of muffin into her mouth and swilled it down with a mouthful of coffee. 'John's flight shouldn't be too much longer.'

'Well, it was nice to meet you, Beth. And good luck with the tigers.' We shook hands.

'Nice to meet you too, Joe. Thanks for the muffin and have a safe trip back.'

After a ridiculously long flight, I passed through customs at LAX and was surprised when one of the officials said: 'Hey, Joe. Good to have you back!'

At first, I frowned at the young man. Did I know him? Not wanting to appear rude or like a victim of dementia, I nodded and thanked him.

When I walked up the ramp and into the arrivals area, an explosion of flashing lights caused me to squint and inadvertently lift my hand to my face. A mass of energy surged forwards—jostling

Flirting with The Moon

faces, microphones and camera lenses were thrust into my face and a sea of questions roared and tumbled like an incoming tide.

'How does it feel to have finally captured The Moon, Joe?'

'Is it true the victims in Australia would still be alive if you hadn't gone over there?'

'What have you got to say to those who doubted you?'

'Are you looking for apologies, Joe?'

'Are you going to demand the LAPD reinstate you?'

I blindly pushed through the crowd with my head down.

A hand grabbed me by the shoulder and yanked me to one side. 'This way, quick.'

I looked up to see my old pal, Burt Williams, leading me with one arm while with the other wafting away the reporters like mosquitos.

We barged through the airport and outside into a waiting police cruiser. The crowd of reporters and TV cameramen followed, engulfing the car. Were The Beatles back in town?

The young police officer skilfully negotiated the airport traffic, weaving in and out of buses and cabs at speed.

'They'll be expecting us to go back to headquarters. They're camped out on the street waiting for your return. Thought you might prefer a bit of peace and quiet instead,' Burt said as we pulled into the driveway of his home.

'Is this really happening, Burt?

'Hell yes. You're the biggest thing since OJ!'

Burt's wife, Nance, welcomed me with open arms. 'It's so good to see you, Joe. And congratulations!'

We sat out the back of Burt's home for most of the day. I soon realised that I was talking more about Candle Stick Bay and its people than the reason for being there. I decided to change the conversation. 'What about Johnny?'

Burt shuffled uneasily in his seat. 'He's not around at the moment.'

I could tell by the continuous fidgeting that there was something on Burt's mind.

'How did he react to the news?'
'John's been working undercover in Pennsylvania with the Amish.'
'Pennsylvania?'
'We had a request from the Pennsylvania State Police department for assistance a few weeks ago. Members of the Amish community were being bumped off. Assistance was required in the form of an out-of-town undercover detective who we could plant in the community to keep an eye on them.'
'You sent Johnny?'
'Yes. He was the right man for the job. And he cracked the case. Turns out old Eli, the patriarch, was receiving messages from God telling him to slit the throats of anyone who questioned his authority.'
'Are you saying Johnny doesn't even know about any of this?'
'That's right. No TV or radios where he's been.'
I knew that feeling. What an irony.
'Where is he now?'
Burt shook his head and shrugged. 'He took some time off. He's not in LA.'

Over the next few days, I made numerous television appearances and radio interviews. I was also photographed and interviewed by a stream of magazines and newspapers. I even hired a part-time agent to manage my engagements, and boy were the offers and cash coming in. I could've easily spent the next few months criss-crossing the country from interview to interview. But it wasn't what I wanted.

I was kept busy—too busy. After a week, I fired my agent and decided to lock myself away in a Santa Monica hotel for a few days. Then came the offer of the book deal. The advance alone would set me up for life. I thanked the publishers for their kind consideration and told them I would need to think about it. 'That's fine, but don't leave it too long!' was their reply.

Saturday was my first day alone. I got up early and strolled down to the pier then decided to walk the length of the esplanade to Venice

Beach and back. Cyclists and runners of all ages passed by in both directions like a human highway. By the time I reached the end of Venice and was heading back, the homeless community was stirring, and the market traders were setting up their stalls. Candle Stick Bay this was not. I realised I was missing Australia like hell.

Upon returning to my hotel, there was only one thing on my mind. I showered and changed, skipped breakfast, headed straight for the nearest travel agent, and booked the next available flight to Brisbane.

58

On the eve of my departure, I'd arranged to take Burt and Nancy out for dinner. Nothing flash. Nance loved Mexican food, so I booked an outside table at Mariasol on the end of Santa Monica Pier.

'So, what time do you fly out, Joe?' Nance asked, bubbling with excitement.

'8.00 pm tomorrow.' I was also excited with the thought of travelling back to Candle Stick Bay, but I noticed Burt was unusually quiet. 'You okay, Burt?'

Before he could answer, Nance cut him off. 'How about we drink a toast?' She lifted her glass of table water and I realised it wasn't excitement she was exhibiting but nervous energy. I suddenly got the feeling I was the object of an unresolved argument between them.

'What's going on guys?'

When their eyes met, I knew my suspicion was correct. Burt's expression said: I told you we couldn't hide this from him! Nance's said: You just couldn't let it be, could you? She looked away and gave a soft sigh of surrender.

'Thing is, Joe, I'm feeling pretty shitty,' Burt said, glaring at his wife.

'Why? Because I'm going back to Australia?'

'No.' He pushed down the piece of lime through the top of his Corona bottle and took a large swig of *La Cerveza Mas Fina*. 'I lied to you!'

'About what?'

Flirting with The Moon

'About John.' He threw back another mouthful of beer, glanced at his wife, then focused on the complimentary bowl of corn chips on the table. 'When I said I didn't know where he was, I wasn't being truthful.'

'You mean he's here in LA?'

'No, he's …' the next glance at his wife was more of a call for help. Nance was having none of it and continued to stare towards the Ferris wheel.

Burt took another swig of beer then blurted it out. 'He's in Australia, Joe!'

'He's what?' I searched Burt's face for an explanation. Was this a joke? Burt's grave expression told me it wasn't.

'But what on Earth would John be doing in Australia?' Then a dreadful scenario occurred to me. Had he found out I was alive and in Australia and stormed out there to confront me?' My mouth was suddenly dry, so I downed my full glass of non-alcoholic Sangria.

Burt seemed to read my thoughts. 'He knows you were there. Think about it, Joe. He's a detective. He's known you've been alive since he joined the police force!'

Burt's words pummelled me like a volley of bullets and the realisation of what he was saying caused my chest to cramp and my head to swim.

'But that's not why he went to Australia. He went out there to join his wife. She's been working over there.'

'If all this is true, why didn't you tell me before?' I finally said.

'I don't know, Joe I really don't. Just an impulsive decision at the time, I guess.' He ordered two more drinks.

Nance, the designated driver, sipped her water in silence.

There were so many questions I wanted to ask but could only manage, 'Do you know whereabouts in Australia?'

I could tell Burt was wishing the waiter would hurry up with his beer. 'Queensland.'

'What?' I couldn't believe what I was hearing. 'Brisbane?'

The waiter arrived with the drinks. I wanted to bat him away like an annoying fly.

'Far North Queensland. That's all I know, Joe.' He cursed as he nervously struggled to push down a larger than usual slice of lime into his fresh Corona.

One question was turning in my mind like the famous Ferris wheel. 'What possible reason would my son have for being in Far North Queensland?'

Then it hit me.

It's funny how a subliminal image can jump into your mind and provoke a random memory—usually something very simple. The trigger on this occasion was certainly that, but as it flashed into my mind, it all made perfect sense.

The largest muffin I had ever seen, cut in two.

ACKNOWLEDGEMENTS

As a proud Queenslander, I'd like to begin by acknowledging the traditional custodians of this land which we inhabit, and pay my respects to the Elders past and present.

I will always be indebted to Australia, in particular, Queensland. The beaches, the hinterland, the people, the weather—a lifestyle I could only ever have dreamt of when growing up in the UK.

As always, a big thank you to my wife, Jane, you truly are the light that guides my ship.

Thank you also to my editors, Sue Pearson, Karen Collyer and Julie Guthrie, for your patience and knowledge, and your positive feedback and encouragement. I'm proud of what we've achieved.

ABOUT THE AUTHOR

ANDY M^cD (aka Andrew McDermott) lives on the glorious Gold Coast of Australia and is the CEO of Publicious Book Publishing. His first novel (*The Tiger Chase* - 1st edition) was published in the US in 2002, which was followed up with the launch in San Diego and a book tour of the US, including LA and Las Vegas. More titles followed.

Andy was born in Nottingham, England. A naturalised Aussie, he has lived on the Gold Coast for the last 32 years with his wife, Jane. He is a patron of the Gold Coast Writers Association, and currently resides at Kirra Beach.